The Valley of Ooga Ooga
and the
Daring Adventures of the Kiddos

Written and Illustrated by
Steven Platt

Steven Platt

"All's well that ends well!"

pottplatt@gmail.com

DEDICATION

This book is based on the stories I made up for my young sons, when they needed something special from their real dad, something they could remember and think about when we couldn't be together.

The stories of Ooga Ooga that flowed into my head while we were camping in a tent in the high deserts of Colorado and Utah were the most imaginative gift I could ever give to my boys. They loved hearing about the adventures of six children, a dog (who wanted to be a cat), and a cat (who wanted to be a bird). For years, they've wanted me to write down the stories, and now I have.

This book is dedicated with love
to my sons, Bo and Sonny,
my daughter, Melody,
and my grandchildren, Gabriel, Juliet, and Hélio

ACKNOWLEDGEMENTS

꙳

When I started writing this book, I thought it would be easy and fun. It was enjoyable but easy ... not so much. Four years later, with the help of many souls, it has come to life.

To all the people who helped bring this adventurous and moral tale into existence, thank you. My wife, Sharon, is at the top of that list – it would not have been possible without her hard work, research, and guidance from beginning to end. My dear friend, Joanne Hunold, read along as the creation of the story unfolded, and her feedback was inspiring, hilarious, and filled with valuable insights.

Special thanks to Kaelyn Stevens, for her priceless feedback from the perspective of a bright young girl who loves to read; Carol Mackay, for her invaluable encouragement and support throughout the process; and Eva Gangnuss, an avid reader, for her expression of delight as she followed the kiddos on their adventures and for her appreciation of the surprisingly powerful endings.

Ragamuffin and Smokey

CONTENTS

෧~෧

AUTHOR'S NOTE

જ્જી

This book was written for readers young **and** old. Just as familiar stories about the Wizard of Oz, the Hobbit, and Harry Potter were written for children, they also found a place in the hearts of older folk.

The main story is about a unique group of children who live in a fantasy world named Ooga Ooga. The story follows the daring adventures of the kiddos and their quest to solve an ancient, unanswered question about the land on which they live.

There is a secondary story line about a boy named Bobby and his girlfriend, Cookie, who experience the adventures of the kiddos and the land of Ooga Ooga in their dreams. There are fourteen Bobby chapters in all, and the name of each chapter begins with the word Bobby, so they are easy to spot.

The 73 chapters about the adventures of the kiddos form a complete story. They can be read in succession by skipping the Bobby chapters as you go. The book consists of many chapters, but they are not long, so a chapter or two can be read at bedtime. After three months of having the book read to him each night, my grandson Hélio was disappointed when he heard there were only six chapters left.

Older readers have enjoyed the parallel plot lines and the complexity that the fourteen Bobby chapters bring to the story as a whole. The Bobby chapters cannot be read on their own for they are dependent on what happens in the Ooga Ooga story line.

This book was written with Bobby in mind, with all the details about how his life became entwined with his dreams. The reader can decide to read this book with or without the Bobby chapters.

I hope you take a minute to curl up, relax, and join the delightful kiddos on their amazing and purposeful adventures.

Now the story begins…

Chapter 1

THE RIVER OF FUN

❧❧

In the Valley of Ooga Ooga, in the Village of Ooga Ooga, far below Ooga Mountain, live the fun-loving children, Topp, Taffy, Walnut, Sugar, and her dog, Ragamuffin.

The kiddos are the best of friends and often spend entire days together. This was one of those days. It was a beautiful morning in the Village of Ooga Ooga. The air had neither a hint of winter's chill nor the brisk winds of spring.

Taffy ran next door to Sugar's house and shouted through her open bedroom window, "Wake up! Wake up!"

"Huh?" Sugar mumbled sleepily. "Wha-what's goin' on?"

"First day of summer – it's time for fun!" Taffy bellowed.

"Okay, okay. But I *was* having fun – *sleeping in*!"

"Fine, but don't forget we're meeting at Poppy Park in an hour."

"I'll be there," Sugar muttered and then plunked her sleepy head onto her cozy pillow. Her sweet puppy, Ragamuffin, cuddled up next to her and closed his eyes.

Three of the kids arrived at the jujubee tree in Poppy Park at about the same time. As usual, they had to wait for the fourth, Walnut, to show up.

When he finally got there, Taffy asked him pointedly, "Walnut, could you *please* try to leave earlier – so you'll be here on time?"

"Works for me," Walnut replied good-naturedly.

"I'm glad you made it," Topp said. "It wouldn't be the same without you."

"That's for sure!" Sugar said. "You're one of a kind, Walnut."

"Okay, okay, time's a wastin'!" Taffy declared. "Grab your stuff, and let's go play at the falls!"

The kiddos took off and hurried along the well-traveled foot path that winds through lush farms and shady woods on its way to the Ooga River.

When they reached a bridge over an irrigation canal, Sugar stopped and said, "Let's go pick popcorn berries from the community garden!"

The others agreed, so they scurried along the canal to the nearby village garden plot.

If you don't know, popcorn berries are large white berries that taste like freshly popped, buttered popcorn. They are just one of the yummy fruits and vegetables grown in the public garden, which is planted and tended by people who live in the Village of Ooga Ooga. The popcorn berries are ripe now and free to all who helped pull the awful piggy weeds from the garden during springtime.

As soon as the kiddos reached the berry patch, they started picking (and munching) big handfuls of the tasty treats.

Suddenly, from out of a nearby cornfield, a weird old man appeared. "STOP! STOP! YOU CAN'T PICK THOSE!" he barked.

The kiddos looked up, but they couldn't manage to say even one word because their mouths and cheeks were chock-full of popcorn berries.

"GET OUT OF HERE! NOW!" the old man crowed angrily.

The kiddos were trying their best to swallow quickly so they could explain when Mrs. Sweet showed up.

"Mr. Bark, these children earned those berries! They were here a couple of weeks ago and worked for most of a day pulling piggy weeds. Who gave you the right to police the field, anyway?" she scolded. "Children, go right ahead and pick all you like."

A disgruntled Mr. Bark retreated, and as he slunk back toward the cornfield, he turned around and grumbled, "Kids! Good-fer-nothin' kids!"

The kiddos thanked Mrs. Sweet for her help and then filled a small bag with berries to share later at the waterfall.

The four kiddos, with Ragamuffin trailing behind, returned along the levee of the canal to the main trail and resumed their journey to the Ooga River. At the river, they followed the rocky trail up to the waterfall.

With the spring runoff at its peak, the falls rumble and roar into a deep swimming hole called the Bubble Bath. This natural pool is always bubbly and fragrant because leaves from the soap trees above the falls are always dropping into the river.

A few years ago, something extraordinary happened at the waterfall. A dreadful storm uprooted an ancient soap tree, and the whole thing toppled into the river. Thousands of soap leaves crashed into the rushing water, cascaded over the waterfall, and exploded into hundreds of enormous bubbles – bubbles so gigantic a kid could climb inside. In case you're wondering, the record for the most kids in one bubble is five!

The Bubble Bath is a wonderful place to cool off and play, so the kiddos were not surprised to see a bunch of friends from school hanging out there.

The kiddos dropped their towels by the pool and climbed the steep path to the entrance of the deep cave underneath the top of the waterfall. At the back of the cave, a wall of ice continually grows and moves forward from within the mountain. The ice comes in all sorts of vivid colors as well as clear (if clear is indeed a color). Surprisingly, each color has a different flavor, like snow cones do. People from the nearby village come to the cave to chip out ice to use at home. Just for fun, children throw handfuls of ice into the Bubble Bath to cool and color the water.

Starting at the back of the cave, the four kiddos ran and launched themselves out through the wall of falling water. When it was his turn,

Topp did a cannonball and landed with a huge splash. Then they swam to shore, climbed out, and scrambled up the hill to jump again.

Without warning, Walnut started a snowball fight within the cave and when it was over, everyone was covered in colored ice. They looked like snow cones with legs. One by one, they jumped through the waterfall again, yelling "Yahoooo!" and splashed into the bubbly pool far below.

Next they took turns going down the slippery water slide above the pool. As they zoomed down the slimy surface, they picked up speed and barely missed each other when they landed willy-nilly into the water.

After that the kiddos ran to the rope swing. Taffy climbed onto the narrow platform, firmly grasped the knot in the rope, and leaped off. She swung over the pond in a graceful arc and at the farthest point, she let go and yelled, "Whoopee!"

"I'm next!" shouted Sugar. She grabbed the rope, flew away gracefully, and landed in the cool water with a big *ker-sploosh*! The boys gladly took their turns as well.

After drying off, the kiddos warmed themselves on a rock, ate popcorn berries, and talked about what to do next.

"I want to go to the fishing hole," Walnut said.

"I want to go birdwatching," Sugar declared.

"I'm going to hike above the falls," said Taffy.

And Topp shared, "I'm going to go help some kids build a new diving platform."

So, off they ran in four different directions.

Walnut walked down river from the Bubble Bath to the Fishin' Hole. The shore was crowded with kids but surprisingly quiet. These kids know that being silent is important if you want to catch the big ones. But whenever someone caught a fish, the wild cheers could be heard all the way up to the Bubble Bath!

Walnut enjoyed watching the kids fishing but after a while, he wished he had brought his fishing pole. *I'll bring it next time,* he thought.

In the meantime, Sugar hiked to the best place for birdwatching near the falls, a wonderful habitat for many bird species. In no time, she spotted one sitting on a low branch. It was a pretty, tiny bird with tan feathers, a pink face, and a yellow beak. When Sugar doesn't know what kind of bird she spots, she makes up her own name for it. She named this one a Pink Fizzywizzy. Her dog, Ragamuffin, is an excellent birdwatching companion because he sits very quietly as he scans the air for birds, bees, and dragonflies.

Meanwhile Topp joined a group of kids building a new diving platform. Last summer, a dam broke upriver and washed away the old diving structure on the edge of the Bubble Bath. Topp helped the others gather building materials from the nearby woods. It took teamwork to position the support posts and lash crossbeams to them. They made progress, but it would surely take another day to finish the job.

Taffy had on her running shoes, so she raced up, down, and all around the trails above the falls. Her favorite path leads to a large rocky outcrop. Taffy stood on top of the protruding boulder and looked down at the spectacular view of the Valley of Ooga Ooga. Gazing at the amazing vista, she felt incredibly lucky to live in such a special place.

Heading back toward the top of the waterfall, Taffy saw that the flow of the river had suddenly tripled in size and turned cocoa brown. She cried out frantically, "RUN! RUN! A FLOOD! THE DAM BROKE!" Taffy waved her arms wildly and shouted as loudly as she could to all the children below.

"RUN! RUN!" shouted everyone, to each other and to themselves. The children at the swimming hole scrambled quickly to higher ground and watched the falls become enormous. The river looked like a giant cascade of chocolate syrup! The roar of the water was deafening for a minute or two, then everything calmed down, and the flow of the mucky river returned to near normal.

Everyone was safe! They watched the Ooga River slowly return to its lovely blue hue. Everybody had a good laugh at the excitement caused by the flash flood.

You might recall this was *not* the first time the small dam up the river had broken. And you might have guessed it – today's flood washed away the half-finished diving platform, just like last year. They'll have to start building it all over again.

Taffy looked down and sighed with relief that everyone was safe. She smiled and whispered to herself, "We never know what's going to happen in the land of Ooga Ooga."

The kiddos and Ragamuffin reunited at the edge of the pool and sat close together on a grassy mound, exhausted and hungry. The daylight began to dim as they began their journey home.

On the way back to the park, the kids came to the little bridge over the canal. In the evening stillness, they heard a distressful call.

"Help! Help! H-e-l-p!"

They trotted cautiously but quickly along the bank of the canal toward the screams.

Looking down, they saw a man up to his chest in the flowing water of the canal. He was waving his arms frantically. "HELP ME, HELP ME! I'M STUCK IN THE MUD!"

Oh my! It was Mr. Bark, the grumpy old man!

"Hang on! We'll get you out!" Topp reassured him. The kiddos linked arms and created a chain long enough for Topp to grab Mr. Bark's outstretched hand.

"PULL, PULL!" Taffy shouted.

Using the children as an anchor, Mr. Bark was able to pull himself out of the mud and climb to safety. "Thank you, oh, thank you," he said. "I would have died if you hadn't saved me!"

"Are you okay now?" Taffy asked kindly.

"I'm fine – I think. Thank you," he said. "Hey, you're the kids from the berry patch this morning, aren't you?"

"Yep, that's us," Sugar said sweetly.

"I thought about you children all day long. I felt so bad about the way I yelled at you. I'm sorry. Yesterday I lost Leafy, my green cat, and I'm not myself right now. I loved that cat *sooo* much."

"I saw a green cat at the gazebo this morning. Does your cat have a pink tail?" Walnut asked.

"Yes! Yes, she does!" Mr. Bark shouted. "You saw Leafy at the gazebo?" He instantly took off running, with mud flying off his shoes with every step. The kiddos could hear Mr. Bark's voice faintly in the distance. "Thank you, thank you!"

"I'm so glad we were able to save him," Sugar said.

"Hey, look over there! What's that weird thing floating in the canal?" Taffy said pointing.

"It looks like a floating bottle," Topp said. He slid down near the mud at the water's edge and reached out. "I got it!"

He sped up the bank of the canal to where the others were.

"It's a bottle all right," Sugar said. "But an *unusual* one."

"Wow, it has a big cork in it and a paper or something inside!" Topp said. He tried to pull out the cork, but it wouldn't budge.

"Maybe there's a treasure map inside!" Walnut shouted. Then he looked around quickly to make sure no one overheard him yell *treasure*.

"Hey, it's getting dark," Sugar said. "We ought to get going and open it tomorrow."

"Good idea," Topp said. "Let's meet at my garage in the morning. I have plenty of tools to get the cork out. Here, you take it home and keep it safe, Taffy. I'm famous for breaking things, you know."

Taffy wrapped the fragile bottle in her towel and tucked it securely under her arm for the journey home.

The kiddos hurried on to their houses for dinner. On their way, they couldn't help but wonder ... *What's inside that strange bottle?*

Chapter 2

THE MYSTERIOUS MAP IN THE BOTTLE

❧❧

Topp, Sugar, and Walnut paced anxiously in front of Topp's open garage as they waited for Taffy.

"There she is!" Sugar shouted, jumping up and down.

Taffy was out of breath as she explained, "Sorry I'm late. I hid the bottle in our basement to keep it safe overnight, but I had trouble finding it again among all the boxes and bags."

The kiddos hustled into the garage and cleared space on the workbench. Taffy unwrapped the precious treasure carefully and placed it gently on the towel. The bottle was blue and semi-transparent, and there were tiny air bubbles in the glass. A large cork was stuck halfway into its wide neck. The bottle was plenty big enough to hold what appeared to be a rolled-up piece of paper.

"The cork should come out if I twist it with these wide-jaw pliers," Topp said. "This'll do it." He gripped the cork firmly and gave it a twist.

"Whoa! The cork just crumbled into pieces!" Taffy exclaimed.

"No problem, I'll dig out the rest of it with a screwdriver." Topp removed the last bits of cork and then tried to pull out the paper with his thumb and finger. But he couldn't reach it.

"Let me try, my hands are smaller," Sugar said. Into the bottle her fingers flew, and out came a rolled-up piece of yellowed paper.

"A treasure map!!!" Walnut yelled out.

The Ancient Map

"Hush up, Walnut," Taffy whispered sternly. "Do you want the whole town to know?"

"The paper looks very old and brittle," Sugar remarked. She slowly and delicately unrolled the fragile paper and flattened it gently.

Topp took polished stones from a jar and placed them carefully on the four corners to keep the paper flat when Sugar let go.

The kiddos jockeyed for position to see what might be written on it. They were strangely silent as their eyes wandered all over the stained paper. They were so quiet, you could hear an ant burp.

"It looks like an ancient map," Taffy said. She read the words written on the map out loud, "It says Happy Vally Oooga, Big Mont, Roc Clifs, Tot Hils, and Jungle. It looks like a map of our valley – of Ooga Ooga!"

"But I don't see an X to show where the treasure is hidden," Walnut said glumly. "Maybe it's just a dumb, old, worthless map!"

"I'm not so sure," Topp said. "It looks old and seems to show places far from Ooga Ooga. And in all four directions it says EDGE, whatever that means. I think we should show it to Grandpa Gabby and find out what he thinks."

Taffy put the map back into the bottle, wrapped it tightly in the towel, and snuggled it up under her arm. Then the kiddos set off for the bench near the Ducky Pond in Poppy Park, where Grandpa Gabby can often be found.

Grandpa Gabby is the oldest living person in Ooga Ooga. Nobody knows how old he is because no one, including him, knows when he was born. He was already old when the other elderly Oogans were mere youngsters. He is a vibrant old man, tall and upright, with broad shoulders. When asked how he stays healthy and strong, he simply says, "Watching the ducks and the children playing in the park keeps me young."

The kiddos were in luck because they found Grandpa Gabby on his favorite bench, tossing breadcrumbs to the ducks. "Hi, young'uns," he said, greeting them kindly. "What brings you to the park today?"

"We have something to show you," Sugar said. "You might know something about it."

Grandpa Gabby's eyes widened in anticipation as Taffy unwrapped the bottle and handed it to him. "We found this floating in the canal. It has a map inside," Taffy said.

"My, my, my!" he said. "Let's take a look." He spun the bottle around in his hands and held it up to the sunlight to look through it. "Oh my! This is an incredibly old bottle, me thinks! I would say it's from Dirt Town, a town of old that no longer exists. I have seen pieces of broken glass from Dirt Town in our museum but a *whole* bottle – my, my, my!"

"Pull out the map," Walnut whispered anxiously. "Could it be a treasure map?"

Grandpa Gabby's long fingers deftly removed the paper from the bottle and unrolled it carefully. He studied it intently for several minutes. The kiddos held their breath so long, they got dizzy waiting for him to say something.

"Most interesting, me thinks," Gabby began. "It came from ancient Dirt Town. I can tell by the ink made from the dust of blue butterfly wings. Quite an amazing find of antiquity, I would say."

"So, does it show where the secret treasure is buried?" Walnut asked.

"I don't know if it's a treasure map, but it does appear to be something very special," he replied. "With your permission, I would like to take it to the Museum of Everything to hear what the curator, Mrs. Smart, thinks about it. Want to come with me?"

Four "yeses" were clearly voiced, so off they went to the museum.

"Hello, Mr. Gabby," a petite woman said as the old man entered the museum with four young'uns and one cute dog. "And who are these handsome youngsters?"

"Friends from the park. They found something you will be most interested in, me bets. They found a map in a bottle from ancient Dirt Town, me thinks."

Mrs. Smart is knowledgeable about all the collections in the museum, but her specialty is the history and artifacts of Dirt Town. She led her visitors into a special room off the main hall, the museum laboratory.

Taffy carefully placed the bottle upright on the spotless countertop. Mrs. Smart put on white gloves to hold and examine the exterior of the bottle thoroughly and then gently pulled the map out with a special tool. She unrolled the piece of paper and placed small weights on each corner to keep it flat.

"Goodness me!" she said. "This is amazing! This bottle undoubtedly came from ancient Dirt Town – of this I am certain! Where did you find it?"

"It was floating in the Village Canal with an old cork in it," Topp said.

"That makes sense. The water in the canal comes from Tot Tot Creek, which flows through the ruins of old Dirt Town," she explained. "Over the years, several artifacts from Dirt Town have been found in Tot Tot Creek and the canal."

"Could it be a treasure map?" Walnut asked hopefully.

Mrs. Smart took a long minute to study the map using a special light and a huge, powerful magnifying glass. The kiddos waited impatiently. Finally, she spoke, "I don't see any indication of the location of a treasure, but this map is undoubtedly a priceless treasure of incalculable historical importance."

The kiddos stood befuddled, not knowing what to say or think.

"What makes it so special?" Grandpa Gabby asked.

"First of all, it's over five hundred years old and in perfect condition!" she said. "But more significant than that, look at what it says in all four directions of the map: EDGE. The majority of Oogans believe that our land goes on forever in all directions. However, there is a legend passed down through the generations that our land is finite and comes to an end – that is, has an *edge,* if you will. This concept has not been proven in modern times. This map is the first written record that there might be an *edge* to our land after all. Amazing!"

Grandpa Gabby reflected on Mrs. Smart's comments, "In my many years, I've heard about a few adventurous Oogans who set out to find the supposed *edge*. Ultimately, no one in my day and time has ever found it – and some have never returned from the search. Truth be told, no one knows for certain if there is an end to our land – as far as I knows."

"Exactly," Mrs. Smart said. "This map is as close as we have come to documentation of the existence of an end to our world in all directions."

The kiddos just stood there, with blank looks on their faces.

"I can tell you are disappointed," Mrs. Smart said. "I'm sure you want to find a treasure."

"Yes'm," Walnut squeaked.

"I've decided to give you something that may lead you to a treasure someday," she said.

That grabbed their attention! The kiddos watched her every move as she walked to a cabinet, pulled something out, and brought it to the table. She said, "This is a map of what lies beyond our Valley of Ooga Ooga. A few years ago, the museum hired a team of mapmakers and explorers to document what is out there in all directions. As a result, they produced two identical copies of a highly detailed, hand-drawn map for the museum archives. Children, I would like to give one of these special maps to you as a thank you gift for finding such an exceptional artifact."

The kiddos were delighted because they had sometimes talked about traveling beyond the valley, but they had no idea what was out there.

"Mrs. Smart, would you like to keep the old bottle and map we found? Your map is far more useful to us than this old one," Taffy said.

"Yes, thank you so very much! These priceless objects would enhance our Dirt Town collection greatly."

Mrs. Smart laid out the colorful, modern map next to the ancient one. The new one showed the seas to the north and south, Candy Mountain, the Chocolate Hills, and many other fascinating places.

"I've heard there are valuable treasures to be found out and about," she said. "Perhaps you will travel to some of these faraway places **when you grow up**, that is."

The kiddos were deep in thought as they trundled out of the museum. "We can't thank you enough for bringing us here, Grandpa Gabby," Sugar said sincerely. The kids smiled and waved goodbye to the wonderful old man. He waved back and then sauntered on to the park to feed a duck or two.

"I have an idea," Topp said. "Let's go to my garage and figure out our next move."

ഇ

Topp laid out the new map on the workbench for all to see.

"This map sure has a lot of interesting places to see, and I don't think we need to wait **until we grow up!**" Taffy said boldly, sneering at the suggestion they weren't old enough to venture out and hunt for treasure.

"Hear! Hear!" the others shouted.

"Who knows, maybe we can go even farther – and find the *edge*," Topp added.

"That's what I was thinking!" Taffy said. "Let's go and see it all – and the *edge*!"

"We can do it, I'm sure of that!" Walnut said. "After all, we *are* the four kiddos!"

"Wouldn't it be amazing if we solved the mystery about the *edge*?" Taffy said. "But even if we never do, we'll have fun going to all of those faraway places, now that we have a map to show us what's out there!"

The kiddos studied the map for a long time, pointing out the unfamiliar and unusual places named thereon. They were thrilled with their new map, and they all imagined awesome adventures in the various lands and seas *beyond* the Valley of Ooga Ooga.

The Valley of Ooga Ooga and Beyond

Chapter 3

BOBBY AND HIS SWEET DREAMS

❧❧

Bobby began waking up from a dream with a broad smile on his face. But when he opened his eyes, he found himself back in his room. "Darn!" he said out loud.

He was quite disappointed to no longer be in that magical dreamland.

He tried to fall back to sleep but he couldn't, so he tried to remember details of the dream instead. It was summertime in that unusual place, and there were lots of kids playing in a swimming hole. He remembered the fun of jumping through a big waterfall, scooting down a water slide, and eating a snow cone in a cave. And he remembered dreaming of four kids who found a mysterious map in an old bottle.

Bobby leaned over and pulled back the window curtain. The sky was dark and heavy and filled with gray clouds. Outside, tree branches were whipping in the wind, dripping with water. *It is so dreary out there,* he thought, *I think I'll stay inside today. But what I really want to do is go back and play with those kids in my dream.*

His muscles ached from top to bottom, and his legs felt stiff. Yesterday he and his friends spent the entire day riding their bikes. They raced, rode up and down on hilly trails, and cruised over miles of country roads.

Bobby thought to himself, *I'll take it easy today. I have lots of things to do inside.* He decided not to invite any friends over but instead spend the day at home with his best friend – himself.

Bobby's face glowed with joy as he looked around at all his awesome stuff: rows of books, stacks of games, tons of toys, art supplies of all sorts, and other wonderful things – like his collection of dead bugs pinned on a board. On his worktable, there was a half-finished puzzle of a monkey in a jungle and next to that, a miniature roller coaster under construction. Everything was organized neatly on bookshelves, so he could easily find anything he needed to start a new project.

Bobby stood up and gently raised his arms overhead. He took in a deep breath and held it in while reaching up as high as he could. Then he released the air through his mouth with a *wooooo* sound.

When he heard her meowing outside his door, he let his cat in. Fluffers pranced across the floor like she owned the place, jumped on the bed, and curled up to take a nap. "Boy, what a life," Bobby muttered to himself, watching his lazy old cat.

Bobby followed his nose to the kitchen where something smelled delicious. "Hi, Mom, what's for breakfast?"

"A cheese omelet with bacon on the side. Does that sound good?"

"It sure does and smells good too."

The kitchen table at Bobby's house is always set for four, but there would only be two for breakfast this morning. One empty place at the table is for Bettykins, his older sister, who is away at college. Another place and an empty chair are there waiting for his long-lost father.

Bobby's father, Rufus, was expected to return after three months on an expedition to study medicinal plants in a faraway jungle, but he has been gone for more than a year. Many search parties have looked for his missing father but with no success. Chances for his safe return are getting slimmer as each day goes by. Nevertheless, Bobby's mother, Mari, is holding onto hope that Rufus will return someday soon.

In his father's absence, Bobby has taken on more chores and responsibilities to help his mom. He tends to stay close to home, to be there for her. And Mari's only daughter, Bettykins, tries to lift her mom's spirits by coming home from school as often as she can.

Bobby cleaned his plate in no time and then had a second helping. He looked up and asked, "Do we have any popcorn and butter?"

"Yes, but why do you want popcorn now?"

Bobby tried to explain, "Last night I had a dream that I can't get out of my head. In the dream, some kids were eating buttered popcorn that grew on a bush. The dream was so real, I could smell and taste it. Mom, are dreams real? Do you know what I mean?"

"Yeah ... I think so."

"The dream last night was as real as this," he said and opened his arms wide to include everything around them. "I didn't think dreams were real, but I do now – I definitely do!"

"I've had dreams that seemed real, too!" she recalled. "It's so mysterious when that happens." She smiled and focused on popping the popcorn, then put it in a bowl and poured melted butter over it.

"Thanks, Mom! I think I'll eat it in my room."

"It's raining, what are you going to do today?"

"I'm going to do stuff with my indoor plants and start new seeds that Cookie gave to me. What are you gonna do, Mom?"

"I'm going to sit in my comfy chair with a cup of tea and finish the sweater I'm knitting for Bettykins. I'm planning to have dinner ready around five, is that okay?"

"Sounds great," Bobby said. He watched her leave the room and then quietly opened the freezer door and pulled out a carton of ice cream. He put ten spoonfuls in a bowl, and then five more, and then the rest of it.

Why am I so hungry this morning? Bobby wondered, with his mouth full of popcorn and ice cream. *Maybe playing for hours in my dream gave me a huge appetite! Yeah, if dreams are real, of course I'd be hungry.*

The idea he could get hungry from a dream seemed silly indeed. Feeling a little guilty for his gluttony, Bobby buried the empty ice cream carton under other garbage in the trash basket under the sink.

With a plump tummy, Bobby waddled like an overweight goose back to his room and settled in to play inside on this rainy day. He read story books, threw darts, and built a house of playing cards with five gum drops balanced on top.

He worked on an activity book full of word games, mazes, puzzles, and connect the dots. He colored the pictures with the brightest crayons in the box – the hottest colors of the rainbow – reds, yellows, and oranges. And for more than an hour, he worked on his pet project, a roller coaster made of toothpicks and glue.

Bobby sat on his bed and wondered what his friend Cookie was doing. She and Bobby have been like two beans in a pod for a long time. She lives across the street, and they hang out with each other almost every day. She is a girl and a friend, so I guess that makes her a girlfriend. Neither of them would disagree with that. They are sweet like candy on each other.

He planted the petunia seeds from Cookie and watered them with care. Then he placed the pot in a sunny spot with the rest of his plants. It takes patience to germinate seeds. It will be a while before they push their delicate leaves through the soil and join him in his room.

Bobby gives each of his plants a name, like Woozy, Bock, and Frit. His favorite one is named Cookie – it is the prettiest. He talks to his plants, too, and says they talk back to him.

He doesn't think anyone else can hear them, but I think I heard them once.

Bobby looked out his window at the flower garden, the fruit trees, the old shed, and the squirrels and birds moving about. He was surprised to see the large sun starting to set behind the tall, purple mountain. There were puffy clouds throwing sunset colors around. He'd been so busy all day, he completely lost track of time. The hours went by like minutes – it was twilight and time for dinner.

At the dinner table, Bobby wanted to tell her more about his dream, so she smiled and nodded and listened, while he went into more detail about the fantasy land he visited.

After dinner, Bobby sat down on the soft rug in the center of his room. Fluffers, purring loudly, curled up next to him. He pulled out his harmonica, played a happy tune, and thought about his day. He'd built a longer run on his roller coaster for his favorite red marble; the monkey puzzle was done; and he'd solved a slew of word puzzles in the activity book.

He sat on the floor, feeling peaceful and content, even more so than usual. Today might have been one of the best days of his life – but there will surely be even better days when his dad comes home.

He got up off the floor and flopped backward onto his bed. He gazed at the glowing planets and stars stuck on the ceiling. He stretched, yawned, and thought about various details of his dream last night. Before this busy day had even begun, he'd spent the whole night playing with a bunch of kids in a dreamy dreamland.

Bobby sank into his soft blankets, and his eyelids grew heavy. Fighting drowsiness, he got out of bed and walked unsteadily into the family room to say good night to his mom.

"Good night, sweetie," his mother said. "Did you have a nice day?"

"A very special day, Mom." He gave her a tender hug and a soft kiss on her cheek. "See you in the morning."

Cozy in bed, Bobby closed his eyes and vibrant visions of last night's dream played in his mind. He wondered if tonight's dream would take him back to that dazzling world and those fun-loving dream-kids.

With boundless hope in his heart, he sighed and deep into slumber he went.

Sweet dreams, Bobby ...

Chapter 4

THE KIDDOS OF THE VALLEY OF OOGA OOGA

⮞⮜

In the Valley of Ooga Ooga, Topp, Taffy, Walnut, and Sugar woke up in the quaint Village of Ooga Ooga. The children's homes are not far from each other and not far from the Ooga River that flows below the towering and pointed Ooga Mountain. The tip-top of this great mountain reaches to the clouds and looks down on everything that happens in the valley below.

In case you don't already know, Ooga is pronounced like the sound of a child who sees a delicious bowl of ice cream: ***Ooooo,*** *that looks good* – with a ***ga*** at the end. In the old days, it was spelled **Oooooga** but after a while, the folks in the valley decided that was a big waste of o's, so they shortened it to **Ooga**. Perhaps they were afraid they might run out of o's someday. Who knows, maybe they would have. Then what? How would they spell cookie or book?

The Valley of Ooga Ooga is shaped like a large square with rounded corners. There are creeks and streams but only one river, the Ooga River, which meanders below the base of Ooga Mountain on the sunset side of the valley. The river's headwaters are in the massive Giant Step Mountains. The river flows through the fertile Ooga Valley, cuts through a gap in the Yeller Cliffs, and continues onward to the Fantasmo Sea.

For your enjoyment, a copy of the map that Mrs. Smart gave to the kiddos is included in this book on page 15. It shows the Valley of Ooga

Ooga and the various lands and towns surrounding it. If you look *very* closely, you might see the kiddos waving up to you. Oh, just kidding – but they are down there somewhere!

The people of the valley are called Oogans. Most of them live in the village, while the rest live in the lush, green farmland that stretches out to the edges of the valley. It's a wonderful place to live, and the kiddos feel lucky it's their home. They believe it's the best place to live in the entire world – even if it's the only place they've ever lived!

The kiddos had agreed to meet in the morning at the picnic table under the gazebo in Poppy Park. Topp was the first to arrive. He looked up at Ooga Mountain and thought, *Wow, what a beautiful day! The birds are singing, and the mountain is glowing like gold!*

Topp is the oldest of the kiddos. He is a friendly boy, about average height, with a commanding, almost manly voice. He's quick in both body and mind, and a natural born leader. His chums appreciate that he is fearless, clever, and talented in so many ways. He has brown hair, with a streak of blonde sun-bleached hair in front, but you will hardly ever see it because he often wears a cap.

On her way to the gazebo, Taffy came running around a blue bush near the Ducky Pond. She's the toughest of the bunch – athletic, confident, and always speaks her mind. Taffy is a little taller than Topp and reminds him of that from time to time. She has brown eyes and wavy black hair which she often puts in a ponytail. She hasn't many dresses in her closet – not much need for those. She wears jeans or shorts most of the time. She's sometimes bossy, but Taffy has a tender side and is a loyal, devoted friend.

Topp welcomed Taffy to the gazebo as Sugar came skipping up the trail.

Sugar is as sweet as honeysuckle in a breeze. She has blue eyes and golden hair. Somehow, she manages to stay clean and tidy no matter what she does. Sugar loves to read and has a wealth of knowledge of many subjects, including history, science, and animals. She has a sunny disposition and is a delight to be around.

Sugar's sweet dog, Ragamuffin, goes everywhere Sugar goes. He has floppy ears and beautiful, expressive eyes. Strange as it may seem, Ragamuffin wants to be a cat. Every day, he practices meowing and tries to jump onto high places like a cat – and he refuses to eat dog food.

Ragamuffin is not very big and not very small. That didn't help much, did it? His coat is thick and furry and belies his actual size. He once chased a dragonfly and fell into a pond. When he came out, he was quite tiny. I don't want to burst his bubble, but Ragamuffin looks nothing like a cat. But he has a girlfriend named Kitty, and yes, she *is* a cat.

On the lookout for Walnut, the kiddos spotted the lovely green cat that lives in the park. Everyone calls her Emerald. She has a white tail (not a pink tail like Mr. Bark's cat, Leafy), hops like a rabbit, and purrs constantly. Folks have tried to give her a good home, but Emerald likes living in the park, close to nature.

Walnut was late as usual, but the faint sound of whistling in the distance meant he wasn't far away. Walnut says whistling makes him happy and it must be true because he is a cheerful young lad almost all the time.

Walnut is the youngest and not quite as tall as Topp. He is roly-poly but strong and healthy. Walnut is kind of goofy, and he likes to make people laugh. Like a turtle, he's never in a hurry. He loves to daydream and may seem absentminded, but sometimes he taps into a special superpower that he calls his magic or *pow pow*.

Topp, Taffy, Walnut, and Sugar have known each other forever – or at least all their lives (which is not such a long time really.) Together they are like a rainbow, different colors that are most beautiful when all together. Each has a unique personality, but on one thing they agree: They want to be together and have fun and adventures every chance they get.

Each one has a favorite color and motto.

Topp: Orange *Life is an adventure with so much to do and see*
Taffy: Red   *Always do your best, and be strong and brave*
Sugar: Yellow *Be kind to all living things, and never stop learning*
Walnut: Green   *Have fun, enjoy every day, and be your goofy self*

The four friends settled in comfortably around the picnic table, while Emerald and Ragamuffin kept each other company underneath the table, purring away. It didn't take the kiddos long to figure out what they wanted to do for their next daring adventure. Glancing up at the clouds, Taffy said, "It's not very hot today. What a perfect day to ride our bikes and get in better shape for our long travels ahead."

"Good idea! It'll be fun to put more miles on our brand-new three-wheeled bicycles," Walnut added.

Chapter 5

THREE-WHEELED BICYCLES

❧❧

Each of the kiddos is the lucky owner of a three-wheeled bicycle – yes, a *three*-wheeled bicycle. And *no*, they are not tricycles, oh no! The three wheels are in a straight line with the third wheel connected directly behind the second one, not like a tricycle with two wheels side by side. The third wheel seldom touches the ground, but it keeps the bike (and rider) from tipping over backward when going up steep hills, which the kids often do for the thrill of it.

The invention of the three-wheeled bicycle was inspired by a terrible accident that Topp had last year. One day while riding his old bicycle up a steep mountain trail, Topp tumbled over backward, crashed hard and broke his arm. He was lucky he didn't break his head!

Topp's dad, Mr. Topper, asked himself if it might be possible to prevent this from happening again. He developed a prototype by rigging up an ordinary bike with an extra wheel in the back, which he called a safety wheel. Before long, all the kids wanted one. And not surprisingly, all the parents wanted a safety wheel on their children's bikes too.

Wouldn't your mom and dad?

Mr. Topper turned his innovative design over to the bicycle makers. Now all new bikes are three-wheelers. Even the new tricycles for little kids have an extra wheel out the back – they're called four-wheeled tricycles.

Get it? I hope so ...

When the new bikes arrived at the bike shop in town, the kiddos were given bikes in their favorite colors. Topp's bike is orange, Taffy's is red, Walnut's is green, and Sugar's bike is yellow.

Does your favorite color reveal something about your personality? Perhaps! Topp is free-spirited and intense like the color orange, Taffy is energetic and enthusiastic like the color red, Walnut is gentle and down to earth like the color green, and Sugar is cheerful and warm like the two suns that shine above them in the Valley of Ooga Ooga.

The kiddos love to ride their bikes all over the Valley of Ooga Ooga. They ride for fun, in search of new adventures.

"Are we going to sit under the gazebo all day?" Taffy blurted out.

"Let's decide where to ride," Topp said. "We need to get in shape, so wherever we ride, we need to ride hard!"

"We could ride to the flower field on the other side of the river," Sugar suggested. "I'm pretty sure the flowers are in full bloom about now. We could pop the pop flowers and run all over the field like we did last year."

The flower field is a twenty-minute ride from the far side of the main bridge over the Ooga River. Millions of wildflowers fill the lush meadow every year. They have appeared every spring and summer for forever – however long that is. They bloom like crazy this time of year, and the kiddos love to play among the flowers.

"Walnut, do you think you can keep up with us on your bike?" Topp asked, teasingly.

"I *am faster* on my bike," Walnut answered, "but not as fast as you speedsters!"

Even on his bike, Walnut tends to lag behind, but the others don't mind slowing down so he can catch up. They are the bestest of friends, after all, and their motto is *All for One – and One, Two, Three, Four for All!*

"Let's run home and get our bikes. We can meet at Riverside Park, at the end of Moon Street near the bridge," Topp proposed. "When we're all together again, we can ride full speed to the flower field. That would be a good workout."

All the kiddos agreed, jumped up, and shouted, "Rainbow kiddos away!"

Three of the kiddos *did* run all the way home to get their bikes. But Walnut, who had hidden his bike in a bush near the gazebo, had a plan to trick the others. He petted Emerald the cat and waited until the others were out of sight, then he hopped on his bike and took off full speed to Riverside Park at the bridge over the river.

Chapter 6

SKIPPING STONES ON THE OOGA RIVER

❧❦

Just as he had planned, Walnut arrived at Riverside Park before anyone else. He walked down the embankment to the edge of the Ooga River and looked for small flat stones. He gathered a few good ones and started throwing them across the calm shallows. "One, two, three, four, five skips, plop! Pretty good – don't ya think?" Walnut muttered to himself or to the river, I'm not sure which ...

At this time of year, the Ooga River babbles and bubbles as it flows over big and little rocks near the bridge. Walnut's whistling was accompanied by the friendly sounds of the river.

"Hey, Walnut! How in the world did you get here so fast?!" Topp yelled from high above on the riverbank.

Before Walnut could answer, Sugar and Taffy rode up, with Ragamuffin close behind. They skidded to a stop and kicked up a little cloud of pink dust.

"What the heck, what are you doin' here already, Walnut?" Sugar asked.

Taffy chimed in, "Yeah! What are you doin' here so soon?"

"Skippin' stones, that's what I'm doin'," Walnut said, trying to hide a smile.

"That's not what we mean," insisted Topp. "How did you *beat* us here?"

"Maybe you were just slow ...," Walnut said, struggling to keep a straight face.

"That's impossible!" Taffy exclaimed. "I ran home and rode here as fast as I could. I should have been here long before you!"

"Maybe it was my pow pow!" Walnut chuckled, clearly enjoying being the center of attention. Then he turned to face the river, whistled, and sent a rock spinning through the air. It skipped more than five dozen times across the surface of the water and traveled so far, the last few skips were a blur.

"See? Pow pow – my magic!" Walnut said, grinning from ear to ear.

Topp, Taffy, and Sugar were amazed. None of them had ever skipped a stone that many times.

Finally, Walnut explained, "Okay, okay, I'll fess up. This morning, I rode my bike to the gazebo and hid it in the bushes. When you guys went home to get your bikes, I came straight here. No pow pow – I just tricked you!"

The kiddos stared sternly at Walnut for a moment and then burst into laughter.

"You win!" admitted Topp. "We tease you quite a bit, so we can't blame you for spoofing us."

"Yeah, good one ...," Taffy added, "but I'm still wondering ... how did you skip that stone so many times?"

"That's *my* secret," Walnut beamed. He didn't want to admit he was just lucky.

The kids were in no hurry to get to the flower field, so they parked their bikes, trotted down to the river's edge, and started skipping stones. Walnut was sure they would try to beat his unexpectedly long throw. He also knew they would ask him to do it again. He doubted he'd be that lucky, so he moved behind a big boulder on the beach and kept busy with a different game. He rolled fist-size round rocks at upright sticks and tried to knock them down – like bowling.

Topp, Taffy, and Sugar tried as hard as they could, but the most skips they could manage was five or six. Finally, they gave up, and everyone agreed it was time to ride on to the flower field.

As they started to climb up out of the riverbed, Topp said, "Hey, Walnut! Show us more of that pow pow and skip another stone."

Uh-oh. Walnut knew he was in a pickle! The other kids stopped and waited. They looked at him in anticipation, to see him try to skip another long one – which they knew he couldn't.

"No problem!" Walnut said boldly, sounding much more confident than he felt. "But just one, I don't want to use up all of my pow pow."

Walnut whistled while he took his time searching for the right stone. He shuffled up to the edge of the water and dug in with his sturdy legs. Then he cocked his arm back and pivoted. His hand came around like a whip, and the stone cut through the air like lightning – it spun so fast, they could hear it whirring before it hit the water.

"Oh my!" screamed Taffy.

"What the, the ...?" Sugar spewed out.

"Are you kidding me!!!" shrieked Topp.

The stone danced across the water as though it was on a frozen lake. It skidded so many times, his earlier throw seemed feeble in comparison. At the end of its journey, the stone appeared to sink slowly and gently in the water, like a soggy leaf.

Even Walnut was astonished by his incredible achievement, but he didn't let anyone know that he was as dumbfounded as they were. Instead, he simply said, "Enough pow pow for today – let's go play in the flowers!"

"Wow ...," was all the others could muster. The amazing things Walnut does sometimes are mind-boggling. Topp, Taffy, and Sugar gazed at the river one more time. Perhaps they thought Walnut's stone might still be skipping along – this *is* Ooga Ooga after all where anything is possible.

They jumped on their bikes and started pedaling toward the bridge when Taffy hollered, "It's a race to the other side!"

"You're on!" shouted the others. And they pedaled over the bridge, high above the sparkling Ooga River.

Chapter 7

THE KIDDOS AND THE FLOWER FIELD

Topp and Taffy were neck and neck as they raced over the bridge. It almost ended in a tie, but Topp crossed the finish line a second ahead of Taffy. "Yay, I won!" he shouted.

Taffy instantly reminded Topp that *she* had won the last three races. And just as quickly, Topp replied, "That's because sometimes you don't play fair!"

"What do you mean, *I don't play fair?*" challenged Taffy.

"Sometimes you don't play fair – because sometimes you're faster than me!" chuckled Topp.

Taffy's face snarled then brightened, and she began laughing at Topp's playful teasing.

Sugar came in third because she isn't into racing. She leaves that to the others. She loves to ride her bike and cruise along but slowly enough to enjoy the birds and other living things around.

On the other hand, Sugar's pup, Ragamuffin, *loves* to race. He beat all of them over the bridge and was not at all pleased when no one noticed that *he* won the race.

Walnut crossed the finish line with a grin and proclaimed, "Better late than never!" He likes to whistle while he rides, which makes it difficult to pedal fast. When it comes to bike racing, you might think Taffy and Topp are the only serious contenders, but Walnut believes he'll be a winner someday, in the same way he believes in fairy tales, and that *wishes do come true.*

The kiddos pedaled hard and rode as fast as they could. They were determined to get in shape for the many long journeys ahead. Carefree and lighthearted, the kiddos pedaled to the flower field in a rose-colored cloud of dust.

(The colorful dust in Ooga Ooga is a healthy thing, and when it goes airborne, it fills the air with delightful fragrances and healthy powders.)

When they reached their destination, they leaned their bikes against a shade tree and paused to take in the spectacular view: a field full of millions of colorful wildflowers, such as red pop pop flowers, white puffy flowers, and fan flowers in every color of the rainbow – and then some.

Pop pop flowers are lovely with their flower pods dangling down like tiny lanterns. If you smash a little pod between your hands, it will pop so loudly, your ears will ring. If you and a friend prefer a quieter game, pull a pod off its stem, and toss it back and forth like a paper ball. Try to keep it afloat by gently bouncing it up with the palm of your hand.

Puffy flowers are unique and look like white cotton candy. Give them a whack and thousands of tiny white fluffies will be set free and billow into the sky.

Fan flowers are used in a game by kids and grownups alike. Start by plucking one petal off a flower and say, "Loves me." Then pluck another petal and say, "Loves me not." Repeat plucking petals and alternating the phrases until there's only one petal left. The game is extra fun because the last petal will *always* be followed by "Loves me." How can that be? It's simple. Every fan flower has seven petals, don't you know? Try the game yourself, and you'll end with "Loves me" every time.

Topp shared a secret that the others had never heard before. "If you pick a fan flower in your favorite color and put it under your pillow at night, it'll bring you good luck the next day."

The kiddos ran across the trail into the flower field with reckless abandon. They were so full of energy, you might think they'd eaten a gob of a Big Ol' Slurp. I think the pollen from the flowers energized them and made them kind of cuckoo. They ran rowdy through the field and created little trails as they stomped around. Every time they collided with the flowers, clouds of fluffy stuff and charming delicate pods were set aloft in the breeze. There was so much stuff floating in the air, they could barely see where they were going. What fun. While the kiddos ran around, Ragamuffin hopped through the flowers like a kangaroo.

After an hour of running and playing, the day turned chilly. Gray clouds were rolling over the valley, so the kiddos decided to go home before it got colder and darker. They hadn't dressed for cold weather this morning because it had been summertime warm but not anymore.

In case you're concerned about the trampling of all those flowers, don't worry. Overnight, all the flowers will grow back and look the same as before. The flower field has its own kind of pow pow, I suppose.

When the clouds of fluffy stuff from the flowers finally cleared, Walnut was nowhere in sight.

"Where is he?" asked Taffy.

"I don't know, we need to find him," said Sugar.

They called his name and waited to hear his voice or his whistle, but they couldn't hear a peep. Walnut had disappeared!

"I'll check the river's edge," Taffy said. "Maybe he's skippin' stones down there."

"I'll check the woods at the end of the field, maybe he went explorin'," Topp said.

"I'll go back to the tree where we left our bikes," Sugar said. "He might be there."

After a few minutes, the three children returned, but there was still no sign of Walnut. What should they do?

At that moment, Sugar pulled out her special whistle (which she always carries in her emergency kit) and blew it as loudly as she could.

Suddenly, Walnut jumped up out of a thick clump of flowers nearby.

"Are you okay, Walnut?" Sugar asked.

"Yeah, I got tired, so I took a nap. I really needed that nap!" Walnut said groggily.

Walnut has done that before. The kids call them Walnut's turtle naps. It's fitting because Walnut is as slow as one. Turtles sleep for months, which is what Walnut would do if nobody woke him up.

"We better get going," Topp advised. "But before we go, don't forget to pick a fan flower in your favorite color to put under your pillow tonight."

Taffy picked a red flower, Sugar picked a yellow one, Walnut found a green one, and Topp picked an orange one. Wasting no time, they ran to their bikes, rode over the bridge, and sped home.

That night, they tucked their fan flowers under their pillows before they went to bed. Everyone had wonderful and colorful dreams that night! Their dreams were so funny, they laughed out loud in their sleep – believe it or not!

Did the fan flowers have something to do with their delightful dreams? They will never know for sure, but even if the fan flowers *didn't* bring any good luck, their hilarious dreams were reward enough.

In the morning, Taffy, Walnut, and Sugar met at the park as they had planned. Surprisingly, Topp arrived last. He rode up on his bike speedily, skidded out of control, and kicked up a lot of pinkish dust.

"I found a brittle$ on the road on my way here! What luck!" Topp shouted with excitement.

(Just in case you haven't heard, brittles$ and coins$ are the money used in Ooga Ooga. The dollar sign at the end of the words brittles$ and coins$ is silent when spoken, so you simply say "brittles" and "coins.")

Topp was thrilled because with a few more brittles$, they could buy a Big Ol' Slurp at the Goody Goody store. A Big Ol' Slurp is a lot like ice cream but even more scrumptious.

"I found a brittle$, too!" exclaimed Taffy. "It was run over by a six-legged horse or something, so it's a little dented and dusty but it's still good, I think."

Then Sugar said, "I found a brittle$ near the bench at the Ducky Pond! There was nobody around, so I figured – *finders keepers*. What luck! The fan-flower-under-my-pillow kind of luck, I suppose!"

Three of the kiddos were overjoyed, but *Walnut* sat there with a long sad face. "I didn't find one!" Walnut lamented. "My green fan flower wasn't lucky at all!"

Perplexed, Topp asked Walnut, "Did you put it under your pillow last night?"

"Just like you told me to," Walnut said softly. "I put the fan flower under my pillow when I went to bed, but when I woke up, it was on the floor!"

"That's it!" Topp shouted. "If your fan flower isn't under your pillow *all* night, it isn't lucky, I suppose."

"Yes, it was! It *was* lucky for Walnut, too!" Sugar shouted. "We found three brittles$, right? That's exactly how much we need for a Big Ol' Slurp, which is plenty big enough for the four of us."

Without another word, they rode off to the Goody Goody store to buy and share a Big Ol' Slurp. Walnut realized that he *was* lucky after all. He got gobs of Big Ol' Slurp, he gets to live in the Valley of Ooga Ooga, and he has such good ol' friends.

Chapter 8

BOBBY AND HIS CAT FLUFFERS

❧❧

In the middle of the night, Bobby was rudely awakened when something landed on his chest. "Ow! Wow!" Bobby yelled. "Fluffers, how did you get in here?"

Bobby pushed his purring cat off and turned on the light by his bed to see what was going on. He noticed that his door was open just wide enough for his fuzzy cat to enter. He must not have latched it tightly enough when he went to bed. Bobby loves spending time with his cat during the day, but he usually keeps his door closed when he goes to bed to keep his rascally cat out when he's sleeping.

Whenever she gets a chance, Fluffers jumps around and plays on his bed day and night. She sleeps during the day and stays awake all night playing silly hunting games. She acts like a great hunter, prowling and pouncing all through the night. But the only thing she ever caught was a fly – and it might have been dead when she got it.

Bobby climbed out of bed and shook his finger at Fluffers, who was now playing on top of his new puzzle of a hundred ladybugs. She seemed to be batting at the picture of the ladybugs on the puzzle box as if they were real bugs.

"Fluffers – stop it – you cuckoo cat!" Bobby said. "I was having a great dream, and now I'm awake – talking to a cat! I should punish you – you rascally cat!" He pointed a finger at her and stared eye-to-eye. Then he melted under her trusting gaze. Bobby knew he could never punish his lively cat, for he loves her dearly. He does enjoy cats – except for the cats that jump on him and wake him up from wonderful dreams!

Cats? Bobby suddenly remembered that there was a cat in his dream – it was a friendly but weird-looking green cat with a white tail. It hopped like a rabbit and lived in a park where the dream-kids often played.

When Bobby began shooing Fluffers out of his room, she raced across his worktable and almost knocked over his toothpick roller coaster. Fluffer's tail disappeared out of sight as she jetted through the open door with Bobby close behind, "Good riddance, you nutty cat!"

Bobby returned sleepily to his bed, crawled under the covers, and plopped his head onto his pillow. He longed to fall asleep and pick up where his dream left off. He turned off the light, closed his eyes, and breathed slowly. He tried to gather up pieces of the lovely dream lingering in his mind and bring it back to life.

As he let his imagination run free, he visualized the green cat in the park and a sandy beach with pebbles by a river bridge. He remembered skipping stones on the wide river and riding bikes with his new pals – the dream-kids.

Bobby fell asleep quickly. Shortly after, a smile appeared on his face.

I wonder what made him grin ....? Sweet dreams, Bobby.

Chapter 9

DARING ADVENTURES APLENTY

❧

After the kiddos gobbled down the delicious Big Ol' Slurp they shared at the Goody Goody store, they headed over to Topp's garage to study the fascinating map they were given at the Museum of Everything.

The kiddos gathered around as Topp spread out the mysterious map on the workbench. They were mesmerized as they pored over every inch of the colorful, detailed map.

"Look, there's a mountain called Candy Mountain," Walnut said. "Wow! I wonder if it's really made of candy."

"And look at those hills – they're named the Chocolate Hills," Sugar said.

"I'd be surprised if they're made of real chocolate," Taffy said skeptically. "Maybe they're just made of chocolate-colored dirt."

"We sure have a lot to learn about what's out there beyond our little valley," Topp mused. "Heck, there might even be an end to our land way out there somewhere, and we could be the ones to find it."

"Hey! Let's take the new map to Grandpa Gabby and ask him what he knows about all these faraway places," Sugar said enthusiastically.

Everyone thought that was a great idea, so they hopped on their bikes and rode swiftly to the Ducky Pond. The map was tucked securely in Taffy's pocket as they coasted up to the bench at the pond. Much to their disappointment, Grandpa Gabby wasn't there.

Undeterred, the kiddos rode on to the giant jujubee tree on a nearby hill. The majestic tree, covered with ripe jujuberries, is out-of-the-way and more private than the gazebo. The long limbs of this grand old tree reach out from its trunk like a giant umbrella, and the longest branches droop down to the ground on all sides. Underneath, there's a secret room (that's what the kiddos call it) where it's dry and cozy — unless it starts to rain, that is.

The kiddos laid their bikes down on a mossy patch and walked briskly up the grassy hill to the jujubee tree.

"Come on in," Taffy said as she held back branches so the others could enter the hideout.

They sat in a little circle, with Ragamuffin in the center. Walnut started the conversation, "It's time we start plannin', and I think the first thing we should do is build a clubhouse with a *real* roof. This one leaks every time it rains!"

"Yeah, I agree!" Sugar said. "We're so lucky that Old Man Gruff gave us permission to build a real wooden clubhouse on his property someday."

"We know that's where our headquarters will be eventually," Topp said, "but we need to get more boards and nails before we can start building."

Suddenly, a weird, black, smoky form appeared out of nowhere. It swirled loudly in the limbs just above their heads. The kiddos were paralyzed with fear as the dark cloud thing began making a high-pitched squeal.

"YOOOW! What's that noise?!" Walnut shouted.

"I don't know! I've never heard anything like it!" Taffy yelled.

"FANG BATS!" Sugar cried out. "KNIFE-TOOTHED FANG BATS! RUN FOR YOUR LIVES!"

The kiddos bashed through the leafy curtain of the tree and ran outside as quick as a flick. From a safe distance, they looked back at the jujubee tree and heard the fang bats still making a noisy racket inside the tree.

"What are ... fang bats?" Walnut asked, his heart pounding in his chest. "Do they bite?"

"Yes, they do!" Sugar said. "They'll suck your blood if they land on you!"

Taffy could not resist the chance to tease Walnut a bit, "Yeah, we like to drink Big Ol' Slurps, and they like ... well, people juice!"

"Whoa! No!" Walnut blurted out.

The kiddos stood there staring at the tree, listening to the screeching, buzzing sounds made by the huge swarm of bats within. Suddenly, one flew out from under the branches and circled directly over their heads.

"It's *not* a fang bat!" Sugar said. "It's *only* a barn bat. They're completely harmless. Haven't you heard of them? My grandma says they usually live in barns and keep the six-legged horses company."

"I still don't like them," Walnut said with a quiver in his voice. "How do you know which kind of bats they are, anyway, Sugar?"

"I read about animals all the time," Sugar explained. "I'm not afraid of them, so I'm gonna go in and shoo them out of our hideout."

Sugar ran around the tree, whacking the hanging twigs, leaves, and berries with a stick as she made her way around and around. Then she held back an armload of branches to create an opening and in no time, out flew a couple of hundred bats. The barn bats wiggled and wobbled through the air as they flew over the Ducky Pond and beyond, to who knows where – some barn, I suppose.

"Well, come on! Back to it!" Taffy shouted.

The kiddos tiptoed cautiously through the opening and sat down. They looked up anxiously at the silent branches above.

"They're gone now ... don't worry!" Sugar said. "They won't get your blood – not today anyway!"

Topp said, "As I was saying, before we were interrupted by those awful bats, we need more boards and nails before we can start building."

"Okay, we need more wood and nails," Taffy said. "So, what can we do next, until we're ready to build?"

"Hey yuck!!!! What's that smell?!" Walnut yelled out, pinching his nose. "It's nasty stinky!"

"STINKY WORMS! WE GOTTA GET OUTA HERE!" Sugar shouted. "They're stinkin' everything up! Get out, or you'll stink for days!"

The kiddos dashed outside to fresh air and safety and looked back at the tree. "What should we do now?" Topp asked.

"Let's sit down right here on this grass and keep plannin'," Taffy said.

"What's next? An attack by killer wasp-bees?" Walnut asked. (Walnut wasn't kidding one bit, but everyone ignored him.)

"I think we should ride our bikes up to Lookout Rock on Ooga Mountain," Topp said. "We almost made it last summer. If it wasn't for those nasty two-headed snakes, we would have made it for sure! If we're going to ride to the far-off places on the map, we better be in shape. A ride to Lookout Rock would be a heavy workout for us. And I can borrow my dad's long-eye telescope, so we can look through it and search for the *edge* when we're up high on the mountain."

After a good bit of discussion, everybody agreed that Lookout Rock would be next on their adventure list.

Taffy asked, "After we go to Lookout Rock and after we build the clubhouse, can we make a raft and go down the Ooga River to the Fantasmo Sea?"

"Okay, and maybe we could ride our scooters to the Tot Tot Hills," Sugar said. "Maybe even go as far as the Jolly Jungle on the other side."

"I have an idea," said Taffy. "We could make a garden and grow yummy food and pretty flowers next to the spot we build our clubhouse."

Topp didn't say a word, he just listened.

"Let's figure out how to get to Candy Mountain and eat you know what – yum, yum!" Walnut said, licking his lips.

"Oh no, it's starting to rain!" Taffy yelled. "Run! Run! It looks like a white rain! Run for the gazebo!"

Damp and cold, the kiddos huddled together under the gazebo roof. Emerald, the friendly green cat, was under the picnic table, purring loudly because she was dry or because she likes the kiddos or both. Ragamuffin sat next to Emerald and purred the best he could.

The kiddos spread out the map on the table and resumed making plans for future adventures. "Maybe we could go to the Ice Bug Sea, after we visit and eat some of the Chocolate Hills," Sugar said with a twinkle in her eye.

"Maybe we could have a parade and afterward have a picnic in the park. We could invite everyone in the village, play games, and give away prizes," Taffy suggested. "And maybe we could go swimming in Wetwater Lake or cruise around the Ducky Pond in a rowboat."

"Or go to that spooky sounding Rat Town place, at night with lanterns!" Walnut said, even though he knew that would be too scary.

On and on, the kiddos pointed out places on the map where they wanted to go. Topp sat there and just listened. After a while, they realized that the two suns were starting their downward journey to the west. The fading daylight let them know it was time to start riding home.

Taffy spoke up, "Topp, you haven't said a word! Which adventure do you think we should have this summer?"

Topp jumped up and shouted, *"ALL of them*! And more!!!"

They all laughed out loud! They laughed so hard, their tummies hurt a little.

Then Topp said, "I think we need to decide which one to do *first* — we can't do all of them *at the same time,* can we?!!!"

They laughed until their tummies hurt a little more.

"For now, we should start getting ready to ride our bikes up Ooga Mountain," Taffy said. "Many times, we've talked about riding higher than we have ever been before. Let's do it the day after tomorrow."

"Good idea," Topp said. "We'll oil our three-wheelers, pump up our tires, and get ready for a long ride."

"That's it, then," Sugar confirmed. "To Ooga Mountain we will go!"

There was a break in the rain, so they grabbed their bikes to head home. On their way out of the park, they spotted Grandpa Gabby sitting by the pond and stopped to ask him questions about the new map.

"Hi, young'uns," he said. "It's gettin' late, me thinks. You're heading homeward, me hopes."

"We're on our way, but we'd like to ask some questions about our map," Topp said.

"Can you bring it and meet me about noon tomorree at the gazebo?" Grandpa Gabby asked. "I'll have something to give to you young'uns when you come."

An agreement was made, and the kiddos hurried home in the last light of evening.

I can't be sure, but I suppose that as the kiddos lay in their beds that night, they were thinking about all the fun and daring adventures ahead of them.

The Valley of Ooga Ooga is full of happy dreams tonight, I bet.

Chapter 10

BEYOND THE VALLEY OF OOGA OOGA

❧❧

The kiddos woke up with visions of mountains, deserts, jungles, wildlands, and mystical seas swirling in their heads. They were excited about riding to Poppy Park to meet Grandpa Gabby to ask him about their amazing map.

"Hi, young'uns," greeted the nice old man. "Right on time, me sees. That's a good thing to observe in young'uns today. Hey, I'd like you to meet my old friend, Captain Float. He might be able to help with your questions too."

"Hello, and ahoy mateys," the Captain said with a tip of his sailor hat.

"Nice to meet you, sir," the kiddos chorused sweetly.

"The Cap'n's been around a long time, like me," Gabby said.

"Not nearly that long, you old relic!" the Captain said, laughing.

Grandpa Gabby glared at the Captain and then asked, "What kin we do fer ya, young'uns?"

"We'd like to ask you about the faraway places shown on the map that Mrs. Smart gave to us," Topp said. "Maybe you've been to those places or know something about them."

Grandpa Gabby and Captain Float took a minute or two and looked closely at the details on the map. Their eyes traveled slowly from east to west, north to south, and all around in circles. They seemed captivated by the wondrous map. Now and then you could hear them say things like: *Hmm, very interesting! Oh my! Fascinating!*

"This is truly an extraordinary map you have here," Gabby said. "I've never seen a map that shows places so far from the Valley of Ooga Ooga. I don't have much to say because I have never been to most of these places. Honestly, the valley is so very nice I haven't wanted to venture out to any hostile places – like the Duney Desert or the Jolly Jungle. I have only heard terrible things about them. The Jolly Jungle didn't sound *jolly* at all, with all the snakes, tigers, and wild critters all over the place!"

"Can you tell us more about the Jolly Jungle?" Sugar asked.

"What I know about the jungle is this: It's dangerous, but it also provides good things to eat, like plananas, bangos, and choco-lattay beans. Wood for construction and pencil reeds come from there too. However, and unfortunately, I've heard that several Oogans went into the jungle and never came back!"

"Yikes!" Walnut blurted out.

"Most Oogans steer clear of those places," Gabby continued. "Same for Rat Town, the Spiky Mesa, the Ice Bug Sea where the dangerous ice bugs live, and that massive Duney Desert!"

"So, all the years you've lived here, you didn't go anywhere out there?" Walnut asked.

"That's mostly true, yep – why should I? The Valley of Ooga Ooga is as good as she gets. There's nothin' out there better'n this place!"

"I suppose that's true," Topp said.

"It's not very wise for any Oogans to go out there, especially young'uns, me thinks."

Grandpa Gabby then pulled something out of a big bag. "Here's a detailed map of the Valley of Ooga Ooga – *just* the valley and all that's within it. I've had it for years. I'd like you to have it. There are lots of places *in* the Valley of Ooga Ooga to enjoy – and it's plenty safe around here, me thinks."

"I agree," Captain Float said. "I'm a boat captain, and I've sailed the seas – like these here I'm a pointin' to – the Fantasmo and the Ice Bug

Seas. There's nothing special out there, just *danger* on them waters, so whenever I was away, I always yearned to get back to the Valley of Ooga Ooga and its beauty and bounty."

When Captain Float was young, he owned a cargo boat named *Lady Luck* and had a business transporting silver coins$ down the Ooga River to the Fantasmo Sea. In Old Town, the coins$ were made of silver from the mines of Mr. Greede. He hired Captain Float to transport them to the far-off Island of Wow and other islands in the Fantasmo Sea.

Countless times, Captain Float successfully navigated the currents of the Ooga River to reach the islands. The trip was always dangerous. *Lady Luck* had to travel past the Village of Ghosts and the Spiky Mesa, which is covered with deep pits, enormous plants with long spines, and nothing else – oh, except the snapping snarks that roam around there.

"If I was forced to abandon my boat and step ashore, I might have fallen into a deep hole or gotten speared by pointy things – *if* I managed to survive the Village of Ghosts," the Captain said with a spooky voice.

"Whoa!" Topp said. "Sounds creepy!"

"Very creepy," the Captain agreed. "But now I'm here, living happily in Ooga Ooga!"

Then Topp asked, "Captain Float, have you ever heard of the legend about the *edge* – where the land comes to an end?"

"Oh yes, I've a heard of that silly notion. I've sailed far out into both of these here seas and never found no edge. I figure there can't be one nohow, otherwise all the waters in the seas would've poured over the edge a long time ago. A few people believe there *is* an *edge*, but their heads are full of nonsense!"

Pointing to the map, Walnut asked, "So, Mr. Gabby, do you know if there's any real candy on Candy Mountain?"

"I've never known for sure. Some say there is, and some say there isn't. As you know, there's a shop in the village where chocolate candy is made from the choco-lattay beans from the jungle, so why would anyone cross that terrible desert to get sweets from a mountain so far away?"

"The map I'm giving to you shows what's right here **in** the Valley of Ooga Ooga. It has details of what's close by and safe, like the flower field, Silly Creek, the Bubble Bath, Wetwater Lake, Happy Harbor where the Ooga River flows through the gap in the Yeller Cliffs, and so much more. I know all these places quite well, especially the tall and mighty Ooga Mountain. I *can* sure tell you many a thing or two about the mountain," Gabby said.

"We're going to ride up to Lookout Rock tomorrow, so we'd like to hear all you know about Ooga Mountain, if you please," Sugar asked Gabby sweetly.

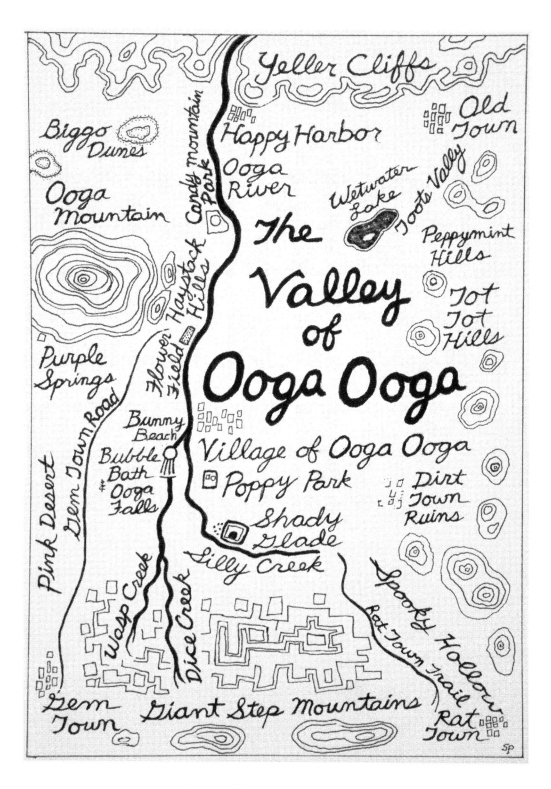

The Valley of Ooga Ooga

Chapter 11

TALES OF MIGHTY OOGA MOUNTAIN

ಹೊಂ

Grandpa Gabby got comfortable on the bench at the Ducky Pond, and the kiddos gathered around. He began telling stories about the mighty Ooga Mountain. He started by saying that he is one of the few Oogans who have climbed to the top of Ooga Mountain twice. Few people reach the summit because the round trip requires an overnight stay high upon the mountain. All kinds of creepy things are active during the night, so most Oogans would rather stay away. In fact, little is gained by getting to the top, except for being able to see and touch the big ball rocks balanced on the top and getting to eat fresh mittenweed and the delicious ice cream that oozes out of a rock fissure at the top. Also, bright red rubies the size of gum drops have been found up there.

Grandpa Gabby said that the Oogans who have climbed to the top of Ooga Mountain wanted to prove to themselves and others that they could do it. If they made it, they were rewarded by the breathtaking beauty of spectacular views in all directions. Sunrise and sunset from the top of Ooga Mountain are the most beautiful sights anyone can possibly see – so they say.

Ooga Mountain is much loved by everyone who lives in the Valley of Ooga Ooga. The mountain provides important things for the valley inhabitants: wood for their houses, rubber from the verystretchy bush, gonzo grapes, the webs of fire spiders, plus too many things to mention.

The most valuable resource of all is the drinking water from the creeks that run down the mountain slopes. The delicious water is carried to the village through clay pipes. The water is sparkling blue, like the blue color of Wetwater Lake. Visitors to the valley think the water looks strange, but after they taste it, they love it!

The Oogans say that strange animals and creatures come out of hiding and roam around on Ooga Mountain, day and night. Of all these critters, fire spiders are the most special. Fire spiders live on the back (or sunset side) of the mountain. They weave strong webs and glow red at night. They might seem scary, but they're not dangerous. They look like exceptionally large ladybugs and are quite friendly, too friendly perhaps, for they are spiders after all! The Oogans harvest their webs and use them to make fabric for clothes, string, and extraordinarily strong rope. The fire spiders don't mind when their webs are taken because the Oogans leave behind jujuberries, their favorite food, as payment.

Only one person has ever lived up on Ooga Mountain – a mysterious, young man who arrived in the Valley of Ooga Ooga several years ago. He hiked up the mountain and continues to live there to this day. He seldom comes down from the mountain, but when he does, he trades gold nuggets and rubies for food and other supplies. Then he *zips* back up the mountain and disappears again. Nobody knows his real name, so everyone just calls him Zip.

No one has ever spotted him on the mountain nor has anyone ever seen something like a cabin or tent where he lives. Perhaps he lives in one of the many caves high up on the mountain. When it's very quiet and still at night, you might hear singing on the mountain or see the flicker of a campfire up there. Zip was a mysterious young man when he came to the valley, and he is still a mysterious young man today.

Maybe the kiddos will meet Zip someday and find out his *real* name.

Grandpa Gabby and Captain Float told a few more stories about Ooga Mountain and then stood up and prepared to leave.

"I hope you learned somethin'," Grandpa Gabby said. "It's time for us two oldies to go now. You have two good maps to use, if'n you want to go on adventures **when you grows up, that is**."

Ignoring his last comment, Taffy said, "Thank you, we will treasure the maps, and now we won't *ever* get lost!"

Grandpa Gabby and Captain Float laughed, waved goodbye, and shuffled off down the trail.

The kiddos looked at each other and then down at the two maps.

"We didn't learn very much about the faraway places, did we?" Topp said. "I guess we'll just have to visit and explore them ourselves."

"For now, our goal is a successful ride up to Lookout Rock, which we've never achieved, of course," Topp said.

The kiddos remembered their first attempt to reach Lookout Rock. On the trail, they ran into dozens of stubborn two-headed snakes that blocked the path and refused to get out of the way. The kiddos couldn't figure out how to get the snakes to move without hurting them or being hurt themselves. Unfortunately, the kids had to turn around and abandon their goal to reach Lookout Rock that day.

Two-headed snakes like to hang around on the mountain trails. These snakes are like most snakes, except they have ten little feet to run around on. Oh, and two heads. They are dearly loved by the Oogans because they eat the bitter bugs that can ruin crops, and the snakes have an especially beautiful fragrance that fills the valley with a divine perfume. Two-headed snakes are seldom harmful, but boy, are they stubborn!

"I'll go to the blobwood forest today and get enough blob oil for our ride up the mountain tomorrow," said Taffy.

"That's great. Blob oil will really come in handy," Sugar said.

The kiddos are planning much better for this trip up the mountain. If they put blob oil on their bicycle tires, it will be easier to go uphill, much easier. Nobody knows and nobody cares why blob oil makes it easier to climb hills, but it does. The kiddos need all the help they can get because the trail is steep all the way.

Sugar said, "Remember, everybody – eat strong beans for breakfast, like we all promised!"

"Yuck!" Walnut said, putting his finger in his mouth as if to gag.

Topp said, "I have a plan for the snakes. My dad thought of a way to get the two-headed snakes to move off the trail. He offered to make a *pea rattle*. It's a hollow gourd filled with dried peas, with a stick for a handle. He thinks it will sound like a rattle-y-snake and scare the two-headers away. I'll bring it tomorrow."

"Wonderful," Sugar said.

"However, my dad did say his idea could backfire! He said the pea rattle might make them angry and even more stubborn!" Topp said.

"Yikes! I guess we'll find out tomorrow on our way up the mountain," Taffy said. "Okay, everybody, let's meet at Riverside Park by the bridge at sunrise."

"Okay!" they agreed.

The kiddos have always been in awe of the height and beauty of Ooga Mountain, partly because it is so imposing, but also because it beckons them to come and seek its mysteries and challenges. The kiddos are determined to reach the very tip-top of Ooga Mountain someday. But even if they never make it to the summit, there are interesting things to see and do on the mountain's lower slopes. Tomorrow the kiddos will make their way up the mountain. Their goal is to go higher than they've ever gone before.

Chapter 12

YIKES! A *THREE*-HEADED SNAKE?!

☙❧

The morning of the bike ride up Ooga Mountain was here. The kiddos planned to meet at the bridge by Riverside Park at first light. They planned to cross the bridge that led to the flower field but they'll go farther down the road to where the Wiggle Canyon Trail begins. It's the best way to Lookout Rock.

Taffy, Sugar, and Walnut arrived at the bridge at about the same time.

"Hey, Sugar, where's Ragamuffin?" Taffy asked.

"I don't think it's a good idea for him to come – too dangerous," Sugar said. "He wasn't too happy about it, so I told him he could come with us next time. He'll probably spend the day with his friend, Kitty, who lives in the house next door."

"Sounds like a lucky dog to me," Walnut said.

"I brought plenty of blob oil," Taffy said. "I hope Topp brings the rattle to shoo away those stubborn snakes."

"Did everyone have strong beans for breakfast?" Walnut asked. "I did, I'm sorry to say! Awful!"

The girls nodded yes and stuck out their tongues in disgust, to express how bad the beans tasted.

When strong beans are cooked properly, they are good for your health and give extra energy for adventures like riding a bike up a mountain. Strong beans boost strength so much, even Walnut will be able to keep up with the others. To say strong beans don't taste very good is being kind to the beans, because they really taste horrible! They taste so foul, people eat them only when necessary, like now. They taste like … oh, never mind! Yuck!

"Where's Topp?" Walnut asked.

"I don't know. It's not like him to be late," Taffy said. "I hope he didn't have a flat tire or have something else go wrong with his three-wheeler."

"Maybe he forgot to wake up early," Walnut said with a grin. "I almost did."

After a whole bunch of minutes ticked away, the kiddos grew worried. Finally, Taffy saw something down the road, far off in the distance. "I think Topp is headed this way in that yeller cloud of dust!"

"Sorry I'm late!" Topp said, breathing hard from pedaling with gusto. "I'd almost made it here when I caught a whiff of perfume from a two-headed snake. That's when I realized I'd forgotten to bring the pea rattle. Silly me! I had to turn around, ride home, and fetch it."

"I hope the rattle thing works," Taffy said.

"Me, too," Topp agreed, with his fingers crossed.

Topp had been more than a little late. Time was getting short for their ride up *and* down the mountain. Everyone knew they had to come down from the mountain before nighttime set in. No one wanted to be up there in the dark, that's for sure. No, not up on Ooga Mountain in the dark! Yikes!

The kiddos hopped on their bikes in a flash and raced across the river bridge. Powered by strong beans, they sprinted as fast as they could. They coasted up to a bench near the sign marking the trailhead. The Wiggle Canyon Trail lay ahead, beckoning them to come.

But first the kiddos took a minute to apply blob oil to their tires. They'll need the help of this special oil because the ride is uphill.

"Wow, this is exciting!" Topp blurted out. "I can barely wait to get up to Lookout Rock and peer out over the whole valley!"

"I'm excited, too!" squealed Taffy. "We'll make it this time, I just know it!"

"Yep, we're ready," Walnut said and began whistling a jolly tune.

In a very quiet voice, so soft none of the kids could hear her, Sugar whispered, "I hope we get back before night fall. I'm afraid of the dark – especially on Ooga Mountain." She hoped no one heard her because she didn't want anyone to worry.

With the strong beans kicking in, the kiddos jumped on their bikes and rode up the trail, yelling, "Rainbow kiddos away!"

The Haystack Hills are at the start of the journey. After that, the trail gets steeper. But with strong beans in their tummies and blob oil on their tires, they flew up the mountain like it was flat terrain.

As they rode along a field of wild gonzo grapes, they saw some Oogans picking grapes. When the kiddos stopped to take a breather, somebody yelled, "Hi, kids, help yourself to some gonzo grapes."

The kiddos gladly accepted several bunches of grapes, packed them in their lunch bags, and thanked the pickers heartily. From there, they followed the trail through a grove of skinny pine trees and came to Whistle Creek, which flows across the trail. The creek was shallow and easy to ride across, but they had to be careful not to get their feet wet as the tires splashed through.

Beyond the creek, the trail wasn't getting steeper, but they began having a hard time pedaling. The kiddos knew something was wrong, so they stopped to check things out. It didn't take long to realize that the ride through the creek had washed off the blob oil. It was now almost impossible for them to pedal uphill, and that wasn't good. But what *was* good was they still had plenty of blob oil with them, so they slathered it on their tires again.

"Next time, let's carry our bikes over the creek," Taffy suggested.

They all agreed with that simple strategy and pedaled onward and upward, much more easily now.

After a while, pedaling got harder again but not for lack of blob oil. The slope was now so steep, the third wheels of their bikes were rolling on the ground behind them. The third wheels worked like a charm, for without them, they would have surely tipped over backward and crashed down the mountain slope.

Feeling unsteady, Taffy got off her bike. She said, "I think this is where we need to walk our bikes – it's too steep to ride!" The others agreed, hopped off their bikes, and started walking them up the incredibly steep incline.

Around a big curve, they came upon a strangely familiar rock formation. The rocks were bright purple and shaped like triangles. Between the rocks were tiny, pink pine trees, no bigger than the kids.

They remembered the purple rocks and little pink trees from their last trip. They knew they were making good progress and that just ahead was the spot where they'd run into the two-headed snakes.

"There they are!" Taffy shouted. "Oh no, there are more snakes than last time!"

Topp quickly pulled the pea rattle out of his bag, raised it high in the air for maximum effect, and shook it wildly. *Clack-a, clack-a, clack!*

Startled by the obnoxious noise, the snakes raised up their heads and coiled, ready to strike. Clearly, they had heard the pea rattle and they didn't like it one bit! The snakes stared at each other with quizzical looks, and then they all shifted their attention to the biggest snake of all, the one with *three* heads! The strange-looking leader of the snakes rose from the ground, fixed its gaze with all six of its eyes on Topp, and hissed loudly. Unexpectedly, the three-headed snake turned abruptly and scurried off into the bushes. All the other snakes followed as fast as their ten little feet could carry them.

"There they go!" Topp yelled. "It worked!"

"Hooray!" Sugar shouted with glee.

The kiddos rode on with great enthusiasm because they knew they were almost to the lofty Lookout Rock. They also knew they had already gone higher than they had ever gone before. "Yippee!" they all shouted.

When they came to the end of the trail, they knew they had made it. Huffing and puffing, they parked their bikes. Joy and excitement were all over their faces as they walked slowly onto the massive overhanging rock. Side by side, the kiddos stood on the rocky promontory and took in the breathtaking view.

Standing and staring outward at the vast landscape, Sugar said, "Wow, look at that, I can see the Ooga River from way up here!"

"You're right, and if we can see the river, I bet we can see the shady glade by Silly Creek," Topp said. "Yep, there it is!"

Everyone looked down and saw the shady glade, the small meadow where they will begin building their clubhouse soon.

"Wow, we really did it!" Sugar cried with delight.

Topp pulled out the long-eye telescope his dad had lent him, and they took turns looking out in all three directions. They couldn't look toward the fourth direction (to the west) because the mountain was in the way.

The kiddos settled in for a while on Lookout Rock. They ate the sandwiches they'd packed and enjoyed the gonzo grapes too. As they filled their hungry bellies, they stared down at the wondrous sights in the valley below.

Straight ahead, toward the east, they saw the Tot Tot Hills and beyond them, they glimpsed the green foliage of the faraway Jolly Jungle.

To the left, toward the north, they saw the Yeller Cliffs and beyond the cliffs, there was the brilliantly blue Fantasmo Sea. To the right, toward the south, they saw the Giant Step Mountains. With the long-eye, they caught sight of the Chocolate Hills, the faraway Chocolate Hills and beyond those hills, they could see the Ice Bug Sea.

They all looked in amazement at the beauty that lay in front of them. This is *their* valley, the Valley of Ooga Ooga, and they realized how truly special it is.

Sugar saw some long shadows and began to worry about the time, so she spoke up, "Isn't it getting late? Shouldn't we be going back down?"

No one budged an inch nor said a word. It was as though they were under a kind of spell.

So, Sugar *shouted* this time, "We gotta get going!"

"Hold on, Sugar, I need a few minutes to look carefully over the land to see if there is any hint of an end to it," Topp said. "Maybe we can see the *edge* from up here."

After a (long) *few* minutes, Topp said, "It looks to me like the land just keeps going and going. Maybe the *edge* can be seen from the very *top* of the mountain."

"We're not going to the top today, I'll tell you that!" Sugar said in exasperation. "We've got to go down now, it's getting late!"

The others looked at Sugar and then down at the ground and sadly nodded in agreement. They glumly said their goodbyes to Lookout Rock and its beautiful views.

I doubt this will be the only time the kiddos come to Lookout Rock. What do you think?

Chapter 13

WILL THEY EVER GET HOME AGAIN?

⤳⤨

There they were, the four young children from the Valley of Ooga Ooga, standing high on Ooga Mountain. They were overjoyed to be on top of Lookout Rock and so sorry that it was time to leave.

"It's nice up here – I don't ever want to go," Walnut said sadly.

Topp and Taffy agreed with Walnut, but they also knew that Sugar was right. It was time to get going – and so they did.

They raced downhill scary fast, partly because the trail was so steep, and partly because they were concerned it would be dark soon. They rode down the trail so fast, they left a puffy cloud of blue mountain dust behind them. At one point, they took a corner too fast and almost skidded off a cliff! So, they slowed down a little for safety's sake.

Suddenly, Topp yelled, "Stop! Stop! Snakes!"

They all applied their brakes, skidded, and nearly lost control. They stopped just short of dozens of the scary wiggly creatures. Topp got out the pea rattle and shook it hard. Finally, after about five shakings, the snakes got onto their ten little feet and slowly shuffled off the trail and into the bushes.

As the kiddos got going again, Sugar yelled back to the snakes, "See you next time!" Then she dumped the last of her gonzo grapes on the trail for the snakes to enjoy as a gesture of goodwill.

Farther down the road, something strange happened. The trail was still steeply downhill, but now the kiddos had to pedal to keep moving! They pulled over to figure out what was wrong.

"I can hardly pedal!" Taffy cried out in alarm. "Something must be wrong with my bike."

"Same for me," Walnut said.

"I just remembered something my dad told me – about using blob oil," Topp said. "It dries out after a while and then acts like a brake."

"It would be fine if we had lots of time," Sugar said. "But we don't have time!"

Taffy then said, "When we get to Whistle Creek, we can wash the blob oil off and go fast again!"

"But Whistle Creek is still so far below us," Walnut squeaked.

Sugar had an idea. "I have rags in my emergency kit. Let's wipe off as much oil as we can and then wash off the rest in the creek when we get there."

The cleaning helped a little, but it also took precious time – which they had little of. With dark shadows falling upon them, they were now having trouble seeing the trail. But they needed to keep going – and fast! They pedaled as hard as they could, but the looming darkness of night was catching up with them. Now all the kiddos could see was a black curtain in front of them.

"Oh no!" cried Sugar. "What are we going to do now? We can't even go any farther, we can't see the trail!"

"I don't like the dark," Walnut said, his voice quaking.

"Oh my, I guess we didn't plan this very well, did we?" Topp said. "We'll have to sleep here on the trail until the sun comes up in the morning."

"That's the last thing I want to do!" cried Sugar.

"Same here," moaned Walnut, his throat tightening with fear.

"Shh, quiet ...," whispered Sugar, "do you hear that?"

"What is it?" Topp whispered back.

"It's the sound of Whistle Creek," Sugar said softly. "You guys stay here, I'll be right back."

Sugar walked away slowly into the darkness. She tapped a stick in front of her to avoid any obstacles in the blackness.

The kiddos wondered what the heck Sugar was doing. They were growing afraid for her (and themselves). They couldn't see her, but they could hear her stumbling and falling somewhere out beyond their view. They were deeply concerned about the predicament they had gotten themselves into.

"Are you okay, Sugar?" Taffy shouted out, not knowing if Sugar even could hear her.

Then they heard Sugar whistling faintly in the darkness. Suddenly, small lights started to glow in the distance. The lights became so bright, the kiddos could see the trail again, and they could see Sugar, standing by the creek whistling.

"What's going on, Sugar?" Taffy asked as she and the others walked their bikes down to her.

"The light is coming from the fairy flowers!" Sugar announced with glee.

"Wow! What are fairy flowers?" Walnut asked.

"My Grandma Mossy once brought me up to Whistle Creek to pick gonzo grapes and collect some webs from the fire spiders. She told me a story about a girl who got lost up here in the dark. Much to her surprise, when the girl whistled, the fairy flowers started to glow. So, she picked a few of the flowers, with their permission, of course, and kept whistling. The fairy flowers lit up and gave her the light she needed to get home safely."

"That's quite a story, Sugar!" Topp said. "So, if we just whistle, these flowers will glow?"

"That's right, just look around," Sugar said, pointing to the dozens of glowing flowers. "Grandma said the flowers glow when the light fairies inside are awakened by the music."

(And no one was more relieved than Sugar because she's afraid of the dark. Aren't we all just a little, maybe?)

"Everyone knows I like to whistle – SO I WILL!" Walnut shouted. He whistled loudly, and the fairy flowers glowed even more brightly than before. Fairy flowers glow like lightning bugs, but the fairy flower light doesn't flicker as much as a lightning bug's.

Few Oogans know that fairy flowers can produce light because only a few have been up on the mountain in the dark to find out. Smart people, those Oogans!

In the wonderful, glowing light, the kids rolled their bikes down to the creek and washed the blob oil off their tires. They picked handfuls of the fairy flowers (with their permission, of course) and then tied a bunch of flowers to the front of their bikes with string from the emergency kit that Sugar always carries with her.

Now the trail was brightly lit in front of them, and they rode swiftly down the steep, winding trail. They went upsie and downsie over the Haystack Hills, bumpity-bump across the river bridge, and then glided smoothly into the village.

They rode to Topp's house first because his was the closest. He let his mom and dad know that everyone was fine. They had made it to Lookout Rock and returned safely – so they were very fine *indeed*!

"Sugar saved the day!" Topp said excitedly. "It got dark so fast, we couldn't ride anymore. Then Sugar started whistling, the fairy flowers started glowing, and we raced home as fast as we could!"

Topp's mom was none too happy to know that Topp and his friends had been up on the mountain in the dark, but she was very happy that they were home, safe and unharmed. "All's well that ends well, I suppose," she said.

"Yay, Sugar!" the kiddos yelled. "You were so brave – you saved us all!"

Sugar blushed a little and said humbly, "The true hero is Grandma Mossy ... and the fairy flowers. They saved us, not me."

Topp wouldn't hear of it. "That's true, but you are a hero, too!"

The kiddos were delighted that they had gone higher on that mountain than they had ever gone before!

Chapter 14

MR. GRUFF'S SPECTACULAR GIFT

৶৶

After a few days of rest to recover from the long and difficult trip up Ooga Mountain, the kiddos gathered at their imaginary clubhouse under the jujubee tree. They brought bunches of fragrant roses to freshen the air inside the hideout and force the stinky worms deep underground. The kiddos were so sleepy, they couldn't stop yawning! If the ground under the tree was softer and cleaner, they might have all lain down to take a nap.

To wake up, the kiddos decided to play tag and chase each other around the tree. That helped a little.

Huffing and puffing and laughing, too, they reentered the hideaway and began discussing how to build their clubhouse in the shady glade.

Sugar was about to say something when it started to rain. "Oh no, we might get wet!" she cried. "But it's only an orange rain. I hope it'll stop."

In the Valley of Ooga Ooga, there are different kinds of rain, and most rains are colorful. Blue and green rains are cool. Yellow, orange, and red rains are warm. White rains are known to have big heavy drops that drench everything and everyone.

The kiddos stayed dry under the jujubee tree for a while because the leaves above their heads were holding the first drops. But as it rained harder, the rainwater flowed down the leaves and started to drip, drip, drip onto their heads.

"Let's get out of here! Run for the gazebo!" cried Topp.

The kiddos and Ragamuffin didn't hesitate and sprinted as fast as they could across the park. The rain which had started out as a soft, orange rain turned into a deluge of white rain. By the time they got to the gazebo, they were completely wet, right down to their socks! Darn rain!

They found Emerald the cat sitting on the picnic table, purring contentedly and dry as could be. When Ragamuffin arrived at the gazebo, he wasn't so lucky or so dry.

Standing under the gazebo roof, safe from the pouring, white rain, the kiddos looked around at each other. Then all at the same time, in one form or another, they yelled out, "A clubhouse, we need to build our clubhouse!"

New adventures will have to wait. If only they had a clubhouse, they could hang out inside, look out the window, and watch everything get wet but themselves. Someday they hope a new clubhouse will be their permanent headquarters for all their daring adventures.

The piece of land on which they have been given permission to build was an impressive, unexpected gift from an old man named Mr. Gruff. He gave them a beautiful parcel of land by Silly Creek, in gratitude for rescuing his best buddy, an adorable dog named Groovi.

A month ago, Groovi went exploring far from home. While wandering down Silly Creek near the Ooga River, he got his paw stuck between two large rocks at the water's edge. He was missing for four whole days, and many of the villagers helped search for Groovi.

The kiddos searched far and wide and eventually found Groovi. He was in terrible shape, hungry, stressed, and exhausted. They wrapped him up in a jacket and carried him all the way home to Mr. Gruff.

Old Man Gruff thought long and hard about how to express his gratitude to the four children. Then he came up with a wonderful idea: Let them build a playhouse in the shady glade, next to the place where they found Groovi.

A glade is a type of meadow or clearing in the countryside. Old Man Gruff's glade is roughly an acre and surrounded by groves of tall trees, which create a great deal of shade in the glade. So, there you go – the shady glade.

Mr. Gruff also gave the children an old shed to take apart, to get started in their quest for the wood and nails they will need to build a shelter.

The kiddos promised Mr. Gruff that they would take good care of the land and keep it clean and build a handsome-looking dwelling. Furthermore, they wanted to grow a garden and share the harvest with him. And they agreed to grow goober peas because they're Mr. Gruff's favorite food. Some people in far-off places call them *peanuts* but in Ooga Ooga, they call them by their *real* name, goober peas.

Mr. Gruff was overjoyed to have Groovi back home again, and the kiddos now have a dream-come-true place to build their clubhouse. Everyone is delighted with the arrangement, especially the kiddos!

At the gazebo, the rain shower had stopped, but it was too late because the kiddos were already soaking wet. They decided to go home and change into dry clothes and then meet at Topp's garage to start making plans for their awesome clubhouse project. So off they went, dripping water everywhere.

Chapter 15

THE AWESOME CLUBHOUSE PROJECT

⤦⤧

In Topp's garage, safe from the rain, the kiddos sat in a circle and discussed all things clubhouse. For one thing, there's nothing more awesome in the imaginations of children than to have a *kids only* playhouse somewhere out behind their house, or even better, deep in the woods – a little shelter that is all their own, a secret hideaway where best friends can get together to share stories and prepare for adventures near and far.

The kiddos decided it would be best to plan their clubhouse carefully. They needed plans on paper that show what the clubhouse will look like and how it will be built. Taffy and Sugar started drawing the plans, while the boys went out to search for more building materials and supplies.

Everyone agreed that Topp should oversee the construction of the clubhouse. Topp has learned a lot about building things, thanks to his dad, Mr. Topper, the brilliant inventor. Furthermore, the Topper family's garage is full of all the kinds of tools they will need to build it.

Walnut was put in charge of collecting building supplies, so he got busy figuring out how much wood they already have and how much more they will need. For a couple of weeks, they had been trying to gather old boards from around the village. When Walnut counted those boards and estimated the wood to be salvaged from Mr. Gruff's shed, he knew they still needed more boards. Maybe not a million more but definitely more!

So, he came up with the brilliant idea of putting posters up around the village that read:

```
┌─────────────────────────────────────────────┐
│            BOARDS WANTED!                     │
│                                               │
│       Big Boards or Little Boards             │
│      Long Boards or Short Boards              │
│      Dirty Boards or Clean Boards             │
│                                               │
│          Thank you very much!                 │
│  Topp, Taffy, Walnut, Sugar & Ragamuffin      │
└─────────────────────────────────────────────┘
```

The wonderful people of the Village of Ooga Ooga are always willing to contribute to a good cause. They started searching their garages, backyards, and everywhere else, and came up with a lot of boards for the kids.

Donated boards came in from all over town, big ones and little ones, long ones and … you get it. The helpful people dropped off the boards in huge piles in the children's front yards. It was a mess, but what a wonderful mess it was!

Within a week, they had enough boards to build the clubhouse. There weren't a million boards but almost. And people brought nails because they knew those would be needed as well. Some of the nails were straight, but most were used and bent and needed to be pounded straight with a hammer. That'll keep the kids busy!

When Mr. Burps heard that the kids were building a clubhouse, he donated a big ol' window.

Mrs. Quilty offered to make curtains for the window, and Mr. Buggity gave them an old door that still had its hinges, blue hinges, three of them. Really nice, don't you think?

Mr. Bark dropped off a large barrel of brand-new nails and thanked the kiddos again for saving him from drowning in the canal. Taffy almost thanked him for getting stuck in the canal because they wouldn't have found the bottle and the ancient map if he hadn't. Instead, she and the other kiddos thanked him sincerely for his generosity.

Bob Bobb donated a shiny brass doorknob. And his wife, Bob (yes, her name is Bob), gave them a cozy rug for the floor. I know it's unusual, but they're called Bob and Bob Bobb – and somehow it works out okay. Mr. and Mrs. Bobb are quite nice, but their son, Bob, and his twin sisters, Bob and Bob, are not so nice. Do I dare tell you the names of their cousins? Maybe you can guess.

Now the kiddos needed to haul the boards to the shady glade and get them out of their front yards. They couldn't carry them on their bikes – that's for sure. They had to figure out another way.

Topp said, "We could make a sled to carry the boards and tow it behind one of our bikes."

"Swell idea," agreed Sugar. "That's the first thing we'll do – build a big sled to move the boards."

Besides letting them keep a big pile of old wood in his front yard, Topp and the kids were also allowed to use any of Mr. Topper's tools, if they used them safely.

Last summer, the kiddos built a doghouse for Ragamuffin with Mr. Topper's help. He taught them how to use saws, jigs, and rigs. They also learned to use drivers, racks, and jacks. All the kiddos learned how to build, but Topp knew the most about how to put things together. Mr. Topper trusts the kids to take care of his tools because they're all good kids (most of the time anyway).

On Topp's hobby table, Taffy and Sugar continued working on the drawings, while Walnut and Topp started nailing boards together to make a sled.

Sugar and Taffy were trying to decide where the window should be and where the door should go.

"I think the window should face Ooga Mountain. That way, we can look up and see the mountain and the sunsets," Sugar suggested.

"Yeah, I agree, and the door should face toward Silly Creek," Taffy said.

"Why face the creek?"

"That way, if we leave the door open, we can listen to the babbling of the creek flowing over the rocks and stones. It's such a peaceful sound."

"Great idea! Hey, what are we going to do about a roof?" Sugar asked. "We need a good roof so when it rains, we can look out the window and watch everything get wet but ourselves."

Just then Topp came inside, with Walnut close behind.

"The sled is done!" Topp shouted excitedly.

"Great news!" the girls sang out.

"How are things going with the plans?" Walnut asked.

"We ran into a problem. We don't know how to build the roof. What are we going to do for a roof? We *have* to keep the rain out!" Taffy said with concern.

The kids didn't say a word for a long minute, for this was a huge problem indeed. After all, they were just kids, so how would they know how to build a waterproof roof? They looked back and forth at each other and rubbed their chins as though that might help them think better.

All of a sudden, Taffy spoke up, "I've got it! In our backyard, there's an old, rubbery swimming pool that we don't use anymore. It's full of leaves, dirt, and bugs right now. It might make a good roof."

"I remember it," Topp said. "We would splish-splash in it when we were little kids."

"I get it!" Walnut said. "We can turn it upside down – *that* should work."

"I think that really *will* work!" smiled Sugar. "If the pool didn't leak when it was filled with water, then it will keep the rain out when it's turned upside down."

"Do you think your mom and dad will let us use it?" Walnut asked.

"I'm sure it'll be all right because my dad is thinking about taking it to the dump," Taffy said, "but I'll ask to make sure."

"I remember playing in your pool. It's round, isn't it? If so, we'll have to design a round clubhouse," Sugar said. "We'll go take measurements and come back and finish the plans."

"While you two are doing that, Walnut and I can start towing loads of boards to the shady glade."

The girls returned with the pool measurements and finished the plans for the clubhouse. They were delighted at how big the pool was because it meant they could build a roomy clubhouse.

In the new design, the girls figured that the wall with the window needed to be straight because the window from Mr. Burp was not curved. The wall with the door also needed to be straight because the door from Mr. Buggity was also not curved.

"When it's done, we can call it a *roundish* clubhouse," Sugar said.

Meanwhile Walnut and Topp loaded a heavy stack of boards on the sled. After they tied the sled to Topp's bike with a rope, they discovered it was too heavy to pull. He pedaled with all his might, but he could only move the sled about a foot. Walnut suggested unloading a few boards, but Topp had a better idea: to tie another rope from the sled to Walnut's bike, so they could pull the sled together, riding side by side. They didn't have any horses, so it couldn't be called horsepower, but it could be called *two three-wheeled bicycle* power, if you like.

Happily, Walnut and Topp pedaled away, towing the first of dozens of loads to the shady glade.

Chapter 16

THE CLUBHOUSE IS A DREAM HOUSE

After Sugar and Taffy finished revising the plans, they jumped in to take turns hauling loads of wood on the sled with their bikes. The kiddos were determined to remove all the piles of wood from their yards in one day.

As they pedaled along, their thoughts were filled with gratitude for the kindness and generosity of their Oogan neighbors.

Throughout the long day they made dozens of trips to the shady glade. With perfect timing, the last load of wood made it to the shady glade just as the two suns disappeared behind Ooga Mountain.

Boy, were they exhausted! All the kiddos went to bed right after dinner that night. They needed a good night's sleep, for they'd already agreed to work on the clubhouse all day the next day.

In the early morning, they met at Topp's house again. The kiddos gathered tools from the garage, loaded the sled, and pulled it to the small, dilapidated shack that Mr. Gruff had given to them. It didn't take long before they had it all apart and finished towing the salvaged boards to the shady glade.

There they stood, right there in the shady glade, staring at a big ol' stack of wood next to the spot where they would build their first clubhouse. There might not be a million boards but almost, I bet.

When Topp's older brother, Ripp, a carpenter, heard that the kids were going to build a clubhouse, he offered to help. Mr. Topper wanted to help too. Surprisingly, all the dads and moms wanted to help.

All the younger brothers and sisters and even Ragamuffin wanted to help, so they came along, too – and got in the way all day long.

Bob and Bob Bobb, and Bob, also volunteered to help build the clubhouse. Bob deftly installed the shiny brass doorknob he'd donated.

By late afternoon of the first day, the clubhouse walls were standing tall, and that was great progress. The door with the three blue hinges was attached and working. The window was in place, so now they could look out at Ooga Mountain from inside. The curtains that Mrs. Quilty sewed were up, and the rug from Mrs. Bobb was down. They were all done – *except* it had no roof!

"Hey, on sunny days, it would be nice to have *no* roof at all," Sugar said, "because it's fun to see the sky."

"Yeah, but on rainy days, it wouldn't be so nice," Taffy remarked.

"Maybe we can make a movable roof, so we can have it both ways," Topp added.

"Huh? How are we gonna do that?" Walnut asked, thinking that Topp's idea was nutty.

"Some other day maybe but certainly not today!" Topp agreed, and the others breathed a sigh of relief.

The kiddos were still facing an enormous problem, however. How would they ever move the heavy, rubbery, swimming pool out of Taffy's backyard to the top of the new clubhouse walls?

Taffy said, "What if we ask Mr. Float of the Float Moving Company? He has those big balloons that move things around. Maybe he could help us."

"How are we going to pay him for his time and such?" Sugar asked. "We don't have any brittles$. We spent what we had on that Big Ol' Slurp."

"I suppose we ought to ask him what he would charge and go from there," Taffy said.

To move big objects around in the valley, the Oogans hire movers who use large balloons that fly the objects high above the ground to where they need to go. Everyone knows that Mr. Float is the best floater around.

The kiddos rode their bikes to Mr. Float's house and knocked on his door. They introduced themselves, and Taffy explained their situation with the swimming pool and their roofless clubhouse. Then she asked what he would charge to move the pool from her house to the shady glade.

Mr. Float stood on his porch and looked upon the sweet, hopeful faces of the kiddos. He knew then that it would be a pleasure to help these lovely children. "Using my very best balloon, *Big Yeller*, I will move the pool shell and place it on top of your clubhouse, if ... you'll pull the piggy weeds from my backyard."

The kiddos gladly agreed.

"Mr. Float, are you related to Captain Float?" Sugar asked just before they left.

"Why yes, he's my brother. We both float. He floats in the water, and I float in the air – I guess *float* is not only in our names but in our bloodlines," he said with a wink.

On roof moving day, Mr. Float and his bright yellow balloon hovered over Taffy's old pool. He lowered long, strong ropes made from fire spider webs, down to the kids on the ground. They took their time and tied the ropes securely to the pool. They gave Mr. Float a thumbs up when the pool was ready to lift.

Up, up, and away went the pool, high into the sky! Pushed by a puff of wind, the balloon leaned and off it flew toward the shady glade.

The kiddos jumped on their bikes and rode off as fast as they could – they wanted to get there before the flying roof!

They made it with time to spare, so they held hands and waited breathlessly for *Big Yeller* to appear over the treetops.

"Look, there it is!" Taffy yelled.

Mr. Float gently and expertly lowered the upside-down pool onto the clubhouse. It was a perfect fit. The clubhouse was complete, and the kiddos could not be happier.

As *Big Yeller* lifted off and flew away, the kiddos ran inside. They jumped up and down for hours – okay, for a few minutes, anyway.

"Home sweet home!" Sugar said as she stood looking out the window. "Now we can look up at the mountain and see Lookout Rock, and when it rains, we can watch everything get wet but ourselves!"

Everybody jumped up and down and had a good laugh.

They yelled, "No more bats, no more stinky worms, no more rain, no more parents!" (Just kidding, they didn't even *think* 'no more parents!')

They fell to the floor in hysterics and couldn't stop laughing. When the excitement died down, they were utterly exhausted. They all lay down on the soft rug from Mrs. Bobb and fell asleep.

Just after dark, Ripp came to the clubhouse to look for the kiddos. He opened the door quietly, and there they were, fast asleep. They were lying next to each other on the floor of the new clubhouse, like a litter of newborn puppies.

"WAKE UP, SLEEPY HEADS!" Ripp yelled. He shouted extra loud, just to shock them.

"Whoa, what's up?" Walnut warbled groggily.

"You need to get home and pronto!" Ripp bellowed.

The sleepy kiddos slowly got to their feet and wobbled out of the clubhouse. Topp carefully closed the door and put a stick in the hasp that Mr. Topper installed, so the door won't blow open in the wind.

They took a few steps down the path and then stopped and looked back at the little building made of wood.

"See you in the morning," Sugar whispered and blew it a kiss.

They had a hard time seeing in the darkness, so they walked their bikes slowly down the trail.

The kiddos made it just in time for dinner and then spent time chatting with their families. They told them about the successful roof installation and thanked them for all they had done to help create their awesome clubhouse.

The kiddos ambled to their rooms and jumped into their cozy beds. As the children lay there thinking about their clubhouse, they knew that this day had been a very special one indeed.

Knowing what I know, there will be many more days ahead just as special, *or even more so*, than this one.

Chapter 17

BOBBY THE FEARLESS PROTECTOR

৵৵৵

Bobby was startled awake by a loud *WHACK*! He wasn't sure what it was. He wondered if something had fallen in his room or the noise came from outside. He had been so wrapped up in his dream, it was hard to wake up and figure out what was what. He propped his head up on his bunched-up pillow and looked around at his shelves. Nothing seemed out of place.

He knew his mischievous cat hadn't made the noise because he'd chased her out and closed the door securely before he went to bed.

There was no doubt *something* was amiss, and Bobby wanted to figure it out.

He sat up in bed and noticed the sound of rain *tap-tap-tapping* on his window. He stood up and looked through the wet glass. His vision was a bit blurry, so he rubbed his eyes but that didn't help. He pressed his nose against the glass and saw the branches of the apricot tree whipping around in a frenzy.

If the crashing noise came from outside, I'm not going to worry about it now, Bobby thought. *But ... what if it was somebody up to no good? What if something bad happens on my watch as guardian of our home?*

He listened for more noises, but there were none. *What would Dad do if he was here?*

He envisioned his dad checking on Mom and inspecting the outside doors. So, he started down the hall without turning on the light. He pretended that he was a night guard silently making his rounds.

SQUEEEEEK! Fluffer's squeaky toy blared out when Bobby accidentally stepped on it. He tripped and fell headfirst in a belly flop. "Yooooow!!!" he yelled. He slowly picked himself up and said to himself with a silly grin, "That was really sneaky, wasn't it?!"

He turned on the light in the kitchen and looked around. All he saw was Fluffers stretching next to her bed, after she was so rudely awakened by Bobby's yell.

Bobby continued onward to the entry, to check the front door. *It's fine here*, he thought. On his way to check the back door, he peeked into his mom's bedroom. She was asleep and had apparently slept through all the noise. He found that the back door was closed and locked. Bobby was relieved that all was well, and he knew his dad would have been proud of him for making sure his mom was safe.

Instead of going back to bed, he opened the back door and walked onto the porch. The cold, wind-driven rain pelted him through the open side of the covered porch. Fluffers stayed back, she wasn't about to go out there and battle the elements.

Beyond the apricot tree near the house, he noticed his old playhouse or what was left of it anyway. Memories came back to him as he stared at the ruins. He remembered that his dad planned to help him rebuild it as soon as he got back from the jungle expedition. Bobby had been waiting for his dad to return but as time went by, he started thinking he ought to rebuild it on his own. Things have stayed that way for six months – nothing more than a thought.

As Bobby turned to go inside, he looked back and saw water flowing through the crumbling roof into the small clubhouse. He thought sadly, *I've gotta get to work on that poor old shack and make it something I can be proud of.*

He sat at the kitchen table and reminisced about playing with his friends in the clubhouse years ago. He started formulating a plan to fix it up and make it larger. After all, he and his friends are bigger now. It would be great to have get-togethers with his friends in their own private kid-space again.

Bobby let out a big, noisy yawn and stumbled back to bed. It was the middle of the night, so he knew he needed more sleep. Before he burrowed into his pile of blankets, he saw the moonlight flicker through his window as the apricot tree boughs swayed in the wind.

His eyelids grew heavier. He was almost asleep when memories of the dream world came back to him. He remembered fragments of the dream – bits and pieces. He recalled being with the dream-kids and feeling afraid high up on a mountain at night in the dark. He knew they got home safely, and after the scary mountain trip, the dream-kids designed and built a whole new clubhouse!

"Oh my ...! What a coincidence, there was a new clubhouse in my dream!" Bobby whispered.

He crawled under the bed covers like a bug until he popped out at the top of the bed. He rolled over, stretched his legs, and nestled his head on the pillow. He tried to remember more of the dream, but sleep overtook him and away he went.

Chapter 18

OH, SUCH STRANGE CRITTERS VISIT

❧

The kiddos and Ragamuffin spent the afternoon at Mr. Float's house pulling piggy weeds from his yard. They were paying him back for the floatation of their clubhouse roof as they had promised. Picking the weeds was fun because the rancher next door let the kiddos feed them to his six-legged horses. Piggy weeds taste delicious to the horses. In fact, it's one of their favorite treats. Wouldn't you eat piggy weeds, if they tasted really yummy, that is?

To be clear, these horses don't have six legs, they have four. But when they gallop, it looks like they have six legs – hence the name. And just so you know, there is no such thing as a two-legged horse that looks like a four-legged horse when it gallops. That would be too weird – even in Ooga Ooga!

Six-legged horses have very strong tails that keep them from tipping over backward. Sound familiar? The Valley of Ooga Ooga has many strange and wacky *unusualalities* – like the word I just made up.

Many odd critters live in the valley. There are whistle birds that never make a sound and dirt lizards that fly and live in trees.

And there are all sorts of interesting rocks and gems in the valley too. Consider the rare, dark red rock found on the peaks of the Tot Tot Hills. They are called no-see-ums because they're hard to find and hardly anyone ever sees-um. There are sparkly white dia-mons, too, which you will find out more about soon.

The day after the kiddos pulled the piggy weeds, Topp left his house and headed for the clubhouse. He figured that Taffy, Walnut, and Sugar would already be there because he was late. He had to feed his swans and clean their pond – Mom's orders!

Everyone was delighted to see him riding up. When one of them is missing, it doesn't feel right – like a square with only three sides.

Would a three-sided square still be a square? I think it would more likely be a U or maybe a triangle – but not a square. What do you think?

The kiddos were so delighted with their clubhouse, they may never want to leave it, unless they're off on a new adventure, that is.

Inside the clubhouse, the kiddos were taking turns looking out the window at Ooga Mountain. Taffy was hogging her turn. It seemed she couldn't stop looking at something out there.

Eventually, Sugar had to ask, "Taffy, what are you looking at?"

Taffy ignored Sugar's question, kept looking through the window, and then finally blurted out, "I want to ride to the very tip-top of Ooga Mountain!"

"Wow, how are you going to do that – fly?"

"No," she shot back. "I'll ride up there on my three-wheeled bicycle or go on foot or both!"

"You're just a kid!" Walnut joined in. "Only grownups get to the top of Ooga Mountain – and not many of them ever get there!"

"No, I have a special plan. I'll go on Baby Gravity Day."

"I've heard of that. It's the day when the big sun and the little sun are right on top of each other, right?" Topp asked.

"Exactly," Taffy said. "On Baby Gravity Day, when both suns are lined up, the gravity in the Ooga Valley is less than half of what it is normally. I've heard it's easy to ride uphill on Baby Gravity Day because everything is so much lighter. Things almost float."

"You're making that up!" Walnut complained.

"I've heard that, too," Topp said, "but I thought it was phony."

"We'll be findin' out soon because there'll be a Baby Gravity Day in a couple of weeks. It'll be the first one to happen in our lives," Taffy said. "It happens only once every seventeen years. I will definitely be ready to ride to the top of Ooga Mountain on that day! Who wants to ride with me?"

"I do, I do, I do!" yelled the others. At the same time, the idea seemed kind of silly. *Ride to the top of Ooga Mountain, hahaha?!* It seemed so silly, they couldn't help but laugh! They laughed so hard that their tummies hurt a little ... all except Taffy.

"You'll see ...," Taffy said defiantly, staring them down.

At that moment, Ragamuffin jumped up and started barking at something outside. The kiddos heard a bird singing. The sound was so unusual and piercing, the kids heard it from inside the clubhouse, even with the door closed. As they ran outside to look, they realized that the chirping was coming from the boo tree near Silly Creek.

The kiddos crept forward very slowly and quietly so as not to scare the strange bird away. They stayed low until they reached, then hid behind a big mossy rock near the boo tree. The bird hadn't made a sound since they left the clubhouse, so they waited patiently for it to sing its weird song again. At last, a sharp, loud bird-like song resounded above their heads. The kiddos looked up, and their jaws dropped at the sight.

"It's a mouse ... a really big mouse ...," Sugar whispered so softly that her own ears were the only thing that heard her. She whispered a little louder. "That mouse is *singing* – singing *like a bird*!"

"Hush up," whispered Taffy. "You'll scare it away."

The oversized singing mouse was in plain sight for all to see. It was unmistakably a mouse – everybody knows what a mouse looks like. The singing mouse wasn't afraid of them because it was out of reach, and kids can't climb trees very fast – at least not fast enough to catch a magical, singing mouse!

The kids stared in amazement as the mouse continued its serenade. They realized that this must be one of those critters they'd heard about. *What-ers* are critters that come into the Valley of Ooga Ooga from somewhere far away. They're called what-ers because people ask "What-er those?" The what-ers that have shown up in the valley are unique. They are critters that have never been seen before, then they suddenly disappear, never to be seen again. They don't stay for long, and they never come back, according to legend, anyway.

These weird critters appear several times a year in different parts of the valley. The people of Ooga Ooga wonder what the heck lives out beyond the mountains, deserts, and jungles surrounding the valley. Someday soon, the kiddos will explore far beyond the valley, and they just might find out. *Maybe the what-ers come from lands near the edge,* they wondered.

Nobody knows where the what-ers come from, and *nobody* knows where they go. *Nobody* sure knows a lot about the what-ers!

The mouse stopped singing and started running. It ran quickly up a branch and then leaped into the air. It didn't fall, instead it flew like a bird and soared above the shady glade as if it had wings, even though it didn't. It turned toward Ooga Mountain and disappeared. Yep, just like that, it was probably gone forever, and for certain it *was* a what-er.

The kiddos thought the large mouse was both fascinating and delightful. They wondered what other critters or *what-ers* they might run into someday in the Valley of Ooga Ooga and beyond.

Chapter 19

THE SURPRISING RICHES OF SILLY CREEK

૱৵৻

After the mouse-bird departed, Topp wandered down to the edge of Silly Creek. He dipped his cupped hands into the clear water and splashed his face. He jumped back suddenly, almost fell and yelled, "I saw a fish! I saw a fish!"

The others came running and peered into the babbling brook. "Are you sure you saw a real fish?" Taffy asked.

"Yeah. I saw a ball fish. I know I did!" he said. "It had lots of colorful squares all over and big ball-like eyes – just like a delicious ball fish!"

"They're very tasty," Sugar agreed. "My mom cooks them on special occasions."

"Maybe we can catch one!" Walnut said excitedly. "I *am* good at fishing because I don't care if I catch anything. I just like sitting around doing nothing. That's why I'm good at fishing."

"What makes you think you can catch a fish?" Taffy said with skepticism.

"Easy, I am more patient than the fish," Walnut said, sounding like Santiago in *The Old Man and the Sea* or something fantastical like that.

"That's silly, Walnut," Topp said with a wry grin. "But you'll have a chance to prove yourself because we're going to catch that fish today."

The kiddos kept their fishing poles and other fishing gear at home because they'd never had a clubhouse before. So, they rode home, grabbed their gear, and rode back to the clubhouse at breakneck speed (which means fast, not that they hurt themselves or anything). After all, they can't catch any fish at home – except a goldfish or two! But it looks like they *might* be able to catch at least one fish in Silly Creek – if Topp really saw one, that is.

Wiggle worms are the best fishing bait in the valley, so the kids rushed to the slimy vines where the worms like to hang out. They dug up more than a dozen worms and then headed to the creek, full of expectations.

They quickly baited their hooks and prepared to fish. Topp, Taffy, and Sugar eased up to the edge of the creek and cast their lines out into the bubbling water. *Splash! Splash! Splash!* went the weights, hooks, and worms when they hit the water. Ragamuffin relaxed on top of a grassy bank and watched their every move.

Why wasn't Walnut fishing? Well, his fishing line got tangled on his belt buckle, and when he tried to untangle it, he tripped and fell. When he fell, he lost his special fishhook in a bush. While he was looking for it, his fishing line got tangled around his arm, the bush, and his fishing pole.

In the meantime, the others were busy fishing.

Topp, Taffy, and Sugar had been fishing for quite a while, patiently doing their best to catch something. They checked their bait often as well they should have. They tried different spots along the creek, and they were very quiet, which you know is important when fishing.

"I haven't gotten one nibble," complained Taffy.

"Me, either!" said Sugar, with a look of disappointment. "Are there really any fish in here?"

"I know I saw *one* when I was washing my face!" Topp said.

Here's a question: Can it be called *fishing* if someone puts a line, hook, and bait into the water but never catches a fish? I would call it *wishing-to-be-fishing* or maybe *putting-small-stuff-in-the-water-on-a-line-ing*. I'm curious, what would you call it?

At last, Walnut was ready, but he nearly slipped and fell again – and this time he would have fallen into the creek! Finally, he threw his line, weight, and bait out into the water, not far from where he was standing on the bank. He looked up at the sky as if he were looking up to heaven (what-ever or where-ever that is) and began whistling. Then he slowly lowered his head, looked into the water, and started reeling in his line.

"Why are you bringing in your line so soon? You just put it in!" teased Sugar.

"Because I need to reel in the ball fish I just caught," Walnut said with a big smile.

The other kiddos watched with their mouths wide open as Walnut gently raised a colorful fish out of the water and put it in his fish basket.

"That's a pretty big one!" Walnut said gleefully. Satisfied with his catch, Walnut lay down on a grassy spot, rested his head on soft moss, and took a nap.

The kids were amazed at the size of the fish Walnut had caught. They put on fresh bait and focused on hooking one themselves. They figured there must be more than one fish in Silly Creek, but time went by with not even one tiny nibble.

"Walnut was pretty lucky, wasn't he?" Topp said, trying to make them feel better.

Sugar agreed but added, "I wonder what special technique he used to catch that fish? And what the heck, he's taking a nap! Crazy!"

"Luck, that's all," Taffy said tersely. "Walnut was just lucky – everybody gets lucky sometimes!"

They got back to their fishing or *staring-at-a-string-in-the-water-ing* or whatever you want to call it. They were about to give up when Walnut woke up from his nap, looked around, and remembered where he was. He got to his feet, prepared his fishing line with a fresh wiggle worm, and cozied up to the creek. He gently lowered his bait into the water again, looked to the sky, whistled a little, then lowered his head and started bringing his fishing line in.

The other kids were silent and frozen – like tree stumps in winter. They stared in amazement when Walnut pulled the second ball fish out of the water and gently placed it in his basket, next to the other one.

"This one is bigger than the first one!" Walnut said with excitement. "How many more do we need for dinner tonight?"

Topp hesitated a bit. "Well ... ah, one each, I guess ... four in all?" He was surprised that he could even talk, and the others were speechless at what Walnut just did.

"Four it is," replied Walnut and then promptly dropped his newly baited hook into the water, right in front of everyone. And once again, he pulled a fish out of the water and put it in his basket.

"Hey, wait a minute. I want to catch the next one!" shouted Topp. "Move over, I'm going to fish right here – right where you were fishing!"

"Okay, good idea," Walnut said agreeably. "I'll fish over there, by that flat rock."

Topp put a wiggle worm on his hook just right, checked his line and put it into the water in the exact spot where Walnut had caught three fish.

In the meantime, Walnut sat down in the shade and nodded off again, this time leaning against a tree. He woke up quickly and looked over at Topp fishing or *sort-of-fishing*. I'm still not sure what to call it when no fish are caught – maybe *zero-fishing*.

Walnut got up, walked over to the creek, and got his line ready again. The girls studied his every move to see if they could figure out his method. The girls were gawking at Walnut when he gently pulled another fish out of the water and placed it in the basket with the other three.

At the same time, Topp pulled his line out of the water. His hook had no fish and no wiggle worm on it. He wandered over to where Walnut was and stared down into his fish basket in amazement.

"Okay, it's time to tell us, how did you catch those?!" Topp pleaded.

Walnut simply said, "I am more patient than the fish."

"That's baloney, you don't wait at all!" Topp said, sounding a bit peeved at Walnut's nonsense.

"I know," said Walnut.

"That doesn't make any sense, either! What do you mean, *I know*?" Topp said.

The girls shook their heads in agreement with Topp. It didn't make sense to them, either – and it doesn't make sense to me – and I wrote this thing!

"I give up!" Topp conceded.

The kiddos rapidly headed up the trail to the clubhouse because they needed to get the freshly caught fish home quickly. Their moms and dads will need time to prepare them for dinner.

They never figured out how Walnut caught the fish, and that's where it was left. Maybe it was Walnut's pow pow or maybe it was one of those crazy things that sometimes happens in the Valley of Ooga Ooga, like the what-ers. Strange and inexplicable things happen in the valley, and they'll just have to get used to it!

Chapter 20

PLANTING SEEDS FOR THE FUTURE

᪥᪥

At dinnertime, the freshly caught ball fish turned into a wonderful meal for all the kiddos and their families. The kids went to bed earlier than usual that night. They had decided to start their garden in the wee hours of morning, like farmers.

What do farmers do? Well, one thing farmers do every day is wake up early in the morning, at the break of day or when the rooster crows at the crack of dawn. Morning must be a fragile thing because it breaks and cracks every day! Pretty flimsy, wouldn't you say!

Oh, be careful, people of Ooga Ooga, don't be too hard on the morning or you might break it or crack it! What did you say? Mornings are going to break anyway, every time the suns come up? Well then, do whatever you want to the morning, good people.

In a discussion, the kiddos reasoned that if they want to have a great garden someday, they will have to start thinking and acting like farmers. But that won't be easy since they have never even met a farmer. They only know the farmers in children's stories, like *The Farmer in the Dell* and *Old MacDonald* (who had a farm).

The kiddos remembered reading that farmers get up before dawn every morning and work awfully hard all day long. That being pointed out, the kiddos squirmed a little. And farmers must plant crops and trees, take care of all of that, and pick the veggies and fruits to put on the family table. The kiddos thought they would probably like the eating part of *farmer-ing*, much more than the *long-days-of-working-hard* part of farmer-ing.

So, early the next morning, Topp, Taffy, and Sugar arrived at the clubhouse (or should I call it the farmhouse) at just about the same time. But Walnut ... oh, never mind.

The reality is that Walnut kind of saunters when he walks, almost like a slow waltz. Speed is not part of his way of doing things. The other kids do the cha cha, while Walnut prefers the waltz.

"Good early morning, Walnut," Sugar said, greeting him. "You got here really fast!" She was being sarcastic and teasing him a little, and the other kids chuckled to themselves.

Rather than being bothered by the joke, Walnut enjoyed her playfulness and retorted with ease, "Yeah, at super speed!" And they all had a good laugh.

Then Topp said sternly, "Settle down, kiddos, you might *break* the day or *crack* the dawn!" They laughed again, a big belly laugh, and their tummies hurt more than a little.

"Well, let's get to it," Taffy ordered. "Didn't we get up early to plan our garden, just like a storybook farmer would? I don't remember those farmers goofing around so much, especially so early in the morning!"

"I agree," Sugar chimed in. "We need to decide where we'll put our garden and what we're going to plant."

"Yeah," Topp added. "We need to draw it up, like keroots go here and plumpykins go there. We need to figure out what grows big and what grows small so that everything has its own space. We don't want the plants to be fighting with each other, so we need to plan carefully."

"I think we should grow taterz, pea-wees, and yeller beanies," Taffy said.

"I think planana sqwish would be nice, and spinooch," Sugar added.

"And we can't forget to plant goober peas for Old Man Gruff," Walnut reminded them.

"We'll need to buy seeds at the Feed, Seed, and No Weed store," Topp said. "So how are we going to get brittles$ to pay for them?" The kiddos became very quiet after Topp's question, and they seemed to be looking deep inside their brains to find a way.

Then Topp came up with an idea. "We could catch fish in Silly Creek, and instead of eating them for dinner, we could sell them at the fish market."

They all perked up at that idea.

"Sounds good," Sugar said. "But I've never caught a fish!" And she wasn't alone.

"I know someone who *can* catch fish!" Topp said, and all eyes focused on Walnut. "Can you catch more fish today, Walnut?"

Walnut stopped whistling and said, "Of course, I *am* a fisherman."

They had stored their fishing poles and gear in the clubhouse the day before, so Walnut went over and picked up his stuff.

Taffy and Sugar left behind their fishing poles but not Topp. He grabbed his pole and fishing box and headed out the door with a determined look on his face.

Sugar called out, "Why are *you* taking your fishing pole, Topp? You won't catch anything."

Topp glared at Sugar and said, "I'm going to catch a fish today, just you watch!" He grunted as he lurched out the door and hurried to catch up with Walnut who was already halfway to the creek. "I'm going to watch you, Walnut, and figure out what you're doing so I can catch fish, too!"

Walnut smiled, gave Topp a nod of agreement, and then they all ambled down the path to Silly Creek, with Ragamuffin playfully leading the way.

Chapter 21

FISHING FOR BRITTLES$

❧❧

Not far from where Walnut was preparing to fish, the other kids and Ragamuffin sat on a flat rock to watch. They stared intently to see if they could glean a clue of how Walnut fishes so successfully. They wondered if Walnut had a magic fishing pole or used some other gimmick.

They watched closely as Walnut fumbled and bumbled around with his fishing line, hooks, and weights – and again he got them all tangled up with his hat, shoe, and a nearby bush. "I wonder if getting all tangled up is part of his secret," Sugar whispered.

"Naw ... no way, that's too nutty," Taffy said.

Finally, Walnut walked down to the very edge of the water, lowered the wiggle worm gently into the water and began to whistle. He slowly lifted his eyes up to the sky, then slowly lowered his head, and started pulling in his fishing line.

"I don't believe it!" Topp said. "Not again!"

Walnut didn't say a word. He just smiled and kept fishing, cool as can be.

Topp was beside himself in disbelief. "How do you do that, Walnut?"

Walnut stopped whistling. "I'm just fishing – aren't I supposed to catch fish?" He knew that would get under Topp's skin a little – at least he hoped it would.

"Let's see you do it again!" Topp demanded, figuring that Walnut couldn't possibly keep catching fish so easily.

Walnut picked up his pole calmly and put new bait on his hook. It took him a long time to get ready because he dropped everything at least five times. He had a hard time finding things because they ended up under his foot.

Finally, he was ready, and he went back to the creek. This time, he went a little farther downstream from where he had caught the last one. He whistled, slowly lowered his line, looked up at the sky, then down, and started reeling in his line.

Their eyeballs almost popped out when the other kiddos saw what came up.

"Amazing!" shrieked Taffy when she saw a big ol' fox fish on Walnut's line.

"Wow, a fox fish, they're even more valuable than ball fish," Sugar said quietly as Walnut put it in his fishing basket. "I don't know how you do it, but I don't care because we need brittles$ to buy seeds."

Topp, clearly more frustrated than amused, blurted out, "Let me use your pole, Walnut, your *magic* pole."

"Sure, do you want me to bait it for you?" Walnut replied.

Topp thought for a second and said, "Sure."

Topp took Walnut's magic fishing pole and stood at the exact spot where Walnut caught the last fish. Then he started to whistle. He'd never whistled much before, but he figured that he wasn't going to leave out any of Walnut's tricks. However, whatever Topp was whistling was not a waltz. It wasn't even music, for that matter. He did his best, but it wasn't very good. If I was a fish and heard that, I would swim away as fast as I could!

Topp, not paying any attention to all the things the others were thinking about him, bravely lowered the bait into the water. He slowly raised his face to the sky, then back down, and started to lift the line. *There has to be a fish on the hook,* he thought as he gently reeled in what was now a heavy fishing line.

"I think I got one!" cried Topp. But to his surprise, it was just a chunk of river moss!

Taffy stood next to Topp and said, "You are good at so many things, Topp, this is just not one of them. This is Walnut's thing."

And to that, Topp gave her a smile.

"Oh well, I tried," Topp said. "We need fish to sell, not moss! We can't sell moss! Walnut, catch us fish – please." Now with acceptance in his heart, Topp sat down on a log to watch Walnut fish.

Walnut went about the business of getting his pole and stuff ready to fish again. He only had two wiggle worms left. *Two worms, two fish, perfect!* he thought.

He dropped his line in the gurgling creek two times and pulled out two fish in two minutes.

He lowered his fourth fish into his fish basket, picked it up, and started walking back to the clubhouse.

All eyes were on him as he started walking away.

"Why are you leaving?" Sugar asked.

"I'm done fishing."

"Why don't you catch more?" Taffy asked. "We need lots of seeds."

"Because ... I made an agreement."

"An agreement with whom?" Topp asked.

"With the fish, of course," Walnut said. "The ones that I am more patient than."

The others became stone silent. What could they say? It made no sense whatsoever, but there were four fish in his basket. If Walnut was nutty and *didn't* catch any fish – that would make sense. But he is nutty and *does* catch fish!

Whether it's pow pow, just luck, or a trick he uses, Topp, Taffy, and Sugar couldn't figure it out. It didn't matter much anyway because they had what they needed – fish to sell at the fish market.

Heading to the clubhouse hand in hand, the kiddos shuffled – or sort of waltzed – to the tune that Walnut was whistling. The kiddos sat for a while inside their clubhouse hideaway and talked about the garden and other stuff. They felt grateful to be best friends and that each of them had special talents. For Walnut, it was fishing and whistling, and he was also very good at confusing everyone!

The kiddos hopped on their bikes and rode speedily toward the fish market owned by Bob Bobb's brother, Bob. Bob is always honest and fair. He paid nine brittles$ in all for the fish: two brittles$ each for the ball fish, and three brittles$ for the fox fish.

The kiddos were delighted with their money largess and headed home.

Later that evening, Sugar's mom asked, "What did you do today, dear?"

Sugar's answer was short and sweet. "Aw, nothin' really." But it was a much better day than that, and Sugar knew it.

Cozy in their soft warm beds, the kiddos reflected on their busy day.

Sugar thought: *What a great clubhouse.*

Taffy thought: *What a great garden we're going to have.*

Topp thought: *Someday I'll catch the biggest fish ever!*

And Walnut thought: *I'm sleepy …*

With sparkles of starlight streaming through their windows and tickling their eyelids, the kiddos fell asleep.

Don't forget – the starlight that shone down on these lovely children is the same starlight shining down on *you* tonight.

Chapter 22

BOBBY WILL NOT GIVE UP

❧

The brilliant morning sunshine shone through Bobby's bedroom windows, illuminating the toothpick roller coaster and the puzzle of a hundred ladybugs. Bobby's head was still burrowed in his pillow and his blankets covered most of his face, when a ray of sunlight crept through a small gap in his bedding. It reached his closed eyelids and woke him up. Sensing the light, he pushed off his covers, turned onto his back, stretched his legs, and wiggled his toes.

He looked around, saw that he was in his room, and realized that his wonderful dream had faded away again. *Oh, that dream, I love that dream!* Bobby thought as he looked up at the stars and planets on his ceiling. *I went back – I was there again – with those dream-kids in that magical land.*

He peeked out the window and saw that the yard was brightly lit, and the wind had stopped as well. The storm had passed through, and the sunshine returned. It was summer break from school, so Bobby was excited that he could do anything he wanted, inside or out. As he became more alert, Bobby's mind started filling up with ideas for this fresh new day.

He decided to have ice cream for breakfast, just like yesterday. Then he remembered there wasn't any because he'd eaten all of it. *Whoops!* So, Bobby decided to make his mom happy and eat the breakfast she would offer shortly.

He stood up, raised his arms high, and stretched to greet the day. He looked around his room and reflected on all the things he'd done yesterday during the rainy weather. He heard a familiar scratching noise on the door and let Fluffers in. His oversized, tan-colored tabby cat purred loudly as she pranced in. "Hi, Fluffers," Bobby said. Then he walked over to his little leafy plant friends and said good morning to them.

He glanced at his roller coaster and recalled how much fun he had working on it yesterday. When he can start the red marble at a point higher than his head, his goal will be reached. In the test runs at waist high, the marble rolled rapidly and smoothly, and stayed on the track the entire way. *I can barely wait to show Cookie how fast it rolls,* he thought.

He considered gluing on more toothpicks this morning, but his better judgement whispered in his ear. *You should do that the next time it rains!*

He found his favorite play clothes in a drawer and put them on. That will make his mom happy because he sometimes forgets and wears his pajamas outside, gets them dirty, and then sleeps in them that night. Good boy, Bobby, at least today, anyway!

He walked down the hall to the kitchen, where Mom was already up and knitting.

"Hi, sweetie, let me finish this row, then I'll make you breakfast. I don't know why, but we're out of ice cream, so how does oatmeal sound?" his mom said with a wink.

"That would be great!" he said.

"Did you sleep well?"

Bobby's eyes lit up when he shared, "Yes, I did. I had that dream again – all night!"

"What's it about?" she asked.

"It's realistic – like I was really there! I was playing with four kids and their dog in an amazing world!" Bobby said excitedly.

"That sounds fascinating," she said with a loving smile that only a mother could give to her son. "The oatmeal is ready. Would you like raisins in it?"

"Sure, Mom, thanks." He scooted up to the kitchen table, poured milk onto his steaming porridge and dripped honey on top. "What are you knitting *this* time?"

"I'm finishing the hat I started for you last winter. I want to get it done before the cold weather comes."

"You know what's so amazing about my dream? It started the night before last, and each time I go to sleep, it picks up right where it left off – three nights in a row now."

"Dreams are usually one-night things as far as I know," she said.

"This dream's not like that," he explained. "It's the longest and most wonderful dream I've ever had. I'm glad it isn't a nightmare – it's just the opposite – it's a fun dream."

He thanked his mom for breakfast, kissed her on the cheek, grabbed his cap, and hopped out the back door. He wondered what Cookie was doing and thought, *Maybe I'll head over to her house this morning.* He walked slowly by the apricot tree and his broken-down old playhouse on the way to the street.

He paused and stared at the tiny clubhouse. The entire roof was falling apart, so much so that most of it had already fallen onto the grass below. He also noticed that there was a freshly splintered board leaning against the house under his bedroom window. He realized the wind must have blown the board there. *That's what made the loud noise last night.*

Bobby stood still and suddenly recalled his dream. He remembered a small field with a newly built clubhouse and recalled the laughter of his now familiar friends, the dream-kids.

His eyes flickered back to reality, back to the sight of the rickety, neglected, bug-infested hovel of a playhouse. Last night, when he was awakened by the crashing sound, he had decided to fix it up. He wanted to make it bigger and cleaner and keep out every drop of rain.

Forgetting about Cookie, Bobby walked through the back yard to a shed behind the garage where tools were stored. As he opened the door, the rusty hinges creaked loudly. He looked at the tools hanging on hooks on the wall straight ahead and saw a familiar hammer and wood saw, covered with dust.

He was overcome by deep sadness. He remembered using them when he and his dad worked on projects together. But now his dad was gone. He tried not to think too much about it but at times like this, it was especially hard. Bobby wiped tears from his face with his shirt sleeve and said quietly, "You'll come home again someday, I know you will."

He left the shed and went around to the back of it. There was a stack of boards leaning against the wall, left over from one of Dad's projects. Then he realized that he had everything he needed to rebuild and expand his clubhouse.

While he was looking at the boards, Cookie showed up. "Hi, Bobby, whatcha up to?"

"Hi, Cookie, I was going to come over … but I got distracted."

"By what?"

"Remember the fun we used to have in the little playhouse by the apricot tree? Well, I want to rebuild it like new and make it bigger, so we can use it again and have our friends over."

"For sure, I remember. It doesn't look too good right now, does it?" she said, glancing over at what was left of it.

"I know, it looks like a pile of rubble," Bobby said.

He entered the shed again, grabbed a hammer, and looked around in the dimly lit space for a crowbar. Peering into a dark corner, he was surprised to see his old fishing pole. He reached into the shadows and brought it out into the sunlight.

"You poor neglected thing!" he said, examining it closely. It was covered in dust and spider webs, and the fishing line was all tangled up.

"Remember when we used to go fishing, Cookie? I'd like to go again. My life kind of stopped when my dad didn't come back. I need to start living and having fun again."

"I know it's been hard ... about your dad," Cookie said softly.

"My dad would *want* me to be happy, I know. But sometimes the sadness just creeps in."

Cookie leaned over and gave him a kiss on the cheek. With a caring smile, she said, "You've got *me* ..."

"Thanks, Cookie, I'm grateful for that every day."

As they walked hand in hand to the picnic table, Bobby brought along his fishing pole. He brushed it off with a rag and removed a dried-out worm from the rusty hook. As he fiddled with it, he told Cookie about his dream.

She was listening intently when they heard someone shout. "Cookie, are you over there?"

"Yes, Mom!" Cookie called back. "I'm in Bobby's yard."

"It's time to leave for town," her mom said.

Cookie gave Bobby another peck on his cheek and took off running. "Comin', Mom!"

Bobby sat at the table and said out loud, "I've got to go fishing again soon!"

Bobby often talks to himself. His mom sometimes thinks she has two sons, the one that's talking and the one that he's talking to. Confused? I hope not ... I talk to myself sometimes, don't you?

He thought about digging up bait worms and heading off to the brook to go fishing. But he decided to wait and go with Cookie another day.

He quickly came to his senses and remembered that his top priority was to start rebuilding his clubhouse.

He hopped up the porch steps into the house, ran to his room, and placed his now clean fishing pole in the corner near his plants. He stared at it and was glad it was in his room now and not in that lonely, dirty, spidery tool shed out back.

Suddenly, it dawned on him. *The dream-kids were fishing in his dream! What a weird coincidence!*

He headed back outside and worked for several hours tearing apart his old clubhouse. His tummy eventually told him it was time to eat, so he headed for the kitchen. After gobbling down two peanut butter and apple jelly sandwiches, he lay down on the nice soft rug on his bedroom floor.

He looked up at the stars and planets on the ceiling and thought about his life. Cookie, fishing, and friendship in a new clubhouse came to mind as well. He knew he had to start finding happiness and joy again. He needed to push through the pain – just let life be.

His eyelids got heavy and slowly closed. He didn't mean to fall asleep, but he did, right there on the floor. There's nothing better than an afternoon nap, especially one with delightful dreams.

Chapter 23

A CRITTERY SURPRISE ON A FOGGY DAY

჻჻

The kiddos in the Village of Ooga Ooga woke up early just like farmers but instead of getting out of bed, they all decided to sleep in. With all the exhausting activities they'd undertaken recently, it was understandable that they did not want to get out of bed. I don't know if *real* farmers ever go back to sleep, but the kids did it anyway.

When they finally got up and left their homes, they met at the Feed, Seed, and No Weed store. This is the all-things-farming store in the valley. They went to see what the store carried in the way of seeds, baby trees, tools, and products that a farmer needs to grow things. Now that they were (pretend) farmers, they were delighted to see so many things available for their little plot of land. They knew that they had enough brittles$ to pay for what they wanted. (Thanks, Walnut!)

As they wandered around the store, Sugar asked, "So, what's the difference between farming and gardening?"

"I'm not sure, but I do know that we'll be farming – not gardening!" Walnut said assuredly.

"Don't dare tell Walnut that he's just a gardener!" Taffy warned and then giggled.

"Bein' a furmer *does* sound more impressive, so we's furmers. So, let's git on with bein' furmers *and* git what we's a needin' for our furm!" Topp said in a silly way.

The kiddos chuckled a bit and then got busy picking out seeds and such. They looked at all the plants and seeds that are possible to grow and that really got them in the farmer mood.

"Well, it looks like they have all the vegetable seeds we want," Taffy said. "I had trouble finding the pea-wee seeds, but I finally found them hidden behind a packet of giant plumpykin seeds."

"What about fruit trees?" Sugar asked. "We want to plant lots of fruit trees, don't we?"

"Right now, we only have enough time to get the veggies in the ground," Taffy said wisely. "Let's start there. We can always come back."

"And we don't have enough brittles$ to buy fruit trees now, anyhow," Topp said. "I looked at the prices, and they cost a lot. After all, they're *real* trees!"

"Someday we'll have fruit trees!" Walnut said. "Especially abbles and sherries!"

∽

With seeds in hand, the kiddos arrived at their clubhouse late in the morning. They had to ride slowly because a thick fog had settled into the Valley of Ooga Ooga overnight. It was so foggy, the only thing Oogans could see outside were their noses. That's a bit of an exaggeration but not by much. The fog wasn't a bother to the kids, since they were only making decisions about where to plant different things. The kiddos were certain that *real* farmers worked in fog sometimes, so they didn't mind it, not one bit.

Topp popped his head out the clubhouse door and said, "It's still very foggy out here. It might be like this all day."

"I kind of like it because it's cool," Sugar remarked. "We won't get too hot when we do the hard farming work."

"I like the fog, too," added Walnut. "It makes me sleepy."

"It's time to get out there and start working!" Taffy said. "If we work hard, we might be able to get all the seeds planted today. There's supposed to be rain coming in tonight, which would be great for the seeds – if they're in the ground, that is."

"Yeah, let's get to it!" Sugar said. "It sure will be fun to watch the little baby veggies poke their heads up out of the soil and say "hello" to us someday."

"I got fire spider string from my dad and wooden stakes for laying out the garden," Topp said. "We'll stretch the string line between wooden stakes where we want the rows."

"Veggies grow faster when they're all in a straight line," Walnut added, with a smile.

"How do you know that?" Sugar asked, figuring Walnut was just making it up.

"The veggies told me!" Walnut said with a straight face, no less.

"Oh my! You sure have an interesting mind, Walnut!" Topp uttered, not believing a word Walnut had said.

"Let's stop jabbering and get to work!" Taffy said, being her practical bossy self.

"Yes, and let's make those rows really straight!" Sugar said with a chuckle, chiding Walnut for his far-fetched remark.

The kiddos finally got to work. They worked *so* hard, the farmers in the children's stories would have been proud of them. They made the rows very straight because Topp, Taffy, and Sugar knew not to completely disregard what Walnut said. They have been friends for a long time and have learned to trust his intuition sometimes.

The fog got thicker as the day unfolded, but it didn't slow them down. Topp and Sugar were down on their knees planting goober peas near Silly Creek, when they heard a weird noise coming from the other side of the creek.

Sugar spoke softly, "Did you hear that, Topp?"

Almost whispering, Topp responded, "Yeah, it sounded like a wounded cat or maybe a sick bird across the creek."

They dropped their garden tools and crept stealthily toward the creek. They stopped and listened and heard the sound again.

"I agree, it's on the other side and sounds like an animal in distress," Sugar said.

"Maybe it's a what-er," Topp surmised.

Just then, they saw something running back and forth through the bramble bushes on the far side of the creek. It was a gray cat, but it didn't sound like a cat. It ran back and forth in a frenzy as if in anguish, trying to draw attention to itself. It stopped a couple of times and looked straight at them.

"We need to help it!" Sugar, the animal lover, cried. "We need to get to the other side of the creek!"

Nearby, they found a fallen tree that bridged the creek. They started to cross over on the log, but they didn't get far. The log started to wiggle and wobble, so they turned around and went back to the sandy bank. They realized the fallen tree was *not* a good way to cross – unless they wanted to get wet, that is!

"I know a better way," Topp said. "There's a bigger fallen tree upstream. It should make a good crossing!"

The cat-critter on the other side was growing more agitated. It followed the kiddos as they worked their way up the trail by the creek. It ran into the bramble bushes, disappeared, and then came back again. It acted like it wanted them to follow it into the bushes.

When Taffy and Walnut saw Sugar and Topp heading up the trail, they ran after them. "What's that weird sound?" Taffy asked.

"It's a sort of a cat, I think. It seems to be in trouble, so we're going up the creek to get to the other side, to see if we can help it," Sugar explained.

All the kiddos hurried up the trail to the fallen log. When they got there, they assessed the situation. This log was bigger and stronger than the other one, but it would still be a difficult crossing. Taffy and Topp, being the most athletic, decided to try it first.

The cat-critter was now right at the end of the big log, looking directly at them. It was clear that the little thing needed help and wanted them to come across. So, they did.

As soon as Taffy and Topp reached the other side, the weird smoky-gray cat took off into the brambles. They followed it, even though they knew they'd get scratched up by the thorny bushes. Fortunately, they didn't go far before they came upon an open field of grass.

As they stepped out into the open, they saw the little four-legged critter climb onto a pile of fabric crumpled on the ground. To their surprise, they saw a young boy in the middle of it all, twisted up in ropes.

"Hey there, help me!" the boy yelled out. "I'm all caught up in a complete tangle! Can you help me?"

Chapter 24

THE FLYING CAT

⮰⮯

Taffy and Topp sprang forward at once to rescue the boy. He was lying on the ground, all tangled up in the ropes and fabric from what they learned was a collapsed balloon. Taffy had a special cutting tool with her and cut the boy free of his bindings. Shaking the ropes off, the boy eventually broke free and stepped out of the pile of tangled up cloth and cords onto the grass.

"Thank you, thank you!" the boy said and breathed a sigh of relief.

Next to him, the cat-critter was chirping, squawking, and hopping around. The kiddos were surprised to see what appeared to be little wings on the cat!

"What's your name?" Topp asked the boy.

"My name is Raffer Daffer Doo, but everyone calls me Balooon."

"Hello, Balooon! Are you okay?" Taffy asked.

"Yeah, just a little banged up, I suppose." He poked and patted all over his body to check to see if all his parts were there. "Yeah, looks like I'm okay. I am embarrassed and a lot humbler, that's for sure!"

"We're glad you're okay," Topp said kindly.

"I was cruising along pretty good in my balloon on the way to pick bramble berries for my Aunt Pet, but when the fog got thick, I couldn't see a thing. We clipped a treetop and down we went! Thank goodness my cat got me out of this fix! Good girl!"

At that, his cat-critter rubbed against his leg, smiled, and made a tweet-like sound!

"My name is Topp, and this is Taffy," he said warmly as he reached out to shake Balooon's hand.

"Come with us to our new clubhouse. We have food and water, if you and your, er, cat … would like some," Taffy said.

"Sure … is it far?"

"No, not too far, just over the creek and down a little. Come on, follow us," Topp said.

They made their way slowly through the bramble bushes and hiked to the creek. When they reached the log, they saw Walnut and Sugar waiting anxiously on the other side.

"We have a new friend!" Taffy shouted across the creek. "He's coming with us to the clubhouse."

Topp, Taffy, Balooon, and the cat-like critter carefully crossed the sturdy log bridge and joined the others. They shared a few friendly moments there by the creek and then started down the trail.

The fog had dissipated, but the skies above had darkened. The kiddos looked up and wondered … *Is it getting late or had the clouds become thick and dark?* The answer came when the first big raindrops hit leaves near their ears and made loud whacking sounds.

"Run, run … rain!" shouted Walnut.

"To the clubhouse!" Sugar yelled and took off sprinting down the trail.

All four kiddos, followed by Balooon and the winged cat, scurried into the clubhouse in the nick of time. They stood in the middle of the shelter, huffing and puffing while the rain went *tappity-tap-tap* loudly on the swimming pool roof above their heads.

The kiddos realized that this was the first rain since their clubhouse was finished. Now the rain sounded like *whack-whack-whack* as the white rain came down extremely hard. But not one drop of rain came into their cozy clubhouse, and the kiddos were delighted. Unlike their meeting place under the jujubee tree, this roof was indeed waterproof!

Sugar went over to the window and looked outside for a long time. Taffy cozied up to her and asked, "What are you looking at, Sugar?"

"Oh, I'm just looking out the window, watching everything get wet but ourselves!" she said with a giant grin. "Our dream has come true!"

Eventually, the rain stopped, and one of the suns peeked out from behind a cloud. The kiddos wanted to go back out and continue planting, but the rain had turned their garden soil to sticky mud. Their planting day was over.

"So, where are you from, Balooon? Sugar asked. "I don't recognize you from school."

"I live in a tiny place called Happy Harbor," Balooon said. "It's right where the Ooga River enters the Yeller Cliffs. It's called a harbor because it has a small pier where boats and rafts traveling down the river can dock. Maybe you've been there?"

"I've heard of it, but I've never been there," Sugar said. "Have any of you guys been there?"

They all shook their heads to say no.

"I saw it on our map," Topp said as he walked to the wall where their two maps were mounted. "See right here, Happy Harbor."

"I live with my Aunt Pet and my Uncle Tunia," Balooon said. "They're known as the *PetTunias* – maybe you've heard of them. They grow flowers and fruit and sell them in the Village of Ooga Ooga. I go to a small school in the Town of Trombone down the river. I go to school one day a week, and the rest of the days I learn at home and work on the farm."

"Work on the farm! Wow, that's cool!" Walnut exclaimed. "Do you grow abbles and sherries?"

"Yes, we grow *plenty* of abbles and sherries."

Then Taffy asked, "If you live with your aunt and uncle, where are your mom and dad – if you don't mind me asking?"

"Oh, they went on a long trip in their giant balloon to somewhere out there," Balooon said. "They'll be back in a couple of years – I hope. They love traveling to distant lands, and it's okay with me because the PetTunias are good to me, they're just like my mom and dad!"

"So, how did you get that balloon?" Topp asked.

"My Granny Bubbles gave it to me for helping Pet and Tunia on their farm. Years ago, my granny invented balloons. When she was a little girl, she loved to blow bubbles with soapy water. She had a vision that if she could make bubbles big and strong enough, they could take Oogans up in the air. She invented the skin *and* the vapor for balloons. She overcooked a batch of molasses which made a gas that nearly lifted off the kitchen roof! With lots of experimenting, Granny Bubbles was able to produce a new, powerful vapor. She named it Vaporgas. She also discovered a wonderful rubbery material made from verystretchy bush leaves. She cooked the leaves, added a couple of secret ingredients, then poured the slop out and created sheets of rubber. She stitched pieces of it together and made a balloon. That's how balloons were invented."

"Interesting!" Topp said.

Balooon continued, "There are four parts to a balloon: the skin, the rope, the basket, and the vapor. My mom and dad make balloons in their workshop. The one I crashed was one of Granny's, and it was old and small. I also have a new balloon from my mom and dad, that I haven't flown yet."

"This is Ragamuffin, my dog," Sugar said. "Tell us about your cat. What's its name?"

"This is Smokey," Balooon said. "You might have noticed she's an unusual cat because she has wings. My mom and dad brought her back from a faraway island, out in the Fantasmo Sea. Her wings are small, so she can't really fly – but she tries. She's always wanted to be a bird, but she's mostly a cat. She stupidly climbs up on high ledges and jumps off as though she can fly – but she can't. It's a good thing she's an expert at landing. She won't eat cat food, only bird food. She is a one of a kind cat-bird. She's very friendly and always wants to fly with me in my balloon."

"I like her," Sugar said, admiringly, "and I think my pup likes her too. Ragamuffin thinks he's a cat even though he's a dog. It's no wonder they get along. Why did you name her Smokey?"

"Smoke goes up, and she goes up – so there you go. She loves to go up in the balloon. She can't fly on her own, so balloons do it for her."

"Hi there, Smokey," Taffy said. She leaned down and petted her gently.

"Smokey has a boyfriend back in Happy Harbor," Balooon said. "His name is Eagle."

"Oh goodness me," Sugar said. "Ragamuffin has a cat girlfriend named Kitty. What kooky pets we have."

"Well, I'd rather stay awhile longer but I've got to get going on home," Balooon said.

"How are you going to do that?" asked Taffy.

"Easy, I'll walk to town and go to Mr. Float's house, and he'll float me home to Happy Harbor. He's a friend of the family. My Granny Bubbles made his yellow balloon."

"We know Mr. Float and his yellow balloon. He put the roof on our clubhouse with it," Taffy said, pointing up to the ceiling above.

Balooon was preparing to leave when he said, "Thanks for saving me – I'll never forget it."

"Hey, Balooon, can you come back and visit us again, maybe the day after tomorrow?" Topp asked. "We'll be at Bunny Beach on the Ooga River at noontime, to hang out, swim, and watch the bunnies run around."

"I'm pretty sure I can. I do have my other balloon at home – I'll get it ready. It was fun being with you today," he said with a big smile. "I'll see you at the beach!"

He took off and trotted down the trail toward the Village of Ooga Ooga, with Smokey at his heels.

The kiddos sat around on the floor, dry as can be, and chatted for a while about Balooon and Smokey. They'd had a wonderful day and met such a nice, new friend. The kiddos were happy indeed, and they looked forward to seeing him again at the beach.

Chapter 25

A NOSE FOR DIA-MONS

❧❧

It was a sunny morning when the four kiddos left the clubhouse for Bunny Beach, a large strip of sand where Silly Creek flows into the Ooga River. It's directly across the river from the flower field where the fan flowers grow. It's also where cute bunnies live. There are pink girl bunnies and blue boy bunnies, and they all have large, fluffy white tails.

When the kiddos arrived and ran onto the beach, the bunnies ran off into the bushes. The kiddos were delighted to see dozens of the fuzzy critters, poking their heads out of the bushes to watch them. The bunnies aren't concerned when the kiddos and Ragamuffin come around because the kids are nice and leave them alone. They *look*, but they don't touch.

"There he is!" shouted Sugar, pointing up. "Yay! Balooon is coming!"

Balooon was a sight to see as he rode underneath his blue balloon in a blue basket. He wore an elaborate blue safety belt to prevent him from falling out when a gust of wind comes along.

Balooon is tall and thin, with long, curly hair that waves in the breeze as he flies. His height is helpful in ballooning because his long arms enable him to work the ropes easily. He and Smokey don't weigh very much and that makes it easier for the small balloon to lift them.

Balooon's balloon floated over the trees, descended quickly, and landed with a thud. It is notable that his balloon, basket, ropes, and clothes are all blue. He told them that he likes the color blue because it's the color of the sky he flies around in. It's too bad that cats don't come in blue, because if they did, he would certainly have one!

Balooon has a blue bike at home, but it's not a three-wheeled one. He leaves his bike behind most of the time because he rides in his balloon whenever he can. On very windy days, he can't fly his balloon because strong winds could blow it miles off course to who knows where: Rat Town, the Jolly Jungle, the Spiky Mesa, or even the Village of Ghosts! Today there was only a gentle breeze, so he arrived by air.

Balooon secured his craft near the beach by tying it to the twisted root of a crooked tree, so it will not blow away. The kiddos ran up to him and gave him a warm welcome. Balooon tossed things out of the basket, including Smokey, and then jumped out onto the ground.

Full of excitement, the four kiddos took off running onto the warm sand and jumped into the shallow riverside pools. "Come join us in the water, Balooon!" Taffy shouted.

"How warm is it?" Balooon asked as he trotted toward the others.

"Like a warm bath!" Taffy said.

He shouted, "Super!" and then ran full speed through one of the shallow pools and kicked up a lot of splatter.

While the others goofed around in the small ponds, Sugar was in a larger one, playing a silly game. She slowly lowered her nose about an inch into the water trying to not get any other part of her face wet. She was holding still, with just her nose in the water when she caught a glimpse of something at the bottom of the pool. "Oh my!" she shouted out.

"What happened, Sugar, are you all right?" Topp queried.

"Yes! Yes! I'm fine! I think I found a dia-mon – a shiny dia-mon!" She popped up, with her arm raised high above her head. She opened her hand and there it was, dazzling and sparkling in the bright sunlight as if it was made of pure light.

"Let me see," Taffy said as she got closer to examine it. "Wow, I think it *is* a dia-mon!"

"Maybe there's more," Walnut said. "Where'd you find it?"

"Right in the middle of this planana-shaped pool," Sugar said and pointed to the exact spot. "Right there, I was having fun putting my nose in the water and looking at the pink pebbles on the bottom, when – *wham!* – a bright light hit my eyes! I kept an eye on it and reached for it, and sure enough, it's a dia-mon!"

"How do you know it's a *real* dia-mon, Sugar?" Topp asked.

"Because it's just like the one that my dad bought for my mom years ago."

Dia-mons are a rare gemstone in Ooga Ooga. They're extraordinary and worth quite a few brittles$, especially the big ones. Yes, dia-mons *are* beautiful, brilliant, and sparkly, but their beauty is just one of their wonderfulnesses. They are also like batteries and can supply power for all kinds of things, like egg cookers, automatic umbrellas, and fig-muggers.

What's a fig-mugger, you ask? Honestly, *I* don't know! There are things about the Valley of Ooga Ooga that I don't know. I mean, do you know *everything*? I didn't think so. But I can tell you one thing about fig-muggers: They need a good dia-mon in them or they don't work very well. So, there you go.

"I learned that dia-mons are not only beautiful and useful, they are also picky," Sugar said.

"How can a rock be picky?" Walnut asked.

"Dia-mons aren't rocks at all, they are a type of living thing," Sugar explained. "They live, think, and are very sparkly and admired by all – and they are picky!"

"Okay, how can a dia-mon be picky?" Walnut asked.

"They are found only when they want to be found and by whom they want to be found. Dia-mons won't let just anybody find them. They like to be found by certain people – the nicest people."

"So, we must be extra nice, or they might be picky and hide from us, is that right?" Walnut asked.

"That's right," Sugar added, "and they make people feel good. They are kind of like pets – but without the mess!"

The other kiddos had baffled looks on their faces. This all sounded very weird to them, but they knew dia-mons were valuable, so without another word, they scattered out around the beach and found their own puddle to search in. Just like Sugar, they stuck their noses, just their noses, into the water and hunted for dia-mons.

They looked and looked until their noses shriveled up, but they didn't find another.

Topp suggested, "I think we need to look *upriver*. The dia-mon that Sugar found was most likely washed down the river from somewhere farther up, maybe from Bon Bon Beach."

"Great idea, let's go!" Sugar shouted, and she and the others took off running up the trail along the riverbank.

They followed the path beyond the Bubble Bath and the Ooga River Falls, until they came to the lower rock formations of the Giant Step Mountains. Bon Bon Beach is a short hike from the falls. This beach has many pools of water in the sandbar, and it wasn't long before all five kiddos had their noses in the cool, clear water.

"I found another one!" Sugar yelled out. "Wow, they must like me – er, us!"

The kiddos jumped up and down and huddled around the newly found dia-mon. It was so shiny, so bright, and so *big*!

"Brittles$! Brittles$! Brittles$!" they all shouted and jumped around all over. Their stomping didn't make any clouds of dust as they often do because sand doesn't do that – only dirt gets to make dust – lucky dirt!

"I found it near those same pink pebbles, just like before," Sugar explained. "I guess pink pebbles and dia-mons are friends!"

So, back to the pools they ran, stuck their noses into the water, and held very still. The kiddos looked until their noses started to wrinkle, but they never found another dia-mon on Bon Bon Beach.

Again, Topp suggested that the dia-mons must come from higher upriver. He shouted, "Let's go up the trail to Wasp Creek, I know there are puddles up there!"

Taffy agreed, "Let's go. There's got to be more of them!" So, she took off sprinting up the trail heading upriver.

Sugar stopped running and yelled, "Wait! We gotta stop! Look at the sky! The day is almost over. If we get caught in the dark again, there won't be any fairy flowers to save us!"

They looked up at the sky to see where the suns were and agreed that they should turn around. Sugar was right.

They are smart kids but even more than that, they are wise. Their wisdom told them it was time to be patient. They decided to head back home and come back the next day. Tomorrow they'll have all day to travel farther up the Ooga River and up the side of the Giant Step Mountains to hunt for dia-mons.

Off they ran, back to Bunny Beach, to get their bikes and the balloon. When they arrived on the beach, the cute bunnies ran away in all directions.

"We'll meet at the clubhouse tomorrow morning – early!" Topp suggested. "Let's go home, eat dinner, and get a good night's sleep."

"I agree," Taffy said. "And we should all eat strong beans for breakfast, even though they taste so bad."

"Yuck, those taste awful!!" said Balooon. And the others laughed out loud.

"You're just like us, Balooon!" Walnut said. "You're our new, special friend."

Balooon's face beamed with dclight, and Smokey cuddled up next to Ragamuffin and flapped her tiny wings.

That night, after a hearty dinner, the five kiddos crawled into their beds and closed their eyes. Visions of bright, sparkly dia-mons danced in their heads as they rested on their cozy pillows and fell asleep.

Chapter 26

CLIMBING THE GIANT STEP MOUNTAINS

❧

Sugar woke up early, climbed out of bed, and looked inside the secret box she had hidden in the closet. She wanted to be sure that the two beautiful dia-mons were still there. "So sparkly," she said with delight as she held them in the sunlight streaming through her window. Ragamuffin looked curiously at the dia-mons, sniffed them, and then went to hunt for *real* food.

After she put the precious gems away, Sugar got dressed for adventure and put on her Super-Tracker hiking boots. She ate the small omelet her mom had made and then forced down a helping of strong beans. She gave her mom a kiss on the cheek and stomped out the door. She had a sense of purpose as she set off to find more dia-mons up the Ooga River.

The four kiddos were delighted when they rode through the tree canopy into the shady glade and saw that Balooon and Smokey had already landed.

"Hi, Balooon," Topp said. "So glad you could make it to our dia-mon quest!"

"This will be such a fun adventure!" Balooon said with a big grin. "I wouldn't have missed it for the moon. Thanks for letting me come along!"

In Balooon's town of Happy Harbor, there aren't many children his age, so he was especially grateful to make new friends in the Village of Ooga Ooga.

Inside the clubhouse, the kiddos filled bag-packs with provisions, including towels and drinking water. They packed their lunches, cat and bird food, and tools and gizmos they might need to stay safe on what could possibly be a long adventure.

Oh no, they need to *stay safe*? Will the journey be dangerous? In a kid's mind, if an adventure isn't a little daring, it isn't much fun. Right, kids? Wise kids are always prepared for anything, and these kiddos are well prepared – most of the time ...

Off they rode (and flew) to Bunny Beach, which is not far from the shady glade. Balooon arrived before the others and tied his balloon to the twisted root again. The kiddos soon arrived and parked their bikes nearby, while the bunnies on the beach scattered into the bushes. Ragamuffin greeted Smokey, and they touched noses in friendship.

Within minutes, the five kids started hiking up the cube-like steps to Bon Bon Beach. From there, they trekked onward and upward until they reached the source of the Ooga River, which is the place where Wasp Creek and Dice Creek merge.

"I remember seeing this place on the map that Grandpa Gabby gave to us," Topp said. "I wonder which creek we should follow. They're roughly the same size, and we don't know which one holds the source of the dia-mons."

"I have an idea," Sugar said. "I'll look for dia-mons in the pools of Dice Creek, and you four try to find them in the pools over there on Wasp Creek."

"Why four of us on one beach, and you by yourself on the other?" Walnut asked.

"The dia-mons apparently like me, considering I found the first two," Sugar replied.

"I get it," Walnut said wryly. "You are more patient than the dia-mons!"

The kids all had a laugh but more like a chuckle because they needed to save their energy for the search ahead.

They got to work hunting for dia-mons in the small pools of the creeks. They stuck their noses into the clear water and searched for a long while. When their noses got bright red from the cold water, they had to take a break.

"We haven't found any dia-mons on Wasp Beach yet," Taffy said, on behalf of the group of four.

Suddenly, Sugar screamed out loudly, "I found one!" Sugar happens to have a piercing scream. At full volume, she could be heard by her mom in the village, but she held back a bit.

"It's a beauty!" Topp said as he beheld Sugar's third sparkling dia-mon. "Now we know they're in Dice Creek! That's where we need to search. Let's go!"

They climbed up the big, bigger, and *bigger-than-that* cubes along Dice Creek. Above them, there were millions of cubes on the Giant Step Mountains to climb. Of course, there are! That's what these mountains are made of – rock cubes by the zillions. Many of the large ones have patterns of round dots on them, so they look like dice that the giants who roamed Ooga Ooga long ago might have played with.

They followed the creek up, but there wasn't much of a trail, just lots of steps, big and small. They came upon waterfalls of different sizes as they followed Dice Creek up the mountain.

When they came across a large pool at the base of a splashy waterfall, Sugar said, "This looks like a good place to search. I think I saw pink pebbles over there near the falling water."

Down went their noses and only their noses into the pool. The water was much colder higher on the mountain, so the kiddos were glad that only their noses were in the water. The kiddos had high hopes. They'd found three dia-mons already. Who knows, maybe there were hundreds more dia-mons high on the mountain.

"If we find the source of the dia-mons, we'll have found what's called the *mother lode*. There could be millions of them there!" Taffy said.

Sugar suddenly cried out, "I just found one … no, two of them! They were next to each other! Wow!"

"Two at the same time? Amazing!" Topp said excitedly.

The kiddos thought they must be hot on the trail of the mother lode. They gathered around Sugar to look at her new find. Taffy gave Sugar a hug, Ragamuffin purred happily, and Smokey was busy looking for tasty bugs to eat.

"What a great treasure hunt!" Walnut said. "Now we have *five* gems! But why are *you* finding all of them?" He was clearly disappointed that he hadn't found any dia-mons.

"Why do *you* catch all the fish, Walnut?" Sugar asked as a gotcha. "Finding dia-mons might be my kind of pow pow!"

"Maybe *I'll* be the one who finds the whole mother lode and proves that the dia-mons love me as much as they love you," Walnut told her with a phony sneer.

"I hope you do find millions of them," Sugar said with a smile.

After Sugar made the latest find, the kiddos ran around laughing loudly like looney birds! It was a good thing that the waterfall was loud because all the critters anywhere around would have run away from all that merriment.

"Onward to the mother lode!" Topp yelled. He put on his bag-pack and started climbing the cubes above the waterfall. The others hurried to catch up with him.

"Boy oh boy, we're high up on this mountain!" Taffy said. "I hope we find the mother lode soon. We're an awfully long way from home!"

This part of Dice Creek doesn't have pools, only fast-moving water, and a whole bunch of waterfalls, big and small. The kiddos kept climbing up, up, and up, stopping and looking down into the water of the creek from time to time as they went.

Eventually, they came to an unusually large cube that overlooked the valley. Everybody climbed onto it and caught their collective breaths. They walked cautiously to the edge of the huge, square rock and looked down.

"There's the village!" Taffy said pointing. "It looks so tiny!"

"Yeah, and there's Ooga Mountain standing tall," Topp said.

"I can see the Yeller Cliffs," Balooon said, "but I can't quite make out Happy Harbor – it's too far away."

"Look!" Sugar said with excitement. "There's the shady glade, and that little speck is our clubhouse! And way out there ... that blue thing must be the sea on our map – the Fantasmo Sea."

Topp took off his bag-pack and dug something out of it. "I brought the long-eye telescope. We're really high up, so I want to take a minute and look for the *edge* from up here."

He scanned the landscape slowly, back and forth, with total concentration. "Nope, all I can see is the land fading into the distance."

Walnut looked down at the valley, stopped whistling and said, "I am a bit tired, maybe I'll lie down for a minute."

"No! No!" the others yelled. "No turtle naps now! We have to keep going! The mother lode of dia-mons must certainly be near."

Off they went again, climbing higher and higher up the Giant Step Mountains. They came upon a small waterfall splashing into a wide pool. The waterfall was small, and the stream flowing away from the pool was much larger, so Topp thought there might be another source of water flowing into the pond. He snooped around and took off his shoes, rolled up his pants, and waded into the pool. He moved up close to the falling water and shouted, "There's a cave back here, with water flowing out of it! There must be a fork in the creek here. One fork that comes from higher up and another that comes from inside the mountain!"

Again, the kiddos had a decision to make. They could continue following Dice Creek or they could follow the stream flowing out of the cave. They decided to continue following Dice Creek because that was the safest and easiest way. A short distance above the waterfall, the kiddos found another pool of still water.

"This looks promising, let's look here," Sugar said.

Only Sugar stuck her nose in the pool. The others stood around watching her. They figured they wouldn't find anything anyway, so they kept their noses warm. Sugar searched the pool carefully and thoroughly, but she found nothing. All she got was a bright red nose.

"The dia-mons must be coming from inside that cave then," Topp said. He started hiking back down to the pond below the waterfall.

He bravely entered the cave and disappeared into the darkness. The others watched him vanish from view and became worried for his safety.

He came back out and declared, "The deeper I went, the darker it got. But I did go far enough to see that the cave is large and goes deep into the mountain."

"Do you think it's safe, Topp?" Balooon asked.

"I don't know for sure, but it looked solid to me. I don't think we have to fear a cave-in," Topp said. "But what we need is *light* to go in there."

"Do you think the mother lode is in the cave?" Taffy asked, dreaming of such a wondrous find.

"Who knows?" Topp said. "But we should call it quits for today and head back down and come back another day with lots of lights. Let's get going, so we don't get caught in the dark."

It took a lot of energy for the kiddos to descend the massive mountain. They had thought that it would be easier to go *down* the mountain than go *up* it – but they learned that *both* are hard.

Without mishap, the weary kiddos reached Bunny Beach at twilight and headed home to get a good night's sleep.

Chapter 27

THE DARKEST OF DARK CAVES

❧❧

Their hearts were beating excitedly as the four kiddos met early at the clubhouse to finish preparations for the return trip up the Giant Step Mountains. Today their plan was to enter that cave and search for more dia-mons and possibly the mother lode. The five dia-mons they had found are a lot, but a million would be a whole lot more!

Four of the kiddos were ready to head out to Bunny Beach, but they couldn't leave just yet. They were anxiously waiting for Balooon to appear and join them in today's daring adventure.

"Look, a balloon's coming!" Sugar shouted.

"That's not Balooon's balloon!" Topp remarked as he carefully inspected the balloon coming toward them. Topp recognized right away that the approaching balloon was not blue and therefore not Balooon's.

"It's Mr. Float's balloon!" Taffy yelled. "It's *Big Yeller*."

Sure enough, it was Mr. Float. He landed softly and professionally near the clubhouse.

"Hello, kids! I'm here to let you know that Raffer Daffer Doo won't be able to come today. The PetTunias needed help planting the new abble and sherry trees. He says he's sorry he can't make it and asked me to let you know."

"Thanks, we were wondering where he was," Sugar said, saddened by the message.

Then Walnut commented pointlessly, "I do love abbles and sherries!"

Mr. Float waved goodbye as he lifted off and floated away over the tallest tree on the edge of the glade.

"Well, let's get going then!" Taffy said. "The mother lode is a-waitin'!"

Off they went, all four of them. Balooon and Smokey wouldn't be coming, and Ragamuffin stayed behind because he was still worn out from the last trip up the mountain.

The kiddos quickly reached Bon Bon Beach, then hiked and climbed up and over the millions of piled-up rock cubes that make up the Giant Step Mountains. They would have no trouble finding the cave, as all they had to do was follow the Ooga River to where Wasp Creek and Dice Creek come together, then continue from there up to the waterfall, the big pool, and the cave.

This time the kiddos arrived at the dark cave fully loaded with light-wands. Each kiddo planned to carry four light-wands in their bag-pack but with Balooon not showing up, they each had five of them now.

Light-wands are reeds that grow in a marsh near the ruins of Dirt Town. When they're fully in bloom, they look like a fuzzy ball on a stick. Light-wands glimmer very brightly when they're fiercely shaken and whacked against a shoe or rock. They are kind of like fairy flowers but light-wands won't light up if whistled to. Light-wands would rather be whacked, which fairy flowers do not like at all!

The kiddos had picked the light-wands the day before. The reeds grow in open marshes that get sunlight all day long. The suns give the light-energy that gets stored inside the light-wands. Once they start glowing, they stay bright for about twenty minutes, and then the light fades away quickly.

The kiddos carried the wands in their bag-packs. They had to be careful not to shake or whack the packs too hard when they moved around. If one of them dropped a bag-pack, the light-wands would start glowing within the bag-pack. What good would that do? The kiddos might need each and every wand while in the dark cave, so they must handle them gently until they are needed.

"Well, here we are!" Sugar said. "I'm ready to find dia-mons, how about you guys?"

"Me, too!" the others said in unison.

Since Topp had been the one to enter the cave previously, he led the way. He entered cautiously, and the others slowly followed him into the pitch-black darkness. Topp pulled out a light-wand, shook it, and then whacked it on his shoe. Amazingly, it lit up right away and was brighter than ten candles. Taking his cue, each of the kiddos pulled a light-wand out of their bag-pack and did the same. The walls of the cave were now glowing brightly, except where the cave disappeared deeper into the mountain.

For a few minutes, the kiddos stood still like they were frozen stiff and looked into each other's eyes. They silently contemplated the danger of what they were about to do. They wondered if they might meet their doom inside this mountain. Oh my ...

Taffy, in her own powerful way, shook them out of their fearful trance and bellowed loudly, "Let's go find the dia-mons, I know they must be in here somewhere!" Her words echoed over and over down the hollow cave.

Step by scary step, the kiddos plodded deeper into the cave. It was a little tricky because there was water flowing down the center of the cave floor. They had to jump from side to side so as not to get their shoes wet as they moved farther into the dark unknown.

The kiddos were somewhat comforted by the fact that they had light with which to see. They could easily spot where they were stepping as they moved slowly over and around the big and little cubes on the cave floor.

"What's that?" Topp whispered as he stopped and stared at something unusual ahead of him.

They approached it cautiously with their slowly dying lights. It was a kind of wooden timber structure, holding up a boulder on the ceiling of the cave.

"This isn't a cave!" Topp said. "This is a tunnel, not a natural cave! This is an old mining tunnel!"

Their first light-wands were fading fast, so they quickly pulled out others from their packs. They shook and whacked them, and presto, there was a brilliant glow once again.

"What would they be mining?" Sugar asked.

"Dia-mons!" Taffy said with concern on her face. "Maybe the mother lode has already been found!"

"Maybe and maybe not. Maybe they *tried* to find them but never did," Topp said wisely. He then reached up to touch the wooden beam to figure out its age. He pushed against it a little but a little too much. The ceiling beam slipped out of place, fell with a thud, and splashed into the water on the floor of the tunnel.

"Wow, that was close! That big thing almost hit you, Topp!" a startled Walnut said.

"I think we should go a little farther," Sugar said. "Maybe the dia-mons didn't like the people who made the mine tunnel. Dia-mons are picky, so they only let people they like find them. I know they like me – uh, and you guys, too, of course – so if there are any dia-mons, we'll find them!"

They moved deeper into the tunnel and farther from the fresh air and daylight they had left behind by the little waterfall. Their lights lost their glow again, so the kiddos all pulled out new ones, shook and whacked them, until each one brought bright luminosity to the dank walls of the tunnel.

RUMBLE!

RUMBLE!

CRACK!

CRUMBLE!!

A terribly loud, thunderous sound reached their ears. It came from where they had just been a few minutes earlier. All the kiddos started trembling in fear, but Topp and Taffy, the bravest of the group, went back toward the sound to find out what had happened.

It was a sight that took their breaths away. The entire tunnel had caved in! There were hundreds of heavy rock cubes blocking the entire tunnel – and their way out!

Topp and Taffy returned with the bad news. "We can't go back," Topp explained, "The tunnel has caved in. We must go forward and look for a way out ahead!"

"We better move fast, because at some point, we'll be out of light-wands and then we won't be able to see a thing!" Taffy warned.

"Oh, my!" exclaimed Sugar. "That would be awful!"

There was no water on the floor of the tunnel at this point, so it was easier to walk. But before long, the light-wands began dimming, so they stopped and started to pull out new ones.

"Hold on!" Sugar said. "We only have two wands each – which means we have eight in all. What if we light only two this time?"

And that's what they did, until they were down to the last two light-wands. They decided to use only one at a time, even though it was harder to see where they were stepping.

"OW! OW!" cried Sugar. "Ooow, my arm! I tripped and fell and twisted my arm badly!"

"Can you still walk?" Taffy asked.

"I think so. I can't stay here, I know that!" Sugar said in desperation.

The kiddos were in a terrible situation now. Dark thoughts filled their minds. They longed to be back home in the valley and in their wonderful houses with their families.

As the final bit of light faded from the last light-wand, despair surrounded them. It became darker than dark. They began shaking, and they were scared to their core.

∽

Some time passed, and the children started to whimper. Walnut stood up suddenly and took off down the black cave. They heard him stumble away into the darkness.

"Where are you going, Walnut?" Topp called out.

"Anywhere but here!" he said with determination. He bumbled down the dark tunnel, fell several times, and yelled "Ouch!" each time.

It was cold and foreboding inside the dark cave. The kiddos were frantic with fear and frigid from the cold, dank air inside the gloomy tunnel.

The others were surprised when they heard Walnut whistling in the distance. To their amazement, they heard Walnut yell, "There's a light ahead. I think it's daylight. I found the way out!" Walnut had found the end of the tunnel and just in time. They stumbled out of the darkest of caves into the heavenly glow of sunlight!

They wanted to yell "Yippee!" or something, but they quickly realized they were a long way from the Valley of Ooga Ooga. They were now lost on the far side of the Giant Step Mountains, miles from anyone!

The kiddos sat on a rock outside the tunnel and decided to eat the food they had brought with them, to renew their strength.

Taffy used her sweater to make a sling for Sugar's arm. Sugar was still in pain but felt a little better. She was grateful for Taffy's loving care.

In silence, they sat on the back side of the Giant Step Mountains and looked around. Now they could easily see the Chocolate Hills below and the Ice Bug Sea beyond. It was a beautiful sight, but the kiddos were feeling too lost and forlorn to enjoy it.

Topp pulled out his long-eye telescope and searched near and far into the distance. "I'm looking for any sign of life or any sign of people, but I don't see any. I looked for the *edge* too, but I only saw land and sea, fading into the distance."

Just then, a huge dark cloud hovered above them, causing the whole area to become dark – perhaps a heavy raincloud was moving in.

"A balloon! A balloon!" Taffy screamed. "It's Balooon! Our friend, Balooon!"

Balooon made a gentle landing nearby. He explained to the kiddos that he'd felt something inside that told him he must go to find them.

He had flown over Bunny Beach, saw their bikes, then floated up to the cave entrance but didn't see them there. He decided to fly over the mountain to the other side to look for them. "And here you are!"

Tears of joy filled their eyes.

"I loaded my balloon with max Vaporgas in case I needed to carry an extra person," he said. "I'll float you guys down one by one to Gem Town, at the end of the mountain range."

Thanks to Balooon, everyone arrived safely at the Floatbus station an hour before dark.

The kiddos climbed on a Floatbus and rode gratefully and joyously back to the Village of Ooga Ooga. When they entered the village, Sugar shouted, "All's well that ends well!"

They all laughed, delighted to be home.

Balooon, the happy hero, lifted off from Gem Town and flew home to Happy Harbor.

The kiddos learned an important lesson: There is something far more valuable than dia-mons – THEIR LIVES!!!!!!

Except for Sugar's wounded arm, everything went well, don't you think? Maybe the next adventure will go just as well. (YIKES!)

Chapter 28

BOBBY CRAWLS INTO A CREEPY PLACE

❧

Bobby awoke to a cat meowing loudly outside his door. "Hi, Fluffers! Yes, you can come in, kitty, just a minute!"

I'm sure that all Fluffers heard Bobby say was: "Blah, FLUFFERS, blah, blah, blah, KITTY, blah, blah, blah." At least she knows her name. The rest of the words don't matter much as long as she has plenty of food and warm places to nap. Everything's perfect in her world if she has those two things.

Have you ever wanted to be a cat? I have.

Bobby doesn't mind waking up from his dream anymore. He has realized that every time he goes back to sleep, it picks up right where it left off. He always returns to that amazing valley and the wonderful little group of kids. He played with them all night – in the dream world, that is. When he wakes up, he knows he has returned to what he now considers his other life – his *real* life.

Bobby had been working the last two days to improve his clubhouse. First he took apart most of the dilapidated structure and salvaged the boards. He planned to enlarge it significantly, so he decided to start from scratch. He made a detailed plan on paper of the new design, and it turned out to be three times bigger than it had been before.

Bobby began to nail the first boards on the floor when his mom yelled something to him from the porch. He couldn't understand her at first, but then he heard her call out. "Bobby, please come help me!"

Bobby could tell by the tone in her voice that it was something important, maybe not a *big* emergency but important. He put his tools down and yelled back, "I'm coming!"

He jogged toward the house where his mother was anxiously waiting. "What's the matter, Mom?"

"Bobby, I accidentally dropped my diamond ring in the sink, and it went down the drain!"

"Uh-oh!" Bobby said. He knew that the only ring his mom ever wore might be gone forever. It was her wedding ring, and it meant the world to her.

"I was washing the dishes and it slipped off in the soapy water. I didn't realize what happened at first, so I ran some water to rinse the soap off my hands, and I was shocked that my diamond ring was gone. It must have washed down the drain!" she moaned.

Bobby ran into the house and went to the kitchen where the tragedy had happened. He looked down into the drain hole but couldn't see anything. He opened the cabinet door to access the sink from below and looked at the trap attached to the drainpipe. He hoped the ring would be in there.

"I'm going to take apart the plumbing under the sink, Mom. I'll find your wedding ring," he said reassuringly.

Bobby started removing all the cleaning supplies and stuff stored under the sink. Once the cabinet was empty, he went out to the tool shed and found two pipe wrenches and a wad of old rags.

He went back to the kitchen and began removing the parts. When he got pieces loose, the soapy water leaked all over him and dribbled out onto the floor. Undaunted, he sopped up the water with the rags and continued to remove the plumbing part that might have captured the diamond ring.

"Doggonit!" Bobby squealed in disappointment. "It's not here, Mom! I'm so sorry."

"What can we do now? I guess it's lost forever!"

"I have an idea, but I don't know if it'll do any good," he said, trying to keep her hopes up.

He knew the priceless ring had been given to her by his father when they were married years ago. Bobby thought about his dad's expedition to the jungle. He was only supposed to be gone for three months, but now nobody knows if he's gone forever or will return someday. Many search parties have gone far and wide to find him but with no success.

"Your Papa gave me that ring, Bobby," his mother lamented. "I would be so very sad if it's gone forever. So long as I had that ring, I still had hope that he would return someday. It's a bad sign that I lost the ring – now he may never come back."

"I still think he will make it home, Mom. He's probably on his way home right now. I'll keep trying to find the ring. It may have gotten caught in the big plumbing trap down under the house. I'll go down and see if I can find it there."

Bobby went back to the tool shed, got an old oil lantern, filled it with fuel oil, and lit the wick. He grabbed more rags, a hammer, and the pipe wrenches, and then headed for the little opening that led into the dark, creepy, spidery space beneath the house.

This is like a cave, Bobby thought as he moved slowly on his hands and knees under the floor of the house. The lantern lit up the area around him but out in the distance, the darkness was daunting, frightening, and spooky.

"I can do this! I can! I can do this!" he chanted quietly to himself as he continued crawling under the house, searching for the big trap where his mom's ring might be lodged. His light flickered and almost went out from all the jostling, so he stopped for a moment and rested.

"My dream!" he said out loud. "In my dream last night, the dream-kids went into a black cave to find diamonds. That's weird because that's what I'm doing right now! "

His light flickered again, which startled him back to his current situation under the dark cave-like subfloor of his house. He moved forward more carefully now, dragging the two pipe wrenches, the hammer, and rags along on top of the filthy dirt under the house. He pushed through mats of spider webs, and who knows what else.

"There it is!" Bobby said when he saw the trap in front of him. "I hope I can take it apart, and I hope, hope, hope I can find Mom's ring."

He banged and whacked at the huge plumbing trap to loosen the fittings that held it together. He tried to turn the part with a pipe wrench, but the rusty old pipe wouldn't budge a bit. He tried again, but it still wouldn't turn, so he rested for a moment and thought about what the dream-kids would do.

"They would get this thing open and find the diamond – that's what they would do!" So, he hit the hammer on the pipe wrench much harder, making so much noise that if there were any critters under the house they certainly would have run away – even the spiders!

Inside the house, his mom could hear the pounding and Bobby talking to himself.

Bobby gripped tighter and pounded with all his might, and the parts suddenly loosened. "Yay! It's loose!" he yelled out.

The big heavy plumbing gadget came apart just right, allowing Bobby to peer into the big trap. It was the only place the ring could possibly be found or else it was gone forever down the sewer under the street.

He held the lantern so the light shone into the trap.

"THERE IT IS! THE RING!" he screamed out. He yelled so loudly, his mom heard him from inside the house.

And Bobby heard her yell back. "Bobby! Bobby! How wonderful!"

He put the plumbing parts back together, and as he was crawling toward the exit, his lantern went out. "Yeowww!" he screeched. He was now surrounded by complete darkness. His imagination suddenly ran wild with scary thoughts of spiders, snakes, and worse! Bobby was afraid of the dark and creepy things, but then he remembered that the dream-kids got out of the tunnel they were trapped in by sheer determination. With renewed confidence, he started moving slowly through the darkness, toward a sliver of light far out in front of him. He was relieved when it turned out to be the little door to the outside. He quickly scrambled out into the refreshing sunlight.

His mom was waiting for him there, and they both jumped up and down in delight. So, off to the bathroom she went, to clean the ring and put it back on where it belonged.

After he cleaned up and the daylight ended, Bobby lay on his bed, looking up at the stars and planets on his ceiling. He thought about the quest for the diamond ring and how good it felt when he found it. He thought about his dream-friends and thanked them for helping him have the fortitude to crawl through the darkness in that ghastly crawl space.

As he stretched to go to sleep, he was certain he would once again enter that wonderful world that lives inside of him.

Chapter 29

THE SPOOKY, FARAWAY, PURPLE HOT SPRINGS

᚛ঌ

After their wild adventure on the Giant Step Mountains and their harrowing escape from the tunnel, the kiddos slept in. When they eventually woke up, they just sat around like lazy lumps.

How tired were the kiddos the day after the quest for dia-mons? Well, Walnut didn't whistle, Topp didn't even *want* to catch a fish, Taffy didn't leave the house, and Sugar and her injured arm went to the doctor and then back to bed. And Balooon? He was a little weary from flying for hours in the sky to rescue his friends, but he had fond memories as he dozed off in the shade under his favorite abble tree in Happy Harbor.

After Sugar had been examined, the doctor wrapped her arm with a medical elastic bandage, not a hard cast. He decided that there was nothing really broken, it was just a bad sprain and deep bruising. He suggested bed rest, ice packs, and for Sugar to just **take it easy**. Sugar didn't like that last part at all. *Sit around and do nothing! No thanks!*

Two days later, all five kiddos met early in the morning at the clubhouse in the shady glade. Among other things, they needed to check the seeds they had already planted in the garden. They wanted to be sure they were all still snug in their garden beds. They also had to get the remaining seeds into the ground, the ones that didn't get planted the other day when Smokey, the winged cat, chirped frantically for help.

The kiddos went out to the garden to get their overdue farming work done while Ragamuffin hung out in a nearby tree with Smokey.

"Ow, ow, ow," Sugar cried, grabbing her arm. "Darn! I can't help because of the pain!"

"Just take it easy, Sugar! Taffy told her. "We can get this done without you. We have Balooon and Smokey to help us now."

"I don't want to take it easy!" Sugar exclaimed loudly with disgust.

"I don't know if it will make you feel any better, but all of us would be frustrated, too, if we had to sit around like you," Topp said kindly.

"The problem is that my arm hurts even when I'm just sitting around," Sugar said with a tear in her eye.

"Do you know about the Purple Hot Springs?" Balooon asked Sugar.

"No, what's that?"

"They are special, healing hot springs on the far side of Ooga Mountain," Balooon explained. "The hot water is purple, and that's how it got its name."

The Purple Hot Springs are low on the southwest side of Ooga Mountain, almost halfway around. From the Village of Ooga Ooga, it takes half a day on a bicycle to get there and back. The springs are cared for by a family named the Indigos, who live in a house next to the springs. The mineral water is hot but not too hot – like a warm bath – a bath you can stay in for a long time.

"The purple water is said to have special healing properties," Balooon explained. "People from Happy Harbor make special trips to the Purple Hot Springs from time to time to cure their achy muscles and joints. However, many Oogans won't go to the hot springs because they're afraid of getting attacked by flying flamboes on the Purple Springs Trail."

"What are flying flamboes?" Sugar asked.

"Flying flamboes may or may not exist. Nobody knows what they look like because nobody has ever seen one or lived to tell about it anyway. Some say they can swoop down like giant hawks, grab people with their talons, and fly off to the top of Ooga Mountain and do something to the people that isn't very nice. Others say that the story was made up years ago by the caretakers of Purple Springs because they didn't want anyone to bother them there. I wouldn't like to meet a flamboe – how about you guys?"

"Yikes no!" Sugar squealed. "So, Balooon, the Purple Hot Springs might heal my arm? Really?"

"That's what I think," he said. "Pet and Tunia had body aches from all the farming. They took a trip over to the Purple Hot Springs and came back with lots of spunk and feeling young again. They go there often and have never had any problems with the mythical flamboes."

"You should go, Sugar!" Taffy said, listening from a distance. "We can all go with you. We are the Rainbow Kiddos, so no creature will bother us! We even have our bikes here, even Balooon has his!"

The kiddos finished their seed planting and took off for Purple Springs, to get Sugar's arm fixed up.

Off they rode as fast as they could, kicking up fragrant poofs of pink dust in the air as they sped away. They crossed the Ooga River Bridge and headed south past the flower field. They were on the main road to Gem Town, but they weren't going that far on this trip. They rode speedy-fast until they were slowed a bit by a steep hill.

At the top of the hill, the kiddos stopped and got off their bikes. They were amazed at what they could see. The Pink Desert was glowing in the sunlight. To the left of that, they saw a tiny bit of the Chocolate Hills peeking out from behind the Giant Step Mountains.

There's a small trail that goes uphill to the right toward Ooga Mountain. They saw an old, weathered sign that was hardly readable:

PURPLE SPRINGS TRAIL - BEWARE!

Before they started up the trail, Sugar asked, "I don't want to spook anyone, but isn't there a possibility that we might run into a dangerous flying flamboe on this trail? It even says BEWARE on the sign!"

138

"No, we won't run into any of those! That I know!" Walnut said assuredly.

"How do you know that?!" Sugar shot back.

"Because I have an agreement with them!" Walnut said, hiding a smirk with his forearm.

"Oh no! Not that again!" Topp said, glaring at Walnut with a touch of disdain.

"Just kidding! Actually, we won't run into any flying *anythings* because they don't exist. It's just an old made-up story!"

Surprisingly, Walnut ran and jumped firmly onto his bicycle, jammed his foot on the pedal, and lurched forward up the trail. The other kiddos quickly followed and pedaled on toward the Purple Hot Springs.

The kiddos rode for miles through the southern foothills of Ooga Mountain on the way to the springs. The trail was wide and easy, however they noticed that there were bushes and rocks that flamboes could hide behind. Everyone except Walnut looked warily from side to side and kept a sharp eye out for those scary flying creatures.

I mean who can really believe Walnut – about anything. He's full of nonsense a lot of the time. This time, the kiddos hoped he knew what he was talking about – they hoped he was right about there being no such thing as a flying flamboe!

Chapter 30
SWEET MISS VIOLET INDIGO

❧❧

The kiddos had ridden quite far on the Purple Springs Trail when they came upon a deep canyon. The trail headed through rocky outcroppings, into dark shadows of tall rock cliffs and large shade trees. Deep within the canyon in front of them, they heard water gurgling. They continued riding through the dark shadows and eventually came to a clearing where there was a gigantic purple boulder sitting in an open grassy area. Next to the huge rock, there was a tiny house surrounded by colorful flowers planted in neat rows. The house and the yard were well taken care of and looked welcoming.

The kiddos coasted up to a small picnic table in front and skidded to a stop. They kicked up a tiny poofette of purple dust as they parked their bikes next to the table.

"I guess we're here," Sugar said quietly.

"We are," Balooon said. He pointed to a colorful sign:

> # Welcome to Purple Hot Springs

A nicely dressed woman emerged gracefully from the house and said, "Welcome. Welcome to Purple Springs. My name is Mrs. Rose Indigo." Three more people came out of the house and stood next to her. "I would like you to meet my husband, Mr. Blue Indigo, our daughter, Violet, and her younger brother, Gray."

The kiddos politely introduced themselves and shared the reason they had come.

"My friend, Sugar, hurt her arm in a fall, and I thought a soak in the hot springs could fix her up," Balooon said. "My Aunt Pet and Uncle Tunia have come here many times with great success to fix what ailed them."

"Yes, I remember them. Lovely people! We will get your friend into the springs right away," said Mrs. Indigo. "Violet, would you please show these lovely children to the dressing rooms and assist them?"

"Of course, Mom," Violet said. "Come this way." The five kiddos followed her to a small building near the sound of bubbling water. "So, which one of you is hurt?"

"I am! My arm hurts bunches," Sugar sniffled. "I hope this can help."

Violet handed swimwear to Sugar *and* the other kiddos. "I know the springs will help you."

Holding up the swimsuit in his hand, Topp said to Violet, "We came here to help Sugar. We don't need to go in the hot springs."

"Everyone gets something good from the hot springs," Violet pointed out. "Just you wait and see. You have a long ride home, don't you? You want to feel your best, don't you? Jump into the purple pools and rejuvenate!"

The kiddos didn't know what *rejuvenate* meant, but they jumped into the steamy water anyway. And boy, did it feel good! Even Violet jumped in and floated around in the deep purply-colored mineral water.

"Come over here," Violet said to Sugar. "Put your bad arm under the little waterfall here, and let it bubble the pain away."

Sugar slid her arm under the splashing suds of the waterfalls to get maximum healing as Violet suggested. The others had fun moving all around in the deep purple water and getting splashed by the many waterfalls cascading into the pools. Walnut whistled a jolly tune. Topp looked for fish in the pool and Taffy swam laps, while Walnut floated on his back and fell asleep. Balooon soaked in the hottest pool and watched the others enjoy the healing waters.

About an hour had gone by when Violet brought them towels to dry off. They slowly wobbled into the dressing rooms and got back into their traveling clothes. They were so relaxed and rejuvenated, they moved in slow motion. And Sugar said that her (now purple) arm felt much better!

When the kiddos were dressed and ready, Violet invited them to have bread and cheese with her at the picnic table. The kiddos accepted her kind offer and headed toward the table. They sat down, looked around, and realized that the house and the big purple rock sat on a broad flat outcropping. There were no trees to the west which left an open view out across what looked like an expansive desert below them. The kiddos munched on their bread and cheese and enjoyed the immense view in front of them. Relaxing together at the picnic table, Violet and the kiddos chatted for a while and got to know each other.

"I've lived out here for several years with my family," Violet said. "I love living here in so many ways but once in a while, I wish I had more friends – like you guys."

"Well, why don't you come visit us over in the shady glade," Sugar said gaily. "We just built a clubhouse, planted a new garden in the glade, and …"

Cutting Sugar off, Walnut blurted out, "Wow, is that Candy Mountain out there?"

"Yes, it is," Violet said. "And between here and there is the Duney Desert."

All the kiddos stood up and stared into the distance at a very interesting mountain indeed. The magnificent, towering mound of candy was far away, but they could clearly see its bright rainbow colors and bands of chocolate brown. Their imaginations were going wild and their taste buds were too.

"Have you ever been to Candy Mountain, Violet?" Taffy asked.

"Yes, I have … once," she shared. "It was two years ago."

"Is it made of candy? Really?!" Balooon asked, licking his lips.

"Yes, the whole mountain is made of candy," Violet said. At that, their jaws dropped, and they all made a sound like *Oooooh!* They never really believed it was made of real candy until now.

"I've been planning to go there again someday," Violet said.

"Maybe we can all go together," Taffy suggested. "What do you think, Violet?"

"Sure, but the best time to go to Candy Mountain is when the weather is colder. When the weather is warm, the candy is soft and sticky, so you might get caught in it and sink in over your head! When the weather is hot, like it is now, the candy is like quicksand – like quicksugar!"

"Wow ... dangerous candy! I've never heard of that before!" Topp said with a grin. He pulled out the long-eye and pointed it at Candy Mountain. "Wow!" is all he said.

"I want to see!" Taffy blurted out.

The kiddos took turns looking at Candy Mountain through the long-eye. They could have looked at it for hours.

"I do know of an adventure that we could do during the warm weather," Violet said. "We could do it right away. It's something I've wanted to do, but I recently discovered that I can't do it alone."

"What's that?" Sugar asked eagerly.

"We could go into the Pink Desert, and in the miles and miles, and piles and piles of pink sand, we can look for pink rockroses," Violet said excitedly. "In the center of a rockrose, there is sometimes a ball of solid pink gold!"

"Gold! That stuff's worth a lot of brittles$, I bet!" Walnut said.

"Yeah, they're out there in the Pink Desert ... and I was given permission to find them!" Violet said. That caught the attention of the kiddos.

"Who gave you permission?" asked Balooon.

"Oh, the pink rockroses, of course," Violet said with a twinkle in her eye.

"Where have I heard *that* before?" Walnut said with a mischievous grin.

And the kiddos laughed and Violet laughed and a good time was had by them all.

Topp asked, "When can we do the Pink Desert treasure hunt?"

"The day after tomorrow would be perfect for me. How about you?"

"Perfect," the kiddos said in unison.

"What time should we come?" Taffy asked.

"As early as you can make it here," Violet said.

The kiddos were energized indeed and looked forward to the exciting adventure and treasure hunt that their new friend Violet had cooked up.

They hopped on their bikes and down the Purple Springs Trail they flew, leaving behind a cloud of purple dust. As they raced home, vivid images of balls of gold filled their thoughts, and they kept an eye out for those scary flying flamboes!

Chapter 31

HIDDEN TREASURE IN THE PINK DESERT

࿇ঙ

On the morning of the treasure hunt, the five kiddos met at the clubhouse and readied themselves for an adventure into the Pink Desert with Violet. They looked carefully at the map on the wall and studied every part of the desert and its surroundings. They had put a push pin in the Pink Desert on their map, to mark it as one of the mysterious places they planned to visit.

Without hesitation, the kiddos ran outside, jumped on their bikes, and sped down the path. They thought about Violet and the adventure ahead of them. They also thought about flying flamboes, Candy Mountain, and balls of pink gold. They rode their bikes swiftly along the road toward the Purple Springs Trail with eager anticipation.

Full of excitement, they arrived at the turnoff and rode up the narrow trail to the hot springs to meet up with Violet. All the kiddos (except Walnut) were on the lookout for flying flamboes, but none appeared.

"There's Violet!" Sugar exclaimed.

The kiddos rode rapidly to the picnic table and jumped off their bikes, well before they stopped.

"Welcome back, friends," Violet said with a big grin. "I'm so glad you could make it!"

"We wouldn't miss an adventure for the stars!" Taffy said.

"Especially a treasure hunt for gold!" Walnut added.

Violet held out a plate of chocolate cookies and offered them to the kids. "Here, I baked them just for you. The chocolate chips are from the Chocolate Hills."

Her guests were delighted and thanked her as they each picked up a freshly baked cookie. The chocolate chips inside them were still oozy and warm from the oven.

Topp was munching on one, when he eyed a bright green rake-like tool leaning against the table. "What's that, Violet?"

"That's Greenie Forkie. It's a sand-rake we can use to find rockroses. I believe the roses are out there, and Forkie can pull them out from under the sand when you can't see where they are!"

"Wow, that's interesting," Topp said. "How does it work?"

"The tines or forks are pulled through the sand, and if the rake runs into a rockrose, it'll pull it up through the sand to the surface. I tried it by myself about a week ago, but I couldn't get it to work. With more of us, I think it will."

"So, why do you think there's gold out there in that barren sand?" Sugar asked. "And what are *rockroses* anyway, are they gold or something?"

Violet began giving the kiddos the whole lowdown.

"I think I should start at the beginning. The Pink Desert is part of the Duney Desert, but it stands out because the sand is pink, like cotton candy. Some say the color came from real cotton candy that was on Candy Mountain years ago, then melted and flowed over the sand and turned it pink."

"Wow!" Walnut said.

"But don't eat the pink sand thinking it will taste like cotton candy – it tastes like gritty sand. I tried it when I was young. It took me a week to get all the sand out from between my teeth!"

"No, I certainly won't," Balooon said. "Thanks for the warning!"

"You asked me why I think there's gold out there. I've heard many stories about the Pink Desert and how there is rare and valuable gold out there. Very few people go into the sands of the Pink Desert

146

because there's no water nor anything else – except maybe wind and pink dust," said Violet.

"There's a lot of sand out there, that's for sure," Topp said, looking out over the Pink Desert from the Purple Springs perch.

"And I should tell you about Gem Town, since that's where there's pink gold on exhibit. Gem Town is a lovely town on the western edge of the Giant Step Mountains," Violet said.

"We were in Gem Town just a couple of days ago," Sugar said. "But it was late, and we never saw anything but the Floatbus station."

"It's too bad you didn't get a chance to go to the exhibit of pink gold. There are also beautiful sparkly jewels and rare stones at the museum in Gem Town. There are various gems that were found in the Giant Step Mountains nearby – that's how the town got its name. The gems are all colors of the rainbow, even sparkly white ones which are called dia-mons. Have you ever heard of those?"

"Oh yes!" Sugar said and then whispered. "Can we share a secret with you?"

"Why, of course!" Violet said and made a gesture like zipping her lips.

"We found five dia-mons a few days ago up the Ooga River!" Sugar revealed.

"Wow! You must be lucky!" Violet said. "With that kind of luck, I'm sure we'll find gold out there!"

"It would be nice to visit Gem Town someday," Topp said.

"Yes! People travel to Gem Town from near and far to buy gorgeous gems, metals, and amazing onyx from outer space."

"There's something from outer space sold there?" Balooon asked. "Really?"

"Where's Outer Space? I've never heard of that town before," Walnut said.

"The best I can tell you is that outer space is that place you would get to if you traveled straight up into the sky forever," Violet said.

"Oh ...," Walnut said, his eyes glazing over trying to imagine what that meant.

"Space onyx is for sale as are the gems and most of the gold. What's not for sale are the two pink gold balls that were found in the Pink Desert! They're displayed in the Gem Town Museum and are very rare and priceless."

"Now you're talkin'!" Topp said.

Violet continued, "Last year, Blubba, a young man from Gem Town, found the two balls of gold. The story goes that he went out far into the Pink Desert with water and food and stayed out there for a while. When he returned, he showed the gold balls to Rocki Pile, the mayor of Gem Town, who collects rare things for the museum.

"In the past, finding gold in the Pink Desert was only a rumor. Those pink gold balls are the only ones that have ever been found. They are very valuable indeed and certainly not for sale!"

"Wow! Sounds like we'd be rich if we found just one!" Balooon said.

"I've heard stories about the pink gold from visitors to Purple Springs. I heard from somebody, who heard from somebody else, who heard from Blubba, that he found the pink gold balls encased in the center of pink rockroses!"

The kiddos' ears were bulging out as they listened.

"I've learned a lot from the Gem Towners who visit Purple Springs," Violet said. "They come to soak in the healing waters, and they don't believe that there are any such things as flying flamboes. They say, 'Show me a flamboe, and I'll believe they exist!' And no one ever has. I heard something else that's weird – Blubba will never go out into the Pink Desert again. Something scary happened to him out there, but he has never told anyone what it was."

"Whoa!" Sugar said.

"What do the rockroses look like?" Taffy asked. "Do you know? Have you seen one?"

"Yes, they're made of pink sand that has been compressed, like sandstone, like a rock. A rockrose is about the size of a hand and shaped like a rose. Now you know as much as I do about the pink gold," Violet said. "I want to find rockroses and then go from there."

Not wasting any time, except to stuff the extra cookies in their pockets, the six kiddos headed down the trail to the Pink Desert. They were on foot, not on their bikes, because the trail is over steep, rocky terrain. And even if they did reach the Pink Desert with their bikes, they would be useless. Bikes don't ride on sand – the tires sink in and go nowhere, no matter how hard you pedal!

As soon as the kiddos arrived at the edge of the Pink Desert, they went out onto the sand and ran around, or sort of slogged around, because their little feet sank deep into the powdery sand with every step. They stumbled and bumbled out there in the sand, especially when they tried pulling Forkie. Walking in deep fluffy sand is always difficult. It's easier to just lie down on it, but you can't get anything done that way.

They worked to pull Forkie through the sand, but it skidded across the surface because it wasn't heavy enough to dig in. Sugar sat on it to add weight but when they realized that Sugar wasn't heavy enough, Walnut climbed on to replace her.

"Down they go!" Violet cried out as the tines dug deeply into the sand.

"Perfect!" Walnut said, riding comfortably on Forkie.

"Perfect for you!" Topp said to Walnut. "Perfect because you're just sitting and not doing any work." They all stopped and had a good tummy laugh.

As worn out as they were, they had one more pull in them.

"What's that? What's caught in the tines?" Walnut said pointing.

The pullers stopped pulling, and they all gathered around.

"Wow, it looks like a rose made of rock!" Balooon exclaimed.

They stood in a circle and stared at the pink rockrose. Then Violet spoke, "Well, now we need to break it with a hammer to see what's inside. Does anyone have a hammer?"

The kiddos couldn't help smiling, and then they frowned. At first, they thought it was a funny notion that a kid would just happen to carry a hammer around. Then they realized they couldn't crack the rose open because nobody had one.

"So," Taffy said, "we better get going anyway, and on the way, we can break it open on a rock to see what's inside."

They eventually found a nice sharp rock and broke open the rose. They held their breaths with great anticipation.

"It's just a dark ball!" Topp moaned. He and the others realized that it was only a ball of lead.

The kiddos were only slightly disappointed because Forkie had worked and effectively pulled up the rose up from the sand. They learned what they needed to bring next time: a hammer and extra-wide shoes that won't sink into the sand.

Before the kiddos headed home, they decided to meet back at the picnic table at Violet's house in two days. There is no giving-up in this group, not with gold out there!

Chapter 32

SAND SHOES OF WARTWOOD BARK

❧

Years ago, Taffy's dad took the whole family to play in the snow bunnies on the Tot Tot Hills after a snow bunny storm. Snow bunnies are the cold white stuff that falls out of the clouds onto the high hills and mountains around Ooga Ooga. Taffy's dad made wide shoes out of wartwood bark, so they could walk around on the snow bunnies. He called them snow bunny shoes, and they worked much better than regular shoes. They were wide and extra-long to keep their feet from sinking into the cold, white, powdery bunnies. They were constructed quite cleverly, and Taffy remembered how he made them.

On a quest to find the right bark, the five kiddos rode their bikes to the Wildy Woods. They planned to harvest the bark from a wartwood tree if they could find one and then go back to the clubhouse and make the shoes.

"I see one!" Sugar said. "There's a wartwood tree over there – it's a big one, too!"

"So, what do we do with it?" Walnut asked. He stared at the bumpy bark on the exceptionally wide tree trunk.

"We chip off big pieces of bark about the size of our pillows," Taffy answered. "Then we make laces and such to hold them onto our shoes."

Taffy brought a special machete knife she had borrowed from her father. Taking turns, the kiddos chipped and chopped with the large blade, until they had twelve big pieces of bark.

As Sugar was whacking away with the knife, Balooon asked, "Doesn't that hurt the tree?"

"No, this kind of tree benefits when it can grow new skin or bark. It likes its old bark to be taken off."

"How do you know it likes it?" Taffy asked.

"Because it told me so," Sugar said, looking directly at Taffy with a straight face.

"Is this kind of a pow pow thing or something?'" Taffy asked.

"Kind of," Sugar said with a twinkle in her eye and gave Walnut a knowing wink.

Sugar laughed, Topp laughed, Balooon laughed, but Taffy wasn't sure if she wanted to laugh. And Walnut whistled.

Back at the clubhouse, after their successful trip to the Wildy Woods, the five kiddos started shaping the wartwood bark into shoes. They created shoelaces by weaving fire spider web twine into sturdy straps.

"I really like Violet," Sugar shared. "She's so nice. She told me that she wants to find the pink gold so she can help people who are poor or sick."

"I heard, that's very kind," Taffy said. "What do you make of the bells she wears around her ankles?"

"I like them – they sound so tinkly," Balooon said. "And I always know where she is!"

"Violet said that the bells keep the fairies close by," Sugar said. "She told me she spends time with angels too! I don't know what that means, but I like it. I like it a lot!"

Working quickly, the kiddos created quite a pile of sand shoes. "How many do we need to make? Let's see: six kiddos, two feet each, that makes twelve!"

"I'll count 'em," Balooon said, "… nine, ten, eleven, twelve, thirteen, … whoops!"

"How funny," Sugar said in delight, "we made one extra!"

They all had a good laugh and then tried on the new shoes. They clomped around like ducks or platypuses, but they were able to walk pretty well considering they had big ol' clodhoppers strapped to their feet. Ragamuffin and Smokey looked on curiously and wondered what the heck these crazy kid-people were doing – they seemed almost dangerous.

"I think they'll do just fine," Topp said as his feet flopped around all over the place. "I can hardly wait to get onto that sand, walk around, and pull Forkie like crazy hard!"

"And pull up those rockroses with gold balls inside," Walnut added. "I can hardly wait!"

"Tomorrow will arrive soon enough," Sugar said wisely, "and we'll be ready!"

And tomorrow did come, and the kiddos arrived at the clubhouse early. They had eaten strong beans for breakfast, packed lunches, and brought water in leather waterbags about the size of a pear. So, without any further delay, the kiddos rode to Purple Springs in record time.

Chapter 33

DANGEROUS QUEST FOR RARE GOLD

❧❧

The kiddos rode up to the picnic table at Violet's house and parked. Violet waved to them as she came out of the cottage. She pranced over to them, fairylike, and greeted them. The tinkle of the bells around her ankles sounded refreshing to the giddy kiddos. They thought the jingling sounds were special, and they knew their new friend Violet was special too.

"Are you guys ready to rake up rockroses?" Violet sang out.

"We sure are! And Topp even brought a hammer," Taffy said.

"Try on these sand shoes, Violet, we made them for you," Sugar said.

"Wow, these are wonderful! They fit just right, thank you!"

Walnut added, "We're bringing an extra one, just in case someone gets a flat tire!"

His silly comment was met with silence. They let it drop like a rock balloon.

Carrying, not wearing the sand shoes, the kiddos ran so fast down the mountain, they almost didn't touch the ground.

When they reached the edge of the Pink Desert, they quickly put on their shoes made of bark and walked around on the sand – like sand ducks or something. The sand shoes worked just as they were designed, so Forkie better be ready for action.

All of a sudden, the sand shoes, all twelve of them, went flip-flopping out onto the pink sand, and took off over the dunes! Oh, and the kiddos, all six of them, went with them ...

The kiddos journeyed straight out onto the rolling pink dunes. They went up and down, down and up, and around many hills of sand. They didn't worry about getting lost because they could see Ooga Mountain clearly. The mountain is so tall, it touches the clouds. The Purple Springs are right at the base of the mountain, thus easy to find.

"Stop! Wait a minute," Violet said. "I think this might be a good place to start raking. But first, I want to tell you what I did yesterday."

The other kiddos put Forkie down, raised their arms into the air to stretch, and then settled their bottoms onto the sand to listen. They were anxious to hear what she had to say, so they were on the edge of their (sand) seats.

"Yesterday I went to Gem Town to see Blubba," Violet said, "the guy who found the two pink gold balls in the two pink rockroses in the Pink Desert. He said he was out in the desert for a couple of weeks. He found many rockroses, but when he broke them open, most of the roses had a dark lead ball inside. Eventually, he found two with a *gold* ball inside!"

"How did he find the rockroses?" Topp asked. "Did he tell you?"

"He noticed that when rockroses wiggle themselves into the sand to hide, they leave a little cone-shaped dent in the sand. When he found those divots, he found rockroses underneath."

"Did he tell you anything else?" Sugar asked.

Violet said in a hushed tone, "Nothing that I want to tell you."

"Uh-oh, is it something scary?" Sugar asked warily. "Tell us ... please!"

Reluctantly, Violet told them, "He said that he was busy digging when suddenly there was a loud *skreeeck* sound – a very loud *SKREEECK!* He was startled to his bones and looked around to see what had made the scary sound. Then a stiff wind started blowing sand like a sandblaster. It was a violent dust storm, and he couldn't see a thing in the swirling sand!"

"What was it?!" Topp asked with concern. "What made the awful sound?"

"Blubba said he never found out because he ran as fast as he could back to Gem Town. He said he left his hammer and all his stuff behind. What he *didn't* leave behind were the two gold balls which he sold to Rocki Pile. He said he will never go back into that desert ever – gold or no gold!"

"Whoa! Scary!" someone blurted out. All the kiddos had concern written all over their faces – all except Violet.

"We'll be okay. I know it!" Violet said confidently. "*They* told me it will be all right."

"Who told you it would be okay?" Sugar asked.

"My fairies and angels, of course," Violet said with a twinkle or two in her eyes.

The jingle of Violet's ankle bells brought them back from wherever their minds had taken them after they heard about the awful *SKREEEEK* that Blubba had heard.

Violet walked up the nearest tall dune and stood at the top. She looked around in all directions. She saw Ooga Mountain to the north and Candy Mountain to the west.

She thought for a second and then realized something unsettling. *What if a wind comes up and blows so much sand around, we can't see Ooga Mountain anymore? How will we know which way to go to get back to Purple Springs? Maybe we should have brought a big ball of string and unrolled it when we entered the desert. Then we could follow it home if a dust storm blocked our vision. Too late now ......*

Just then, Taffy yelled out, "I think I found a dent, maybe where a rockrose dug itself in!"

They all ran to where she was pointing and put the rake into position quickly. They pulled Forkie as hard as they could with Walnut riding on top. The forks dug in deeply and in no time, they pulled up a rockrose. They broke it open with the hammer and found a ball of lead inside. They were disappointed but not at all deterred from continuing their quest for gold.

The kiddos found dents in the sand and raked them all. They found ten rockroses, which was exciting, but each one contained lead, which was not so exciting.

They kept at it and pulled up a rockrose that was a little darker than the other ones. Topp smashed it and jumped back. "WOWIE-ZOWIE, A BALL OF GOLD!!!" It was the prettiest thing any of them had ever seen.

With success in their pocket (literally), they dug up another rose with a gold ball inside. "That's two!" the kiddos shouted.

They continued raking different areas of sand here and there. It might be hard to believe, except in the land of Ooga Ooga, but they found a third gold ball! "YIPPEE!" they all shouted.

"We can help the poor now!" Violet shouted with gratitude.

They continued to rake up more roses, so unless you really like lead balls, it wasn't worth "yippee-yaying" about. They searched persistently but never found another gold ball.

At one point, they gave up and sat down to rest, when out of nowhere, there was an extremely loud *SCREEEEEECK!!!*

They all jumped straight up out of their sand shoes, frightened by the hideous sound.

"Oh no!" cried Sugar.

"Oh no!" cried the others.

A fierce wind kicked up at once and filled the air with sand. The wind got stronger, and the sand and dust were blowing everywhere now. The kiddos could only see a few meters in front of them, but fortunately they could still see each other.

"We better get out of here!" Walnut said.

"But we can't see which direction to go! What direction is Ooga Mountain?" Topp asked.

The kiddos knew they were lost now, and they were also worried about a big monster coming to get them. Maybe it was a flying flamboe or something even worse, or maybe it was a mean what-er! There they were, deep in the Pink Desert, lost and alone, with a fortune of gold.

Oh, what they would pay to get home safely! They huddled together with their heads down, to protect themselves from the blasting sand as best they could. But that didn't assuage the pervasive fear and forlornness that they all felt. They worried that they would end up buried in the sands of the Pink Desert ...... *forever!*

Chapter 34

VIOLET'S NOSE

శ్రీ

The kiddos, all six of them, were completely lost, far out in the Pink Desert, and none of them knew how to get out. With the blinding dust storm upon them, they were trapped and surrounded by thick billows of sand, which obscured any view beyond a few feet.

The kiddos were breathing in too much sand, so Sugar pulled out a small towel and a pair of scissors from her emergency kit. She cut the towel into six pieces and handed them to the others to use as filters to breathe through.

When someone asked, "Which way do we go to get home?" Each of the six kiddos pointed in a different direction. Five of them were wrong, and one was right – but which one? Oh goodness, how are they *ever* going to get home?

Violet spoke with a firm but caring voice, "Stay together and hold hands. Possibly the fairies and angels will come and reveal the way home."

The six kiddos stood in a circle for a scary long time. They looked around the circle at each other and appreciated the fondness they felt for each other. There were no tears, just the strange, overarching contentment of being in this together.

The wind died down a little, but that didn't do much to help clear the dust cloud around them. Violet climbed up to the top of a dune, and the others followed her for fear they might get separated.

When Violet raised her hands high above her head, the stiff wind got even stronger and began to howl! The kiddos knew that they were clearly in big trouble now.

"Do you smell that?" Violet asked the others. The kiddos all stuck their noses up in the air and sniffed like dogs. *Sniff, sniff, sniff* ...

"I do smell something, something sweet!" Walnut remarked while sniff-sniffing into the dusty desert wind.

"That's the sweet sugary smell of Candy Mountain!!!" Violet exclaimed. "That smell comes to Purple Springs when the wind blows east from Candy Mountain. Now I know which way we need to go — that way!" She pointed her finger definitively and started slowly walking, er, clomping with her sand shoes in that direction.

"I get it," Taffy said excitedly. "If Candy Mountain's aroma is coming from that direction, from the west, and Ooga Mountain is to the north, then we need to go in the direction you're pointing!"

"That's right!" Violet confirmed. "Let's get moving and get out of this disgusting mess!"

The kiddos followed Violet, hoping she was right. If she was wrong, the kiddos knew they could end up walking for days out in that lonesome desert, and they would get thirsty and hungry indeed! Even worse, they could be forever buried by the blowing sand. To be saved, the kiddos possibly needed to believe in fairies and angels, like Violet does.

"Look, look! It's Ooga Mountain, I can see it! *Hell-oooo Ooga Mountain*!" Sugar cried out.

Knowing that they were going in the right direction gave the kiddos a boost of energy. They had worn themselves out clomping through the powdery sand for so many hours, but somehow they found the strength to keep moving.

Eventually, they reached the edge of the desert and were at last on solid ground again.

"Why didn't that monster eat us?" Sugar asked. It had been on her mind ever since she heard the terrible *SCREEEECK!*

"Maybe it doesn't like the taste of kids!" Walnut quipped with a silly smile. "Maybe it only eats adult people, and we're *anything* but adults, that's obvious!"

"That's for sure," Topp said. "Only kids would get into the messes we've gotten ourselves into … again and again!"

The kiddos were too tired to be in a laughing mood, but that certainly made them smile.

"All's well that ends well," Balooon declared.

"That's one way to look at it," Sugar agreed. "But we've certainly had close calls!"

The kiddos still had the three pink gold balls, but Forkie the rake was left out there somewhere in the dunes, hoping to be found by somebody someday. Poor Forkie!

"Your fairies saved us, like you said they would," Taffy said in appreciation.

"They are *our* fairies, not just mine," Violet responded with a bright, flashy twinkle in her eyes.

"I know we're tired, but we must get home," Topp said. "There isn't much daylight left!"

Everyone agreed. They took off their sand shoes, put on their regular land shoes, and started walking up the hill. They climbed up the trail to Purple Springs as fast as they could to get back to their bikes. The darkening twilight was rapidly creeping upon them and turning everything the color of deep indigo. That presented them with another problem – darkness – another 'kids just being kids' problem.

After they arrived at Purple Springs, they huddled around the picnic table in front of Violet's house.

"It'll be pitch-black very soon!" Topp said in a worried voice.

"You can stay overnight here," Violet offered. "We have extra beds in the guest house."

"That's great, and thank you, but someone needs to get back to the Village of Ooga Ooga to tell our parents where we are and that we're okay," Topp said, talking and thinking a lot like an adult. "I'll go and tell all your parents. There are fairy flowers at the start of the trail, so they'll give me light if I need it."

"If *we* need it!" Walnut blurted out. "I'm going with you! When I whistle, those fairy flowers light up big time!"

As they were leaving, Balooon said, "Let Mr. Float know where I am. He'll tell the PetTunias."

"Got it!" Topp said. He jumped with his full weight on his bike pedal for maximum acceleration, and Walnut did the same.

The boys coasted up to the fairy flowers and politely asked for permission to pick them. Without lighting them up, Topp and Walnut headed for the Village of Ooga Ooga. There was a touch of twilight glow in the sky, but it wasn't going to last much longer. They rode as fast as they could go, down the Purple Springs Trail.

This ride was much scarier for Topp because if a flying flamboe was going to attack, it would mostly likely do so when it's dark. Walnut wasn't scared at all – he didn't believe in them.

Without any incident, the boys arrived at the main road between Gem Town and the Village of Ooga Ooga. They lit the last two fairy flowers and hurried to the river bridge. They zoomed over the Ooga River, and then put out the word that Taffy, Sugar, and Balooon would be sleeping comfortably and safely at Purple Springs that night. They had a note from Mrs. Indigo, who reassured the parents that she would take exceptional care of their children.

Their parents were glad to hear that the kids were cozy. They trusted their children completely and knew they wouldn't do anything risky. They weren't concerned one bit.

Really ......?! Shush ......!

Topp and Walnut were given permission to stay at the clubhouse that night, so they went there to conk out. Taffy and Sugar plan to stay there someday soon. Their parents know the children want to have adventures out and around, and they want their children to learn all they can about nature and the land they live in. And that's what the kiddos are doing – each and every day. They learned a great deal about the Pink Desert today, like ...... DON'T GO THERE!!!

Chapter 35

BOBBY'S SANDBOX SURPRISE

੭੭੭

Bobby woke up bright and early, but he didn't get out of bed right away. He wriggled around in his blankets and ended up on his back. He looked up at the stars on his ceiling, and he knew where he was. His thoughts had been full of dreams but now were focused on his new clubhouse. He was going to work on it all day, once he got up and got going, that is.

Eventually, he shuffled his way sleepily into the kitchen.

"Good morning, dear son," his mom said lovingly. "Thank you for saving my ring, Bobby. I'm so happy to have it back, and I shall never lose it again!"

"It was a fun adventure, really," Bobby said with a smile. "And one with a happy ending."

His mother made him a delicious breakfast with extras. There was a slice of apple pie with ice cream on top and whipped cream on top of that and a cherry on top of that! I suppose his mom wanted to express how happy she was with her son and how special he is to her.

His belly was full to the top when he finally walked out the back door to start working on the clubhouse. He's looking forward to getting it finished so he can have friends over to enjoy it, like the dream-kids enjoy theirs.

Because Bobby is making the floor area more expansive, he needs to get rid of his old sandbox, next to the old clubhouse. His dad built the sandbox years ago. Bobby remembered his dad made a stout wooden frame and then brought in a giant truckload of sand to fill it. The sand came from a desert miles away, on the other side of the Happy Hills. Bobby was small at the time so when the dump truck unloaded the sand, it seemed to him like half the desert had shown up in his yard.

It's a large sandbox as far as sandboxes go, and now it's in the way of progress. Bobby either had to get rid of the sand or move the whole thing, frame and all, to a new location.

He had not played in it for years because he outgrew it and the sand got too dirty. Leaves and rotten fruit from the overhanging apricot tree have landed in it for years and never been cleaned out. Fluffers and other neighborhood cats have played a role in making the sandbox *extra* dirty, but that's a yucky story.

He rolled the wheelbarrow carrying a shovel and a rake over to the messy moldy sandbox. Bobby's first thought was to just get rid of the sand completely. He considered spreading it in the vegetable garden because sand improves garden soil. It aerates the dirt and allows more water to sink in where the roots of the plants are (as you know).

However, his final decision was to move the whole sandbox rather than get rid of it altogether. He had fond memories of the fun he had with his friends in the sand – before the cats took it over for their litterbox. Yuck!

He scraped off the top layer of dead leaves and then raked deeper into the sand. With a deep stroke of the rake, he hit something hard. He used his shovel to dig out whatever it was. "Oh my, it's the pink pogo stick!" Bobby shouted to himself.

His mom peeked out the window and asked, "Is everything okay out there?"

"Yeah, Momma. Just talking to myself again."

"Oh good," she said, remembering that sometimes it's like she has two sons talking to each other.

Bobby gently pulled the pogo stick out of the damp sand and stared at it. Fond memories came flooding back, of how he and his sister shared the pink pogo stick years ago. He had looked for it from time to time but never knew where it went.

He decided to clean the pogo stick, oil its moving parts, and try it out. To his surprise, it still worked! Bobby thought, *When Bettykins comes home next week, I'll show her what I found.* He looked at the now slightly rusty, pink jumping stick and remembered the good times they had taking turns hopping all over the driveway.

He continued the laborious work of moving the sandbox by digging around the wooden frame to set it free. He then moved the whole thing to a good spot near the peach tree. He was determined to clean up the sandbox because his friends have younger siblings who might play in it when they come to visit. (But before that happens, he will definitely mix in several boxes of Sand-itizer!) *They certainly will come over when the big new clubhouse is finished!* he thought.

Bobby spent the whole afternoon shoveling the sand into the wheelbarrow, rolling it down (not up, thankfully) to the new location by the peach tree. The work wasn't complicated, but it was tiring – and dusty. Sand was going everywhere as sand does when it's shoveled around in a breeze.

When a sudden gust of wind blew sand in his face, it went into his eyes, mouth, and inside his shirt! "Yuck! Patooey!" Bobby complained. "Sand doesn't taste good at all!" Then he had a weird thought that it would be nice if sand tasted like candy, then it wouldn't be so bad to get in his mouth. Silly Bobby.

"Oh, my gosh!" Bobby said. His dream from last night flashed in front of him. He remembered that the dream-kids had been lost in a pink desert of sandy dunes, surrounded by miles of sand. They were raking through the sand for some pink things.

"Wow!" Bobby cried out. He remembered that the dream-kids had raked up a treasure last night. It was a kind of rose made of rock with gold inside. He realized he'd also raked up a pink treasure from his sand – a pink pogo stick!

"Everything okay out there?" Bobby's mother asked again, leaning out the kitchen window.

"Yes, Momma, everything is really … fascinating!" Bobby shouted.

Fascinating? I wonder what he's talking about, she thought. Then she went back to work making a sandwich and a purple blueberry cake for Bobby.

It took Bobby hours and lots of effort to move the massive amount of sand. When it was finally all set up in the new location, Bobby took a well-deserved break. He went into the house, took a shower, and changed into clean clothes.

Bobby's mom had set the table for him and offered a sandwich and a veggie salad for a late lunch. For dessert, there was a large piece of purple cake with ice cream on top.

After he ate every bit of it, Bobby slowly sauntered with his bulging tummy in front of him, down the hallway to his room. He decided to rest on his bed a bit before he got back to work before evening set in. He walked over to the window and talked briefly to his plants. He told them about his latest dream in the sandy desert, about the sand he moved today, and how bad it tasted.

He stretched out on top of the covers on his bed and stared up at the ceiling. And, just like that, he fell asleep! In days past, he had not liked to take naps. He thought sleeping was a waste of time, especially during the daytime. But now, with the amazing dream he's having, he doesn't mind a bit.

So long, Bobby, see you in Ooga Ooga …

Chapter 36

THE TREEHOUSE AND THE GIANT BUTTERFLY

෯෧

All *six* kiddos met at the clubhouse in the shady glade a few days after their wild and scary adventure in the sandstorm. Violet requested they stand in a circle and hold hands as they had done back in the desert. Once again, they looked into each other's eyes and relished their strong bond of friendship.

The moment was solemn and quiet, until Walnut blurted out, "Hey, we really are the rainbow kiddos! Now we have blue and violet, so our rainbow is complete! Red, Orange, Yellow, Green, Blue and Violet!"

The others couldn't help but smile at Walnut's insight.

The kiddos strolled over to the bank of Silly Creek, sat down, and discussed expanding the clubhouse. Violet and Balooon were given permission from her parents and the PetTunias, to stay some nights at the clubhouse in the shady glade. This way, the two kids who live far away could spend more time with their new friends without having to travel such long distances. The kiddos came to the realization that they would need to enlarge the clubhouse to have room for *all* of them to sleep there.

"What if I build a *treehouse*?" Balooon suggested. "I like to be up in the air, up with the birds, and Smokey does too!"

Balooon's idea of a treehouse brought broad smiles and unanimous agreement from the others.

"Bravo!" Topp said. "That's perfect."

"I can use the skin of my old broken balloon for a waterproof roof," he said. "And there'll be plenty of extra roof material for the addition of Violet's new room."

"We'll have to get a lot more boards, a couple of doors, and a window or two," Topp pointed out.

The kiddos had brittles$ to buy things now, thanks to the five dia-mons and three pink gold balls they'd found on their treasure hunts. They sold three of the dia-mons and one gold ball to Rocki Pile, the mayor of Gem Town, in exchange for a bunch of brittles$.

Two dia-mons and two gold balls were given to Mayor Kee Kee of the Village of Ooga Ooga as a charitable donation to the town. Violet had taught the other kids about giving to others and suggested they donate much of their treasure for the public good. Even in Ooga Ooga, there are people in need, and the town always has expenses for building and repairs. In fact, the village now has the funds to enlarge the Museum of Everything.

What wonderful kiddos – don't you think?

The kiddos were well known around town for the charitable gifts they gave. The Oogans heard the stories about how the children had found dia-mons and pink gold, and how wonderful that was. But only one of their schoolfriends and his girlfriend knew the whole story. Only those two were aware of the extreme danger the kiddos were in when the tunnel caved in and when the sandstorm enveloped them. If you must know, their friend's name is Bob, but he is not Bob Bobb's son, Bob, nor Bobb Bob's son, Bob. The kiddos knew they could confide in their close friends to keep secrets of the dangerous perils they had gotten themselves into. *All's well that ends well* is the motto that the kiddos use to justify their secrets.

The kiddos headed back to the clubhouse because a few drops of rain starting plopping on their heads. Once inside, they sat down on the floor in a circle and continued discussing strategies for enlarging the clubhouse.

Bang! Bang! Bang! There was a fierce pounding on the clubhouse door. It shook the whole building and made the windowpanes rattle.

Topp rushed to the door and cautiously cracked it open. He found himself standing there staring at a giant blue butterfly with its wings spread out. It was standing up on weird feet, and it was twice as tall as he was. Topp stood there with his mouth wide open, not believing what he was seeing.

Then the big blue butterfly spoke, "Have you seen a green bumblebee around here – a huge green bumblebee?"

"Uhhh, nooo ...," Topp said slowly.

"Are you sure?" the butterfly asked in an accusatory tone.

"I'm *sure!*" Topp responded with attitude. "I would certainly remember seeing something like that!"

Just as the other kiddos came to the door and without another word, the blue butterfly quickly rose into the air and flip-flapped away.

"Who banged on the door, Topp?" Sugar asked.

"You wouldn't believe me if I told you! It was a big blue butterfly thing that was taller than me – and it talked!"

"It must have been a what-er," Walnut said.

"It asked me if I had seen a green bumblebee, so I said I hadn't, then it flew away. That's all I can tell you!"

"What's a what-er?" Violet asked. "I've never heard of such a thing."

"They're creatures that suddenly show up in the Valley of Ooga Ooga and then leave quickly and never come back again," Taffy explained. "They're called what-ers because when they show up people ask, 'What-er those?' We met one here in the shady glade a few weeks ago. It looked like a mouse but sang like a songbird. Then it flew away into the sky, but it didn't have any wings!"

"Very interesting," Violet said. "I wonder if my friends, the fairies and angels, are what-ers."

"Do they leave and never come back?" Topp asked.

"No, not really, I've known them for years," Violet said.

"Then they aren't what-ers," Topp told her assuredly.

"That's good, very good!" Violet said. She was relieved that her friends, the fairies and angels, were not what-ers. "Maybe I'll get to see a what-er someday – I'd like that."

"You probably will. They seem to come to our clubhouse door from time to time," Taffy said. "Okay, enough with the distractions, it's time to finish our new clubhouse plans."

Chapter 37

THE BIG ABBLE IS BORN

಄಄

After the encounter at the door with the what-er butterfly, the kiddos came up with clever ideas about how to accomplish adding space to the clubhouse.

Bang! Bang! Bang! There was another loud pounding on the door.

Topp jumped up, ran to the door, and opened it angrily. He shouted out the door, "I told you that I didn't ...!" In mid-sentence, he stopped shouting. "Mr. Gruff! Mr. Gruff! Ohhh, hello! I thought you were that annoying blue butterfly!"

Mr. Gruff smiled and remarked, "I've been called a lot of things, but I've never been called a blue butterfly before! Very interesting – *a butterfly*." He looked down the front of his body and raised his arms to see if he had somehow changed into an insect.

"Come on in, Mr. Gruff. I'd like to introduce you to new friends you might not know," Topp said warmly. "This is Violet from Purple Springs, and this is Balooon from Happy Harbor."

Mr. Gruff cordially shook their hands and welcomed them to the shady glade. When he entered the room, he noticed that the kiddos were sitting on a smallish rug on the hard floor. He thought they looked a bit uncomfortable, so he asked, "How would you kids like a table and chairs, so you don't have to sit on the floor anymore? If you want, I'll bring them to you."

"Wow, that would be wonderful!" Taffy said with delight. "Of course, we want them!"

"Is there anything else you need?" Mr. Gruff asked. "I heard around town that you kids gave a generous donation to the Village of Ooga Ooga. Now Oogan folk want to give you the things you need for your little house. If you tell me what you need, I'll put the word out."

So, the kiddos told Mr. Gruff about their desire to enlarge the clubhouse and what they needed to do it. So, he wouldn't forget anything on their wish list, Mr. Gruff took notes on a piece of paper.

"It's a long list, but it's what we'll need," Sugar said sweetly. "We do have brittles$, we can pay for it."

"It's a reasonable list," Mr. Gruff said, then excused himself politely. "I'll go get the table and stools and bring them back shortly." He waved to the kids as he trotted away on his stout six-legged horse.

The kiddos were working in their garden and talking to their newly sprouted baby plants, when Mr. Gruff showed up with a big cart. His wagon was pulled by two six-legged horses and full of wooden objects. The kiddos all gathered around as his cart came to a stop.

They were delighted. They helped unload the table and stools and carried them into the clubhouse. "Look," Taffy said, "the table's almost round like our clubhouse."

The table had six sides so it wasn't round. Round is like a circle. This table has six sides, which is called a hexagon. It's kind of like a *bumpy* circle.

The stools were carried in, and one was placed on each of the six sides of the table. Just to try it out, the kiddos took their places around the table, one by one. There were grins galore circling this gift, and Mr. Gruff beamed with delight seeing the children so happy.

"Thank you *so* much, Mr. Gruff!" Violet said sincerely. "It's perfect – and much more comfortable than the floor!"

Mr. Gruff hopped onto his wagon, whistled to his six-legged horses, and off they galloped with Mr. Gruff hanging on for dear life!

While the kiddos were working in the garden that afternoon, they heard horses neighing in the distance. *Had Mr. Gruff forgotten something?*

In a billow of dust, five loaded wagons came roaring up to the clubhouse. The Oogan villagers came with wagons full of stuff the kids had put on their wish list. The wonderful people unloaded the wagons near the clubhouse, and the kiddos were surprised and delighted to see that they brought just about everything on their list, including a kitchen sink.

Bob Bobb, his brother Bob, and his son Bob had come to give them two more brass doorknobs. Mrs. Quilty brought two lovely blankets and two large soft rugs, and Mr. Buggitty came with two doors with matching green hinges. Mrs. Clear donated two windows, and Mr. Stick brought a huge stack of lumber.

There was lots of other stuff brought by the village people, but I can't remember who brought what. Oh yeah, Mr. Bark brought another box of shiny new nails and a basket full of popcorn berries for all to enjoy.

Mr. Topper was also there. He brought a wagon full of tools, screws, and all such things to build with. He told the kids that he would be back tomorrow with a whole crew of workers to "Build, build, build!"

Tap-tap, bam-bam, saw-saw, whack-whack were all the sounds in the shady glade that busy day. Mixed in with the construction sounds, there were "whoopees" and "yippees." Topp's dad had gone over the plans with Topp, Violet, and Balooon. The plan was to build two new bedrooms, a treehouse for Balooon, and a big ol' kitchen to keep the kids fed.

Balooon's treehouse would be built upon a huge branch of an umbrella tree which grew over the clubhouse. The plans for the lofty treehouse included a long ramp for going up and down, perfect for Smokey and even Ragamuffin to get up to the treehouse easily.

"Look, it's Mr. Float and his balloon!" Sugar shouted. "What's he doing here?"

"He's here to bring my old broken balloon over the creek to the shady glade," Balooon said. "We'll use the skin of the balloon for our new roofs, and the fire spider ropes can be used to make a swing and lots of other things."

It took three full days to build all the new additions and upgrades. Now the kiddos have a clubhouse that is far beyond what they could have imagined in their wildest dreams. The main room has cushions to sit on, the table and stools, two desks, and three bookcases stocked with donated books. Additionally, there are two new rooms, each with a window and three real beds. One room is for the girls, and the other one is for – you know.

When it was all done, Mr. Colours, the owner of the paint store, painted the clubhouse bright abble red, as the kiddos requested. The roundish-shaped clubhouse, now painted red, looked like a giant red abble.

"I think we should give our clubhouse a name," Sugar suggested. "I read about a big town in a faraway land called *The Big Abble*. What do you guys think of that name, The Big Abble?"

"Yes, I like that, and we could give it a nickname, the Big A!" Topp said. "And this will be our *adventure headquarters*!" With that awesome thought, the kiddos had smiles as big as Ooga Mountain.

The kiddos ran in circles around the new clubhouse like it was a merry-go-round. As they raced around the room, they shouted out the names of all the exciting places on the map that they were eager to explore: "Candy Mountain! Fantasmo Sea! Jolly Jungle! Island of Wow! Chocolate Hills! Ice Bug Sea! The *edge*, the *edge*, the *edge!*"

Chapter 38

DELICIOUS YELLER PLANANAS

ҩ⚬ᕗ

When their parents heard about the generous gift the kiddos had given to those in need, they were very proud and thus very supportive of their pursuits. The parents granted the kids permission to sleep overnight in the Big Abble from time to time. This made the kids happy, especially Violet and Balooon, whose homes were so far away.

The Valley of Ooga Ooga has no crime, if you don't count the squirrelies who steal acorns from the oaken trees. The valley is so safe, their parents have few concerns about the kiddos sometimes staying overnight in the clubhouse, and that includes Topp, Taffy, Walnut, and Sugar, who live nearby.

A very nosey neighbor once asked Taffy's mother, "Why would you give Taffy permission to sleep at that shack?"

And Taffy's mother answered, "Taffy is an excellent student and does all her chores. Oh, and she does everything with a smile. We trust her to behave and take good care of her health and safety. Have you ever visited their playhouse? It's like a real house, very safe and cozy."

The nosey neighbor heard similar answers from the parents of Topp, Sugar, and Walnut, and decided to keep her nose out of their business from then on. Good idea! Maybe the nosey neighbor doesn't trust her own children, and maybe she should. Your parents trust you, don't they? They should, shouldn't they?

The kiddos did keep some of the dangerous details of their adventures from their parents. They knew that they would get themselves out of the messes some way or another, and they did. When everything ends well, then that's well enough, I suppose. They'll be wiser and more careful on their next adventure.

Really?

The six kiddos gathered one morning around the hexagon table in their fancy, expanded clubhouse to discuss their next big adventure.

"How about we make a raft and float down the Ooga River to Happy Harbor and then to the Town of Trombone – maybe even all the way to the Fantasmo Sea!" Topp proposed. "We can swim, fish, and play games along the way."

"What about we go to the Biggo Dunes in the Duney Desert and slide down the mega dune really fast on sleds?" Violet said.

"I've had enough of sand for now!" Sugar said. "How about searching for the lost silver coins$ in the Yeller Cliffs near Old Town?"

"Or how about going around the Giant Step Mountains to get chocolate from the Chocolate Hills?" said Walnut, licking his lips.

"We could even go farther south, to the Ice Bug Sea, and see ice bugs – from a distance, of course. I've heard they're mean and scary!" Balooon added.

"I think we should spend a day or two planting fruit trees," suggested Sugar, "to grow abbles, sherries, pearettes, burple blums, and affricots. We have enough brittles$ to buy trees now. If we want to have our own fruit someday, we gotta plant them right away! Adventures don't need to be planted and grow, but trees do!"

"Exactly," Taffy said in support. "The planting season is almost over, so we better plant them soon!"

Sugar was delighted that Taffy agreed with her, and the others went along with the plan as well. She thought for a moment and then said, "You know, I love plananas! I love those sweet, long, yeller plananas! We need to have at least one planana tree, don't we?!"

Balooon responded kindly but realistically, "I've heard that plananas can't grow here, it's not hot nor humid enough. They only grow in the jungle – the Jolly Jungle."

If you had seen the frown on Sugar's face after Balooon broke her heart, you would have cried. However, Sugar raised her head high and said, "I *WILL* grow a planana tree in the shady glade. I WILL!"

"How will you grow one in a climate where they can't grow? I know they won't grow in the Pink Desert," Violet said.

"I will use my special power or something!" Sugar replied, wiping away a tear. "I can sometimes influence the behavior of living things."

"What?!" Topp blurted out. "You can?"

"I can communicate with plants and trees and even animals," Sugar explained. "The life blood of trees is their sap, and I have a special relationship with tree sap and the hearts of trees … that's all."

There wasn't a sound to be heard in the clubhouse. It was so quiet, they could hear the mouse under the sink breathing. The kiddos just sat there and soaked up the fact that Sugar had just declared she had special powers. Their silence told Sugar that she was heard and understood.

"That's neato," Walnut said and left it at that.

The kiddos took a vote about planting fruit trees for their next activity. They are a democracy, after all, and the vote was six ayes and zero nays.

The kiddos rushed outside, jumped on their bikes, and headed for The Deep Roote, a tree nursery not far away. They brought the brittles$ they had hidden away in a secret rag, in a secret bag, in a secret box, in a secret place.

I can't tell you where that is because … *it's a secret!*

The nursery owner, Mrs. Roote, handed the kids a list of all the trees available, along with a description of how to grow them and what fruit they bear.

After Sugar looked over the selections, she asked, "I have a question, Mrs. Roote. I don't see any planana trees on the list, aren't they available?"

"No, I'm sorry. Planana trees only grow in the jungle where it's hot and muggy."

"Isn't there *any* way to grow them here in the Valley of Ooga Ooga?" Sugar persisted.

"I doubt it, but they might grow in a glasshouse," Mrs. Roote said pensively.

"What's a glasshouse?" Sugar asked with hope in her voice.

"It is a little room or building made of glass," she said. "The suns shine through the glass and heat up the space inside. The room is closed on all sides, so the heat and humidity build up when the rays of the suns pass through the glass."

"So, that makes it hot and sticky inside?" Sugar mused quietly, more to herself than to anyone else. She pictured a glasshouse room in her head and thought about how she could go about building one at the shady glade.

After the kiddos made their selections and paid for them, Mrs. Roote loaded the trees onto a wagon pulled by a yellow six-legged horse. She delivered the young trees to the shady glade where the kiddos happily unloaded them and spread them out on the ground.

Mrs. Roote was nice and exceptionally helpful. She moseyed around the shady glade and made suggestions as to where they should plant each tree and how far apart they should be from each other. She explained that the trees need to be planted in such a way they have enough room when they reach full size. The kiddos thanked her and waved as she slowly disappeared down the road.

For the rest of the afternoon, the kiddos dug holes for the trees in various parts of the shady glade. They planted the trees around the edges of the glade, so their vegetable garden in the center won't be shaded by the fruit trees when they grow tall and wide. Once the baby trees were in the ground, the kiddos hauled buckets of water from Silly Creek to each one as Mrs. Roote had suggested.

While five of the kiddos looked with satisfaction at their new orchard, Sugar was not in sight. She was on the sunny south side of the clubhouse, planning the new glasshouse for the planana tree.

Topp walked over to Sugar and asked, "You really want a planana tree, don't you?"

"Yep, very much, yep!" Sugar said passionately. "I will build a glasshouse and grow one inside."

"I'll help you build the glasshouse," Topp said. "Building is *my* special skill. I can build things so fast, your head will spin like a ballerina!"

"How are we gonna do it if we don't have any glass to build it with?"

"We can check at the Junkitty Junk store," Topp suggested. "I'm certain Mr. Stufff has old used windows. We can go check right now if you want."

So, off they went on their three-wheeled bicycles at breakneck speed to meet Mr. Stufff and look at his collection of various windows.

Mr. Stufff's Junkitty Junk store is a massive yard full of tons of stuff. For example, if you need a kitchen sink, Mr. Stufff has several types and colors to choose from. They are used but still good, most of them anyway.

"Hello, young children, how can I help you?" said Mr. Stufff, after Sugar and Topp parked their bikes and entered the store.

"We want to build a glasshouse next to our clubhouse," Topp explained. "Do you have any old windows?"

"I do!" said Mr. Stufff assuredly. "I do have a bunch. A school in Old Town was torn down, and Mayor Boof gave me all the windows from it. They will be perfect for making a glasshouse."

"How many brittles$ do they cost?" Sugar asked with concern.

"Hey, are you the children that made that generous donation to the Village of Ooga Ooga?"

"Yes, we are," Sugar said humbly. "But it was nothin'. We like to give to others, and we have plenty of brittles$ left over to pay for what we may want to buy."

"Nay, nay, nay!" Mr. Stufff said sternly. "I will not only give the windows to you, but I will also have my worker, Bobb, carry them to where you want them."

(Just to make it clear to the reader, this Bobb is not Bob Bobb. This Bobb is Bobb Bob, who is not to be confused with Bob Bobb. That should clear that up nicely!)

"Thank you," Topp said. "That's very generous of you."

"My joy!" smiled Mr. Stufff. "I'm glad I can help special children like you."

The next day, Bobb brought the windows to the shady glade on a big wagon with six wheels, pulled by six, six-legged horses. When Topp saw the large windows, he knew right away they would be perfect for building a glasshouse.

After Bobb unloaded the windows, he started to leave. Sugar spoke up, "Thank you, and please thank Mr. Stufff for us!"

For the next few hours, the kiddos stood back and watched Topp use his special building skills. The glasshouse went together nicely and was finished late in the morning the next day.

Sugar was delighted to now have a place in the shady glade to grow a planana tree. Sugar loves lots of critters, and she loves planana trees – even though she has never even seen one. Sugar likes the planana fruit because it's the same color as her golden hair, and oh, they taste good too!

Many farmers around the Valley of Ooga Ooga have said plananas won't grow outside of the Jolly Jungle – even in a glasshouse. Sugar wants to prove them wrong. After all, they don't have the ability to talk to trees like she has nor do they love plananas as much as she.

Sugar stood there and stared at the now completed glasshouse, with a concerned look on her face.

"What's wrong, Sugar?" Topp asked. "Is something wrong with it?"

"Yes … very much so!" Sugar said sadly. "There's no planana tree to put in it!"

That *is* a problem. Poor Sugar.

Chapter 39

JOURNEY TO THE JOLLY JUNGLE

☙❧

One morning, Sugar and Walnut coincidentally left their homes at the same time on their way to meet the others at the shady glade. They ran into each other near Poppy Park, and since they had plenty of time to get to the clubhouse on time, they decided to stop and visit Emerald, the cat, for a minute or two.

As they approached the gazebo, they saw and heard a strange man dressed in black, talking to three other men. Intrigued, they ducked behind a bush where they could hear the stranger talking about a fortune of silver coins\$ hidden near Old Town.

Suddenly, the strange man seemed to sense that someone might be listening, so he leaned in toward the other men and began whispering. Sugar and Walnut crept forward quietly and hid behind a low fence. The darkly dressed stranger continued talking to the men in a quiet voice. The men's faces revealed that they had heard something exciting. The hushed conversation went on for a bit longer, and then the three men scurried off. The man in black got up quickly and headed in the opposite direction – straight toward the petrified kiddos hiding nearby!

With quick thinking, Sugar and Walnut clapped their hands together and started playing patty-cake, being careful to ignore the man as he passed by. The man in black hardly noticed them and went on his way.

"Did you hear that, Walnut?" Sugar said. "A fortune of old silver coins$ hidden somewhere near Old Town! Wow!"

"Yes! I heard it, too!" Walnut said. "The man said the treasure was in the Yeller Cliffs, and I think I heard something about an eagle's nest."

"I heard eagles and nest, too," Sugar said.

"Eagles and nest …," Walnut whispered. "Sure! It must have been *eagle's nest*. It must be a secret clue."

"That's what I was thinking!" she said. "A clue to find the silver coins$, no doubt!"

"Hey, let's go ask Grandpa Gabby if he knows anything about the lost silver coins$," Walnut said, pointing toward the Ducky Pond.

Much to their disappointment, Grandpa Gabby wasn't there, so the kiddos walked on with extra pizzazz to the Big Abble.

The kiddos were sitting around the table when Sugar and Walnut entered, later than expected.

"So, now you're going Walnut's speed, I see, Sugar!" Topp said playfully.

"Funny …," she said. "But what Walnut and I overheard is worth the wait!"

"That's right," Walnut said. Then they told the others what they'd heard.

"I guess we know what we're doing next!" Taffy said.

"But what about the promise we made to get a planana tree for Sugar from the Jolly Jungle?" Violet asked.

"No problem, according to the map, we'll pass through Old Town on our way to the jungle," Taffy said.

"Yeah, we could have two adventures in one!" Balooon said. "We'll get Sugar's planana tree and then look around Old Town on our way back."

Since they still had brittles$, the kiddos decided to go the fast and effortless way to Old Town – on a Floatbus. Floatbuses give rides to Oogans on the roads around the valley. They hover about a foot above the road surface and often tow small trailers behind them to carry luggage, bikes, boxes, and other cargo.

The kiddos will certainly bring their bikes with them in the bus trailer because they will need them to ride from Old Town to Bog Town down in the jungle.

To get to Bog Town, the kiddos plan to ride over the Peppy-mint Hills, the reddish mint-scented hills that are at the very northern tip of the Tot Tot Hills.

The kiddos realized that they couldn't get the planana tree back to the shady glade on their bikes, so they devised a clever plan. Balooon will fly from his home at Happy Harbor to Bog Town in the jungle where they'll meet up. After they get a planana tree, he'll fly it to the shady glade while the other kids go to Old Town to snoop around for the whereabouts of the silver treasure.

The kiddos got up early the next day and headed out to catch the first Floatbus leaving for Old Town. The early morning air was chilly, and the kiddos were shivering as they boarded the bus. They'd dressed for the hot and sticky jungle climate but forgot they would need warmer clothes before they got there. Oh, silly unprepared children ...

Once the kiddos had loaded their bikes onto the trailer and climbed inside the bus with Ragamuffin, they warmed up a bit.

"All aboard!" shouted the Floatbus driver. "We leave in one minute – exactly one minute!" And the driver must be an honest man because the bus left at *exactly* the time he said it would.

The kiddos had gotten up earlier than usual and were still sleepy during the bus ride to Old Town. Topp, Taffy, Walnut, and Ragamuffin all fell asleep on the journey but not Sugar and Violet.

Sugar wasn't sleepy because her mind was spinning with ideas and thoughts about plananas. She envisioned the bright yellow fruit hanging on her very own planana tree.

Violet was a little sleepy, but she wanted to see all there was to see out the windows. She had never been to this part of the Valley of Ooga Ooga before. She was fascinated by the views of the Tot Tot Hills,

Wetwater Lake, and the pastoral farmland along the road to Old Town.

"We're floatin' through the lovely Toots Valley, Tot Tot's to the right, Wetwater Lake to the left!" the bus driver shouted, so loudly that it woke up the sleepers. "There be a giant fish in Wetwater Lake that can chomp a boat in half – with the boater inside! Don't dare go near that lake, or you might get snatched up by Crunch, the monster fish therein!"

Whoa, they thought as they looked out the windows at the pretty but dangerous lake.

The Floatbus arrived in Old Town exactly on time. This is as far as the bus travels before it turns back. It can't go to Bog Town in the jungle because the Peppy-mint Hills Trail is too narrow, steep, and rocky for a passenger bus.

The kiddos unloaded their bikes from the trailer and looked for a sign pointing to the Peppy-mint Hills Trail. They couldn't find any such sign, so they asked a boy for help. He pointed to a grocery store down the street and said, "Turn left there at that store to get to the trail. Then head up the bright pink hill – it's a bumpy ride and a little steep at times but rideable."

"Thanks," Topp said, straddling his bike.

"Oh, and when you get to the top of the hill, beware of the swampy crocks! They were originally from the jungle, but years ago, some got lost and climbed up the Peppy-mint Hills. They were too dumb to figure out how to get back down, I guess. They have a bad temper, so watch out! They are surprisingly fast, and their long jaws seldom miss when they snap at someone."

"Thanks for the warning!" Sugar said in shock. "How will we know if we come across one?"

"Oh, you'll know, and you better scram!"

The kiddos hopped on their bikes and rode up the dirt street to the corner grocery store.

"Oh, my gosh!" exclaimed Sugar. "Look at the name of the grocery store!"

"Wow! Eagles Nest!" Walnut said.

"Well, when we come back from Bog Town, we know where to start our search for the hidden coins$," Taffy said.

The kiddos knew they couldn't linger now because they needed to meet Balooon at Bog Town in the jungle.

The kiddos made good time because the Peppy-mint Hills are not nearly as steep as the Haystack Hills at the base of Ooga Mountain. The kiddos were in good shape and had lots of pep to ride quickly to the Jolly Jungle.

They arrived at the top of the tallest hill on the Peppy-mints and coasted to a stop.

"Wow! Look, it's the Jolly Jungle down there!" Taffy said, huffing and puffing.

"There must be a zillion plants, and they're all bright green!" Topp remarked.

"I've never seen anything like that!" Violet said in amazement. "I've seen a lot of deserts and mountains, but I've never seen nor ever been in a jungle! Hey, what happened to Walnut?"

"Oh, he'll be coming along shortly," Topp remarked. "He rides at the speed he is most comfortable with – it's called *slow speed*. He isn't far away, I can hear him whistling."

Taffy said, "It sure smells minty good on this hill, even nicer than the perfume of two-headed snakes."

"I think I see Bog Town down there, at the edge of the jungle trees," Sugar said pointing. "Oh my, no! What's that coming toward us?"

"Ride, ride, ride!" Topp yelled. And the kiddos, including Walnut, took off in a big hurry.

"What a weird-looking beast – and huge!" Taffy said as they coasted to a stop to take a short break.

"We got outta there just in time! I'm sure it was a swampy crock!" Topp said. "What an ugly and mean-looking creature!"

"I bet it looks beautiful to its mama," Sugar said with a grin.

They slowly bounced their way down the poorly maintained gravel trail into Bog Town. On their way down, the air kept getting warmer and stickier the farther they went. They were feeling the hot, humid, muggy jungle climate for the very first time.

When they cruised into the park in the town square, the kiddos saw Balooon's blue balloon, so they rode over to him.

"Hi, guys, welcome," Balooon said. "Hey, why are you guys all wet? Did it rain on you?"

"Not really, we're sweaty from the bike ride, I guess. It's wet and sticky down here, just like we were told," said Topp.

"What do we do now?" Sugar asked.

"Let's talk to that young chap over there," Taffy said pointing. "Maybe he can tell us where we can get a planana tree."

The young chap smiled widely and giggled as the kiddos, Ragamuffin, and Smokey came up to him. He had a wheelbarrow full of bright yeller, ready to eat plananas and offered some to the kids.

Sugar asked the chap, "Do you mind telling us where we can get a planana tree?"

The young chap had a startled look on his face as though she spooked him. "I do know, but it's dangerous, very dangerous!" Then the boy followed his comment with a weird toothy smile and a short laugh. "You can have some of these plananas – they're not dangerous."

Uh-oh! Dangerous, very dangerous?! The kiddos looked around at each other and pondered, *What are we getting ourselves into this time*?

Chapter 40

THE DEADLY HONEY BOG

ও৵৽৬

The young chap in the Jolly Jungle told the kiddos, "I didn't mean to scare you when I said it was dangerous to get a planana tree, but they don't just grow on trees!" The chap laughed out loud at his own silly comment. But the kiddos didn't laugh. They still had the word *dangerous* right in the front of their minds.

There's nothing funny about dangerous, is there?

"Very funny," Topp said, but he didn't mean it. The chap may have thought that would amuse the kids but to them, it was not funny at all. "So, do you mind telling us how we can get one planana tree, maybe in a way that isn't so dangerous?"

"For one thing," the chap said, "you don't have to buy them because nobody owns them. Well, nobody owns them unless you consider the blue snakes, the jungle tigers, and the gobbling gators. They keep an eye on all things in the jungle. In a way, they own the planana trees." Then the chap started laughing again and laughed and laughed at his own remarks. He seemed quite amused by himself.

"Tigers and snakes, oh my!" sputtered Sugar.

"They're not too bad – when they're sleeping," the chap said and then laughed loudly again and grabbed his bouncing tummy.

The young chap seemed to think everything was outrageously humorous, but the kiddos didn't think any of it was funny at all. They wondered what was wrong with this chap and thought that they ought to talk to someone else, but there was nobody else around.

"So, how do we get a planana tree? That is, if we still *want* one," Walnut asked, glancing in Sugar's direction.

"Yes, I still want one!" Sugar pleaded. She turned to the chap. "By the way, what's your name, young man?"

"Oh sure, my name is Vine Boy – at your service!" he said. He tipped his floppy hat and replaced it crookedly.

The kiddos all introduced themselves and told Vine Boy about their clubhouse, the glasshouse, and the garden. Vine Boy seemed interested and appeared to be a nice chap – even though he laughed at his own bad jokes.

"So ... how can we get just *one* planana tree?" Topp asked, more seriously this time. "We only need one."

"There are two ways to get one," Vine Boy said and started giggling. "One way is to go straight out into the jungle, dig one up, and bring it back here."

"What's so dangerous about that?" Topp asked.

"It's not dangerous if you don't get bitten by the snakes, nibbled on by a tiger, or stung by a million fire-ants – and oh yeah, the gators!" Vine Boy said laughing out loud, then he laughed some more, and brasher yet.

"Okay, very funny ...," Topp said dryly. "And what's the second way?" He hoped the second way would be better than the first.

"Well, look over yonder," Vine Boy said, pointing to what appeared to be a long lake next to the tree line of the jungle. "That big lake is a bog. It's called the Honey Bog. Have you ever gotten all sticky with honey? Well, it's like that except it's stinky slime and a mile deep!"

With that comment, Vine Boy went into hysterics, an all-out laughing fit. "If you get in it, you won't get out, you'll sink to the bottom!" And Vine Boy laughed a lot more, to the chagrin of the kids.

The kiddos started to think Vine Boy *was* funny but not in a good way. This chap was such a ridiculous clown!

"So, what does the Honey Bog have to do with us getting a planana tree?" Sugar asked, not wanting to play Vine Boy's silly game any longer.

"Well, to get a planana tree, someone needs to walk along the edge of the bog until they find one. The bog is very close to the edge of the jungle, so there is the danger of stepping into the bog while trying to stay away from the dangerous jungle critters. They might even chase you into the bog!" Vine Boy said and once again broke into uncontrollable laughter.

"Oh, is that all there is to it?" Sugar said. Then she started giggling. Yes, Sugar started laughing! She laughed and laughed and could not stop. The other kiddos stared at her in amazement, and Ragamuffin ran behind them to hide.

"The jungle mist is fun, isn't it?" Vine Boy said with a broad smile. "Do you smell that sweet smell? That's the jungle mist. When you breathe it in, everything seems funny!" He broke into another uncontrollable laughing spell.

Topp started giggling, even though he tried not to. Taffy, Violet, Balooon, and Walnut did everything they could to *not* laugh, but they busted loose with boisterous laughter anyway. It was the silliest thing you could ever imagine. It would make you laugh too!

Ragamuffin started laughing, too, laughing like any ol' cat-dog would, and Smokey joined in as well.

Sugar, laughing and having a good time now, grabbed the shovel and started walking along the edge of the Honey Bog. She was on her way to find a planana tree. She thought how unlikely it would be for a snake or tiger to bite her when she was laughing and having fun. So, she kept deeply inhaling the jungle mist and laughed as she walked carefully along, with the bog on her left and the jungle on her right.

As they watched Sugar wander off along the bog, Topp asked, "Vine Boy, have you ever heard of anyone going so far out into the jungle that they reach a place where it ends – like an *edge*, where the land comes to an edge?"

"That's a funny question!" Vine Boy said, grinning with delight. "As far as I know, the jungle goes on forever. It never ends. If anyone ever found an edge as you call it, I'm sure I would have heard about it."

Topp was disappointed, but he thought it was funny and chuckled at the notion that the jungle went on forever. He realized then that the jungle mist was powerful indeed.

Sugar walked safely along the bog. When she got near the end, she came upon a young healthy tree with broad wispy leaves. It looked just like the picture of the planana tree that Mrs. Roote had shown her. Upon closer inspection, she could see a clump of tiny green planana fruits growing under the leaves.

She ran up to the tree with a big smile and said, "Hi, do you mind if I take you home with me to the shady glade?" Then she stood for a few seconds as if waiting for it to answer. Then she nodded her head and started digging. She worked a little trench around the tree until she loosened the roots. She pulled the young tree free and then lifted it onto her tummy. She yelled to the kiddos in the distance, "Look I'm growing a planana tree from my belly!" She started laughing again and almost dropped the tree in the bog.

She had a hard time holding the shovel and the tree at the same time, especially when she started walking back along the narrow trail between the lake-like bog and the jungle. She made slow progress as she walked cautiously toward the kiddos, laughing all the while.

The kiddos were at the other end of the Honey Bog, laughing so loudly they didn't realize that Sugar had stopped laughing.

Finally, Sugar yelled, "HELP! HELP!" so loudly, the kids looked her way. Somehow, Sugar's right foot had gotten stuck in the Honey Bog. The more she wiggled it, the more stuck it got. She was in dire trouble now but because of the jungle mist, she started laughing again, even in her predicament.

"I'm coming, Sugar!" Balooon shouted. He ran to his balloon, set it loose, and jumped into the basket. He rose and headed in Sugar's direction. He hovered over her and lowered his balloon directly above her. "Grab the rope, Sugar!!!"

"I can't! Both hands are stuck in the bog now!" Sugar cried out and started laughing again!

The kiddos watched in horror at the peril their sweet Sugar was in.

Violet walked to the edge of the bog and shook her ankle bells, first one and then the other. She leaned forward, took one step onto the surface of the bog and then another. She kept walking over the bog toward Sugar. Somehow, she was walking on top of the sticky bog without sinking in! She moved quickly as if she was walking barefoot on a hot road.

Violet moved gracefully across the entire length of the bog, all the way to Sugar. When Violet reached her, she pulled one of Sugar's arms out of the bog, giggled a little, and yelled, "Grab the rope, Sugar!"

Sugar took hold of the rope, and Balooon lifted her up out of the muck. He helped her into the basket and secured the planana tree as well. With Sugar and the tree safely in the basket, he floated over the sticky bog and landed back in the park.

Sugar jumped out of the basket as Smokey jumped in. "I'll see you guys at the shady glade!" Balooon said and laughed freely as he slowly floated upward.

By this time, Violet had successfully walked back along the path to where the others were. The five kiddos gathered in a circle and held hands. They were stunned by the danger Sugar had been in, and they were amazed by Violet's ability to walk safely across the top of the deadly bog to save her.

Up above, they heard Balooon laughing and yelling, "All's well that ends well!"

The kiddos looked back and forth at each other. At first, there was a snicker, then a chuckle, then a giggle, then a guffaw, and then they all broke out into hysterical laughter! They laughed and laughed, until their tummies couldn't take it anymore!

A few feet away, Vine Boy stood watching the kids. He looked as though he'd seen a clan of ghost creatures or something. When Violet had walked across the bog, he didn't laugh, even with the jungle mist everywhere. Vine Boy went running off as fast as he could, shaking his head – and he never looked back.

With their pockets full of the plananas given to them by Vine Boy, the kiddos jumped on their bikes and rode. They were full of joy because they had succeeded in getting a planana tree, and they still had Sugar to give it to.

Now it was time to head back to Old Town, to follow the secret clue and find the treasure of silver coins$.

Chapter 41

BOBBY GOES BANANAS

❧

Bobby was groggy when he woke up on his bedroom floor. He looked up at the planets on the ceiling and once again knew where he was. The dream had continued while he was napping and was fresh in his mind as he sat on the edge of his bed. It was like he was living in two parallel worlds at the same time. *Perfect,* he thought to himself, *I love my home and my mom,* **and** *it's delightful playing in that incredible valley with the dream-kids. What a wonderful double life I live!*

He stood up and looked out the window to see if there was any sunlight left in the day. In the summertime, the days are long, so there was enough time to get back to work on the clubhouse and finish filling the sandbox.

When Bobby sleepily stumbled into the kitchen, his mom said, "Welcome back, I made you iced tea. That might help you wake up."

"Thanks, Mom," Bobby said. "You always make such refreshing tea."

He took the big glass of iced tea with him as he headed out the door. He was delighted with the progress he was making on the new clubhouse. He was almost done nailing boards on the last wall when somebody called out to him.

"Hi, Bobby! What are you working on?" Cookie said. She walked up and looked over the large structure he was busy building.

"I'm building a new clubhouse," Bobby said. "It's a big project but when it's done, we can have get-togethers with our friends like in the old days."

"Wow, that's super!" said Cookie as she stepped inside. "It looks like you're almost ready to put the roof on."

"Yep, the roof, a door, a couple of windows, and she'll be done. My mom has a nice old rug she'll donate. It certainly will be cozy inside."

Bobby's mom called out from the kitchen, "I'll bring out banana bread and iced tea for Cookie."

"That would be nice, Mom. We'll be at the picnic table."

"What's that sound down by the new sandbox?" Cookie asked.

"I don't know. It sounds like running water. I better go check it out!"

Bobby ran toward the sound of water down by the new sandbox. The hose had a large crack in it and had been leaking a great deal of water into a low spot near the peach tree. The faucet was in that low area and now submerged in a large deep puddle. He slowly stepped into the middle of the puddle to shut off the water.

"Oh my!" he screeched as his feet started sinking into the mud. His left foot sunk into the soft mud and was stuck, so he tried to get a firm stance with his right foot. But his right foot also squished into the mushy mud. Now both of his legs were in so deep, he couldn't move them. He was down to his knees in soft slimy mud.

"Hey, Cookie, I need help! Come quickly!" Bobby called out. "I'm stuck in this mud – this quicksand – this sticky stuff!"

Cookie hurried over, saw the mess Bobby was in, and asked how she could help him.

"Grab the shovel over there and hold it out to me!" Bobby said. "Do it from near the faucet, so I can turn the water off!"

Cookie got the shovel and held out the handle for Bobby to grab. He held on as she pulled, and little by little, he was able to free his legs, reach the faucet, and turn the water off. He continued to struggle through the mud until he reached solid ground.

"Wow, that was like a bog of quicksand!" Cookie said. "I wonder how deep you would have gone if I hadn't been around."

"I hate to think what might have happened," Bobby said. With both legs caked in mud, he wobbled over to a garden hose near the house and cleaned the crud off. "That's better!"

His mom had watched it all from the window. She came outside and brought Bobby a towel, dry socks, and shoes. "You two get cozy at the picnic table, and I'll bring out some tea and banana bread in a few minutes. And, just so you know, I'm making banana pudding for tonight's dessert. I also dipped bananas in chocolate and put them in the freezer. It's supposed to be hot tomorrow."

"Wow, that's a lot of bananas, Mom!"

"They were on sale, so I bought bunches! I know how much you like bananas," she said.

Bobby dried off the best he could, put on socks and shoes, and checked his shorts for mud. He sat down with a faraway look in his eyes, deep in thought. He was in a trance.

"Are you okay? You seem in a daze!" Cookie said.

Bobby looked her in the eyes and asked, "Do you believe we can live inside a dream? I mean, can dreams be part of what happens after we wake up from them?"

"Uh, I'm not sure what you mean," Cookie said with a puzzled look.

"Okay, you're a good friend, so I can tell you. I have been having this dream that keeps going and going and going, night after night. When I go to sleep, I end up in this most fantastic dream, and when I wake up, I remember it clearly. When I go back to sleep hours later, I go back to the same dream, right where it left off. That's crazy, isn't it?"

"I don't know," she said. "I've never had that happen to me, so I don't know. What's the dream about?"

"Well, it's a wonderful dream, a fun and exciting dream. It's about a valley in a fantasy-like world. The kids in the dream have the most amazing adventures, and it's like I'm there with them every night."

"Sounds interesting, tell me more."

"I took a nap this afternoon and had the dream again," Bobby said. "I dreamed that the kids went to get a banana tree in a jungle and got stuck in a muddy bog! Sound familiar?" He pointed to his muddy shoes to illustrate. "Then they brought a banana tree back to their clubhouse to grow it there. Do you see? I dreamed about a bog and bananas, and right after I woke up, I got stuck in a mud pit and my mom has lots of bananas!"

"Wow! That *is* interesting!" Cookie said.

"It's not the only thing from the dream that's shown up in my life. There was my mom's diamond ring, the sand and pogo stick, the clubhouse, and many other things that were first in my dream and then happened in this life after I woke up."

"That sounds fascinating, for sure," Cookie said.

"I look forward to sleeping now because I go back to that land and the kids every time. It's like I'm living in two parallel worlds! It's amazing, and I'm getting more used to it too."

Bobby's mom came out of the house with a tray of goodies. "Here you go, kids, iced tea and banana bread." She placed the tray on the picnic table and beamed a sweet smile toward the children. Taking in a breath of fragrant summer air, she headed back to the house.

They enjoyed the treats, hung out for a while, and talked. The sky turned darker. Heavy gray clouds filled the sky. Cookie headed home to help her mom clean their house, and Bobby put the tools away in the shed in case it rained. He was a bit tired from all the construction work, so he headed in to wash up and have supper with his mom.

That night, Bobby took a shower to make sure he got all the mud off, got into his favorite pajamas, and jumped into bed with glee. With bleary eyes, he looked up at the make-believe stars on his ceiling and fell fast asleep.

Chapter 42

OLD TOWN AND THE SECRET SILVER STASH

ॐॐ

After the kiddos rode out of humid Bog Town, they decided to stop and take a break on the highest point on the Peppy-mint Hills. They were wary of the swampy crocks, so they looked in all directions for any sign of them.

From this high vantage point, they could see the Jolly Jungle on one side and the Valley of Ooga Ooga on the other.

"Wow! The Valley of Ooga Ooga! What a sight to see!" said Taffy.

"Better than the jungle, that's for sure!" Sugar said.

"Now I get it! I know why it's called the *Jolly* Jungle," Topp said with a giggle. "The jungle mist!"

The others laughed but continued watching out for those grumpy old crocks. "I think those swamp creatures miss the happy-go-lucky jungle mist. Maybe that's why they're so snappy," Walnut said.

Topp pulled out the long-eye and looked around purposely in all directions. He knew he wouldn't be able to see the *edge* of their world from this low spot, but he looked anyway.

They had a good laugh one more time before they rode on to Old Town in search of silver riches.

ॐ

The kiddos coasted into the town in a cloud of red peppy-mint dust. They made an immediate bee line to the Eagles Nest Grocery to start their sleuthing.

As they rolled through the streets, Taffy said, "Oh my, look at that!" The other kiddos stopped and looked at what she was pointing to. "It says Eagles Nest Barber Shop!"

"Look at *that*!" Topp said, pointing to a sign that said Eagles Nest Bank.

"And that!" Walnut said, pointing to a sign that read Eagles Nest Pet Store.

"And ... Eagles Nest Shoes, over there," Taffy said. "Well, so much for the great clue we had. What do we do now?"

"I'm hungry!" Walnut said, holding his tummy. "Let's go to the Eagles Nest Grocery and get something to eat."

So, off they rode to the grocery store to get snacks and figure out what to do next. Finding the hidden silver coins$ was not going to be easy without a *real* clue.

Oh, the silver treasure of Old Town is sneaky and hard to find, don't you think? Have you found any silver coins lately? I didn't think so.

The grocery store had a deli with a garden patio, so the kiddos settled in around a table and ordered some planana bread. They were openly discussing the hidden silver coins$ when a young gal at the table next to them overheard their conversation.

"Hi, my name is Goldie," the girl said in hushed tones. "I overheard you talking about the lost silver. I know secrets about the treasure that nobody else knows."

"Please sit down with us, Goldie!" Taffy said with extra sweetness. "We're interested in hearing more about that. We thought we had a clue, but it didn't get us anywhere."

"I bet the clue was *eagle's nest*, right?" Goldie remarked.

The kiddos were stunned. "Yes, how did you know?" Topp asked.

"It's a big joke around here. We made up the clue of *eagle's nest*. It really doesn't mean anything. It fools the treasure hunters who all too often come and dig up the hills outside of town."

"However," Goldie said. "I know things that are *real* clues."

That certainly caught their attention, so the kiddos listened intently as she told stories about the lost silver coins$ and the history of Old Town.

Goldie started, "Old Town was settled long ago when the first Ooooogans came to the Valley of Ooga Ooga and began living in Toots Valley near Wetwater Lake. It was named Eagles Nest back then, and the settlers built their homes in this lovely valley. Why there weren't any inhabitants in the valley before the Oogans first came is a mystery. Some say evil giants roamed the area, and others say the Rat People kept the Oogans out. Some historians think the Oogans were originally from ancient Dirt Town. But no one seems to know for certain. It's been left to history buffs or the imagination to figure it out."

"Fascinating!" Sugar said.

Goldie continued, "The Oogans named the new town Eagles Nest. They farmed the little Toots Valley and grew vegetables and fruits in abundance and caught plenty of delicious fish in Wetwater Lake.

"Many years ago, silver was found up in the Yeller Cliffs by a prospector named Mr. Greede. He smelted the silver and turned the metal into silver coins$. The coins$ were sent by boat on the Ooga river and sold to merchants on a faraway island named Wow in the Fantasmo Sea.

"Mr. Greede owned and operated the one and only silver mine in the Yeller Cliffs. He lived like a very poor person, even though he wasn't. Some thought he lived outwardly like a pauper so nobody would steal from him. It didn't really fool anybody because it was obvious that he was getting rich from the silver mine. The weight of the silver that came out of the mine was much more than the weight of the silver coins$ that were shipped away. There were rumors that Mr. Greede kept the rest of the coins$ for himself — lots of coins$ — and hid them away somewhere in the Yeller Cliffs."

"Fascinating!" Walnut said.

"Many have dug up the cliffs looking for them, but nobody has found the hidden coins$. That's why it's still a big shiny mystery."

"Please go on, tell us more, Goldie," Violet pleaded.

"Okay, I will. The Oogans prospered in Toots Valley for several years, but then the weather changed. It stopped raining, and everything dried up. No one knows for sure why the rain stopped, but some thought the giants were hogging it somehow. Perhaps the giants needed it for their baths, but that doesn't make sense – everyone knows that giants smell like they have never taken a bath!

"This long dry spell was very bad for the Oogans of Eagles Nest," she went on. "Wetwater Lake was the main water source for Eagles Nest but when the dry time came, Wetwater Lake was hardly wet anymore. The few fish living in the small puddle left of the lake didn't want to be caught anymore. The Oogans needed to move closer to a good source of water, so they moved to the banks of the Ooga River, built a new town there, and named it the Village of Ooga Ooga. It's where you live, I suppose."

"Yes, that's right. Quite fascinating!" Topp said.

Goldie finished up, "All the buildings of Eagles Nest were still there, but it became a ghost town – nothing but old buildings, with nobody there. The Oogans called it *The Old Ghost Town* for a while, but it got shortened to Old Town because the Oogans feared ghosts."

(Do you believe in ghosts? I almost do ...)

"After many years passed, the rains started falling again. Toots Valley turned green, and Wetwater Lake filled up to the top. Many Oogans moved back into the houses of Old Town. Now we live here in peace – except for all the treasure hunters who tear up the hills around town."

"Wow, that's an interesting story – quite a history lesson," Violet remarked.

Then Topp whispered, "Did you say that you know something that no one else knows about the whereabouts of the silver?"

"Yes, I do," Goldie said. "I've never told anyone because I've never liked the treasure hunters. But you seem nice, and because you are kids, I'll tell you what I know."

"If you don't mind my asking," Taffy said. "Why haven't *you* found the silver?"

"I've tried, but I guess I've never known enough to find it," Goldie explained. "I decided to tell you because I'm tired of strange people coming here all the time looking for it. I figure if *you* find it, none of those bad people will come around anymore!"

"I'll tell you what, Goldie," Topp said. "If you tell us a good clue, and we find the silver, we'll give you a share of the loot. What do ya think?"

"Sounds fair to me!" Goldie said. "My *great*-grandfather was a friend of Mr. Greede and knew where the coins$ were hidden. He promised Mr. Greede that he wouldn't tell anybody until twenty years after Mr. Greede passed away."

"Did he tell anyone after the twenty years were up?" Taffy asked.

"The twenty years have long passed, but nobody knows if my *great*-grandpa passed the secrets down to my grandpa. I was told that some of the clues might have been just lost in time ... whatever that means."

"Wow, so what is the clue you *do* know?" Walnut asked. "Maybe we can figure the rest out by ourselves."

"There are two things that could be helpful," Goldie said. "The silver coins$ are hidden in the Yeller Cliffs, true but not at all near Old Town. They are hidden high up on the cliffs. That's all I know, but it isn't enough because the Yeller Cliffs are long and massive. I tried, but I never found them."

"The Yeller Cliffs do go for miles and miles. I saw them with my long-eye telescope from Peppy-mint Hills," Topp said.

"There is one more thing," Goldie shared. "My Grandpa Gabby, who lives in the Village of Ooga Ooga, may have a clue or two. He once said he wouldn't tell me the most important clue because it would put me in danger. If you can find him, he might share what he knows with you – if you tell him you talked to me, that is."

"We know Grandpa Gabby! He hangs around the Ducky Pond at the park in our village!" Sugar said.

"Well, that's all I know," said Goldie. "But that's more than most treasure hunters know! I gotta get back to work. It sure was nice to meet you all, and I hope you find it."

"Nice meeting you, too, Goldie," Sugar said sweetly. And the rest of the kids said a cordial goodbye to Goldie.

"Okay then, let's head back to Poppy Park and see if we can find Grandpa Gabby," Topp suggested. "It's getting late anyway."

With their tummies now full, the kiddos headed to the Floatbus station to catch the last bus back to the Village of Ooga Ooga.

Chapter 43

GRANDPA GABBY AND THE HIDDEN LOOT

❧

After their journey to Old Town, the kiddos and Ragamuffin returned to the clubhouse just before dark. Balooon and Smokey welcomed them warmly when they arrived.

Sugar saw the planana tree leaning against the wall next to the front door. She had a huge smile when she walked up to it and said, "Welcome to the shady glade." She reached out and shook its hand (its leaf, that is). "I'm sure you will like it here. I'll take good care of you, I promise! Yes, it was difficult getting you out of the jungle." She turned her ear to the tree and nodded as if it was thanking her. "You can thank Violet and Balooon, too, they helped a lot!"

The kiddos overheard Sugar and couldn't help but smile. They went inside the Big Abble and sat around the table. They drank pearette juice that Balooon had brought from Happy Harbor and talked about what's next.

The kiddos filled Balooon in on what Goldie had told them in Old Town, and he was delighted. They discussed farming chores: plant the planana tree, pull weeds, and water the baby trees. However, they knew that the most important thing to do was somehow connect with Grandpa Gabby at the park the next day. They would need more clues to have any chance of finding the hidden treasure.

The kiddos weren't sure what time of day Grandpa Gabby would arrive at the park, so they decided to hang out there in shifts. Each of them would go for an hour, and then another would take over. Someone would be there every hour of the day so that they could talk to him before the day was done.

Grandpa Gabby arrived when Violet was on her shift at noon. She was very direct and told him that they had met his granddaughter, Goldie, in Old Town, and that she said he might have clues to find the coins$ hidden by Mr. Greede.

Grandpa Gabby looked at Violet for a long while and then asked, "Are you one of the young'uns who recently gave generously to the village and the people in need?"

"Well, yes, I am," Violet said. "We're glad to share the wealth of our treasure hunts with others. We believe that giving is better than receiving – especially if you have as many blessings as we have."

"What will you do with the silver coins$ if you find any, do tell?" he asked her pointedly.

"We've made a pact to share half of any valuables we find on our adventures with charity," Violet explained. "We go on treasure hunts mostly for the thrill of it, and sometimes we're rewarded with things of great value. Oh yeah, we promised your granddaughter Goldie a share if we find the hidden loot."

"That's nice of you, young'un. Me do want to help you, but me don't want to tell you right here where we're a-speakin'. Bad peoples could overhear us, me thinks. Do you have any idea of where we can do our yakkin' alone?"

"Why yes I do if you don't mind coming to our clubhouse in the shady glade. That would be a great place, and it's not too far from here. We can talk in secret, and you can see the other kids as well."

Grandpa Gabby agreed and walked very, very slowly toward the clubhouse. Violet strolled at Gabby's pace and realized that by walking so s-l-o-w-l-y, she could see and enjoy delightful things on the way. She saw things she had never noticed before. She often rushes full speed on her bike on this part of the trail and never sees anything but the road ahead of her.

They eventually arrived at the clubhouse, and the kiddos gathered around. They reacquainted themselves with Grandpa Gabby and he with them. They offered him pearette juice and cookies, both of which he gratefully accepted and fully enjoyed.

Violet said, "Mister, er, Grandpa Gabby, told me he will tell us clues. He wants us to find the silver coins$!"

"That's right, by cracky!" the nice old man said.

"He also said that the coins$ aren't doing anybody any good," Violet said. "Right now, they're hidden in a dark hole somewhere and they'll stay there until the end of time – unless someone finds them."

"That's right! Me knows there are lots of scoundrels out there, and I really don't want them to find them silver goodies. I tell them fibs that they're hidden low in the Yeller Cliffs. They've torn it all up for nothin'. Silly, greedy fools! Now you know why nobody has found them – hahaha!!!"

Grandpa Gabby laughed as if he'd just inhaled a whiff of jungle mist. The kiddos were tickled by Gabby's laughter, and they were excited about the treasure hunt about to begin.

For the next couple of minutes, the kiddos were quieter than the napkins on the table as Grandpa Gabby began telling his secrets. "The first thing is that the treasure is nowhere near Old Town. It's at the other end of the Yeller Cliffs – all the way west – *beyond* the Ooga River. Nobody has ever looked there because it's so far from Old Town. There's a pinnacle named Silver Peak west of the Ooga River in them Yeller Cliffs. That's where she be, all shiny and such, and me *thinks* it's still there."

"*Think* it is? Have you ever seen it?" Topp asked.

"Well, no ... I tried to find it once when I was a young'un – but I never did. I knew I was close but never laid eyes upon it.

Balooon spoke up, "I know exactly where Silver Peak is! It's not too far from Happy Harbor where I live – but on the other side of the Ooga River and way up high."

"That be right," Gabby said. "I know clues that someone might figure out someday. Let's see what you can do with them."

"Okay!!!" chorused the kids.

"Another clue is that it's hidden deep in a tunnel near the top of Silver Peak. To get to it, someone needs to slither through a hole, like a snake. Also, to find the tunnel, you must follow your heart. When you find the silver coins$, they will be all stacked up in tall towers."

"How do you know all of this?" Taffy asked.

"I know because my father told me. He was friends with Mr. Greede. In fact, he was his *only* friend. Mr. Greede was a mean old tart and nobody much liked him at all. My father felt sorry for lonely old Mr. Greede, so he did his best to be a friend, out of pity."

"That's nice," Sugar said sincerely.

"Mr. Greede gave my father the clues to where the coins$ are hidden with special conditions: Don't tell anybody until twenty years after I have passed away, and only tell someone who is very special – someone with a good heart – like you young'uns," Gabby said.

"You just touched *my* heart, Grandpa Gabby," Violet said.

"Is there anything *dangerous* about getting to the coins$?" Sugar asked.

"The yeller glizards can be pesky and mean. They bite thunder hard, but they never bite children, only adults," Gabby gabbed.

"Whoa!" Balooon said.

"Also, you must watch out for rocks rollin' down from Silver Peak. It's steep, and the rocks are roundish, so shoes can knock 'em down and hit peoples below. Oh, and you don't want to be up there in the dark-time. The glowy-eyes do come out at night, thousands of them! You will see them because their eyes glow brightly in the darkness. Nobody knows what glowy-eyes look like in the daytime because they disappear in the light. At night, all you can see are their spooky eyes. They make a weird noise that's quite eerie. Other 'n those things, there's no danger at all!"

Sugar's eyes were wide with alarm as Grandpa Gabby stoked her fears.

"Oh, don't you worry, you are quite robust enough, me thinks," Grandpa Gabby said. "I don't think anything will mess with you toughies!"

"I agree!" Taffy shouted. "Don't mess with us! We *are* the rainbow kiddos, and we *have* special powers!"

Grandpa Gabby thanked them for the treats and said he needed to get back to the park, so Violet walked back with him at his usual snail's pace. Along the way, she fully enjoyed every flower, bird, bug, pebble, and grain of sand. Once they arrived at the park, she thanked Grandpa Gabby and told him that if he ever needed their help, they will always be there for him.

Grandpa Gabby winked and grinned as Violet bid him adieu.

She ran back to the shady glade as fast as her powerful legs could take her. She knew that the other kiddos would already be working on plans to travel to Silver Peak.

She was right.

Chapter 44

THE FRIGHTENING CLIMB TO SILVER PEAK

❧

The kiddos worked hard in preparation for their journey to find the silver coins$. They went to the marsh to collect light-wands, to have light inside the tunnel after they find it. They also ate a big breakfast including those not so tasty, but powerful, strong beans. Yuck!

Their plan was to take an early Floatbus to Happy Harbor where they will begin the hike. They don't need their bikes this time. They'll be wearing their hiking boots because Gabby had mentioned that there aren't any maintained trails on the cliffs. They also brought gloves because Gabby said that the slope up Silver Peak is steep, and they'll need to crawl on all fours as they ascend to the top.

As they boarded the Floatbus, they were very excited, but they understood that they best keep quiet about what they were about to do. They needed to keep it a secret.

You can keep a secret, right? You aren't going to tell anybody what the kids are going to do, are you? I certainly hope you can keep a secret.

After arriving in Happy Harbor, the kiddos went to PetTunias Farm so the kids could meet Balooon's aunt and uncle.

The PetTunias had a special message for Balooon – a very wonderful one. They told him that his parents would soon be back from their voyage and that he would get to see them later that evening. Balooon was exceptionally happy to hear about the return of his parents and looked forward to seeing them. But for now, there was treasure to find.

A secret is a secret, so the kiddos didn't tell the PetTunias that they were going to hike up the Yeller Cliffs to bring back silver coins$. The kiddos told them that they were going to look for special *minerals* on Silver Peak, which is the truth because silver is a mineral. The kiddos might do a lot of crazy things, but they don't tell lies – maybe a few fibs when they must – but no *lies*!

With warm goodbyes, the kiddos headed off to find the treasure. Balooon served as their guide because he grew up near there. They shadowed Balooon as he headed up the road that follows the Ooga River through the Yeller Cliffs. Close to Happy Harbor, there is a rickety bridge across the deep gorge over the Ooga River. The bridge was built with thick cables, made of what you might expect: fire spider ropes braided together. There are thick planks or boards laid between the cables for people to walk on.

When the bridge was built years ago, it was sturdy and steady. Time, wind, and rain have taken their toll on the bridge, and it's just about to fall apart to the point it can't be crossed safely anymore. Since this old bridge spans high above the Ooga River, people still risk using it from time to time.

The bridge was originally built for transporting special cube-shaped rocks from the other side of the river to construct the road from Happy Harbor to the Town of Trombone. After the road was built, few people dared to use the bridge. The only other way to cross the river is to climb down to the bottom of the ravine, ford the swiftly flowing river, and then climb up the other side.

Standing on the bank of the river where the bridge begins, Taffy looked down at the rickety, weather-beaten excuse for a bridge and asked, "*Who* is going to go first?"

"I'm glad *Who* is going to go first as you just said – because, I don't want to go first," Walnut said, trying to cheer them up.

The kiddos couldn't help but feel a little uncomfortable about crossing this bridge.

"I'll go first!" Sugar said, showing unusual courage. "I'm the lightest, and I think it would be good to go one at a time because it doesn't look very strong."

"Sugar's right about the weight. One of us isn't very heavy, but all six of us together would weigh as much as a giant!" Topp said with a grin.

Off went Sugar, wobbling and bobbling across the ramshackle bridge. She went slowly but deliberately and eventually jumped the last meter to solid ground on the other side. "Hooray!" Sugar said. "No problem, come on over!"

The kiddos crossed the bridge, one by one. When Violet crossed with her ankle bells jingling, she took her time. She wanted to enjoy all the little flowers, frogs, and butterflies she saw below as she crossed.

Walnut, the heaviest, was hesitant at first but then started to whistle. He gracefully cruised across the bridge like he was dancing. Ragamuffin and Smokey hipped and hopped at Walnut's heels and leaped to the other side with big cat-like grins.

After the kiddos crossed safely, they followed Balooon as he started up a steep rocky slope. He led the kiddos straight up from the bridge along a route that was more like a stairway. Their hiking boots dug into the soil nicely as they quickly advanced up the yeller-colored cliffs. Upon reaching a ledge about halfway to the top, the kiddos stopped and looked around. In one direction, the Valley of Ooga Ooga was laid out before them, and behind them was a tall, rocky peak towering above them.

"There it is!" yelled Walnut. "Silver Peak!"

"Shush!" Topp whispered but loud enough that the others could hear him. "Quiet down, I saw something move in that yeller bush!"

"Maybe it's a yeller glizard!" Walnut said, looking in the direction Topp was pointing.

"Grandpa Gabby said they don't hurt children," Taffy said quietly. "And we are obviously just kids."

"But how does a glizard know how old someone is?" Sugar asked with alarm. "What if the glizards think we are just small adults?"

"I guess if it eats us, we'll know," Walnut said as if that was funny. "We are the *kidd-os*, not the *adult-os*! I'm not worried about them glizards!"

Just then, a glizard came out from behind a bush! It glared at them from a short distance. It was yeller like the dirt and the bushes. It looked like an ugly lizard with floppy ears and three tails. Its middle tail had a stinger like a scorpion. The kiddos had never seen anything like it before. It sniffed the air like a dog and then walked away as if it had no interest in the kids.

"I guess it knows we're kids," Violet said with relief.

"Or, maybe it knows it's outnumbered, and it's gone back to get more of them to attack us!" Balooon said. The level of danger was on the minds of everyone, especially Sugar. "Just kidding – I believe Grandpa Gabby."

"Well, let's go then," Topp said. "The hidden treasure is waiting."

The kiddos remembered that they could not follow each other during the climb due to rolling rocks. So, they spread out and climbed next to each other. Sure enough, rocks were dislodged by their boots and rolled dangerously down the steep cliff. *Good safety tip, Grandpa Gabby!* they thought.

As they approached the top of Silver Peak, they were climbing on all fours. The rocks were sharp, so they were glad to be wearing gloves as they climbed up the last bit of slope to the domed apex.

They were breathing heavily when they finally stood on top. "Wow, what a view!" Violet said, looking down at the Valley of Ooga Ooga and up to Ooga Mountain.

"Well, we made it! But now what'll wc do?" Violet asked.

"We slither like a snake into the tunnel, like Grandpa Gabby told us," Walnut said.

"I don't see any tunnels to slither into," Topp said, looking around.

Sugar reminded them, "There was one other clue – *follow your heart* – whatever that means."

"I thought about that one but if I go in the direction of my own heart, I just go forward in the direction I'm facing – every time," Taffy said.

While the kiddos tried to figure out where to slither, Topp pulled out his dad's long-eye and started looking in all directions to see if he could see an end to the land.

The others took turns looking through the telescope to see what they could see as well.

To the west, they saw the Duney Desert, and to the north, the Fantasmo Sea, with far distant islands. To the south, they saw Ooga Mountain and the Valley of Ooga Ooga, with the Giant Step Mountains in the distance. And to the east, they saw the Tot Tot Hills. Beyond them, they saw the Jolly Jungle and all its endless greenery. What they did *not* see was an *edge* to their land, no matter how hard or in what direction, they looked.

"I found something on the ground! Come look!" Sugar yelled.

The kiddos rushed over.

"What does that rock look like?" Sugar asked, pointing down to a large rock at her feet.

"It's shaped like a heart!" Violet said.

"And that one, the one below it?"

"Another heart," Taffy said.

"Maybe the clue is *follow the hearts!* Look, there's another one!" Sugar said.

The kiddos started scooting on their bottoms down the steep slope below the top of Silver Peak. They followed a series of heart shaped rocks, with the point of each heart aimed at another one below it. Before long, the kiddos came to a flat rock shelf where there was a large stone shaped like a heart pointed directly at a huge tumble-bumble bush.

Topp reached his hand deep into the big bush, grasped the main stem, pulled hard, and yanked the bush out by its roots. He flung it to the side. It bounced and careened down the steep slope until the kiddos couldn't see it anymore.

"Look! There's a slither hole!" Topp yelled.

The kiddos stood in a semi-circle and stared at a dark, narrow opening under the large rock they had just been standing on. There they were, the rainbow kiddos, high on a pinnacle in a faraway wilderness with scary creatures all around. As they looked at the opening, they felt a sense of excitement, trepidation, and raw fear.

"Let's go in and get the treasure!" Topp implored. He hoped that Grandpa Gabby was right about the coins$ and even more importantly, he hoped that Gabby was right about the yeller glizards he could hear rustling in the bushes nearby.

Chapter 45

THE BOTTOMLESS BLACK ABYSS

❧

"I'll crawl in first!" Walnut said bravely. "I'm the biggest around, so if I can slither through that hole, we all can."

"Wow, okay, Walnut," Topp said. "I'll fire up a light-wand for you as you start in."

Walnut got down on his belly in front of the opening and grabbed the light-wand as he began wiggling into the dark unknown. All the kiddos were super quiet as Walnut's feet disappeared from view. The dark hole brightened as the light-wand lit it up. The silence continued as the light in the hole flickered from Walnut's movements inside.

Topp couldn't wait any longer, so he blurted out, "What do you see, Walnut?"

They heard his faint voice coming from the hole. "There's a deep tunnel in here … come on in … bring all the light-wands."

Taffy was next to go. She shook and whacked a light-wand, and it lit right up. Then she quickly and fearlessly wiggled her way through the small opening and disappeared inside. The other kiddos did the same and crept into the skinny entrance, one behind the other. Ragamuffin and Smokey followed them in.

The tunnel was small but so were the kids. The ceiling of the tunnel was low. They couldn't stand upright, so they crouched down as they moved forward. The tunnel turned left, then right, then up, then down. It was slow going with all the twists and turns. The floor of the tunnel was uneven and had to be negotiated carefully. When they went too fast, they would stumble and fall, bang their heads, or scrape their arms on the jagged walls.

They were so far from the entrance, the spookiness was magnified with every step. If you count Ragamuffin and Smokey, there were eight hearts beating double time inside the strange tunnel.

Balooon was well ahead of the others when he shouted, "STOP! Something's wrong! HELP!"

The kiddos crept ahead cautiously, and when they got closer to Balooon, all they could see was the top of his head. Ragamuffin and Smokey ran back and forth, meowing frantically with concern.

"I'm okay ... barely!" Balooon shouted.

When the others got to where they could see all of Balooon, they couldn't believe their eyes. He was standing in a pit, on the edge of a deep dark hole, an abyss. It looked like it went straight down – down, down, down into blackness.

The pit was shaped like a funnel, wide at the top and narrow at the bottom, with the black hole at the very bottom. The sides of the pit were sloped and covered with rocks and gravel. In the middle of the funnel, there was dark nothingness – a seemingly bottomless abyss. The hole had vertical walls that went straight down, down to who knows where or what.

Quickly, Sugar, Topp, Walnut, Violet, and Taffy made a chain with their arms, so they could help Balooon climb back up to the level of the cave floor. All five locked arms but came just short of Taffy being able to grab Balooon's hand.

"I have a safety rope in my emergency kit!" Sugar cried out. "I'll toss it to you, Taffy!"

Taffy caught the rope, gripped it tightly, and threw the other end within Balooon's reach. He held on and climbed carefully up the slope. Once he was connected to the chain of kids, he didn't have any problem getting back up.

"Boy, was that a scary stumble!" Balooon cried. "Thanks to you, I'm safe! I almost went into that horrible black abyss! I do love to fly but not down there!"

They were relieved that none of them fell down into the deep black hole which now loomed in front of them. It took a while for their rapidly beating hearts to slow down so they could think straight.

"This is the end of the tunnel," Walnut pointed out. "Even if there wasn't a big hole, this is where the tunnel ends."

Walnut picked up a rock about the size of his head and heaved it down into the black hole. He wanted to know how long it took before the rock hit bottom to get an idea of how deep the hole was.

They waited and waited and waited, but they never heard it hit bottom. It was an endless, bottomless pit!

"Where are the silver coins$?" Violet asked. "After all this – no coins$?!"

"I guess this big deep hole was a cave-in, and the coins$ went to the bottom," Taffy said. "It must have swallowed them right up!"

They were on their third light-wands by now, and some of those were starting to dim. They weren't worried about running out because they each had a dozen, and twelve should be plenty enough, they figured.

The kiddos really weren't overly disappointed that they hadn't found the hidden treasure of silver coins$. They had a good time getting to where they were up on Silver Peak, and they hadn't lost Balooon or anybody else down the deep pit. And, they hadn't been eaten or stung by yeller glizards – at least not yet!

Sugar lit a new light-wand and then wedged it between two rocks, so that she had two hands free to retie her loose shoelaces. When she was done, she looked down and saw something shiny – just a flicker or sparkle is all she saw. She had to take one step down into the funnel to look more closely at whatever it was. She reached down, picked it up, and brushed the dust off the now shiny object. "I found one! A silver coin$!" she shouted.

The kiddos were incredulous and looked down to where Sugar was holding the coin$. "Wow!" the others yelled out.

"Maybe there's more!" Taffy said. She started looking around in the crumbly rocks, stones, and dirt on the slope of the funnel.

"I see one," Walnut said and scooted on his bottom over to a spot near Sugar. He picked it up, shook off the dusty powder on it, and held it up high.

"Grandpa Gabby said there were hundreds of coins$ in here," Violet said. "I suppose most of them fell to the bottom of the hole."

Very carefully, and using the emergency rope, the kiddos looked for more coins$ along the edge of the drop-off. They found thirteen in all!

"A dozen coins$, plus one. Not bad!" Balooon said with glee.

They lit two more light-wands as they continued searching for more. They searched for a long time and even looked *under* rocks, but they never found another.

They had spent quite a bit of time in the tunnel, so they began feeling antsy to get out of there. They still had six light-wands each, and they knew that ought to be plenty to get them out of that deep dark tunnel with their loot and their lives.

They started out quickly but carefully. They were so pumped up with all the excitement, when they reached the opening to the outside, they were a little winded but fully energized.

After they exited, they covered the opening back up with branches and twigs. They might want to come back someday to look for more coins$.

They stretched their bodies a bit because they had been hunched over in the tunnel. They paused and lookcd out at the beautiful sights of the Valley of Ooga Ooga and Ooga Mountain. To the right of Ooga Mountain, far across the Duney Desert, they saw Candy Mountain in the distance.

"We'll be seeing you soon, Candy Mountain!" someone said.

Based on how much time it took to climb to the top of Silver Peak, they thought they had just enough time to cross the rickety bridge before dusk.

They realized quickly that going down was not as easy as they thought it would be. The rocks were loose and slipped out from under their boots as they worked their way down. Also, Ragamuffin and Smokey kept moving below them because they didn't understand the danger of rockfall. The loose rocks created miniature avalanches as they slid and tumbled down in clusters. Several of the kiddos slipped backward, landed hard on their bottoms, and yelled "Owie!" each time. The yeller glizards stayed away, perhaps they were scared by their cries.

By the time they reached the ledge above the bridge, the daylight had faded to a dull orange glow from the setting suns. They stopped to rest and tend to their minor bruises when Ragamuffin started yapping at a yeller bush nearby.

"I see three yeller glizards over there. Go get 'em, Ragamuffin!" Sugar shouted, pointing to the bush.

And he did. At least he must have barked at them loudly enough because the glizards backed off and ran away.

"Good boy, Ragamuffin!" Sugar shouted. "They don't want to tangle with you, do they, buddy?!"

They continued and descended the steep steps down the hill to the landing at the bridge without a problem. But by the time they reached the start of the bridge, it was dark.

"YIKES! LOOK UP!" Violet cried out. "Look at all the eyes!"

"They must be the glowy-eyes," Taffy said. "Look at how many there are! There's three or four dozen of them – probably fifty or more!"

The glowy-eyes were gathering on the ledge that the kiddos had just come down from. The glowy-eyes made a very creepy sound that really shook them up. The sound was similar to the growling our tummies make when we're hungry, except louder – much louder!

There the kiddos were, caught between a rickety bridge and what seemed like a million glowy-eyes staring at them.

"Everybody, light a wand quickly!" Topp shouted.

The area where they were standing at the start of the bridge lit up brightly. It didn't deter the glowy-eyes, however. They were still there staring at them, but they didn't look as scary in all that bright light. What *was* scary was that all six kiddos still had to cross the Ooga River in the dark, over an old decrepit bridge. The other choice was to spend the night where they were, with horrible glowy-eyes surrounding them.

Oh no! Poor kiddos!

Chapter 46

A BILLION GLOWY-EYES STARING!

❧❦

From the cliffs above, the glowy-eyes glared menacingly at the frightened kiddos. The hideous creatures were also looking up at them from the darkness below the bridge. They appeared to be everywhere and moving slowly toward them.

The kiddos had to create a strategy to get to the other side. For one thing, each kid would be heavier this time due to the added weight of the silver, so they decided to carry two coins$ each to spread out the weight. Sugar would carry three coins$ because she weighed the least.

To light their way across the bridge, Sugar tied strings around their foreheads like headbands to hold the light-wands. When they started across the bridge, they would have light to see their way, and their hands would be free to balance and hang on to the cables of the bridge as they crossed one at a time.

Spooked by the glowy-eyes, Ragamuffin and Smokey took off running over the bridge ahead of the kids. The kiddos were worried about them, but Sugar reminded them that cats can see in the dark. Ragamuffin is part cat or at least he thinks he is, and Smokey *is* a cat. The pets gracefully traversed the bridge and leaped safely onto the other side. They waited for the big animals they live with to catch up.

Once again, Sugar offered to go first. She stepped forward and showed the others how the headband worked. She crossed the bridge with great caution and jumped safely onto the far bank of the river gorge.

One by one, the kiddos went over the bridge while the glowy-eyed creatures watched them intently. Fortunately, the kiddos will never know what would have happened to them if they had spent the night by the bridge.

When Sugar looked back across the river, she saw billions of glowy-eyes staring across the gorge at them. Surprisingly, she yelled out, "Thank you, glowy-eyes, and I wish you well!" Sugar was expressing her gratitude that the creatures which outnumbered them, did not do them any harm.

"Maybe they only attack adults," Topp said. "Kids don't taste good, I guess. We probably eat too much candy ..."

"Well, we did it!" Balooon said, exhausted but relieved.

As they started up the road toward Happy Harbor, the glow from their last light-wands was fading. They were safe now and heading to PetTunias Farm. The night was calm and peaceful as the kiddos strolled up the road but suddenly, there were weird noises right above them.

"HELP! THE SKY IS FALLING ON US!" Taffy shouted as she looked up. "RUN! RUN!"

Without warning, something huge and dark was descending upon them from above. They looked up and saw it was the bottom of a house about to crash down on top of them! The giant thing from the sky came down with a violent thud right next to them! The crash landing created a massive cloud of green Happy Harbor dust.

From inside the dust cloud, they heard voices. "Hi, Raffer Daffer Doo! It's Mom and Dad! We're back!"

Balooon's parents had landed their house-sized basket out of control and almost smashed the kids. His parents climbed down a rope ladder from the edge of the tall basket, ran to their son, and gave him a big hug. The other kiddos enjoyed the loving reunion and were dazzled at the size of the balloon that towered above them.

After introducing themselves to the kiddos, Balooon's parents invited them to climb up into the roomy basket. They said their giant balloon was named *Miss Blimpy* and told the kiddos they would fly them back to their clubhouse. Mrs. Balooon suggested they sit down on the comfy seats inside the basket to relax. They climbed up the ladder and got on board. A small woven basket on a rope was lowered to bring up the dog and cat. The kiddos were offered popcorn berries to munch on (to their delight) as they prepared to take off.

"Hang on tight!" Mr. Balooon shouted. Up and off they flew into the dark sky. They floated up, up, up so high, all the kiddos (except for Balooon) had butterflies in their tummies. They were fascinated as they looked down on the flickering lights of the houses so ridiculously far below them. They soared over the lights of Happy Harbor. In the distance, they could see a cluster of lights from the Village of Ooga Ooga. What a heavenly sight to see.

After they reached cruising altitude for the flight, Mr. and Mrs. Balooon asked the kiddos to tell them what they had been doing during the summer.

Topp smiled and then spoke, "The biggest thing happened on the first day of summer. We found an ancient bottle with an amazing map inside. And when we gave it to Mrs. Smart at the Museum of Everything, she gave us an even better map of what surrounds the Valley of Ooga Ooga."

"That's interesting, anything else?" Mrs. Balooon asked.

That opened the floodgates to all the adventures they'd had. They told Mr. and Mrs. Balooon about how they skipped stones on the river, how they played in the flower field, and all about the lucky fan flowers they'd slept with under their pillows. They told them how they followed a trail of dia-mons up into the Giant Step Mountains, and about the tunnel they explored to find the mother lode. They didn't talk about the cave-in, but they did say that Balooon flew them home from the mountain.

The kiddos continued by describing the clubhouse, the garden, and the fruit trees in the shady glade.

Balooon told them how he'd crashed into a tree in the fog and how the kiddos saved him by cutting off the ropes he was bound up in.

The kiddos then asked Mr. and Mrs. Balooon about their journey, the one they had just returned from. "We'll tell you all about that someday," Mr. Balooon said. "I'd rather hear more about what you adventurous children have been up to."

So, the kiddos continued.

They told about Purple Springs and how they met Violet. They described the Pink Desert, the rockroses, and the three gold balls. They did not say a word about the sandstorm and how lost they were because they ended up finding their way out to safety.

They told about the ride up Ooga Mountain to Lookout Rock, and how Sugar rescued them with the light of the fairy flowers when it got dark on the mountain.

They told of the adventure at Bog Town and Vine Boy, and about bringing back a planana tree from the Jolly Jungle.

Mr. Balooon then said, "My-diddly-doo, you children have been very busy! I must ask why you kids were at the foot bridge in the dark. This ought to be interesting!"

And it was. The kiddos explained that they had not been looking for *minerals* like they'd fibbed to the PetTunias but were looking for coins$ made of silver instead, which they brought out and showed to them. The beauty of the thirteen shiny coins$ dazzled them all.

Balooon's parents listened intently to the stories of the kiddos' adventures as they floated gently through the evening sky. Then Mrs. Balooon made a mistake and asked, "What will you be doing for the rest of the summer?"

The kiddos started talking and shouting over each other about the adventures that still lie ahead of them, like their desires to travel to the Chocolate Hills, Candy Mountain, Wetwater Lake, the Fantasmo and Ice Bug Seas, and many more destinations. They were getting jump-up-and-down excited just thinking about all the things they still wanted to do.

"Wow!" Mr. Balooon said and then joked, "Is that *all*?" He was sorry he asked because the kiddos started right up again.

"We want to raft down the Ooga River to the Town of Trombone – but not as far as the Village of Ghosts!" Taffy said. "We also want to return to the Jolly Jungle and sneak around Rat Town – from a safe distance, of course. We want to have a big picky-nick in Poppy Park and invite everybody to come and go on rides, play games, and win prizes. And someday we want to go back to the Ooga River Falls and the Bubble Bath!"

Just then, the kiddos felt like they were falling. The giant balloon descended rapidly but safely over a group of trees and into the shady glade. *Home at last*, the kiddos thought, *home at last*!

The kiddos hopped out of the big basket with happy hearts. They asked the Balooons to come in and see their clubhouse. However, they declined, saying they needed to get back to Happy Harbor. They promised to stop by again and stay for a while. They made it clear that they were anxious to see the clubhouse, the glasshouse, the garden, and nearby Silly Creek – but not tonight – it was too late.

With the kiddos waving wildly, the giant balloon *Miss Blimpy* slowly rose with Mr. and Mrs. Balooon, Raffer Daffer Doo, and Smokey in the basket suspended below.

Balooon yelled to his friends as he sailed away, "See you tomorrow!"

The Balooon family, together again, disappeared into an ebony sky, full of the brightest stars that had ever been seen.

Chapter 47

BOBBY AND COOKIE GET SURPRISES
OF A LIFETIME

இ~

Bobby woke up early in the morning and thought about the visit he had with Cookie the day before. He was surprised that he'd told her all about his dreams because they're hard to explain and very personal. It was odd to live half the time in a dream and the other half as a real boy in a real world. It was hard for him to understand what was going on, but Bobby was aware that he'd been given a rare gift. *Both lives are fulfilling and wonderful, so what's wrong with that!* he thought.

His imagination was running away with him, so he stood up by his bed, stretched his arms high in the air, and wiggled his whole body. He went into the bathroom and threw chilly water on his face to wake up and brushed his teeth to start the day.

Bobby's mom calls teeth 'mouth jewels' and told him to treasure them and keep them clean. You brush your teeth when you get up in the morning, don't you? You better!

Bobby went back into his room and put on what he calls his power clothes. He has pairs of pants and several shirts that fit that distinction. They are commonly called work clothes – clothes that'll get plenty dirty doing outdoor projects.

He went into the kitchen and noticed that his mom wasn't up yet. He paused for a second and then quietly opened the freezer and pulled out a new carton of ice cream his mom had bought. "I am a good kid, I am!" he said quietly. "I do deserve ice cream for breakfast – *sometimes.*"

So, he ate just the right amount of the peach ice cream, not too much and not too little. He thought to himself, *If I eat too much, then I am no longer a good kid, and if I eat too little, then I don't get all I deserve for being such a good kid!*

Bobby is a thoughtful boy, isn't he?

He still had room in his tummy, so he looked in the refrigerator, saw the banana bread and helped himself. He sat at the kitchen table for a minute and reflected on his latest dream and then headed outside to work.

Bobby was high on a ladder framing a new roof for the clubhouse when he heard a familiar voice call his name.

"Hi, Bobby!" Cookie shouted. "Lookin' good up there!"

"Yeah, it's going pretty well," Bobby replied. "What are you up to today?"

"I came to see if you need help, and I also have an idea I want to talk to you about."

Bobby needed a break, so he came down and met her at the picnic table. "So, what's your idea, Cookie?"

"I was wondering if you could build a small greenhouse on the south side of the new clubhouse. I'll help you build it – the best I can, anyway."

Bobby thought for a few seconds and then asked her, "Why do you want a greenhouse?"

"For one thing, I've always wanted one. I like growing little plants inside the windows of my house as you know. I've always wanted to grow more plants and bigger plants, but I can't do that inside my bedroom. You said that the kids in your dream wanted to grow a banana tree. I found that to be very interesting, and I thought if we had a greenhouse as part of the new clubhouse, maybe we could try growing one too!"

"Well, I never thought about it, but I don't know why not. In the dream, they planted a pla-nana tree, but it seemed like a ba-nana tree to me," Bobby said. "There are a bunch of old windows in the garage that used to be in our house before the remodel. I'm sure I'm free to use those."

"That's super-duper!" Cookie said excitedly. "So, Bobby, did you have that dream again last night? I'm curious to find out what happened next."

"Yes, I most certainly did! It was amazing once again!"

"Tell me about it – if you wish to, of course."

"I don't remember a lot of the details, but I do remember that the dream-kids, that's what I call them, went up a pointed hill in search of silver coins!" Bobby recalled. "The kids went into a dangerous tunnel, found some coins, escaped from big-eyed creatures, and then crossed a dangerous bridge in the dark to get home. They got a ride back to their clubhouse in a big balloon-blimp thing. Pretty crazy – huh?"

"It sounds amazing!" Cookie said. "I wish I had dreams like that."

Bobby's mom came outside to the table where they were sitting. She brought them drinks and frozen bananas covered in chocolate.

"It's getting hot out here today, so I thought you might like something cold," she said.

"Thanks! I do love bananas," Cookie said with a smile and gave Bobby a little wink.

Bobby and Cookie discussed the idea of the greenhouse and what it would take to build one. They would need to construct a foundation of cement blocks set solidly into the ground to hold up the outer wall of glass. They decided to start with foundation blocks, and Cookie offered to dig the rectangular holes.

"Let's mark out the location for each block, so you can get started digging, and I'll get back to the roof," Bobby said with fresh energy.

Bobby marked out four places to dig the holes and got a shovel for Cookie to use. She eagerly started digging to the depth they had discussed. Bobby climbed back up the ladder and continued nailing the final roof boards on.

"Oh my gosh-a-roonie!" Cookie screamed. "I found something interesting! Come look!"

Bobby flew down the ladder and rushed over to Cookie, who was holding something round and shiny. Bobby held the object and looked at it carefully in the sunlight. "It's an old coin of some sort. It must be old because it isn't like the coins we use today."

"It's very shiny – like silver!" she said as she examined it more closely. "I don't think they've made silver coins like this for a long time."

"Oh my! In my dream last night, the kids found silver coins! My dream came to life again! Oh, golly, golly!"

Bobby remembered that the dream-kids had found *several* silver coins, so he went to the place Cookie had been digging to look for more. Right away, they found another one. They continued digging for an hour and made holes all over the place, but they never found another.

"Well, we found two of them, one for you and one for me!" Bobby said. "Now all we need is a big balloon to show up and we'll be right on script with my dream."

Bobby's mom came out of the house to pick up the dishes on the picnic table. As she started back, she looked up and said, "Look kids, the blimp from the county fair is going by!"

Cookie and Bobby looked up and there it was – a blimp, a big round blimp.

The surprised looks on their faces said all that needed to be said. They stared up in fascination. His dream had manifested in his real life once again.

"Life is full of surprises, isn't it?" Bobby said with a twinkle in his eye.

"You got that right!" Cookie agreed and gave Bobby a fist bump.

"I can barely wait for what's next. Life can be very full, can't it?"

"As full as we want to make it, I suppose," she added. "We shall fully enjoy the surprises when they come, won't we Bobby?"

The balloon-like blimp floated out of sight behind tall trees, but it left behind quite an impression for the two friends to ponder. Bananas, balloons, and bogs – oh my!

What happened next was even more miraculous.

Bobby's mother came running out of the house, screaming at the top of her voice! "DADDY'S BEEN FOUND!!! DADDY'S SAFE!!! HE'S COMING HOME!!!"

Bobby and Cookie lay in their beds that night and sensed a joy they hadn't felt in a long time. They thought about dreams and how they sometimes come true.

What will happen in their minds tonight? Only sleep can answer that, so they closed their young eyes and floated away into the misty world of dreams.

Chapter 48

IS THERE REALLY CHOCOLATE IN THEM HILLS?

∽∾

The six kiddos slept in the next day and didn't get together until half the day was gone. After Balooon eventually landed in the glade, they sat around talking at their special table, in their spectacular clubhouse. Their bodies were sore all over from their adventure up to Silver Peak and back. The good news was that they had no injuries from those awful glizards or the glowy-eyes, and nobody had fallen into the awful abyss.

With the thirteen silver coins$ stacked up on the table in front of them, they had a good time chatting about how they found them and how they just made it back before the glowy-eyes got to them in the dark. They celebrated the safe return of Balooon's parents and shared how much they enjoyed the balloon ride home from Happy Harbor on *Miss Blimpy*.

"Well, what's next?" Topp asked the group eagerly.

"I really want to go to Candy Mountain," Walnut shouted out. "Candy Mountain! Whoop! Whoop!"

"I do too, but the weather is still too warm to go there – unless you want to get stuck forever in the sticky candy," Violet said. "We need to go there at the *end* of summer, when the chilly winds blow in from the west."

"We could raft down the Ooga River to the Fantasmo Sea," Balooon said.

"What's down there?" Taffy asked.

"I don't know," Balooon said. "That's why it would be so exciting – it's unknown! Maybe we could find the *edge* out there somehow."

"My sweet tooth is calling me!" Sugar said. "That's why I'm called *Sugar*! I want to go to Candy Mountain, too, but that will have to wait. So how about we go to the sweet Chocolate Hills and get chocolate – I hear it's good!"

That suggestion sounded just right to all of them. They agreed to travel to the Chocolate Hills at last.

"So, what's the best way to get there – does anybody know?" Topp asked.

"I overheard Grandpa Gabby talking about the Chocolate Hills a while back," Taffy said. "Maybe we should go talk to him. We also need to give a silver coin$ to Goldie in Old Town for her reward. Maybe Grandpa Gabby can give it to her."

The kiddos decided to hurry on over to Poppy Park to see if Grandpa Gabby was there. They planned to pick his brain about the Chocolate Hills and give him a share of the silver coins$ in return for the clues he had given them.

In an instant, they hopped on their bikes and left at full speed, with a puffy of shady glade dust billowing up behind them.

"Lucky us!" shouted Taffy, looking ahead to the Ducky Pond. "He's there!"

Grandpa Gabby welcomed the young'uns and asked them about their journey to Silver Peak. The kiddos told him the whole story and handed him seven of the silver coins$, one for Goldie, and six for him.

"I'll certainly give one to Goldie," he said. "But you keep the rest – I don't need 'em." With that, the kiddos told him that they would donate half of their coins$ in his name to Mayor Kee Kee as a gift to the Village of Ooga Ooga. The topic then changed to the Chocolate Hills.

"Grandpa Gabby, what can you tell us about the Chocolate Hills?" Sugar asked, licking her lips. "We want to go there next and eat the delicious chocolate we've heard so much about – if there's really chocolate there."

"Me knows things about them Chocolate Hills," Grandpa Gabby began. "The first thing is there is indeed a lot of delicious chocolate in them thar hills."

"Wow!" Sugar declared. "My tongue loves hearing that!"

"That's funny," Walnut said. "Tongues can't hear!"

"Mine can!" Sugar shot back.

Grandpa Gabby laughed at the silliness and continued, "From a distance, the hills seem to be all chocolate, but most of what is seen is just sandstone and dirt that *looks* like chocolate. Me knows that there are veins and pockets of real chocolate in them big ol' hills. There's dark, light brown, and white chocolate too."

"I like the sound of that!" Topp said as the others jumped up and down with glee.

"The *easiest* way to get to the Chocolate Hills is not the *best* way," Grandpa Gabby explained. "Taking the nice smooth road from the Village of Ooga Ooga to Gem Town is easy. However, there is no chocolate at that end of the hills. There's only rock and dirt. The real chocolate is at the other end, the east end. It's very hard to get to the real chocolate from Gem Town for there are dozens of deep canyons to cross, with violent biting chiperoos in all of them!"

"Whoa! That's good to know!" said Balooon. "Is it hard going around the Giant Step Mountains to the east to where the real chocolate is?"

"Listen carefully, kidlings. There is no road, just a trail around the Giant Step Mountains. It goes through Spooky Hollow, close to Rat Town!"

"Oh my, that doesn't sound good at all!" Sugar shuddered.

"The trail is easy to ride on, and there's a narrow pass called The Gap in the tall Charcoal Cliffs that extend from Rat Town up to the Giant Step Mountains. The Gap is the best way to go, but it's patrolled by the people who live in Rat Town. There are only two ways to get to the Chocolate Hills on the east side: one way is on the trail through The Gap, and the other way is through the middle of Rat Town. You don't want to go through Rat Town – unless you don't ever want to come back again. Just kidding!"

"Uh-oh! That doesn't sound good at all!" Topp said.

"Years ago, I went through The Gap by paying the toll with brittles$. The people from Rat Town, now called Rooogans, guard The Gap. They were pleasant and fair and didn't charge me very much, so it worked out all right. On the return trip through The Gap all they wanted was chocolate, but they didn't want very much of that, either. So that's it, you shouldn't have a problem."

"We have brittles$!" Violet said. "And we *will* have chocolate, too, after we get to those yummy hills."

"Very few Oogans go through Spooky Hollow and Rat Town because they are afraid," Grandpa Gabby continued. "I thought the people from Rat Town were quite nice really. Some Oogans think they are Rat People, but they aren't. The Rat People left when the giants came to Spooky Hollow many years ago. The people who live there now are Rooogans. They moved from Ooga Ooga into the abandoned Rat Town a long time ago. They are a little different from us but not in a real bad way."

"I'll tell you that there *are* lots of rats around that area because there is a low pass from the Jolly Jungle into Spooky Hollow. Large rats live in that area of the jungle and in Spooky Hollow as well. Some are as large as dogs!"

"Goodness me!" Sugar blurted out and the kiddos' faces grew pale.

"Me thinks you kids'll be fine," Grandpa Gabby said with confidence. "You are very brave kids and smart too. There are six of you, so I'm sure you will do just fine on the Rat Town Trail. If you leave early on your bikes, you can get back in one day. The trail is smooth, and there are just a few ups and downs along the way.

"Oh, and one other thing, keep a look out for the biting chiperoos. They only have a small bite but once they bite someone, they'll follow that person around to get more bites. I've heard they're cute but troublesome. They live and hide in Rusty Canyon below the Chocolate Hills."

The kiddos stood there in silence and looked back and forth at one another. They were weirded out by all the rat and chiperoo talk.

"If we go there, it must mean we love chocolate!" Taffy said, breaking the silence. "I love chocolate — but I don't love rats or weird biting things!"

The kiddos thanked Grandpa Gabby and headed back to the Big Abble to discuss what he had told them. They must decide whether to go get chocolate or choose a different adventure.

I bet they go get chocolate. What do you think?

You're right — it's time for chocolate! Yum yum!

Chapter 49

ON THE WAY TO THE CHOCOLATE HILLS

ॐ♥ॐ

The kiddos decided that nothing, not even rats, could keep them from the delicious chocolate waiting for them in those brown-colored hills. Violet told them that her fairies and angels will keep them safe from the Rooogans *and* rats as they journey around the Giant Step Mountains.

Having seen Violet walk across the Honey Bog to save Sugar, the kiddos knew her powers were incredibly strong. "If Violet says we'll be safe, I believe her," Walnut said.

Wow, these kiddos are really something, aren't they? They seem to have special powers and fortitude galore.

The kiddos planned to leave early the next morning. They will take food with them but just a little bit because they don't want to get their bellies too full. They wanted plenty of room for the delicious chocolate they hoped to find.

The kiddos were taking their bikes because they learned that there would be good trails to ride on. They were also wearing their hiking boots because Grandpa Gabby told them that they would be challenged by the arroyos in Rusty Canyon where they wouldn't be able to take their bikes. Because they weren't sure of what might happen on this new adventure, they decided to leave Ragamuffin and Smokey at the clubhouse.

The next morning, they jumped out of their beds so early there was still darkness hanging around from the night before. A cool dank fog was floating over Silly Creek.

They were quite sleepy as they started on the Silly Creek Trail in the direction of Spooky Hollow. They sped along, past the big log lying across the creek, the one they had crossed when they followed Smokey, the cat. The trail went in and out of groves of wild trees and across fields of beautiful grain planted by Oogan farmers. The kiddos appreciated farmers more than ever now that they are (sort of) farmers.

The trail also ran along fruit orchards where the trees were loaded with fruit not quite ready to pick. There were abbles, pearettes, figwigs and several other fruit trees – but no plananas.

The trail left the lush and irrigated farmland and started up a long gradual incline. The plants surrounding the trail became scrubby bushes and dry scraggly weeds. It looked more like a desert but occasionally they found seeping springs and ponds of water where clusters of lush green reeds and willows grew.

The kiddos had never been in this area before, so it was exciting *and* a bit scary too. They were just kids in a strange land and giant people-eating rats might not be far away!

"Stop!" shouted Topp. "I saw something moving behind that bush. Hush!"

The kiddos jumped off their bikes and stood still. They looked where Topp was pointing. Suddenly, a huge deer leaped over a hedge and pranced toward them. They didn't realize how tall it was until it came close. It was at least ten feet tall, so tall the kiddos could have walked right underneath it (if they had any desire to do that – which they didn't). The giant deer had bright blue ears as well. It was very strange indeed!

The tall deer-critter stopped short of them and spoke! Yes, it spoke and said in a deep voice, "Ga da, fro fro, you you, ba ba, rick rick?"

The kiddos stood there like blocks of solid steel and stared at the totally weird creature that was obstructing the trail. A dead silence continued for a long moment, and then the deer-critter spoke again. "Oh, you don't speak *Wa Lu Lu*, do you?" the deer-thing said in perfect Oogan and smiled.

"Have you seen a giant blue butterfly on your journey?" the deer-creature asked, looking back and forth at each of the kiddos.

"I did see one," Topp said meekly, wishing he had never seen it and wishing he had kept his mouth shut!

"Where did you see it?" the deer-like creature asked.

Topp quickly realized that this was another what-er, so he pointed and said, "That way, down the trail about an hour."

"Perfect!" the what-er muttered and leaped right over them, then bounded higher and higher down the trail until it disappeared.

"What was that all about?" asked Sugar.

"A reminder that we are in a strange place," Taffy said, "and we better be prepared for anything as we head through this strange Spooky Hollow on our way to the Chocolate Hills!"

They hesitantly mounted their bikes to continue down the trail, but when they thought about the chocolate, they picked up the pace and hurried on toward Rat Town and The Gap.

They rode over a hill, one of many rocky hills at the base of the Giant Step Mountains to their right. They looked down into a small valley to their left and saw a town with houses scattered here and there. As they looked more closely, they saw that all the buildings were painted in dark unfriendly colors. There were no whites, pinks, or tans, just shadow colors.

"Rat Town!" Balooon squeaked meekly, like a cricket with a sore throat.

"It looks like a nice town, from what I can see," Sugar said. "There are nice trees and gardens in their yards."

"Looks spooky to me!" Balooon argued. "Rat Town!"

"We must be getting close to The Gap," Topp said. "We better keep moving."

The kiddos came to a fork in the road. The fork to the left was clearly the road to Rat Town. They were a little confused when they saw a sign pointing down that direction that read:

ROOOGANVILLE   2 MILES

The fork in the road to the right went straight ahead to who knows where, The Gap?

No one uttered a word as they rode on, up and over a rise. They saw a jagged cliff of solid gray rock in front of them.

The massive rock formation is called the Charcoal Cliffs. It's dizzyingly tall and slopes down to the left toward Rat Town and up to the right to the Giant Step Mountains. In the imposing rock wall in front of them, they saw the shadow of a cut or opening in the huge cliff. They realized that the trail they were on went right through that opening. "It's The Gap!" Topp said with apprehension.

The tall cliff was spooky indeed as it towered over them. There wasn't anything but the dusty trail and lonely-looking bushes below the tall charcoal-colored monolith.

The kiddos stopped their bikes and put their feet down to balance. The beautiful sunny morning had turned into a gloomy day, and now the giant shadow of the cliff surrounded them. Most of the kiddos had second thoughts about going farther through the narrow, spooky opening directly in front of them.

However, one of the kiddos showed no concern at all and started to whistle in the stagnant silence. It was Walnut, of course, and he shouted, "Chocolate Hills, here I come!" He quickly jumped onto his bike, bolted forward, and continued whistling as he entered the dark shadows of The Gap.

Chapter 50

RATS, RATS, RATS ... AND CHOCOLATE

శ్రీశ్రీ

The kiddos slowly entered the mysterious gap through the tall foreboding Charcoal Cliffs. They knew this gateway stood between them and the Chocolate Hills. They looked all around because they were afraid that rats or worse might jump down on them from rock ledges above. There weren't any such critters, but the kiddos have good imaginations, so there may well have been hundreds of them if you saw the frightened looks on their faces.

They proceeded slowly, walking their bikes until they came to what looked like a toll booth with a little window. On the wall of the toll booth, there was a sign that said: Wellcome. That put the kiddos a little bit at ease as they put their kickstands down and walked up to the window.

"Hellloo!" said the little girl inside. "Wellcome to The Gapp!"

"Hello," replied Taffy uneasily. "We're traveling to the Chocolate Hills and would like to pass through, if we may."

"Yyess, that would be ffine," said the girl with a cute accent and a lovely grin.

Just then a smiling young boy popped his head up from inside the booth and said, "Thhat'll be one half a britttle$, pllease."

"Oh, this is my brother, Ddandy, and my name is Pperfume," the girl said sweetly, with that unusual, yet endearing accent.

"We only have a *big* brittle$," Topp said warily. "Sorry, we don't have any half brittle$."

"Wwe have chhange," said Ddandy. "Nno probblem."

The kiddos were surprised at how nice and friendly these children were. They weren't scary at all. They spoke perfect Oogan, although they spoke the language with a lovely musical accent the kiddos had never heard before.

As Sugar handed Pperfume a brittle$, she noticed a little mouse pop its head out of Pperfume's top pocket. Pperfume handed Sugar her change and smiled again. Sugar wasn't alarmed by the mouse. *It's a very cute little mouse*, she thought.

"Is that a pet mouse?" Balooon asked politely.

"Nno, it's a bbaby hhamster," Pperfume said. "And there's her mmother, behind me." Pperfume moved a little out of the way, so Balooon could see the large rat on the table behind her, sniffing the air in his direction.

Balooon jumped back in shock. "That's a rat!"

"Nno it's not, it's my pet hhamster," Pperfume said. "Hher name is Fuzzette."

The kiddos started to feel uneasy at this point. They said a polite "thank you" and slowly walked backward so they could keep an eye on Fuzzette the rat as they moved toward their bikes. Because they were walking backward they clumsily bumped into each other and their bikes. Some of the kids and bikes fell, but eventually they all mounted up and pedaled on through The Gap.

They rode for a while in silence, looking side to side, fearing there might be rats hiding in the bushes around the trail. They eventually came to a nice open area with low grass and a broad shade tree, Underneath the tree, there was welcoming picnic table. So, they stopped, rested, and ate the sandwiches they had brought with them.

"That was scary!" Balooon said.

"Fascinating," Violet said pensively.

Topp added, "Interesting young kids – very nice really."

"I liked them," Taffy said. "But they had a strange way of speaking."

Walnut stopped whistling and said, "If all the Rooogans from Rat Town are like those kids, they are just like us – except for the rats that they call hamsters!"

"I thought their pets were cute, especially the little one," Sugar said. "I love animals, you know."

Topp climbed up onto a tall rock by the trail and told the kiddos to come see what he was looking at. Down the trail, they saw a long range of dark brown hills. "The Chocolate Hills at last!" he said.

Seeing the Chocolate Hills helped them forget the Rooogan kids and their pet rats. They jumped onto their bikes and sped onward toward the brown hills. The hills had not looked very big from a distance, but close up, they were quite massive.

As they rode farther, they were surprised to discover that the trail ended. Grandpa Gabby had mentioned that they would need to hike through canyons and ravines at the base of the Chocolate Hills. They parked their bikes and prepared to travel on foot to what they hoped was yummy chocolate. They were excited when their noses got a whiff of chocolate as they hiked through the canyon to begin their climb to the brown hills above.

Coming around a boulder, they saw smoke rising from a gully in front of them.

"Look at the smoke!" Taffy exclaimed. "I wonder what's going on down there."

The kiddos quietly crept to the brow of a mound and looked down to where the smoke was coming from.

"It's a young lad roasting what looks like marshmallows," Balooon whispered to the others.

The young lad saw them (even though the kiddos thought they were well hidden) and waved to them in a friendly gesture.

The kiddos reluctantly hiked down into the gully where the boy was sitting alone by a fire.

"Welcome to Rusty Canyon. Come on down, I don't bite!" said the lad with a grin. "Only the biting chiperoos bite!" The lad grinned again when he saw the kiddos were a bit taken aback, "I'm roasting marshmallows to go with my sweet crackers and chocolate. May I offer you a bite?" the lad asked. He had a very friendly voice and a strong but understandable accent.

Walnut said, "I love chocolate! Sure, I'll try some!"

Just then, a lovely young lass came around a nearby rock with an arm load of small sticks.

"This is my sister, Cricket," the lad said, "and my name is Buggy. We're from a small village in *that* direction, on the other side of the Chocolate Hills." He pointed toward the tall brown hills to the south.

As Cricket dropped the sticks she had gathered, the kiddos introduced themselves and settled in around the flickering fire. They explained to their new acquaintances that they had come from the shady glade in the Valley of Ooga Ooga to get chocolate to take home with them.

The kiddos eventually found out that Buggy and Cricket were Buggans. They lived in Bugg Town, on the edge of the Ice Bug Sea. They spoke the Oogan language but with an accent – yet a different accent than the Rooogan kids.

"Wow, these are such delicious treats – I'm sure I'd want *some more*," Violet said in appreciation.

"Funny, that's what we call them. We call them *s'mores*!" Cricket said with a jolly laugh.

"So," Topp asked. "What's the best way to get real eatable chocolate out of those hills – if you don't mind telling us?"

"There is a trick to it," Buggy explained. "The chocolate looks just like the chocolate-colored rock and dirt all around it, so it's difficult to find it without getting a mouthful of dirt now and then!" He made a funny face as he remembered all the times he'd had to spit out dirt.

"How do you find the good stuff?" Balooon asked.

"Okay, listen up. For one thing, the best place to find the chocolate is near the top of the hills," Buggy said. "The farther you go toward Gem Town, the less you'll find. Right above us is the best place – right up there." He pointed to the tall hill directly above them. "There's plenty of chocolate if you can figure out how to avoid the chocolate-colored dirt!"

The kiddos enjoyed hanging out with Cricket and Buggy, but they were aware they needed to get back to the shady glade before dark. They politely thanked the two kids and started climbing up the amazing hills of chocolate.

They climbed up and up until they reached a plateau near the top and noticed places where it looked like others had dug before. With their little picks and tiny shovels, they pulled out chunks of what looked like chocolate.

"Wow, that's really good!" Sugar exclaimed. "It's a little gritty, but the chocolate is delish!"

The kiddos didn't find much chocolate, but they found enough to fill their tummies, and they had extra to give to the Rat Town kids when they passed back through The Gap. They realized that they'd spent a lot of time with the what-er deer, the kids from The Gap, and the Buggan kids, so they decided to take a little chocolate today and come back for more in a couple of days.

With their tummies full of chocolate (and chocolate-colored dirt), they headed back down and climbed out of the rusty-colored canyon to reach their bikes.

They rode hard to The Gap, where they paid the toll to the Rooogan kids who were still very pleasant. A small chunk of dark chocolate is all they wanted for the toll. The kiddos told Pperfume and Ddandy that they would be back in a couple of days to get more. The Rooogan kids were happy to hear that. "See you then!" Pperfume said. And the kiddos disappeared down the Rat Town Trail.

They coasted into the shady glade, a little winded from the long journey. However, they were energized by the delicious chocolate and yummy s'mores they had eaten!

Chapter 51

HOME SWEET HOME

❧ ❧

The kiddos returned from their journey to the Chocolate Hills with fresh ideas for the future. Their adventure to get chocolate was a success because everything Grandpa Gabby had told them turned out to be true. They wanted to return to those sweet chocolatey brown hills soon but not yet.

Considering all the messes the kiddos had gotten into during other daring adventures, the trip went about as well as it could. After all, the kiddos came back in one piece, and they had never been in any danger as far as they knew. And they'd never encountered the biting chiperoos that Buggy had warned them about.

The kiddos took a vote and decided six to zero to go back and get more chocolate in two days. For one thing, they knew they needed to spend time at their *real* homes with their moms and dads. To show appreciation for all their parents have done for them, the kiddos decided to spend a day doing chores and helping around their real houses and yards. That's what good kids do – they help their parents with chores. Right?

They also knew they needed to work on their garden at the shady glade. The young fruit trees and vegetables needed watering, and they needed to clean up their clubhouse. (Kids can be messy – imagine that!)

The next morning, they sat around the table to discuss details of their future trip back to those yummy hills. Topp took the lead and shared the ideas he was excited about. Topp said he had been working on an invention to get chocolate out of the hills without any grit. The kiddos were all ears and eyes as Topp proceeded to lay out what he had in mind.

Bang, Bang, Bang! There was pounding on the door. Then again, louder! *BANG! BANG! BANG!* All the kiddos got up this time and huddled near the door as Topp opened it slowly. At the door, there was a giant purple frog. It was taller than the door and three times wider than that. It said in a very pleasant voice, "Hello there, my name is JoJo. Have you seen a large deer with blue ears – a deer that speaks *Wa Lu Lu*?"

Topp spoke up, "Yes, we saw a deer like that, up that trail over there. We saw it yesterday, about a one-hour bike ride from here."

"Thank you very much!" shouted the frog. It let out an ear-piercing *CROAK*, took a giant leap over the tallest tree on the edge of the glade and disappeared.

The kiddos thought the frog was totally weird. But stranger yet, it went the wrong way when it left.

"I guess what-ers go what-ever way they *want* to go!" Topp remarked with a grin.

The kiddos walked back to the table giggling and resumed their discussion.

Then before Topp said a word, there was a tiny *tick, tick* at the door. The kiddos got up quietly and slowly opened the door. No one was there. They saw no giant butterfly, no giant deer, and no giant purple frog.

Sugar looked down at her feet and said, "Hello, little elf, can we help you?"

The elf, who was only as tall as a brittle$ on edge, looked up at all the kiddos who were now looking down at him. He said, "Sorry to bother you, but have you seen a big purple frog named JoJo around here?"

"Are you a what-er?" Violet asked the elf, rather bluntly.

"What's a what-er?" the tiny elf asked.

"Oh, never mind! Yes, there was an immense purple frog at our door a few minutes ago – you just missed it. It hopped that way, over those trees," Violet said, pointing to the trees in the direction of Ooga Mountain.

"Jolly good!" squeaked the elf. "Jolly good!" The little guy ran as fast as he could through the garden. He zigged and zagged, so as not to step on the young veggies and disappeared into the woods yelling, "Jolly good, jolly good!"

The kiddos started laughing, even though they were a bit annoyed at all the disruptions by the what-ers.

"How many of those things are out there?" Violet asked.

"*Who* knows? Go ask *who*!" Walnut said giggling.

The kiddos decided not to answer the door again and got back to business.

Topp, the kid inventor and builder, brought out a roll of paper with plans on it. He spread it out on the table.

"What's this all about?" Taffy asked him.

"It's my new invention," Topp said. "I'll show you."

He explained that he had designed a special tool to take to the Chocolate Hills the next time they go. The plan showed a drawing of a long, skinny, pointed metal rod. He said he will get it red-hot in a fire and then poke it into one of the chocolatey hills. "If the hot steel rod doesn't do anything, then that is just dirt. But if it's chocolate, the chocolate will melt and the rod will penetrate the hill. We won't have to eat any more dirt – only pure chocolate!"

"Brilliant, Topp," Sugar said. "But how are we going to build a fire?"

"We'll gather firewood like Cricket did," Topp said. "Then we'll carry the wood up the hill and build a fire to heat the chocolate-melting rod or what I call the hot-rod."

"Great idea!" Violet said. "The chocolate up there was good, but I still have brown grit stuck between my teeth!"

"I have an idea," piped in Sugar. "What if we find a good vein with lots of clean chocolate inside and bring back a lot of it. Then we can make our own brand of chocolate bars and sell them around Ooga Ooga to earn brittle$."

"Great idea! We can call them KIDDO BARS!" Taffy said excitedly.

The kiddos got down to figuring out a two-day plan. They would water the garden (bucket by bucket is hard work), fertilize the planana tree and the other fruit trees, and pull the weeds that decided to be greedy and crowd out the veggies in the garden. Then they would head home to their *real* houses and enjoy the rest of the day and all the next day with their *real* families.

On the third day, they would meet early at the Big Abble and leave for the Chocolate Hills again. They would bring Topp's hot-rod invention and a flint to start a fire. This time, they would each bring a large bag-pack for carrying gobs of chocolate.

Having made their plans, they got on with their farmer work and daydreamed about the grit-free KIDDO BARS that would soon fill their tummies.

Chapter 52

PEANUT BUTTER AND JELLY ZOOOMS

৵৽

The kiddos arrived early at the clubhouse well prepared for the long journey back to the Chocolate Hills. Topp brought his steel chocolate melting rod, fire starting flint, and a bit of wood kindling. The kiddos put lube oil on the wheels of their bikes to make them spin more smoothly. It isn't a hilly ride, so they don't need blob oil.

Riding in single file, the kiddos sped past the log over Silly Creek and never even noticed the fruit orchard as they zoomed on to Spooky Hollow. Not thinking about rats (or hamsters), they passed the sign to Roooganville at top speed. The kiddos were eager to melt that chocolate with Topp's new invention.

Coming to a rise in the trail, they saw the Charcoal Cliffs not far ahead. They rode on and confidently entered The Gap and jumped off their bikes while they were still rolling. As they approached the toll booth, they anticipated that Ddandy and Pperfume would be there.

Suddenly, their smiles turned to fright when they saw a tall man with big rat ears in the booth. Yikes!

Topp demonstrated his bravery and said to the scary rodent-man, "Ahhh … we would like to pass through The Gap, if we could … please. Here's a half brittle$ for our fee." Topp reached out to pay the rat-man with a trembling hand.

"Wellcome, I was expecting yyou!" the towering brute-of-a-rat said with an unexpected smile. "Ddandy and Pperfume told me you would be coming along, and here you are!"

Just as the kiddos were about to slink away, a young girl rushed inside the toll booth. "Wellcome, friends," Pperfume said sweetly. "I see you've met my dad, Mr. Fflop."

Just then, Ddandy yelled a big "hello" to the kids. Ddandy grabbed the hat off his father's head and explained, "My dad likes to wear this silly hat with ears. I bet it spooked you when you saw him!"

"Uhhh ... yeah," Topp muttered.

"Sometimes I like to pretend I'm a hhamster. It seems to me that hhamsters really enjoy life!" Mr. Fflop said with a wide grin of perfectly white teeth.

Mr. Fflop became a lot shorter when he left the booth and came around to greet the kiddos face to face. To their amazement, Mr. Fflop wasn't much taller than they were. Inside the booth, he had been standing on a platform designed so Ddandy and Pperfume could reach the window.

The kiddos felt more comfortable and made small talk with Mr. Fflop. Pperfume spoke in perfect Oogan and told the kids that she and her brother can speak pure Oogan when they want to, so they did that from then on.

"Did you guys see any biting chiperoos the last time you were in Rusty Canyon at the base of the hills?" Ddandy asked.

"No, not a one," Taffy said. "I guess we were lucky."

"Yes, you were," Pperfume said. "You don't ever want one of those to bite you. Once one gets a taste of someone, it'll never let that person out of their sight."

"That's what we were told by an old friend in our village," Topp said. "We'll be careful when we're in the canyon."

"Here's another warning to heed!" Ddandy said. "If you get near Bugg Town or the Ice Bug Sea, whatever you do, don't you dare go near an ice bug! They'll tear you apart with all their claws! They even have a sharp spike on their nose!"

"We've heard they're stinky and ugly and make a weird humming sound!" Pperfume said.

"Have you ever seen one yourself?" Sugar asked.

"Uh ... no. And I don't ever want to," Pperfume said.

"On your way back later today, you're invited to come to our house and meet Mrs. Fflop. She makes the best s'mores for miles and kilometers around!" Mr. Fflop said.

The kiddos felt more and more comfortable with the Fflops, for they found them to be very nice people – and the kiddos do like s'mores. "If our trip works out like we hope it will, we may have time to visit your house on the way back through. But we better get going – time's a-wanderin' on!" Taffy said.

The kiddos didn't stop for anything as they continued their journey for chocolate. They rode rabbit fast until they reached the end of the trail at Rusty Canyon. They parked their bikes quickly and headed into the ravine with their empty bag-packs, fire building stuff, and Topp's chocolate melting rod.

They didn't see any smoke in the canyon, so they assumed that their friends Cricket and Buggy from Bugg Town weren't there this time. But they were wrong. The kiddos came around a jagged rock crag and saw Cricket and Buggy looking intently at an object they were holding.

So as not to startle the two friends, the kiddos rattled nearby bushes to catch their attention.

"Hello again!" shouted Cricket. "Back for more chocolate?"

"Yessiree! Can anyone have too much chocolate?" Walnut said.

"What do you guys have there?" Violet asked. "It looks sort of like a sandwich."

"It is," Buggy explained. "They're called zooom sandwiches. They are a kind of plant that looks and tastes like a sandwich."

"What do you do with them?" Sugar asked.

"We eat them. They're full of special nutritional vitamins and other healthy stuff. They make us zoomy, healthy, and strong!" Buggy remarked. "You wanna try one?"

"They make you strong, you say?" Topp said. "We have strong beans for that where we come from."

"I've heard of them," Buggy said. "The word is that they taste awful!"

"You got that right!" gagged Sugar. "Yes, yucky ... but they *do* give us special nutrition!"

"We collected plenty of zoooms – you want to take a bite?" Cricket asked.

All the kiddos said, "*Yes.*"

"They taste like a peanut butter and jelly sandwich. Delicious!" Taffy said.

While the kiddos munched on the zoooms, Balooon asked, "Where and how do you find them?"

"They hide in the shadows of the big rock cubes that are jumbled around all over the south side of the Giant Step Mountains," Cricket said, pointing to nearby block-like hills at the base of the large mountain. "You will find plenty of them ... if they like you."

"How will you know if they like you? Violet asked out of curiosity.

"Because if you find one, they must like you."

"Uh ... okay," Walnut said, his head spinning a bit.

"So, where did you get that firewood the other day?" Topp asked. "We need firewood before climbing up to get chocolate."

"In the same place the zoooms live – at the base of the Giant Steps," Buggy explained.

"Is that far away?" Taffy asked.

"No, it's just over there. But watch out for the biting chiperoos. Don't let one bite you, not even a little nip, because it will like your flavor so much it will follow you around everywhere you go and take another bite now and then!" Buggy said.

"Yikes!" Sugar blurted out.

"If you need firewood, we have quite a bit," Cricket said. "There's a bundle of it hidden around that corner under a fallen tree. It was left over from a couple of days ago. You're welcome to it. Some other time, you can replace it."

"That's super!" Taffy said. "We gotta get going soon, we have chocolate to harvest!"

The kiddos said goodbye to Buggy and Cricket and then hiked to the fallen tree and grabbed the bundle of firewood.

They raced through the canyon and ran up the hills like they were flat. When the kiddos reached the top of the Chocolate Hills, they were hoping to find a vein of pure chocolate big enough to make a million KIDDO BARS.

Chapter 53

THERE IS NEVER ENOUGH CHOCOLATE

❧❧

Searching the Chocolate Hills, the kiddos found an area where part of a bluff had broken off recently. That gave them a good fresh place to start their dig. Topp unloaded the firewood, the wooden kindling sticks, and the dry fire-starting moss.

He didn't want to build a fire right on top of chocolate (which would melt), so he put a little of it in his mouth and then spit it out. "Yuck!" he shouted. "That certainly isn't chocolate so this is a good place to build the fire." He made a ring of small rocks to put the fire in.

Violet took over the fire making process. She set up sticks in a teepee shape over carefully placed kindling. Beneath the kindling was the fire-starting moss. The kiddos gathered around to watch Violet jingle her ankle bells and call on her fairies to help ignite the fire with a wafer of flint.

Violet chipped and chopped her pocketknife repeatedly against the flint and created bright sparkles. One hot spark settled on a bit of moss, and a tiny glow appeared. She gently blew on the little glowing ember, and it grew. Just then, a little flame burst forth and started the kindling on fire which then caused the bigger wood to burn.

"Hooray!" shouted the kiddos. "Violet made a fire!"

She put on bigger wood until there were flames as high as their tummies.

"We gotta let it burn for a while," Topp said wisely. "We need a bed of hot coals to heat the hot-rod on." While the fire was burning with gusto, the kiddos left the fire pit and climbed up onto a high mound.

"Look at that!" Taffy said excitedly, pointing off in the distance. "There's the Ice Bug Sea! I can see ice bergs and even Bugg Town, where Cricket and Buggy live."

"Wow, look over there!" shouted Violet, pointing in another direction. "It's the Tot Tot Hills and the Jolly Jungle beyond."

"And look over there!" Walnut said, looking upward and outward. "The Giant Step Mountains are right there, and boy, are they wide and tall! No wonder the giants liked them so much."

"Look way off there! It's the Pink Desert and Candy Mountain in the far distance! We'll see you soon, Candy Mountain!" Sugar said excitedly.

All the kiddos laughed at Sugar's comment and danced around, kicking up chocolatey dust and singing, "Candy Mountain, Candy Mountain!"

Topp heated his hot-rod on the fire coals until it glowed red and then declared, "It's hot enough. I'm gonna try it out." He gripped the wooden protective handle so he wouldn't get burned. He walked over to a vein in the newly exposed rock face and poked it against what he thought was chocolate, but it didn't do a thing. "It didn't melt – darn, just dirt!"

He poked a couple of more places, and then finally his hot steel rod started penetrating the hill. "Chocolate!" Topp cried out, and the others came a-runnin'.

"That's a nice wide vein of chocolate," he said. "Let's dig it out."

The kiddos dug at the newly discovered mass of chocolate and pulled out large chunks of the best and most grit-free pieces they had ever tasted. Yum!

So, they kept poking the rod and continued digging out pure chocolate until they had a full load in each of their bag-packs. The kiddos descended the mountain carefully, but the weight of the chocolate on their shoulders forced them down the hill at a fast pace.

They were still feeling strong from the zoooms, so they reached the bottom of Rusty Canyon in no time, crossed through it, and hiked up the other side.

They were still giddy and yelling, "Yippee yay," as they crested the top of the canyon where their three-wheeled bicycles were parked.

"OUR BIKES ARE GONE!!!" Balooon shouted, so loudly it echoed throughout the canyon. Their joy quickly faded away when the kiddos realized that all six of their bikes were no longer where they had left them. They looked around in all directions, but they were nowhere.

"What are we going to do now?" Sugar cried. "How are we going to get home?"

"We're going to have to walk back!" Topp said. "That's about all we *can* do."

Burdened with the heavy weight in their bags, they started slogging up the Rat Town Trail toward The Gap. The zoooms had nearly worn off by now, so the going was slow.

Dragging their tired feet on the dusty trail, they came around a bend and saw something coming toward them that they couldn't recognize at first.

Walnut said, "I hope it isn't another stupid what-er! I've seen enough of those critters for a lifetime!"

"Look! There are two kids on bikes riding toward us!" Taffy said. "Hey, it's Buggy and Cricket, and they're riding our bikes!"

"Hi, Ooga kids, we found your bikes!" Cricket said when she skidded to a stop.

"The Rachett brothers took them," Buggy shouted as he coasted up. "We saw them riding away on your bikes, so we ran after them and stopped them and then chased them away."

"How did you ever catch them?" Violet asked. "They were on bikes, and you were only on foot!"

Cricket laughed and said, "Zoooms!"

All eight of the children laughed and laughed, until they couldn't laugh any longer.

"Thank you so much!" Taffy said gratefully. "We owe you big time!"

"We'll pay you back with chocolate – we have a ton of it!" Violet said. The kiddos pulled out big chunks of pure chocolate and gave it to their heroes.

"You'll find the other bikes down the road, about ten stones-throws from here, behind a purple bush." Cricket informed them. "Those six rascally Rachett brothers from Bergville are harmless, but they play too many pranks. I think they drink too much water from the Ice Bug Sea. That water can make a brain go wacky!"

"Thanks for the chocolate," Buggy said. "Hey, we found a bunch of rare Rusty Canyon mushrooms. Would you like to take a bunch home and try them? They're hard to find but ten times better than candy!"

The kiddos thanked Cricket and Buggy for the mushrooms, then their two new friends waved goodbye and headed home to Bugg Town with their pockets full of pure chocolate.

The kiddos found the other bikes easily enough. They jumped on and then rode quickly to The Gap.

The kids found Pperfume and Ddandy at the toll booth and told them the story about the stolen bikes. "I've heard about those Rachett brothers," Pperfume said. "They've never come around Roooganville, at least not that we know of. I think they're afraid of rats, and that's a good thing. They don't know it, but there are no rats here, only hhamsters."

The suns were getting a bit low in the sky at this point, so the kiddos thanked the Fflop kids and said their goodbyes. Before they took off, Topp pulled out a piece of zooom from his pocket and gave it to Walnut to eat. Then they began the long ride home.

Off they went through Spooky Hollow and onward to the Silly Creek Trail with Walnut in the lead. Walnut rode so fast, the others could hardly see him ahead of them.

"Boy, those zoooms really are healthy!" Balooon said as he watched Walnut disappear into a speck in the distance. "On our next trip to the hills, we should bring back a bunch of zoooms and Rusty Canyon mushrooms, too – if we like them."

"Great idea!" Sugar said. "No more strong beans for me!"

That evening in the clubhouse, Violet cooked up the mushrooms for dinner, and boy, they were great.

"I don't know if they're better than candy — but they are delicious. I'd eat them for dinner every night if I could," Sugar said. And the others agreed.

While Violet melted a large pot of chocolate, the others carefully laid out the molds they had carved out of wood. They poured the liquid chocolate into the molds to make chocolate bars. You've heard of those before, haven't you?

They became a candy factory that night, pouring batch after batch of chocolate into the molds they had made. When the liquid chocolate cooled off, they eased it out and placed the fresh bars on the table. What was special was that they had carved the words KIDDO BAR in each of the molds, so when they were right side up, the name could be seen.

The kiddos made about two hundred bars that night. They wrapped them up in wrappers and stacked them up — ten in a stack and twenty stacks in all. They set aside a small pile of imperfect bars which they didn't bother to wrap. The kiddos called them Our Bars, and they tasted just as good as the wrapped ones.

The kiddos decided to donate one hundred KIDDO BARS to the Oogan Scouts, an organization of boys and girls dedicated to doing good deeds around the Valley of Ooga Ooga. The scouts will sell them to raise brittles$ to support the health and well-being of all children, near and far. Once again, the exploits of the kiddos were the talk of the town.

The kiddos will sell fifty bars at Poppy Park. The brittles$ they earn will be used for their clubhouse and anything they will need for future adventures, such as rope; tools for farming, hiking, and fishing; and healthy food for their tummies.

They deserved to be rewarded for their cleverness, don't you think?

Chapter 54

BOBBY'S BEST GIFT EVER

෨෧

Bobby's cat, Fluffers, woke him up early in the morning by jumping on his belly and purring loudly. Bobby didn't mind, she was just being a cat. Then Fluffers started kneading her paws on Bobby's chest. It felt good at first, and then one of her claws penetrated his pajamas. "Ouch!" Bobby cried out. "Fluffers, go be a cat somewhere else – scoot!" Then he shoved her gently off the bed.

She looked up at him as though to say, "What's your problem?" Then she waltzed away with her tail high in the air, with the white tip swishing back and forth.

Why in the world would anyone want a cat that doesn't act like a cat? We wouldn't want them to act like gophers, frogs, or cows, would we? *Cats need to be cats*, I'm sure that's what Fluffers thinks.

Bobby didn't mind being awakened this morning. He was fully confident that his epic dream will continue the next time he goes to sleep. He also needed to get up early to help his mom get the house and yard ready for his father's return that evening.

After a delightful breakfast of mushrooms, cheese, and eggs, he was ready to go outside and clean up the yard.

"Did I tell you that Aunt Ferny is coming this morning to help me cook and get the house all cleaned up? She wants to help us get ready and be here to welcome your dad home," said his mom.

"That sounds great," Bobby said. "I'm sure Dad will be surprised and very glad to see her. How about Uncle Roy, is he coming too?"

"No, but we're going to visit him at his new house tomorrow. Your dad will be happy to see him as well. Dad told the searchers who found him that he was bringing home a special medicine from the jungle to help Roy with his hiccup problem."

"That sounds interesting," Bobby said. "It will be fun to see Uncle Roy and his house by the sea. I love being seaside."

Bobby thanked his mom for breakfast and then rushed out the back door. He hopped down the steps into the yard and started raking the leaves that were piling up on the grass. He also pulled the weeds that were growing where they didn't belong, which was everywhere.

Then he heard his mother's voice in the distance. "Hi, Ferny dear! I'm so glad you could come!"

To be polite, Bobby trotted over and greeted Aunt Ferny with a brief hug. Young boys aren't too keen on hugging their aunts, but he did it anyway. "Hi, Auntie, it's nice to see you," Bobby said politely. They shared a few pleasantries, and then he left the ladies and hurried outside to do more cleanup.

A few minutes later, his mother poked her head out the window and shouted, "Bobby, in about a half hour, please come in to have lunch with us. Oh, and Aunt Ferny brought a special treat for you."

"Okay," he answered reluctantly. Bobby likes Aunt Ferny but when she and his mom get together, they talk up a constant word storm! He would have rather stayed outside, chasing butterflies, looking for lizards, and even weeding, but the *treat* she mentioned was intriguing.

When the time came, Bobby jogged to the house and washed up as was expected (but not because he wanted to). A little dirt is just fine with him but not so fine with his mom.

After lunch, the ladies started gabbing, so Bobby excused himself from the table, forgetting about the treat he was promised.

"Hold on, Bobby! I brought you something," Aunt Ferny said. "Here are some special chocolate bars that I made in my candy factory! I know you *love* chocolate!"

Bobby was stunned! He stood frozen to the spot, not saying a word, as he remembered that the dream-kids made chocolate bars. Eventually, he said, "Wow! Thank you, Aunt Ferny!"

"For a second there, I wondered if you still liked chocolate," Ferny said smiling.

"Oh, I still do! I was just thinking about a dream I had last night. It was about kids who found a bunch of chocolate and made candy bars out of it – that's all," Bobby said. "Just a strange coincidence, I guess."

"Ferny makes all kinds of chocolate candies. The big chocolate bar is called the FERNY BAR," said his mom.

"That's wonderful, Auntie! You must like chocolate as much as I do!" Bobby said with a laugh.

The ladies joined in and had a laugh too. There was much joy in the house with the imminent return of Rufus in just a few hours.

"Here Bobby, I made four peanut butter and jelly sandwiches for you. I'm sure you're working hard out there," said his mom.

Bobby thanked her politely and went back outside.

He was expecting Cookie to come over with things she made to fancy up the new clubhouse. She said she would also bring flowers to plant in the new greenhouse.

Cookie had sewn curtains for the windows in the clubhouse. And her mother had given her some old pillows, so Cookie recovered them with pretty fabrics to brighten things up.

"Hi, Cookie. What's with the wheelbarrow?" Bobby asked.

"I couldn't carry all this stuff here without it! I have eight pillows, one for each of us and six for our friends," she said. "Since you made eight stools to go around the table, these cushy pillows will make them more comfortable."

Bobby and Cookie took a break, sat at the table on the new comfy seats, and chatted for a while. Bobby shared a FERNY BAR with her while he told her about the dream-kids digging chocolate out of a mountain. "They made a couple of hundred delicious chocolate bars with it," he said.

Cookie has become more interested in the stories about Bobby's dreams. She wanted to hear all the details, and Bobby enjoyed telling them. They both sensed that something special was going on every time Bobby fell asleep.

"Well, I gotta go," Cookie said. "I'll come by in a couple of days with more plants for the greenhouse and flowers to grow outside the door. I'm painting a picture of the big purple mountain west of town that I'd like to hang in the clubhouse, if that's okay."

"Sure, sounds great. It's *our* clubhouse! Thanks for all your wonderful touches," Bobby said with a joyful heart.

"I'm sure you'll have an especially great time with your dad. Have fun on the trip to see your Uncle Roy tomorrow," she said and scooted away.

Bobby went inside and noticed that his auntie and mom were still talking a blue streak. So, to pass the time until his dad arrived, he went to his room to glue more toothpicks on his model roller coaster.

Rufus arrived just before dark. When Bobby heard the front door open, he ran straight there. The hugs and kisses were plentiful, and the gratitude was abundant! Having Ferny there to welcome him home was an extra special surprise for Rufus.

Mari served refreshments as Rufus told stories about his disappearance. "In a heavy rain, I got separated from the other fellows in a dense part of the jungle. After hours of searching for them, I realized that I was lost. Not only was I alone, but I also couldn't tell which way was what. I had no compass on me. It was like putting a blindfold on, spinning around in circles a dozen times in the middle of a dense jungle, and then trying to figure out which way is home. I was healthy and feeling good, but I had no idea which way to go. The canopy of the jungle was so thick I could hardly tell if it was day or night, and I had no idea in what direction the sun came up, either."

Rufus was sitting in the chair that had been waiting for his return, and the family was listening intently to the stories he told.

"After about a week of chopping through the incredibly dense foliage with a machete, I came upon a small village in the jungle. That's where I stayed for months. I had no way of knowing which way to go and neither did the villagers. Eventually, a man from another jungle tribe offered to show me how to get back to what he called the *dry land*, where our town is."

"Fascinating," Bobby said.

"There are more stories to tell, but I'm a bit worn out. I ought to go to bed soon, so we can get a fresh start in the morning. I'm glad Bettykins is coming with us tomorrow. Our little family will be together for the first time in a long time, and our reunion will be complete."

Before departing, Ferny asked Rufus to please say "hello" to Roy from her. And she reminded Rufus that she hopes he will come and visit her someday soon.

Bobby knew the moment had come for him to disappear and leave Mom and Dad by themselves. He gave his dad a long firm hug, said goodnight, and went joyfully off to bed.

Someday soon, he'll tell his dad about his intriguing dreams, but now it's time to get back to the dream-kids and the wonderful land they live in. With his tummy full of chocolate and his heart full of love of family, he fell asleep, very content indeed.

Chapter 55

WHAT'S NEXT?

࿇

The kiddos spent the morning sitting around the hexagon table, eating mushrooms and chocolate, and discussing their next adventure. Some expressed their desire to go back to get more chocolate and mushrooms, but they decided they had enough to last for a week. They weren't getting tired of the sweet treats ... but almost.

They also discussed going to find a bunch of good-tasting zoooms to replace the strong beans, but they'll get those the next time they go to get more chocolate.

I'll bet the next time they eat yucky strong beans they'll wish they had gone right back to get a stash of zoooms.

This morning, something was different. For some odd reason, the kiddos started talking rapidly while sitting around the table. They talked and talked, like little motormouths, just blabbing and blabbing. They had talked a lot around the table before but not like this – they were talking a kilometer-a-minute and hardly taking a breath.

"Wow, we're talking so much and so fast!" Sugar remarked. "There must be something in the mushrooms or chocolate or something that's making us yak so fast."

"That's what I was thinking!" Topp said. "Maybe we're not eating *choc-o-late*, maybe we're eating *talk-a-lot*!

With that joke, the kiddos could be heard laughing in the clubhouse all the way to the Ooga River ten stones-throws away! Life was great for the friends as summer moved along.

In the discussions of what adventure to do next, Candy Mountain was high on the list. The weather was beginning to get cooler but according to Violet, it was not yet chilly enough for that trip. She's the one who knows about Candy Mountain and how sticky it can be. With all the intense summer heat this year, it will take a while for the mountain of candy to cool.

Some say that Candy Mountain used to be ten times taller, but it melted down to its present size. Some say that the giants ate the entire top of it off years ago! Maybe that's why the giants are no longer around. Maybe they only ate candy and no veggies, so they got sick and died.

Perhaps the lesson is: Eat your veggies or you might go extinct!

Topp then suggested, "I think we should do the raft trip on the river next because it's still warm, and swimming in the river would be cool."

"I agree," Taffy said. "We could ... "

"The doorbell is ringing!" Walnut interrupted. "Who's gonna get the door?"

"We don't have a doorbell, but I'll go see what this is about," Taffy said.

She opened the door with suspicion and jumped back a full step when she saw it.

"Uhhhh ... can I help you?" Taffy asked meekly as she looked at the hovering jellyfish-like creature in front of her.

"I hope so," it said. "Have you seen any gobble-D-goops around here?"

"What are gobble-D-goops?" she asked.

"I am a gobble-D-goop," the goop said.

"I have seen *one* – I see you," Taffy said. "Hey, don't you belong in the water?"

"Water is good, air is good, and outer space is good. Thank you for asking," the goop said.

Taffy was fascinated by this floating flowy critter, so she called the others over to look at something most weird. The creature that looked like a jellyfish was colorful, and its tendrils shimmered handsomely as they dangled and swayed in the breeze.

The kiddos all stood there with expressions on their faces like they were looking at the strangest thing they had ever seen.

"I shall deduce that you have not seen another gobble-D-goop this day, so I shall be on my way," the well-spoken goop said. It lifted off and floated to the left, then back to the right, making its tentacles flow from side to side. It rose with flits and flaps like a butterfly, then flew in the direction of Silly Creek.

"That's a what-er if ever there was such a thing!" Sugar said. "Kinda creepy – but *polite* at the same time!"

No one disagreed with her as she reached to lock the door. They returned to the table to plan for the raft trip on the Ooga River.

"I've been talking to my dad about rafts," Topp said. "He told me everything we need to know to build one. The raft my dad suggested would be made of logs that float high on the water, with a deck or platform on top of that, and a small shack on top of that. I drew pictures of it – wanna see?"

The kiddos gathered around the table eagerly and looked down at the amazing plans Topp had drawn based on his dad's ideas. There were sketches of the raft from all angles and a list of the items needed to build it. The kiddos had never built a raft before, so it was swell that Topp's dad and now Topp knew the best way to do it.

"The first thing we need are twelve bubblewood tree trunks about four meters long," Topp said. "I know where there is a grove of bubblewood trees right on the edge of the Ooga River. They're about twenty stones-throws up from Bunny Beach. We can cut 'em down and float 'em down to where we'll build the raft on the beach."

"What are bubblewood trees?" Violet asked Topp.

"Oh, you know, *pop pop* trees!"

"I know what those are!" Walnut said. "They have those leaves that are like bubbles that you can clap your hands on to make a *pop* sound!"

All the kiddos know exactly what pop pop trees are because they have popped *millions* of the leaves! The fact is that the leaves on the trees will never get near the ground because if kids can reach them, they'll certainly get popped!

"My dad said they are really called bubblewood trees or sometimes raftwood trees," Topp explained. "He said there are thousands of big bubbles inside the trunks. There's more air than wood inside. They float on the water because of all the air bubbles."

"From the list it looks like we'll need a lot of fire spider rope and twine, too," Taffy said. "We don't have many brittles$, but I think we have enough to buy the supplies for this adventure."

Now the kiddos knew how to *build* a raft, but they realized that they didn't know *how* to raft down a river, especially a big river like the Ooga.

"I bet Captain Float knows something about rafting on the river," Taffy said. "Remember, he used to run a boat on the Ooga River."

"Let's go find him. We should be well prepared for this daring adventure," Walnut said. "We certainly don't want any scary mishaps – we've had enough of those already."

Sugar agreed, "Good plan ... let's go!"

The kiddos jumped up, raced out the door, and hopped on their three-wheelers to go find Captain Float.

Chapter 56

OLD SHIPWRECKS ON THE BEACH

᷾ᗛ

On the ride to Captain Float's house, the kiddos crossed paths with Timmy Haywire and his sisters, Tulip and Toesie. The kids know the Haywires from school.

They decided to hang out together for a while and chat about the summer fun they've been having. The kiddos told the Haywires about the raft they're going to build and about the plan to go down the Ooga River in a couple of days.

"We built our own raft, too, and rode down the river last year," Tulip said. "We went from the Mountain Bridge to the Town of Trombone. It took two whole days. We swam, fished, and dove off the raft all the way down. We spent one night camping on a sandbar on the bank of the river and sang songs by a campfire. It was quite a thrilling adventure."

"It was safe and easy," Toesie said. "But, whatever you do, don't dangle your feet in the water off the raft!"

"Why? What will happen?" Sugar asked.

"The gobble-D-goops might nibble on your toes, or they may even bite one off!" Timmy warned.

"Yow! Do you know what a gobble-D-goop looks like? Did you see one?" Balooon asked.

"It looks like any ol' goop, I suppose – although we never actually saw one," Toesie said.

"We …," Violet started to say that they had met one but didn't finish her sentence. She thought they'd better keep it a secret. Who would believe that they saw one anyway, especially a *flying* gobble-D-goop?

"Thanks for the info," Topp said. "It sounds great – all except the gobble-D-goop part."

"Rafting is a wonderful thing to do," said Tulip. "There's many interesting things along the way, and there's lots of time to pull over and play on the bank."

The kiddos thanked the Haywires and continued on their way to find Captain Float.

While they were riding through the park, they spotted him on a bench tossing breadcrumbs to the birds. When Captain Float saw them ride up, he had a welcoming smile for them. "What are you pip-squeaks up to now?" he asked. "Oh, and don't mind the word pip-squeak. I call people younger'n me pip-squeaks, and that's just about everyone."

"What does it mean?" Walnut asked.

"I knows not," Captain Float said. "I just calls it out."

"We came to see if you could help us plan a raft trip on the Ooga River," Taffy said.

"Oh yes, the River, the mighty River! Sure, what do ya wanna know?" Float's eyes sparkled when he started talking about the river. "I have rafted the Ooga River many-a-time, so gather around, pip-squeaks, and I'll tell you some *dos* and some *don'ts* about river cruisin'."

The kiddos sat in a semi-circle around the wonderful old man and opened their ears.

He warned the kids about snags or shallow things in the water that can catch or jolt the raft as it flows along. Snags can be fallen trees or big boulders hidden just below the water's surface. He mentioned that the spring runoff is ending, and the water level drops this time of year. He explained that the hidden objects in the river can break the raft into pieces, or if the raft gets stuck, it could end up stranded for a week or more.

He described the monster storms called *monstros* that can drop enormous amounts of rain very quickly over the Yeller Cliffs. He said raging waters would flow down from the canyons and flood the Ooga River in an instant. He warned that monstros storms can quickly turn the gentle river into a dangerous, frothy torrent.

Whoa! they all thought.

He also mentioned that they must avoid getting snagged anywhere near the Village of Ghosts, but he wouldn't say why. When they asked, he replied, "You don't want to know ..."

"*Whoa!*" they all said.

The Captain also told the kiddos about lost silver coins$, and *that* really grabbed their attention. Old man Float said, "Years ago, Mr. Greede from Old Town shipped his silver coins$ to the Island of Wow by boat. Over the years, there had been several shipwrecks in the Fantasmo Sea. I was *on* one those doomed ships but was rescued after four days at sea holding onto a piece of wood."

Whoa! the kiddos thought.

"Some boats floundered and broke up in the high seas," the Captain said. "Several of the damaged ships were blown to shore and wrecked on Fantasmo Beach, the beach where the Ooga River flows into the Fantasmo Sea. Many a silver coin$ is hiding there in the sand, waiting to be found by anyone who goes there and digs."

"Wow!" the kiddos said.

"That's about it," Float said. "Nothing to it, really. You don't need no motor no how."

"Captain Float," Walnut said, "you never mentioned the dangerous gobble-D-goops that bite toes off."

"Oh goodness me, is that old phony story about the gobble-D-goops eating toes still going around? That's just a fable made up to scare kids. There is no such thing as a gobble-D-goop!"

"Aaaaaaaah ...," Topp stopped himself before he spoke. He figured they would tell Captain Float about their encounter with a gobble-D-goop some other day. And they certainly will not dangle their feet into the river from the raft – ever!!!

The kiddos thanked the kind old man for his info and headed back to the clubhouse. On the way, their heads were spinning with thoughts of silver treasure once again.

They sat at the table to discuss their next move. Topp began by saying, "I think we need to go past the Town of Trombone and go all the way to that beach and hunt for coins$. What do you guys think?"

"I agree, but how are we going to get back to Ooga Ooga once we get to Fantasmo Beach?" Taffy asked.

The others fully agreed to go hunt for the coins$, but they realized that this longer journey would require a different strategy than the short trip they had first imagined. Their original plan had been to have a nice leisurely float to the Town of Trombone and finish the voyage there. They had planned to tie down the raft at the dock and catch the last Floatbus back to the Village of Ooga Ooga that evening.

"The trip to Fantasmo Beach will take another day or two," Sugar said. "We gotta plan for all of that."

"We can't use the raft to get home because rafts can only float *down* rivers, not *up* them," Violet said wisely.

"I know what we can do," Balooon offered, "we can spend the first night at my parents' house in the Town of Trombone. Then early the next morning, you five continue the journey down the river to the beach and hunt for coins$. Later that afternoon, I'll fly *Miss Blimpy* there and pick you all up. We'll stay until sunset and then head home that night or even the next. Sound good?"

"You can fly that thing at night?" Violet asked.

"Yep-erooo! Granny Bubbles taught me all about it."

"I like that idea," Topp said. "We definitely *cannot* walk back. We would have to travel through the Spiky Mesa, where the dagger plants and sink holes are. And, if we were to make it past all those dangers, we would still have to pass through the Village of Ghosts – *on foot*!"

"Okay then, tomorrow we'll build the raft," Taffy said. "Then off we go for the silver coins$ that are just waitin' for us!"

"Sounds easy peasy and fun, fun, fun!" Walnut sang out.

Uh-oh ...! Sugar thought.

Chapter 57

BUILDING A BUBBLEWOOD RAFT

❧

At Bunny Beach, the cute pink and blue rabbits scurried off into the bushes as the six kiddos ran exuberantly onto the sand. The kids found that the broad sandbank along the Ooga River was the perfect location to assemble the raft. The river is wide at this point, and the currents are gentle.

As the kiddos walked to a level spot next to the river, Topp said, "This is the perfect spot to build on. We can roll her easily into the flow when she's done. We'll need twelve bubblewood logs for the base. Who wants to go upriver to the forest to chop them down with me? I know where the forest is, and I have the axe."

"I will," Sugar said. "I'm friends with all trees, you know!"

"Taffy and I'll go to the store to buy the rope we need," Balooon offered.

"Walnut and I will stay on Bunny Beach to pull the logs to shore when they come a floatin' down," Violet said.

Once in the Bubblewood Forest, Sugar searched around for the best trees to cut down. She chose fat, straight trees that were overly shading little trees underneath. "This will make the young bubblewood trees happy. When the big ones are gone, there'll be more sunlight reaching them, allowing them to grow up and be big themselves," she said.

Topp quickly chopped down the trees that Sugar had marked for him. They were easy to fell because they were mostly made of air bubbles. Sugar followed behind as Topp whacked off the branches with a hatchet. Several of the branches would be used for a rudder, oars, poles, and other parts for the raft.

In no time, Sugar and Topp moved the pop pop tree trunks to the edge of the river and pushed them out into the current, one at a time. They waited about three minutes between launchings, so Violet and Walnut would have time to grab and beach them before the next one came down.

Balooon and Taffy rolled up to the Super Stuff Hardware store at about the same time the first log hit the water. It didn't take long for them to find the items they needed but when they went to the counter, they realized that they didn't have enough brittles$ to pay for everything. They offered five KIDDO BARS to the clerk to make up the difference. Fortunately, Bobbette Bob, the store owner, was the clerk that day, and she was quite satisfied with the barter of chocolate bars for the rest of the payment. After all, her four children can each have one, and she'll keep the extra one for herself. She smiled broadly, took a bite of the chocolate, and said, "*Yum*eee."

The kiddos thanked her and went swiftly on their way. With the rope and twine slung over their shoulders, they raced their bikes down the trail to meet the others at Bunny Beach. When Balooon and Taffy rode up with the supplies, Violet and Walnut were pulling the last log out of the river.

"We have the logs and the rope, so as soon as Topp and Sugar get here, we'll start putting 'er together," Violet said.

Once Topp got the project started, the kiddos' frenetic movements at the construction site were like a beehive whacked with a stick. Using his building powers, Topp directed the kids to lace the logs together into one amazing base for the raft.

The bunnies were very amused by all the activity and left the bushes to watch more closely.

There wasn't room for everybody to tie the logs together, so Taffy stood watching nearby. She wandered over to a pool and waded in to cool off. She looked down, picked something up and shouted, "I found a dia-mon, a *big* dia-mon! It's the first one I've ever found. Yahoo!"

"You go, Taffy!" Walnut yelled. "It's our lucky day!"

"Keep looking, Taf, maybe you can find more," Sugar said. "We can use more brittles$, that's for sure!"

The kiddos worked on the raft for hours. They lashed together the main logs to form the bottom float. Then they went up the river's edge a short distance and cut dozens of bambooboo reeds to use for the deck. They all joined in the task of hauling reeds to the construction site. The bambooboo pieces were laid across the bubblewood logs and then lashed on securely to make a surface they could easily walk on.

With the remaining branches and reeds, they built a little shack in the center of the raft. The tiny room is for storing all their belongings and for keeping themselves safe from falling off the raft, in case the river gets rough. If the sun gets too hot, the kiddos can go inside for shade as well.

The raft was completed and ready to push out into the river current. They were anxious to get going, but it was too late in the day to start the journey. They had *not* taken a break all day. They were very tired gals and guys, indeed.

Looking at the finished raft, Topp shouted with delight, "What a great day!" He then let his body go limp, fell straight backward, and flopped harmlessly onto the soft sand. His face glowed with satisfaction.

The other kiddos collapsed backward onto the sand just like Topp did, gazed up at the blue sky, and daydreamed about tomorrow's daring river adventure.

Chapter 58

RAFTING DOWN THE MIGHTY OOGA RIVER

❧❧

The kiddos arrived at Bunny Beach early the next morning. They brought stuff they thought they'd need on the raft. They brought baskets of food and chocolate, of course. Sugar brought her emergency kit. She always carries that, and she had Ragamuffin too. Smokey stayed back at the clubhouse because she would rather not be on water. After all, she can't swim as well as a rock.

Topp brought a set of tools of all sorts, and Walnut showed up with a strange gray bag with something inside.

"What's in the bag, Walnut?" Sugar asked.

"Are you sure you want to know?" he asked in an odd way.

"Yes! What's in the bag, Walnut?!" Sugar demanded an answer this time.

Walnut reached into the bag and pulled out eighteen light-wands. "I'm bringing these on the raft trip in case something goes wrong, like ending up in the dark somewhere."

"Oh my!" Sugar squeaked. She was afraid of the dark, and a scary thought came into her head. *What if we get snagged going through the Village of Ghosts and get stuck there at night!*

"Don't worry," Walnut said. "These are for the Fantasmo Beach treasure hunt for the coins$. We may find so many silver coins$, we might decide to stay another night to find more."

"Oh, that's a relief!" Sugar said.

Balooon ran off into the bushes and brought back a long bambooboo pole. Then he securely attached a square cloth that read *KIDDO PRINCESS* to the top of it. He had given the raft a flag and a name.

"Why did you name it *Princess*, a girl's name?" asked Violet with a cheeky grin.

"Well, boats and such have girl names, I've heard," he explained. "And I really *like* girls – heck, they are *all* princesses to me!"

"Oh, how sweet!" the girls said, smiling and blushing a little.

"Hey, let's get going!" shouted Topp in a bossy tone. "The suns will start going down if we keep yapping like this!"

"Aye aye, captain!" someone chirped.

With a big heave-ho, the kiddos slid the large raft into a deep eddy at the edge of the river. One by one, they climbed onto *Princess*. Topp pushed her out gently into the river current and then jumped aboard himself.

"What a great raft!" Taffy said. "Your dad knows his stuff."

The raft did have notable features. There was a rudder on the rear or stern, to steer the raft. It also had oars on each side and brackets or oak locks to hold each oar. There were two, very important, long poles called guiding poles. These were to be managed by two kids, one on each side of the raft. They will be essential to keep the raft in the strongest and deepest currents, by pushing off the river bottom when needed. The strong heavy rudder and the steering poles will be used to keep the raft from hitting the riverbanks or getting snagged on bad stuff just under the water.

The raft floated nicely out in the deep river current. It was high out of the water and very stable. The kiddos felt safe wandering about on the deck, and they enjoyed looking at the interesting things on the banks of the river as they passed by.

"Hey, there's the flower field!" Walnut yelled out as he pointed ashore.

"And I see fan flowers!" Taffy said with delight.

"Put *Princess* ashore, I want to pick fan flowers – for good luck!" Sugar cried out.

"Okay, I'll try!" Topp said. "I'll use a steering pole to beach the raft at the flower field."

Topp jumped off and secured *Princess* to a large tree stump. Sugar hopped off and hunted for six fan flowers. She came aboard with one fan flower in each of the six distinct colors of the rainbow. Ragamuffin, who had jumped off with Sugar, barely made it back onboard before the raft was pushed back into the swiftly flowing river.

Sugar reminded the others that fan flowers will bring good luck the next day if placed under their pillows that night. They just *might* need extra good luck on this challenging, overnight river voyage to the Fantasmo Sea.

Princess was cruising along with ease when Violet shouted, "Look, it's the bridge ahead!"

Near the bridge, there's a large sandy beach, so they pulled over and grounded the raft on the bank effortlessly. They decided to have a stone skipping contest to see who could get the most skips. All eyes were on Walnut to see if he could skip it a million times – like he'd done before.

They decided to do only one throw each and then get going again. Five kiddos threw their stones, and some of them did well. When it came to Walnut's turn, he hoped to at least have a respectable throw. He picked up a stone, rubbed it as if to warm it up, whistled loudly, looked up at the sky to possibly summon a little luck (or pow pow), and then he let it go.

Once again, the other kiddos were speechless as the stone skimmed across the water as if it had no desire to ever dive in. It finally disappeared as it approached the other shore of the river.

Walnut was happy, not because he won the contest but because he knew his pow pow was still intact, and that it would be there again if he needed it.

They all jumped onto the raft, pushed off into the river, and floated toward the bridge. There were three children waving at them from the bridge railing. It was Timmy, Toesie, and Tulip Haywire. "Hi there, friends!" the Haywires shouted. "Have a great voyage on that amazing raft!"

The kiddos responded with a lot of *hellos, see yas, toodle-oos, and yahoos* as they began going under the bridge. Just then, there was a loud *CRACK!* and then a *WHACK*!

The tall flagpole hit the bridge! It broke loose and crashed violently down on the deck. When it fell, it looked as though the heavy pole was going to hit Violet smack dab on her head but at the last second, it fell to the side of her.

If you were to ask Violet, I bet she would tell you that her fairies and angels kept her safe. I, for one, would believe her.

After they were clear of the bridge, Walnut reattached the flagpole in a way that it could be lowered while going under bridges and low tree branches. They'd had good luck on their voyage so far – *Princess* still had her flag, and Violet didn't get whacked on the head!

The raft flowed considerably faster after passing under the bridge. With Sugar at the rudder, and Balooon and Taffy working the steering poles, the raft moved swiftly under control. Working as a team, they kept the raft clear of the protruding rocks and stumps that showed up often and unexpectedly. Then ...

THUD! CRUNCH!

The raft jolted violently and sent the kiddos crashing hard onto the deck. They hung on to whatever they could to keep from falling overboard. Once the raft settled down and became stable, the kiddos stood up and looked behind to see what they had hit.

"Wow, everyone okay?" Topp shouted. "I don't see anything. It must have been something invisible under the water."

"Looks like we better be on alert all the time on this journey," Taffy said. "We got jolted by something we couldn't even see."

Walnut said, "Maybe it was a gobble-D-goop ... "

The day was gloriously warm, and the water was as well. When the kiddos reached The Big Hole, a favorite swimming spot, they stopped and dove off the raft and went swimming.

If there is anything more fun to do than that in the summer, I can't think of what that could be. What they did *not* do was dangle their feet in the water off the raft. Maybe there aren't any gobble-D-goops in the river, but they *did* meet one recently. Maybe that goop is looking for toes to eat!

On this stretch of the river, the raft bobbed along slowly at the perfect speed for fishing. Topp, Violet, and Walnut pulled out three fishing poles, baited the hooks, and dropped them in.

"I got one!" shouted Walnut in less than ten seconds.

He caught one fish and another ... and then a third. Topp and Violet, on the other hand, caught waterweeds, river moss, and ... nothing.

The fish Walnut caught were very tasty blubberfish. Instead of releasing the fish back into the water (because they had no way to cook them), they decided to dock in Happy Harbor and give them to the PetTunias.

They passed under three more bridges without incident and put into Happy Harbor in high spirits. After tying up to the pier, Balooon jumped off the raft and delivered the three fish Walnut had caught to his aunt, who had been waiting on the dock. "What a fine watercraft," Pet said admiringly.

"So, it's *Kiddo Princess*, is it?" said Tunia. "Lovely name. Pet is *my* princess, so maybe I'll call her Princess Pet!"

Pet smiled and blushed a little and gave her hubby a peck on the cheek.

"Well, we better be off," Balooon reminded the others. "We have a dinner date in the Town of Trombone tonight."

As they pushed off again into the flow of the river, Pet shouted from the dock, "Thanks for the blubberfish, they are the best. Be safe!"

It wasn't long before they looked up and saw they were cruising under the dilapidated walking bridge they had crossed on their hike to Silver Peak. "Wow!" Sugar said in amazement. "We actually crossed over that poor excuse for a bridge."

They stared up as they flowed under the old bridge and were glad that they weren't on it anymore. After all, the raft can't fall out of the sky like they might have done from the rickety old bridge. And it was still daylight, so they didn't have to worry about those freaky glowy-eyes.

The raft picked up speed as it entered the wide cut in the towering Yeller Cliffs. Walnut figured that Mr. and Mrs. Balooon could use fish, too, so he whistled quite loudly and began throwing his line in the water once again. In no time, he pulled in a couple of full-grown whopperfish, the best eating fish in the river. Neither Topp, Violet, nor any of the other kiddos bothered to fish ...

The kiddos arrived in the Town of Trombone without incident. They met up with the Balooons, who had a great dinner feast ready for them. They thanked the children for the two large fish and said they would invite friends over the next night for a special grilled whopperfish dinner.

The kiddos went to bed that night in *Blimpy*'s giant basket which was tied down in the center of town. As they settled into their beds, they were excited about what they would be doing the next day: floating through the Village of Ghosts and searching in the sand on Fantasmo Beach for lost silver coins$.

They each put their fan flowers under their pillows when they went to bed. They might need good luck tomorrow – *who knows* ...

Chapter 59
UH-OH! ... **OH NO!!!**

৵৵৶

The kiddos woke up early in the Town of Trombone the next morning. They were eager to get to that faraway sandy beach to hunt for lost coins$. They quickly left *Blimpy*'s basket where they had been sleeping and headed to the raft. They climbed on, took their places, and shoved off.

"Be careful, kids," Mr. Balooon warned as they floated away. "Make sure you keep going through the Village of Ghosts – don't get caught on any rocks or snags as you pass by!"

"Don't worry, we won't!" Sugar said rather hesitantly.

With Topp and Taffy on the steering poles, and Violet's steady hand on the tiller, the kiddos navigated this stretch of the Ooga River easily, and *Princess* wound through the Yeller Cliffs on its way to the Fantasmo Sea.

The raft quickly picked up speed and surged forward through a series of gentle rapids. Water splashed over the bubblewood logs onto the deck, and a few drops even made it into their shack.

When Sugar, Topp, and Taffy realized that their steering poles and rudder were not effective in the rapids, they headed inside. "Nobody warned us that there would be rapids!" Topp moaned as he firmly hung onto the swaying door frame.

In a short time, the rapids ended but by the time the three kiddos got back to their steering posts, it was too late. The raft had skidded directly over a large boulder, hidden just under the waterline!!!! They hit it with a violent jolt!!!

Fortunately, they were all unharmed. And miraculously, the raft stayed in one piece. But they were petrified that the raft had run aground near the river's edge. They looked up at the bluffs above and were mortified. They were stuck on a massive rock, smack dab in the middle of the Village of Ghosts!

"Oh no!" gasped Sugar. The others were full of fear as well.

Violet gently shook her ankle bells to call her fairies and angels in case they were needed. She also looked carefully at the cliffs above them and saw five houses up on top. "This is a village?" she questioned. "There are five houses! Can five houses be enough to be a village?"

No matter, the raft was truly stuck, and their various attempts to rock the raft side to side to set it free were fruitless. They stood there exhausted and out of ideas when Walnut whispered sternly, "Look! Ghosts are coming!"

Along the low rocky banks of the river, below the towering cliffs, two figures in long white robes were walking along the rocks. They appeared to be headed to a place where steppingstones led directly to the raft. The kiddos were frozen with fright – all except Violet, who knew her fairies and angels would protect them, even from ghosts!

"I think they are child ghosts!" Violet said, looking closely at the small childlike figures in white. The little ghosts approached the edge of the river and started to hop over stones toward *Princess*. With their hands covering their eyes, the other kiddos peeked between their fingers and dared to look at the monsters who were hopping on rocks on their way to get them.

"Hi there!" shouted one of the spooky ghosts as it approached.

"You kids, okay?" the other little monster asked.

"We're okay – sort of ...," Violet answered. "We are stuck on this boulder in the middle of the Village of Ghosts!"

"Don't worry!" said the ghost that looked like a little girl. "I'm Tammy Toast, and this is my brother, Teddy Toast. We can help you get off this boulder."

The kiddos were in a world of uncertainty with these ghost children so near. The ghost children looked and talked like ordinary kids, but they can't be – they're ghosts!

The ghost kids, Tammy and Teddy, stopped on a flat boulder close to the raft. "Oh, you kids think we're *ghosts*!" Tammy said. "We aren't ghosts, we're Toasts – Tammy and Teddy Toast! You are in the tiny Village of *Toasts*, not Ghosts."

The kiddos had the most quizzical looks on their faces as they absorbed what the spooky little kids were telling them. The kiddos were truly puzzled at what was going on. They felt dizzy and frightened and didn't want to be there anymore … but they were stuck!

"So, where are the ghosts?" Violet asked the ghosts, er … Toasts, bravely.

"There aren't any ghosts!" Tammy Toast replied. "There never *have* been any ghosts. Somebody made that up or couldn't say the name Toast or *something*."

"We are no more ghosts than you are!" Teddy Toast said, wanting to put the kiddos at ease.

Violet fully believed the young Toast children and invited them aboard the raft, to the dismay of the others. They relaxed a little when they heard the jingling of Violet's ankle bells and remembered her special powers with the fairies and such.

After boarding the raft and having small talk with Violet, Tammy and Teddy invited the kiddos to come to their house for lunch and meet more Toast people from their village.

Before they could answer, the loud rumbling of thunder rocked the sky. They looked up and saw ominous dark clouds swirling above them.

"We gotta go, Teddy!" Tammy shouted abruptly. "I think there's a monstro about to hit. We better scram to higher ground!"

"You kids better get in your little room there and hang on!" Teddy warned the kiddos. "When the monstro hits, you won't have any trouble getting unstuck off the boulder, I can tell you that for sure!"

The Toast kids took off quickly and jumped from rock to rock. When they reached the shore, they shouted back, "Stay safe and come see us sometime! It was nice to have met you!"

Tammy and Teddy were swift on their feet as they scampered up a small canyon to a high bluff overhanging the river gorge. The Toast kids knew that they were high enough – a safe distance from what they knew would soon be a raging river.

The kiddos took the advice of the Toast kids and tied down everything loose, including themselves, and crowded into the little shack just in case the monstro hit.

And did it ever! The sky turned darker than black. Lightning flashed and thunder rumbled, like the kiddos had never seen nor heard before. Then the sky poured down buckets of white rain, and it pounded down on them with frightening sound and fury!

The raft suddenly lurched forward and was now free of the boulder, which *was* good but it began violently spinning and rushing down the swollen river. There was nothing to do but hang on. The raging river was totally in control of their speed and direction. The raft bobbed wildly in the raging torrent as it lurched through the canyon below the Yeller Cliffs.

Peeking out the cabin door, they couldn't see a thing. The rain was coming down in heavy sheets. Fortunately, the raft held together through it all, at least so far. It was well built, and the strong fire spider rope flexed where the logs were lashed together. Even when it hit submerged rocks and whatever else, it stayed in one piece.

After a period of constant heavy rain a few windows of blue sky opened above them. The clouds lightened, and the lightning and thunder became distant. The suns shone down through the spaces between the clouds and created a huge rainbow. However, the kiddos didn't have time to celebrate the passing of the downpour because they were still in the rampaging, churning, swiftly moving flood that was the Ooga River.

"Hang on tight!" Topp yelled at the top of his lungs. "Stay together, *Princess*!" The raft flexed and contorted but held its own against the violent thrusts of the river.

"The ropes are holding!" shouted Taffy. "I love fire spiders more than ever!"

The river widened, causing the rushing water to calm down significantly. The raft was still careening at a rapid clip, but the viciousness of the now muddy river was behind them.

They were now able to venture out of the shack into the sunlight. They looked all around. They had not yet reached the Fantasmo Sea, but they knew from the speed that the river had been moving, it couldn't be far away.

Cliffs no longer surrounded the river. On the low banks, they saw big spikes sticking up. Between the sharp protruding spear-like plants, there were wide pits and holes. They wanted to get off the raft for sure but not here in this prickly, pitted land.

"That must be the Spiky Mesa out there!" Walnut said wearily.

"Yeah, I think you're right," Taffy said. "I heard that there are sharp spikes everywhere and deep sink holes. Nobody dares go there, that I know!"

The river further widened, and the current began to slow down. The kiddos jumped to their steering stations to keep the bow of the raft pointed downriver. They were determined to keep it from running aground in this hostile terrain. With Violet at the tiller and Topp and Taffy on the steering poles, *Princess* bobbed along nicely now, fully under their control.

Sugar climbed up on top of the now wobbly little shack and became a lookout scout. She turned her head in all directions but focused mostly on the direction the river was flowing. "I see the sea! I see the Fantasmo Sea!" she yelled.

"And look!" Topp said, pointing to the shore. "There's a sandy beach!"

"Let's park this thing!" Taffy shouted and pushed hard on her pole to steer *Princess* to the sparkling white sand. Topp worked a steering pole, Violet was on the rudder, and together they forced the raft to the beach.

The raft responded to the maneuver and went *SCRUNCH* as it got hung up on a protruding sandbar. "Great landing! Everyone off!" commanded Captain Topp.

Topp jumped off first, gripping a rope holding the raft onto the edge of the beach. The others began jumping off the sturdy craft, one by one. Sugar, Ragamuffin, and Walnut hurriedly plopped onto the sand and danced around with delight. Violet and Taffy ran back into the shack to grab some things before jumping off.

Without warning, a huge tree trunk floating in the river hit *Princess*. The collision made a loud *THUD* and caused the raft to lurch forward abruptly.

"Hurry! Hurry! Jump off!" Topp screamed as the rope began slipping through his grasp from the force of the river pushing on the raft. The rope pulled him into the water up to his chest to the point where he had to let go or he would have been swept away in the strong current.

The force of the impact of the tree trunk violently knocked Violet and Taffy down inside the cabin. By the time they ran to the edge of the raft, it was too late – they couldn't jump to shore!

"Oh, no! Oh nooooooooo ...!" they all yelled.

The three kiddos on the beach could only watch as *Princess*, with Violet and Taffy aboard, slowly disappeared out into the expansive Fantasmo Sea.

Chapter 60

ARE THE GIRLS LOST FOREVER?

৵৶

Topp, Walnut, and Sugar watched helplessly as their friends Taffy and Violet floated beyond view to who knows where. They were so concerned about their friends' perilous situation, it was of little comfort that they themselves were safe and warm on a beautiful sandy beach.

Now that the short but ferocious storm was over, the three kiddos on the beach knew that Balooon would be coming to pick them up. The plan they had devised was working perfectly – almost. They never planned on *Kiddo Princess* floating off into the Fantasmo Sea with two of their friends marooned on it. All they could do now was wait for Balooon to land the giant balloon and go from there.

They weren't really in the mood to search for silver coins$, but because Balooon wouldn't arrive until late in the afternoon, they started to wander around on the sand. They half-heartedly scoured the beach for any signs of a shipwreck.

The only items from the raft that ended on the beach were Walnut's gray bag and a couple of bags of food. There were more than eighteen light-wands in the gray bag, and Walnut had put a homemade rake in the bag as well. The rake was like Forkie in the Pink Desert but considerably smaller.

Since they couldn't do anything about Taffy and Violet's predicament until Balooon came, they finally decided to hunt for coins$ to keep their minds off the plight of the girls.

Where are the girls? What has happened to them? Are they okay? These were the constant thoughts in the minds of the kiddos.

❧

Unknown to the others, Taffy and Violet were comfortable on the raft. They were a long way from Fantasmo Beach but safe and dry. The raft, pushed by the wind, kept moving farther out to sea. They could barely see the shore they'd left behind.

They looked all around because that's about all they *could* do. Their flag was still flapping on the tall flagpole, so they hoped that someone on a passing boat would see them. However, there were no boats as far as their eyes could see.

Taffy climbed up on top of the shack to see farther out. She saw nothing but water, so she climbed down to eat a sandwich, drink a swig of water, and hang out with Violet. The girls were comforted by the fact that they had food and water that would last for a couple of days. With nothing else to do, the girls decided to take a nap and conserve their strength.

Violet woke up first and climbed up on the roof of the shack. She looked around and tried to see where the flood waters had washed them out to sea, but she didn't know which direction to look.

"I see land! I see land!" Violet shouted.

Taffy, still half asleep, stumbled out of the shack and looked out to where Violet was pointing.

"I see it. There's a tall mountain!" Taffy said. "Maybe we can row there!"

Neither girl had ever rowed before, but rowing isn't difficult, so they started working the oars with good success. The raft was large but floated high on the water, so the oars worked well. When they got closer to the land, they saw a town surrounded by a forest. This land had trees and a mountain, so they knew it wasn't Fantasmo Beach, which had neither.

They were getting closer to the land but feeling fatigued, so they took a break from working in the sun and went inside the cabin.

Violet joked, "I hope there aren't any flying flamboes over there!" Though they were concerned about the predicament they were in, they had a good laugh but not such a good laugh as they'd had back in Ooga Ooga.

The girls thought they heard voices and quickly exited the shack. To their surprise, there was a boat coming toward them with two boys and two girls on board!

"What're you doin' out here ways, out in the blue splashy?" the tall dark-haired girl called out. "Where's your motor?"

Before either of the kiddos could speak, or maybe because they'd hardly understood what the girl had said, the tall dark-haired boy spoke up, "It don't have nothin' for a motor! It's a floater is all."

"We don't get many of those 'round here," the shorter, light-haired girl said.

"I do say that it's a nice one, it is!" the short light-haired boy said. "You folksens from Oogoo Oogoo, I supposes?"

Taffy and Violet were kind of amazed at these kids and the way they spoke, but they didn't seem threatening.

"Oh, we will helpen you get to shore – suren begosh! My name is Polly, and her name is Golly, and his name is Rolly, and the big guy there is Tolly," Polly said in a friendly voice. "We all're brothers and sisters of the this here Wowette family. We like when visitors come-un to the island to where we live, the Island of Wow."

"Can we have a lookity see on your raftie?" Tolly asked politely. "Very nicely made, I can tell sure is!"

The four young people looked friendly enough to the girls, so they allowed them to come aboard. The Wowette kids looked around and were quite impressed. They liked the name *Kiddo Princess*.

"So how did ya get out here, fine kidlets?" asked Golly.

Taffy began the story from the beginning. The Wowette kids listened intently, with all four of their ears. They had two regular ears on each side (like normal) and two hardly visible smaller ones tucked in near the big ones. The Wowette kids were interested in the saga of how the kiddos ended up so far out into the Fantasmo Sea.

"So, can we towen you into Wowton, our villagie?" Rolly asked kindly.

"Uh, why yes, that would be nice," Taffy said. She figured that staying out in the sea, floating listlessly around, was about the worst choice at this point. Violet wholeheartedly agreed with Taffy.

Tolly pulled out a big fat rope stored in the hold of their boat. He attached it to the front of the raft and the stern of their bigger boat. The kiddos stayed on the raft, and the Wowette kids returned to their boat, which had a steamy engine.

They were making good progress until the rope snapped and the raft broke loose. They had to stop to tie the two broken ends together and then start pulling again. This happened four or five times and each time it did, the two watercrafts got closer and closer to each other because the tow rope was shortened each time.

"We have rope – very strong fire spider rope!" Violet said. She tossed a long coil of their rope to the Wowettes on the steamyboat.

After the new rope was attached, there were no more breaks, and the Wowette family's motorboat pulled hard and fast. In no time, they entered the seaport of Wowton. The girls placed their feet on the land of the island with tremendous gratitude. They knew they were safe now because they can't drown in dirt.

"Wow, that ropie is strong," Golly said. "The ropie we havette here is made from stringy trees and breaky-breaks all the time."

"You can have all the loose rope we have on the raft for being so nice," Taffy told Tolly. Or was it Rolly?

"I bets you probably want to get backie to the mainland dirt," Tolly said. "We can take you by steamyboat tomorrow time."

"That's wonderful!" Violet cried. "Wow! ... Oh yeah, this is the Island of *Wow*!" she said, playing with words and laughing. Taffy chuckled too.

"There isie one problemette though," Polly explained. "We can't takie you back to Fantasmo Beachland because of the water-works pushing from the Oogoo River and entering the sea. The best we can dozie is takie you to Swampyville which is a longie-long way from the beach where your friends beekins."

Then Tolly said, "From Swampyville, you can walkie-walk ziggy-zag around the swamps for most of a day to Jollyberg. From there you can take a Flowbus to Olden Town."

Taffy and Violet didn't like the sound of the swamp too much, so they stood there and stared off across the Fantasmo Sea.

"Look, Violet!" Taffy screeched. "Smoke signals. It's the other kiddos sending us smoke signals to show us where they are!"

"That doesn't do much good because we can't get there," Violet said. "Hey, what if we send back smoke signals to them! That way they'll know where we are, and that we're on land. If we were still on the raft we couldn't make a fire, and they would figure that out."

Tolly, Polly, Golly, and Rolly were listening to the girls and understood their idea. "We can helpie you make a flamie here in our firery pit, and you can send a smoke-ity signal all rightie," Rolly said.

"Also, youse can stay in the guestiroom house tonight," Polly said. "That's what it's for, and it'll be nighty-time soon."

It didn't take long for the fire to burn strong and hot. Violet knew how to send smoke signals. She threw water from a bucket onto the fire five times, which made five big billows of smoke rise high into the air.

Violet and Taffy hoped that the kiddos would see their smoke signals and understand that they are alive and on land somewhere, not floating farther out to sea.

But they had a question on their minds. *How will we ever find each other again*?

Chapter 61

A FARAWAY FANTASMO NIGHT

கூ

When the kiddos on the beach saw Balooon approaching from the sky, they jumped up and down and waved their arms wildly. They were relieved to see that an important part of their plan was still working. Balooon landed *Miss Blimpy* with a loud thud on the beach, not far from the three excited kiddos and one quirky dog. The appearance of Balooon boosted their spirits, but they were still concerned and sad about the situation Taffy and Violet were in – lost at sea!

After the big basket landed and was secured, Balooon climbed down the ladder and greeted the others. They ran up to him and expressed how grateful they were that he had come. Without delay, they let him know the plight of Violet and Taffy. It's true that *Blimpy* was ready to fly them home at any time, but they knew that they couldn't leave until they found the lost girls.

It was late in the afternoon and if it weren't for the missing girls, the kiddos would have climbed into the basket and taken off just before dark. Staying the night was never the original plan, but the big basket has ample room for the four kiddos to sleep. There was room for more, but there will be two empty beds in the basket tonight.

"Look! Look!" shouted Topp as loud as he could. "Smoke signals from across the sea!"

"Five puff balls of smoke! That must be from Violet and Taffy! They saw our smoke signals and sent a reply!" Walnut shouted. They started dancing around like wackadoos as they raced around the big basket.

"They must be on land out there! They couldn't build a fire on the raft. They must be on land or on an island!" Sugar said.

The smoke signals gave the kiddos hope that Taffy and Violet were okay. They celebrated for a while and then put a new plan in place. In the morning, the kiddos will take off in the giant balloon and head out over the Fantasmo Sea in the direction of the smoke signals. They had heard there were islands out there somewhere, and tomorrow they need to find the one where the girls landed.

"Hey, it's about an hour before dark, so why don't we look for silver coins$?" Topp said.

They put Walnut's rake to work again to see if they could find buried coins$. Soon it will be dark, and they'll have to head into the basket-house for the night.

RAKE – RAKE – RAKE was the sound of the sand tool in the soft pearl-colored sand. They took turns pulling the fork as deeply as they could and found more than a dozen coins$ before dark. Ragamuffin let his dog side out (rather than his cat side), started digging, and found a coin$ of his own.

"... fourteen, fifteen, sixteen, and Ragamuffin's makes seventeen! Pretty amazing!" Topp said.

Despite the kiddos' success in finding a mess of coins$, their thoughts were focused on Taffy and Violet as they settled into their beds that night.

౨

Meanwhile on the Island of Wow, Taffy and Violet were *better* than just fine. The four *Olly* kids, Tolly, Rolly, Golly, and Polly had the two Oogans settled comfortably in the guest house. They brought them so much delicious food, the girls couldn't have possibly eaten more.

Before the Wowette children left the guest house, Taffy asked, "What do you know about how far the Fantasmo Sea goes to the north of your island – the direction away from Fantasmo Beach? Is there land up that way? Does the sea end somewhere?"

"Yes, it does," Golly said. "There was an explorette named Holly who was away from home for a year and a halflet. She said that she did founded land and another seawater beyond that. The watery was red and warm and had steamin' smoke coming up from it. She didn't have a boat nohow to go on over the hot-wet sea, so she turned back around and came again to the Island of Wow."

"Why did you twose want to know? Are you twose going to try to adventure up there or something?" Tolly asked.

"After what you just told us, I don't think we'll want to go there at all," Taffy said. "I asked because we are trying to find out if there's an end to our land, to our world, in that direction. Does it end at an *edge*, or does it go on forever? That's the question we want to answer. There's an old legend that our world is kind of flat and comes to an end where it drops off. But we don't know for sure."

"Never heard about that – nope! We've always figured that it just goes on up there forever and more. That's what our elderkins say anyhow," Polly said. "We're very happity with our little part of the worldy – the Island of Wow."

"You twose have a great sleep tonight, and we'll be gettin' you to Swampyville in the mornin' time," Golly said.

As the Wowettes turned to leave, Taffy and Violet said, "Thank you for all you did for us today. Many gobs of thanks!"

With full bellies and feelings of gratitude for the kindness they'd been shown, the girls laid their heads down on the lovely pillows on the cozy beds and snuggled in for a restful sleep. They hoped for safe and easygoing dreams as they headed into the world of night.

There will be a tomorrow on the Island of Wow *and* on Fantasmo Beach. Sleep well, kiddos. Tomorrow might be full of surprises.

Chapter 62

BOBBY'S PERILOUS VISIT TO UNCLE ROY'S

ॐ

A ray of light shone through Bobby's window and brought his mind back into his room. A glow of love filled him when he remembered that his dad had returned.

Bobby had missed his dad a great deal as they had often hung out together like best friends – Bobby being his only son. His broken heart was now mended, and he prayed that nothing like that unexpected separation would ever happen again. He felt grateful and blessed as much as a young boy could be.

He knew that he was awake before his mom and dad this morning, so he waltzed into the kitchen (after brushing his teeth of course). He looked around the room with hungry eyes. He saw several FERNY BARS and a note with his name on it, so he munched on one while he scooped ice cream from the freezer into a glass bowl. He knew he wouldn't get into any trouble for gorging on ice cream because nobody would break the spell of joy that filled their house this glorious morning.

Bad Bobby? Yeah, a little bit!

After he had eaten more chocolate and ice cream than he should have (because his tummy was almost bursting), he waddled back to his room like a fat-bellied duck.

When he thought about showing his dad the toothpick roller coaster he'd built, he knew his dad would be impressed. Bobby had made progress on it recently, and now the starting point for the marble was as high as he is tall. He had built a full loop in the run, so the marble now whizzes upside down as it does the loop de loop. *Pretty cool!* he thought as he watched his favorite red marble flying along the rails. He put a bell at the bottom that would *ding* when the marble reached the end.

He talked to his plants and asked them what they thought about his fancy roller coaster. He acted like they said something back to him, but I didn't hear anything, did you?

He looked outside through the window and saw that today was a beautifully clear sunny day. "A great day to travel to Uncle Roy's house," he told the plants. He paused for a moment to listen to their response. Either Bobby can hear them, or he will make a great actor someday!

Bobby sat on his bed and thought about the fruit farm where Uncle Roy used to live. He remembered well the old-time farmhouse with an odd, musty smell. Bobby was always fascinated by the dark and creepy root cellar under that old house. He used to go down there in complete darkness and make up stories in his head. He had a great imagination, and it really flourished down in that private space. His daydreams in Uncle Roy's cellar were very real to him – much like the exciting dreams he is having now.

Sitting there on his bed, he thought about the dream he had last night. The dream-kids had roared down a flooding river on a raft, and two of the dream-kids ended up lost, out in a faraway sea. *Oh my,* Bobby thought. He felt worried for the kids.

When Bobby heard tapping on the front door, his daydreaming ended. He glanced at the clock and figured it must be Bettykins. He glided through the house and threw open the door to find his sister with her arms wide open.

"Sweetiekins!" Bobby said as he wrapped her in a big hug.

"Bobbykins!" she softly said as they walked arm in arm into the house. "Nobody ever calls me *sweetiekins* but you, Bobby. It's so very good to see you and your joyful smile. How's Dad?"

"He seems just fine and delighted to be home. I think they're sleeping in."

"Makes sense, so let's go catch up a little," she suggested.

Bobby and Bettykins sat in the kitchen for an hour or more, discussing current events in their lives. Bettykins talked a great deal about her new boyfriend and college, and Bobby talked about Cookie a bit. Bettykins also spoke at length about her schoolwork, and Bobby told her all about his amazing dreams.

"That's really fascinating!" Bettykins said. "Especially the way your life events seem to follow the dreams you're having. It seems to me that it would make more sense if events in your life happened, and then you had dreams about those things. The other way around is quite weird."

They heard noises coming from down the hall. It was Mom and Dad coming to welcome Bettykins. The room glowed with the love of family – a better moment was never had by any of them.

Eventually, Dad said, "There will be plenty of time for me to tell the tales of my disappearance, but for now, let's just get on with the day and head over to Roy's. I can assure you of one thing, I won't be going into that jungle again!" Everyone smiled and let out a sigh of relief.

Rufus and Mari ate a quick breakfast then started packing. Bobby's stuff was ready, and Bettykins had everything she needed in the suitcase she'd brought home.

When Bobby and his family went outside, he looked up at the sky and then looked again more closely. "Dad, we better get going if we're going south over the river bridge, there's a big rainstorm coming!" he said firmly.

"Why are you so anxious, Bobby? The sky has lots of blue and only a few clouds," his mom said.

"I just know – we better hurry!" Bobby said.

They didn't have any reason to just hang around anyway, so they loaded up the car and took off down the road. Just as they made a turn to the south, raindrops began hitting the windshield.

"Rain! You guessed that one right, son! Good call!" his father noted. Rufus picked up the pace as they headed toward the bridge. Suddenly, the sky opened and torrents of rain came down, making visibility almost nil.

"There's the bridge!" Bobby shouted. "Go!"

As they sped across, the water in the river was so high, spray came up onto the roadway and made it slippery. Rufus skillfully drove the car over to the other side and then pulled over to watch the swelling river roar under the bridge.

"It's taking out the bridge!" Bettykins screamed. "We could have been on it!"

They watched as the entire bridge rose and tore loose from its anchors on the banks. The bridge broke into pieces as it took off down the raging flashflood.

"Oh my!" Mari said.

The rain continued but not so hard they couldn't continue to drive on to Uncle Roy's. As they moved closer to the sea, the rain eventually slowed down to a few droplets.

When they arrived at Uncle Roy's house, the sky was a surprisingly clear blue. Roy was waiting outside to greet them.

"Wow, this is some place you have here, Roy!" Rufus said. "Right on the edge of the sea!"

"You got your dream, didn't you?" Mari remarked to Uncle Roy. "You've always wanted to live by the sea."

"Ya got that right, ya did!" Roy said happily. "Me and the sea – it's gotta be!"

Rufus told Roy all about the drive over and the bridge washing out. His brother listened with his mouth wide open and said, "Oh lordly!"

"Bobby, how did you know that the storm would arrive suddenly – and be so dangerous?" his mom asked.

"I don't think you'll believe me even if I tell you," Bobby said, staring down at the ground.

"You knew somehow. You really knew! How in the world did you know?" Rufus asked.

Mom glared at Bobby and gave him *that* look – the look that moms give to their sons when they intend to pull it out of them one way or another.

"Okay, but if you don't believe me, that's fine. I understand," Bobby said.

There was a long moment of silence. Then Bettykins said, "Go on, Bobby, tell us how you figured that out."

"I knew it was going to be a fast and dangerous storm because of my dream last night," Bobby explained. "I'm having very unusual dreams."

The family settled in around a picnic table by the edge of the shimmering sea to listen to Bobby's story. He started at the beginning and told them about his dreams, how they take place in a fantasy land, and how he has become friends with the kids who live there. As Bobby continued, his family became oddly silent. Eventually, he told them about the dream he'd had last night, when the dream-kids rafted between jagged cliffs, and what happened when the monster storm hit.

"That's how I knew that there was going to be a heavy flood," he said. "That's it, that's how I knew. What happens in my dreams often foretells events that happen in my life when I wake up."

There was a long silence among his audience. The only sound was the gentle splashing of the nearby waves.

Bettykins broke the awkward silence, "I believe you, Bobby!"

Dad, Mom, and Roy just half-smiled with blank looks on their faces.

"So, after the storm," Bobby continued, "four of the dream-kids and their dog were stranded on a sandy beach while two other kids drifted out to sea. Just like with us now, we are going to have trouble getting home. With the bridge out, we're a bit stuck – like them. But I'll admit, this is a nice place to be stranded!"

Rufus, Mari, and Bettykins nodded in agreement and knew *that* was true at least. Bobby had no idea if any of them believed him, but *he* knew it was true.

Eventually, they all headed into Roy's house. Roy had planned on their two-day stay, but if they needed to stay until the bridge was fixed, that would be fine too.

That night, when Bobby started to slide into bed, he saw a light flickering through the window. He got up and peeked out the door to see what was going on. Uncle Roy and Dad were out on the bluff in front of a campfire. Bobby watched as Roy waved a beach towel to fan the flames. Billows of smoke rose in balls, one after the other, like smoke signals in the night sky.

Bobby decided not to say anything to them about the smoke signals in his dream, and he went back inside to go to bed. He was eager to get back to his dream life to find out if the dream-kids on the beach were able to save the two who had floated out to sea.

Chapter 63

THE MAJESTY OF MOUNT WOW

Topp, Walnut, Sugar, Ragamuffin, and Balooon had a comfortable night's sleep in the basket of the big balloon on Fantasmo Beach. They awoke early and wandered out to the edge of the sea. They looked out over the vast body of water and thought about their two lost friends.

Now that Balooon had arrived, the kiddos on the beach had only one worry and that was the wellbeing of Taffy and Violet. Because they'd seen smoke signals the evening before, they assumed Taffy and Violet were on land. That gave them comfort as they made plans to find them.

Fortunately, the sky was clear and bright on this new day. Looking off across the calm water, the kiddos on the beach could see the tip-top of a very pointed mountain in the distance for the first time. There were no smoke signals now, so the kiddos could only assume that the mountain they could see was where the girls were stranded. It was a good place to start anyway. Being able to see land was a great new development, so they discussed plans to take *Blimpy* out over the mysterious sea to save them.

What the four kiddos on the beach didn't know was that Taffy and Violet had enjoyed a wonderful night's sleep as guests of Tolly, Rolly, Polly, and Golly Wowette. They also didn't know that the Wowettes had a plan to get their new friends back to the mainland at Swampyville early in the morning.

To get the day started, the Wowettes served a delicious, however unusual, breakfast omelet for the two Oogan girls. It was made of boiled fuggit bird eggs, with diced boneless funfish mixed in. They were also served a delightful breakfast salad made with colorful, edible flowers that grow on the slopes of Mount Wow. It was so delicious, the kiddos kept *oohing* and *aahing* as they ate, to the delight of the Wowettes.

Right after breakfast, the two kiddos and all four Wowette children boarded the steamyboat at the Wowton dock and pushed off about an hour after the two suns rose.

The sea was calm, nary a ripple on the surface, on this fine morning. As they moved away from the island, Wow Mountain revealed how tall it was. "Wow!" Taffy exclaimed. "Wow – what colors! Your mountain is so beautiful!"

"That's why wez calls it Mount Wow," Golly said.

The clearly fertile mountain was completely blanketed in brightly colored flowers. Viewed from out at sea, it sparkles from its peak in the clouds, to the edge of the sea. It looks like a kaleidoscope of colors.

"I think it's taller than Ooga Mountain!" Violet told Taffy, "and Ooga Mountain is sooo tall!"

"You know what, Violet?" Taffy said, feeling delightfully energized. "In a week it will be Baby Gravity Day, so when we get home I think we should start preparing to climb to the very tip-top of Ooga Mountain."

"Really?!" Violet asked excitedly. "What is Baby Gravity Day, anyway?"

"Baby Gravity Day happens every seventeen years. It happens when the two suns, the big one and the little one, are right on top of each other. The gravity in Ooga Ooga becomes much less than normal. Climbing uphill on foot or on bikes is much easier on that special day."

"Let's do it!" Violet said. "But first we need to get back to the shady glade."

As the kiddos steamyboated smoothly across the Fantasmo Sea, they passed a chain of six small islands about an hour from the Island of Wow. The islands were in a row and looked interesting. "What are those cute little islands? Do Wow islanders ever visit them?" Taffy asked.

"Oh yesie! Those islandies are named: Who, What, When, Where, Why, and How," Molly said. "There's goodie herbs and spices growing on them, and there's super fishin' around them toos."

"You all live a lovely life out here in the sea," Violet said. "It's magical!"

"Whatee do that mean, *magical*?" Polly asked.

"Something unusual, something surprisingly special that feels good," Taffy replied.

"Uhhh, okay ... *magical*," Rolly said, adding it to his vocabulary.

On Fantasmo Beach, Topp, Sugar, Walnut, and Balooon were preparing to take off. They were about to cross over the vast Fantasmo Sea to the mysterious land where Taffy and Violet might be stranded. They had no way of knowing that the girls were well rested and content – and currently cruising in a comfortable boat to the mainland.

The giant balloon lifted off from the beach and then headed directly toward the land they saw. They floated just above the small swells of the azure-colored sea. Their progress was slow because the breeze was but a whisper. The four kiddos were hopeful that they'd find their friends there, and that they were safe. They figured they'd load the girls up onto *Miss Blimpy*, then head back to the Valley of Ooga Ooga straightaway.

As the balloon came closer to the mysterious small bit of land on this giant sea, Sugar shouted. "Wow, it's an island! Look at the colors on the mountain! I think it's covered in millions of brightly-colored flowers! Wow!"

The four kiddos stared in silence as Balooon piloted *Blimpy* closer to the magnificently beautiful Island of Wow.

As they approached, Balooon noticed dwellings in what appeared to be a town. He saw a grassy park and lowered the large balloon right in the center of it. It hit with an abrupt, bone-jarring *THUNK!*

"Whoops!" Balooon said. "I'm still learning, sorry!"

"You did great!" Sugar said. "We got here safely. Good job!"

Two young island children came running up to the basket. "Thaten there is the specialist gizmo I've evar seen!" shouted a petite girl.

"Surie is!" a tiny boy said. "Who're youse kids? I'm Biff, and she's my sister, Kiss. We's Biff and Kiss Wowette."

"Hi, we're from the Valley of Ooga Ooga. I'm Topp, and they are Sugar, Walnut, Balooon, and Ragamuffin, our dog. Hey, have you seen two girls floating on a raft?"

"Yep, they tookity off this mornin' time," Kiss said. "They went by boatie to the bigland at Swampyville."

"Are they okay?" Sugar asked.

"Sure! They spent the night in the guestihouse, had brekkie, then tookity off," Biff answered.

"That's great news!" Walnut said. They were all relieved to hear that the girls were alive and well.

The kiddos were anxious to take off and find the girls in Swampyville, but they were told that the wind direction was wrong. The Wowette children said that the wind would change in a few hours so they might as well relax for a while. The generous children invited them to have breakfast before they left.

As they all sat down to eat, the two little Wowette kids told the kiddos stories about this and that, and the kiddos understood them. The kiddos were served a delicious flower salad and an omelet. While the kiddos were having breakfast, they told stories about the Valley of

Ooga Ooga and the shady glade. They mentioned the big picky-nick they are planning for the last day of summer. They invited Biff and Kiss and everyone on their island to come for the festivities.

The four kiddos were a bit nervous and impatient for the correct winds, but they passed the time by sharing more stories of their two very different lands.

At least they were safe here on the island, and apparently Violet and Taffy were safe as well. The kiddos expected to join them soon in Swampyville.

Chapter 64

THE WICKED, WOEFUL SWAMP

❧❦

Taffy and Violet fully enjoyed the smooth journey by boat to Swampyville. They landed without incident and asked the Wowette kids how they could repay them for all they had done for them.

Polly said, "Naw, you guysies left us strong ropety *and* your whole raftie! We are real happity about that, and we's certainly glad we could helpity. We are nice peoples, after it all."

"Yes, you are! And you make excellent omelets and salads, too!" Violet said warmly. "Thank you again for everything."

The Wowettes introduced the two girls to the Mayor of Swampyville, Mr. Funny. Then the Wowettes loaded a stack of dry firewood for the steamyboat's burner, jumped aboard, and took off right away toward their island home.

"They sure were nice, weren't they?" Violet said with a chuckle. "I hope-ity we'll see them again someday."

"Like maybe at the pick-ity nick-ity," Taffy said giggling.

"What are we going to do about the other kiddos?" Taffy asked. "They might go looking for us, but they don't know where we are."

"I hope they saw our smoke signals and figured that we're okay," Violet said. "I think that they're okay and will eventually float back to Ooga Ooga. If we get to Jollyberg and take the Floatbus back to Ooga Ooga, we'll meet them there soon enough."

"I suppose that's right," Taffy reluctantly agreed. "We just need to get back safely. That's the most important thing we can do."

Mayor Funny of Swampyville was a nice young man and laughed and smiled a lot. He was very informative and helpful. He understood that the two girls wanted to get to Old Town and then to the Village of Ooga Ooga without delay. He drew a map to help them navigate the walking trail through the swamp, which lies between Swampyville and Jollyberg, where they can catch the Floatbus.

Mayor Funny said that he and the whole Funny family have lived around here for over a hundred years.

"Your family name is very interesting. Do you know where your name came from?" Taffy asked.

"Have you ever heard of the jungle mist in the Jolly Jungle?" he asked.

"Yes, we have – it is quite funny down there in the jungle."

"We think our ancestors came from there. Funny, isn't it?" he said with a chuckle.

"Makes sense to me," Violet said with a big grin.

Mayor Funny mentioned one thing that wasn't funny at all. He said there is one danger on the journey through the swampland to Jollyberg: the hissing eels. Mayor Funny warned them in a whisper, "If you talk to each other, do it *very* quietly, or the hissing eels will certainly appear – and you don't want that to happen! They do hiss, but that's not all they do with their mouths!"

"Why? What will they do?" Taffy asked.

"Just be very quiet, and you won't have to worry about that. If you're quiet, you will never see one – not a one!" He didn't want to spook them too much and reveal the gory bite of the hissing eels.

"I see ...," Violet said.

"Oh, and one more thing. The water in the swamp is high lately from that big monstro storm we had recently, so the trail could be a bit narrow in spots."

The girls left Mayor Funny and walked cautiously toward the beginning of the trail. They glanced at each other with a look that said,

"That didn't sound too good, did it?" The only things the girls had with them were the clothes and the shoes they were wearing. The girls had left most everything else behind on the raft because that stuff was useless for hiking through a swamp.

With map in hand, the two girls followed Mayor Funny's directions and took off into the swamp on a wide, well-defined path – at least at the beginning!

᪥

Meanwhile the kiddos on the Island of Wow were preparing to leave to find the girls in Swampyville. The wind had finally shifted to a better direction, but the Wowette kids didn't think the wind was quite right yet. Biff and Kiss suggested they wait another two hours for the best wind, but Balooon decided not to wait any longer.

Up and away they went, climbing into the sky higher than usual because Balooon wanted to be able to see the mainland from high up as they floated in that direction. Biff and Kiss said Swampyville is located on a finger of land or peninsula covered in bright green grass, thus it's easy to spot from far away. The kiddos figured they'd be in Swampyville in no time and that the girls would be delighted to see them. Then all six of them could head for home as safe as could be – if the wind conditions were right.

On the trail through the swamp, Violet and Taffy found that the going was surprisingly easy. The pathway was well-maintained, broad, and flat. But it zigzagged around the wet swampy lagoons, and they got a little disoriented. They figured that they just needed to follow the trail wherever it went, and they would be fine.

The girls were purposely quiet as they shuffled along, until Taffy yelled, "Yikes!" when she tripped on a protruding root and almost fell into the dark slimy water. The girls huddled together and listened warily for hissing eels. They were scared out of their wits when they saw ripples in the water out in the swamp and heard leaves rustling above them in the trees. They stood there silently as still as Ooga

Mountain, hoping that the hissing eels would not know they were there.

To fool the eels, Violet picked up a loose stick and hurled it into the swamp a good distance from them. It made a loud splash, and she hoped it would distract any eels that might be coming after them. She then whispered *very* quietly, "Let's get going …!" And they did.

As they advanced on the walkway, the water became higher, and the trail became narrower. The water crossed over the path in spots, and they had to hop over those rivulets. The farther they went, the more the water covered the trail until they weren't even sure where it was anymore.

Alarmed about the condition of the walking path, Violet looked around and remarked that they had passed the same dark-colored tree with the broken branch once before. They then realized that they had been going around in a circle! "Oh my!" Violet whispered. The girls came to the realization that they were disoriented and lost, deep in this nasty woeful swamp. They were lost in a maze, a truly deadly maze.

They were getting tired, so they stopped and rested. After all, if they were going in circles, why waste their energy? But what should they do now?! Was this the end of them? Would they ever find their way out? How could anyone find them here in this massive swamp? *Help us,* they prayed …!

They sat down on a fallen log on a tiny dry spot. They were deep in despair and cried a little. Violet whispered to Taffy, "Why don't we build a fire and make smoke signals? My fairies can do that for me. Maybe the other kiddos will see it. If not, I think we're doomed!"

So, the girls gathered all the dry twigs they could find on dead trees and started a fire. They threw on bigger and bigger sticks until the flames rose above their heads. They took large swamp leaves and dipped them in water. In a rhythm, they held the leaves over the fire to create smoke balls. The damp wood they threw on the fire made a ton of smoke, and the leaf technique worked perfectly. Big blobs of dark gray smoke rose high above the swamp. They thought that smoke signals were their only chance, so they kept the smoke balls rising.

The girls made smoke signals for a long time, but nobody came and they ran out of wood to burn. They realized that the whole situation was hopeless, so they slumped to the ground, completely exhausted and forlorn.

Just then, a dark shadow blocked out the sun. To their great surprise, it was *Miss Blimpy* right above them!

The girls jumped up and down, waved their arms and yelled, "Here we are! Here we are!" Then they realized that the yelling would bring out the hissing eels, so they shut up quick!

A sturdy rope ladder was lowered from the balloon, and the girls jumped on. They didn't dare look back down when they heard the splashing and hissing sounds below. When they were securely on the rope ladder, Balooon raised *Blimpy* up a bit so the girls wouldn't hit any trees as the balloon swayed back and forth.

The girls were overcome with gratitude as they scrambled aboard the basket and were greeted joyously by their friends. The rope ladder was pulled in, and the six kiddos began celebrating. And boy, did they whoop and holler as Balooon raised the giant balloon high above that slimy, scummy swamp! The balloon caught a stiff breeze blowing toward the Valley of Ooga Ooga, and off they went.

They were safe and together, and the difficult adventure had come to a happy ending. They had seventeen silver coins$ as their reward. While swooping along in high air currents, they could see where the Ooga River cut through the Yeller Cliffs, and they could also see Ooga Mountain in the distance. Looking behind them, they saw the Fantasmo Sea and the tiny image of a colorful mountain on the now faraway Island of Wow.

As the balloon drifted toward home, Taffy remarked, "Are you guys ready for another big adventure? Let's hike to the top of Ooga Mountain after we get home!" They all started laughing, and they didn't stop until the basket landed gently in the shady glade.

Chapter 65

THERE'S NO PLACE LIKE HOME

❧❧

The kiddos slept until late morning at their own homes and in their own beds. After their wild and weird adventure to the Fantasmo Sea, they knew that they needed to take a break and spend quality time with their moms and dads and help with work around the house and yard.

The kiddos are special like that. They're always thinking of ways to help their parents. You do that, too, don't you? Glad to hear it.

The kiddos agreed to stay home with their families for two days and lend a hand – if they ever got out of bed, that is. Their parents don't mind when the kiddos are at their clubhouse, and they trust them when they're off on their adventures. However, I'm not so sure their parents want to know all the details of the dangerous situations the kiddos have encountered. The kiddos only recount the *good* results when they return – like finding silver coins$, dia-mons, and pink gold.

Only two of their friends know all the scary details of the dangers they've encountered during their adventures. But the friends keep their secrets, so the kiddos can continue searching for treasures and possibly the *edge* of their land.

All's well that ends well is the kiddos' motto. That's the most important thing they think because here they are, healthy and safe as can be.

The kiddos worked diligently with their families those days, but they daydreamed about new and faraway places to visit. They could hardly wait to meet at the clubhouse the next day to discuss new plans for the weeks ahead.

That night, the kiddos gladly went to bed early. They felt good about all the chores they'd accomplished and enjoyed the loving smiles they'd shared with their parents. Now they're free to fill the next three weeks with as many adventures as they can – before summer ends and school starts once again.

They had decided to meet at the shady glade at *kid-farmer time* the following day. Due to exhaustion from both the saga of the sea and the family chores, Topp, Taffy, and Sugar headed to the Big Abble at a turtle's pace, while Walnut oozed there at a snail's pace. Balooon flew to the glade early with his small balloon and took a nap while waiting for the others. He waited and waited, then fell asleep again in his treehouse, with Smokey napping on his lap. Violet had left early from Purple Springs, but she was running late because she had the farthest to go, and she picked exotic flowers to beautify the clubhouse on the way.

The kiddos did arrive eventually, but their arrival time was more like a real farmer's early suppertime. Another way to put it – both suns had gone more than halfway across the sky by the time all the kiddos were settled in around the table inside the clubhouse.

The kiddos got cozy and started discussing what the next adventure would be. Wanting to be responsible farmers, they discussed what chores they needed to do around the shady glade before they headed off to faraway places. The discussions about the work they needed to do ended quickly. It sounded too much like work and not enough like fun, that's why.

"We need to carry water from Silly Creek to water the veggies and baby trees," Violet said. "But maybe it will rain, so we might not have to do all of that hard watering work."

"The veggies seem to be getting along with the weeds," Balooon said. "No need to pull the weeds, I suppose."

"We can't pick the veggies yet, they aren't ready, and the fruit trees are little and won't have any fruit until next year," Taffy added. "Well, that settles that. I guess it's adventure time." And everyone agreed.

Suddenly, there was a *BANG! BANG!* on the door.

"Don't answer it!" Topp said. "It's probably just one of those annoying what-ers!"

BANG, BANG, BANG! sounded the wooden door again, more loudly this time.

The kiddos sat there in silence, pretending they weren't there. They kept quieter than the rug on the floor. However, Walnut decided to get up, and his chair made a loud screeching sound on the floor. The noise had blown their cover, so he quickly tiptoed to the window and peeked out.

"It's Mr. Stufff!" Walnut shouted. He bolted to the door and opened it just as Mr. Stufff was about to climb onto his six-legged horse. "Mr. Stufff, we're here! Welcome!"

Mr. Stufff turned around in surprise and then ambled back toward the clubhouse with a smile. The kiddos warmly welcomed him inside and offered him chocolate pancakes that Violet had made for late lunch.

"Thank you, but my tummy is still full of Mrs. Stufff's cooking, especially the stuffing," he said with a wide grin. "I've brought things that you children might like. Come on outside to my wagon, and I'll show you."

Mr. Stufff strutted outside and headed in the direction of his wagon. The kiddos followed like six little ducklings after their mommy. Mr. Stufff climbed up into the wagon, opened a green box, reached in, and pulled out something. "These are backpacks, new backpacks," he told the children. "Some guy dumped a big load of stuff in my driveway, and this green box was in the pile. It's full of new backpacks. I thought you kids would like them. They're a gift." He grabbed one and tossed it down to Violet.

"Wow, these are nice," Violet said as she put the backpack on her shoulders and adjusted the straps. "These are fantastic! They're much bigger than our old bag-packs, and they have all kinds of different pockets too."

With a toothy grin, Mr. Stufff said, "I thought you would like them!" He slid the box out of his wagon and lowered it to the kiddos, who thanked him profusely.

Mr. Stufff jumped down to the ground, hopped up onto his six-legged horse, waved goodbye, and rode away.

The kiddos each grabbed one and put it on. The backpacks were in different colors, of course – how perfect. Each kiddo chose their own special color. They are the rainbow kiddos, after all. There were two extra packs that were white, and the kiddos decided to call them guest packs in case other friends, like their close friend, Bob, and his girlfriend, want to join them sometime in the future.

The kiddos settled in around the table again and discussed the important business of adventure planning.

"I know you all want to go to Candy Mountain," Violet said. "When I was home, I was told that it's been an exceptionally hot summer out west in the Duney Desert. Candy Mountain will have to wait at least until a cold spell rolls across the desert."

"Aw shucks!" squealed Sugar. "I can hardly wait, I can taste it already!"

"Hey, hey, hey," Taffy said. "In a few days it will be Baby Gravity Day. That's the perfect day for us to finally reach the very top of Ooga Mountain. We can play among the ball rocks, taste the delicious mitten weed, and eat that rare mountain-top ice cream!"

"Okay then," Topp said, "if we all agree to climb to the top of Ooga Mountain, we need to start preparing for that challenge right away."

"I have a suggestion," Walnut said. "Since none of us wants to eat strong beans, we should take a trip back to the canyon below the Chocolate Hills and bring back a stash of zoooms. If we leave early, we can be back in one day."

"That's a great idea!" Taffy said gleefully. "No more strong beans for me!"

The kiddos started dancing around inside the clubhouse yelling, "No more strong beans! No more strong beans!"

Again, there was a loud *BANG* at the door.

Violet ran to the door, figuring maybe Mr. Stufff forgot something. She flung open the door and to her amazement, there were three large rainbow-winged swans at the door.

"Falooop gaddie foo foo?" said the largest swan, the one in the middle.

Violet looked at it blankly. Not only had the appearance of the colorful, giant swans mesmerized her, but what the swan had said was mind-boggling nonsense. Violet didn't say a word, she just stared at them.

The swan said, "Oh yeah, in Ooga Ooga you speak Oogan not *Whacka Whacka*! So, my question in Oogan is, have you seen a big purple frog named JoJo around here?"

"Yes, there was a purple frog who came to our door," Violet said. "But I didn't know its name was JoJo!"

"Yep, that's the one!" said the swan. "Is it inside your house?"

"Heavens, no!" Violet shrieked and then pointed her finger in the direction of Ooga Mountain. "It went that way!"

The three swans turned around, took five floppy steps, elevated off the ground, and then flew away in a cloud of colorful rainbow glitter.

"Those what-ers sure are weird," Violet mused. "But I suppose they think that we are just as strange."

"That's an interesting thought," Sugar said with a grin.

"Now it's time to get back to planning," Topp said, annoyed at all the interruptions.

Eventually, the plans going forward were clear to the kiddos. First they would venture back to the Chocolate Hills to get more chocolate and even more importantly, they would gather zooms. The zooms would give them extra strength for the trip up to the top of Ooga Mountain.

Violet spoke up, "Hopefully, after Baby Gravity Day, the weather will have cooled off, and it will be the perfect time to go on a balloon ride to Candy Mountain."

They also discussed having a grand picky-nick or festival, after they returned from Candy Mountain. They planned on having the picky-nick on the last day of summer. By that time, they will have brought back tons of sweets from Candy Mountain for all the guests to enjoy.

The kiddos, satisfied with their plans, settled into their beds in the clubhouse early that night. They planned to leave for Rusty Canyon at first light the next morning because they *definitely* need to be back in the shady glade before dark. They don't want to spend another night sleeping out there in a strange land – because *there's no place like home!*

Chapter 66

WHY ARE THE ZOOOMS HIDING?

❧❧

The kiddos rode out of the shady glade on their bikes with only enough early morning light for each kiddo to see the rider in front of them. Taffy was in the lead and used a light-wand to see the trail. They made good time leaving the Valley of Ooga Ooga and soon entered Spooky Hollow. When the morning opened for business, the kiddos were well on their way.

They weren't startled when they arrived at the turnoff to Rat Town, like they had been on their previous visit. It wasn't Rat Town, the kiddos learned, it was Roooganville, and they all agreed that the Rooogans they'd met were quite nice.

The dawn's golden light was now glowing over the land as the kiddos rode hard and fast. They passed by the place where the tall blue-eared what-er deer had leaped over them, but it wasn't anywhere around this time. Ahead in the distance, they saw the top of the massive Charcoal Cliffs. They knew The Gap was not far away. They hoped that Pperfume and Ddandy were at the toll booth, and this time the kiddos remembered to bring a half brittle$ to pay the toll.

The kiddos rolled down the road with such speed that when they finally stopped to pay the toll, they kicked up a great deal of charcoal-colored dust, that blew onward through The Gap.

Pperfume saw them coming and called out to her brother, "Yay-ee, the kid-soos are back, Ddandy!"

"Helllo there, wellcome back!" Ddandy said.

"Good to see you again!" Sugar said. "It's early in the morning. We weren't sure you would be open yet, but here you are!"

"Where are you going this time?" Pperfume asked.

"Well, we're going mainly to find zoooms to take back home," Taffy explained. "We'll be bringing back chocolate too. There'll be ample for you when we come through later today."

"Hey, have you had breakfast?" Ddandy asked. "Why don't you come on down to our house and have a Rooogan breakfast and meet our mom. Oh, and she made fresh s'mores this morning!"

Did they hear s'mores? The kiddos didn't hesitate a second and went along with the two kids.

They hadn't walked far when they came to a colorful flower garden surrounding a glistening azure pond. On a small island in the middle of the little lake sat a small stone cottage. The whole scene was so adorable, it could have jumped right out of a children's fairy tale.

Pperfume and Ddandy bounded, hop by hop, on the steppingstones leading to their quaint home. The kiddos followed, hop by hop, to the cottage's front porch. The Rooogan children's mom saw them coming, opened the door, and welcomed them in.

The kiddos had possibly the best breakfast they'd ever had and the best s'mores. Still licking her lips, Sugar said, "You and your family are officially invited to our grand picky-nick. It will be held in Poppy Park, in the Village of Ooga Ooga, on the last day of summer."

"Yes, please come!" Violet pleaded.

"We will if we can!" said Pperfume and Ddandy.

"Glad to hear you will consider coming. Invite all your friends – everyone from Roooganville is invited, too," Topp said.

"We need to be on our way now, if we're going to be home before dark," Taffy said. The *thank yous* and such were quick, and the kiddos hustled back up to their waiting bikes, hopped on, and sped off as quick as a dash.

They soon came to the rim of Rusty Canyon, the deep ravine, and rough carved gullies below the Chocolate Hills. They parked their bikes and this time, they chained them together. The rascally Rachett brothers won't be able to take them this time. They skedaddled down into the canyon where the zoooms live and hide, and oh yeah, where the dangerous biting chiperoos reside in the shadows!

Once in the canyon, they searched in dark areas for zoooms, all the while keeping a wary eye out for those scary chiperoos.

"I found a zooom!" Balooon shouted as he brought something out into the bright sunlight where they all could see it. "It looks and smells like a peanut butter and jelly sandwich – it's definitely a zooom!"

"We found the first one quickly, so there must be tons of them around," Taffy said excitedly.

However, when they started searching again, it didn't go so well. They looked and looked, but no more were found. Even with all six kiddos searching every shadowy cranny and crevasse, they came up empty. It came into their minds that *something* must be wrong.

"It's like the zoooms are hiding from us! There must be a reason we can't find any more of them," Topp said to himself, but loudly enough that the others overheard.

"Maybe they're hiding from the … biting chiperoos!" Sugar said, glancing around with concern!

"I think we need to go to Bugg Town," Violet said. "We need to find Cricket and Buggy. It seems to me there must be something more we need to know about gathering zoooms. Maybe there's a trick to it."

The kiddos agreed that they should have found more than one by now, and they knew that just one zooom for climbing Ooga Mountain would not do.

They climbed out of the canyon lickety-split to where their bikes were parked. The bikes were still there waiting for them, unlike the last time!

The kiddos hopped onto their three-wheelers in a flash and rode toward the Ice Bug Sea and Bugg Town.

Chapter 67

THE ENCOUNTER WITH VICIOUS ICE BUGS

❧

The road to Bugg Town is narrow but well kept. It loops around the eastern end of the Chocolate Hills, crosses an open plain of short grasses, and then meanders through rolling hills to Bugg Town. This seaside hamlet lies on the eastern shore of the Ice Bug Sea and is the home of Buggy and Cricket. The ride to Bugg Town is long but not hard – it's flat for the greater part of the way.

The kiddos made good time getting there because they are strong riders, and they were helped by the one zooom that they had found and shared.

The kiddos glided into Bugg Town and stopped their bikes in a park near the wharf.

Staring out at the unfamiliar surroundings and the Ice Bug Sea, Sugar said, "I hope we don't get clawed by those nasty ice bugs while we're here!"

"Me, too," Balooon said. "I wonder if they are as terrible as the flying flamboes!"

"You two are silly. There aren't any flying flamboes, and there might not be any ice bugs, either," Walnut said with his cheeky grin.

"That's not what Pperfume and Ddandy said!" Sugar spouted tersely, to remind them of their warning about ice bugs and their claws.

319

Their attention shifted to three children playing on swings. Taffy walked over and asked them, "Do you know Buggy and Cricket?"

The young children smiled but didn't say a word, they just pointed down the street and held up three fingers.

The kiddos got back onto their bikes and rode down the street for three blocks. They were delighted when they saw Cricket and Buggy climbing a tree in front of what they assumed was their house.

"Lookie there!" Buggy said to Cricket, pointing his finger at the kiddos.

"Wow, you came to Bugg Town! Welcome!" Cricket said. "What brings you travelers here from far away?"

Topp said, "We were searching for zoooms in Rusty Canyon, but we only found one. We never found another, no matter how hard we looked! We thought we must be doing something wrong, so we decided to visit you to ask why we haven't found even one more."

Buggy smiled and asked, "Did you say 'thank you' to the zooom you found and bow down to it like this?" He held his hands together like in prayer or reverence, then bent slowly at the waist and made a cute bow to a pretend zooom.

"Why ... no, we didn't," Sugar said with a quizzical look. "Do they have ears that can hear and eyes that can see?"

"Sort of," said Cricket. "It's a kind of spiritual moment that the zoooms can sense. That's about the best I can tell you, but it works and you'll feel good about doing it. It's an expression of gratitude for the gift they give."

"Wow, we'll have to try that!" Walnut said. "Do you think they'll like whistling?"

"I don't know, but I'll ask them the next time I see them," Buggy said.

"Huh?" Balooon mumbled to himself, wondering if the zoooms can talk as well as see and hear.

"Take a look over there," Cricket said, pointing to the dark Ice Bug Sea. "If you look, you can see ice bergs floating around out there. They are the size of mountains. I bet you don't have those in the Valley of Ooga Ooga!"

"You got that right!" Violet said. The kiddos looked mesmerized as they peered out at what appeared to be huge white ice cubes floating in the brackish sea.

"Also, see that town over there across the water? That's Bergville, where the Rachett brothers live. You don't want to go there. Most of the people from that town are crotchety and unfriendly."

"We won't, if you say not to," Topp said. "Hey, is there any way you can show us an ice bug while we're here – from a safe distance, of course?!"

"You want to see an ice bug? Okay, come on into our house and we'll show you one. In fact, we have two of them," Cricket said.

Whoa! Ice bugs inside their house?! they thought.

"They must be in strong cages then," Violet said.

"Why is that?" Cricket asked.

"Because of their claws," Sugar said.

"Yes, they have claws, but that's not a problem. They are great house pets really," Buggy said.

"Yikes," mumbled Balooon.

The kiddos followed Cricket and Buggy down a long winding path to their house and entered with great trepidation. This is the last place the kiddos thought ice bugs would be – in a *house*. They were said to be nasty vicious creatures, with sharp teeth, dangerous claws on all four of their feet, and one on their nose as well!

When all the kiddos were standing side by side in the living room, Cricket said, "Stay here, I'll go find one."

The kiddos stood there with their eyes wide open in anticipation of seeing their first ice bug. The tension on their faces was clear as the seconds ticked away. They heard shuffling noises from deep inside the house. Cricket suddenly appeared from the hallway with something white and hairy in her arms. They were shocked that she would be holding a dangerous ice bug. *Shouldn't it be in a cage?!* they thought.

"Here's Smoothie, our white ice bug," she said, lifting the critter up high so they all could see it.

"That's a cat!!!" Sugar said in disbelief.

"What's a *cat*?" Buggy asked.

"That! *That's* a cat!" Walnut said, pointing to what clearly appeared to him to be a cat.

"No, it's an ice bug, a white one," Buggy said with a smile. "I still don't understand what a *cat* is. What is a *cat*?"

"An ice bug, I guess," Sugar said, staring at the cuddly white cat in Cricket's arms. It didn't have a claw on its nose, but it was making the humming sound that Pperfume warned them about.

"It's purring, just like a cat!" Taffy noted.

"Oh! And here comes Buzz Wuzz, our other ice bug," Cricket said. A big gray cat pranced into the room and strutted in front of them like it was modeling on a runway.

"Oh, I get it! You must have heard stories about how terrible and mean ice bugs are. That's just a stupid story made up by the Rachett brothers to scare little kids. Ice bugs are friendly and sweet," Buggy said.

The kiddos were fully amused at this point and petted the purring cats. They now thought the whole thing was funny. They had thought that ice bugs were strange and scary creatures, but they're just cats, called by a different name.

Balooon quietly stared at the two cats and said, "I wonder if Smokey knows she's an ice bug?"

The kiddos laughed at how funny that sounded.

"Why are they called ice bugs, anyway?" Sugar asked.

"I don't know. I wasn't around back then," Cricket answered slyly.

"Hey, you two, on the last day of summer we're going to have a grand picky-nick in Poppy Park in the Village of Ooga Ooga, and we would like you to come! Oh, and *all* the people of Bugg Town are invited too. Be sure to tell them," Taffy said.

"Sounds wonderful. We'll try to be there!" Cricket said.

Topp then asked the kids a question, "Out on the Ice Bug Sea, if someone sailed in a boat straight out for a long, long time, what would they find? Does it end at another shore of land, or does it just keep going?"

Buggy's eyebrows rose in surprise. "Just the other day, I overheard two old sailors down on the dock talking about that exact thing. One of them mentioned that their great-great-grandfather had crossed the sea and found land on the other side. The story was that he beached the boat and kept going on foot across the strange distant land and eventually found another sea."

"Did they say anything else?" Taffy asked.

"One of the seafarers said that the explorer never went any farther. They said that everyone figures that it just goes like that – a sea, and then land, a sea, and then more land. They concluded that the land and seas just go on forever."

"But they didn't know for sure, did they? They didn't keep going," Topp said. "We found an ancient map in a bottle that showed that our world ends somewhere out there. The map showed an *edge* to the land in all four directions. However, that was an ancient map. In modern times, nobody has proven that there's an *edge* or end to our land, anywhere."

"I've never heard anything different than what the sailors on the dock said, and they know a lot," Buggy explained.

"We hope to find that *edge* someday – if it exists," Taffy said.

"Nobody around here has ever mentioned an edge. We wish we could help you more, but I guess we can't," Cricket said.

"That's okay, we'll have a fun time adventuring, whether we find an *edge* or not," Walnut said.

With feelings of goodwill all around, the kiddos were grateful to Buggy and Cricket for their hospitality and the knowledge they shared about how to properly honor zoooms. Now it was time for them to ride hard and get back to Rusty Canyon because the day was moving along more rapidly than they were.

Chapter 68

CREATURES IN THE DARK SHADOWS

❧⚜

When the kiddos coasted up to the bluff above the canyon, they had a hunch they would find zoooms because there are shadows everywhere this time of day. Yes, the biting chiperoos hang out in the shadows too, but the kiddos will deal with them, when and if they must.

Thanks to Buggy and Cricket, the kiddos now know the trick to find and gather zoooms. They also learned from the Bugg Town kids that the zoooms can see, hear, and maybe even talk. Zoooms have great awareness of things going on around them. The kiddos also learned a life lesson about taking things. They learned to express gratitude for all things they receive. That's the right attitude to have in life, don't you think?

The kiddos locked their bikes and hurried down into the canyon on swift feet. They stayed together as a group while hunting in the shadows for the fabulous zoooms. Within a minute, Violet found a very nice, smiley one.

The kiddos gently removed it from a dark crevice, put it on a flat rock, and circled around it. They felt a little silly but then gracefully bowed and said "thank you" to the zoom with sincerity. It seemed to smile like it was glad it had been found.

Buggy and Cricket told them interesting things about zoooms. Not only do zoooms like to be found, but they also don't mind being eaten!

It gives the zoooms their purpose for existing. The zoooms would not want to live for years, get old and wrinkly, and then wither away without giving generously of themselves. The kiddos learned that the zoooms are delighted to serve a special purpose: to give their lives for the greater good of others. The kiddos know now that the zoooms are special living things because they care.

You want to do something special with your life, don't you? And you'll be able to do special things for others – without being eaten!

So, what do zoooms taste like? Do they really taste better than strong beans? Yes! A million yeses! They taste like peanut butter and jelly sandwiches, while strong beans taste like ... never mind. Give me zoooms, any day!

The true test of harvesting zoooms was still ahead of them because they had only found one so far on this search. Moving around in a group, they looked in the shadows, and it didn't take long before they found one. And again, they bowed and thanked it.

"Buggy was right! We must express gratitude for the gift that they are. They are wonderful living things," Violet said.

Sugar wandered away a little and suddenly yelled out, "Hey! Come look at this cute critter, it looks like a chipmunk. It came right up to me! It's friendly – sort of!"

The critter showed no fear at all. When Sugar reached a hand down to pet it, the critter took a forceful peck at her fingers.

"Whoa! It tried to bite me!" Sugar shrieked.

"OH NO! IT MUST BE A BITING CHIPEROO!" Balooon shouted.

The kiddos were frozen in amazement. Somewhere in their minds, they had imagined that the biting chiperoos were large scary beasts. Now they see that they are small and rather cute.

"Did it hurt you, Sugar?" Taffy asked, concerned about Sugar's well-being.

"No, not really!" Sugar said. "It was more like a rough kiss! It doesn't seem to have any teeth."

"Wow, how fascinating!" Walnut said. "It looks as though it likes you. It keeps hanging around."

"I guess it likes the way you taste," Taffy said with a smile, remembering that once a biting chiperoo gets a taste of someone, they want to keep tasting them all the time.

"The bite didn't bother me," Sugar said with a grin. "It tickled! I guess it's like a pet, and it wants to be near me – like a puppy dog. Maybe I'll take it home with me … naw, my planana tree would be too jealous, and it might not get along with Ragamuffin!"

"I think you lost your mind, Sugar! Maybe the chiperoo ate your brain somehow," Topp said in jest.

"Naw, I don't think so," Taffy said, standing up for Sugar. "She's always been a little daffy about critters! Maybe this is just a *new* daffy!"

"It's time to get back to work, fellow kiddos," Topp directed. "We have a lot to do today before it gets any later. Let's get going!"

They started the hunt again – all seven of them. (Don't forget the chiperoo.)

It didn't take them long to find six more zoooms. "We should each eat one, so we have lots of energy to collect more of them," Topp said. "We still have a lot more to collect, then get chocolate, do all that, and get back before dark."

"Let's spread out and hunt for them separately," Taffy suggested. "We'll find them faster that way."

"Good idea!" someone said.

So, the kiddos took off through the rocky canyon and continued searching. After a while, they got together again, showed their zoooms and laid them out.

"I only found two more, then I never found another," Taffy said.

"Me, too," the others said.

"Buggy said there is likely a limit of a certain number per person," Balooon remembered. "If we count those we ate, we each found three. There are six of us, which makes eighteen in total."

"That's a lot, certainly enough for us to go up Ooga Mountain," Taffy said with satisfaction. "Let's go get chocolate, leave the chiperoo behind, and then head for home."

After scrambling up the steep Chocolate Hills, the kiddos found a good vein of chocolate to dig. Violet lit a fire, and Topp heated the steel rod. It didn't take long before their strong new backpacks were full to the top with chocolate and zooooms. They hurried down the steep hillside into Rusty Canyon and up to their bikes.

When they arrived, they saw Sugar's chiperoo sitting next to *her* bike. "Oh my!" squealed Sugar. "My pet chiperoo really does like me. It even knows which bike is mine!"

When they got up to full speed on the ride to The Gap, the chiperoo just couldn't keep up with them. Sugar breathed a sigh of relief when she looked back and didn't see it anymore. She also felt a little guilty for abandoning the sweet little critter.

As they rode rapidly down the narrow trail, they stayed in a line with Violet at the back. At one point, Taffy looked around and was surprised to see that Violet was nowhere in sight. "Hey! Violet isn't behind us anymore!"

The kiddos all stopped abruptly and shouted out to her, "Violet! Violet!"

There was no response at all.

"I'll go back and find her," Topp said with concern. "Wait here."

The kiddos waited and waited, but neither showed up.

"I hope they come back soon," Sugar said, looking up at the fading light in the late afternoon sky. "It will be getting dark soon, too soon!"

Chapter 69

BOBBY'S TROUBLESOME NEW PET

❧❦

In Uncle Roy's house by the sea, Bobby wiggled around under the bed covers before he left the bed. He heard the breaking waves cracking though the quiet of the early morning by the sea. The first light of day began peeking through a gap in the window curtain and splashed across the foot of his bed.

He was relaxed and comfortable, so he lay there for a while with his mind pondering. He began going over the events of his latest dream. The wild raft adventure the dream-kids had endured came to a happy conclusion. They had made it home and were safe at last. *What a relief*, he thought. Then the dream-kids took off to get more chocolate and unusual sandwiches. They had also gone to visit friends in a town by a faraway icy sea and petted two cats. He smiled, with warm thoughts of the children he has grown so close to in his dreams.

Bobby got out of bed and strolled into the hallway. He sauntered outside through a side door to a small pathway leading to the edge of the bluff overlooking the sea. *What a big world it is*, he thought to himself as he looked out over the vast sea and saw an island on the distant horizon. He sat down on a bench and thought about all his many blessings: his family, his home, his cozy room, his girlfriend, Cookie, and Fluffers, his cat. As he sat there, he realized how good his *real* life is and how special and real his dreams have become.

He looked up the coast, saw a mountain, and thought of the mountain in his dream and the other one made of candy.

"Daydreaming, Bobby?" his sister asked, walking up behind him. "You looked like you were in a trance."

Bobby slowly turned his head and looked at her with a welcoming smile.

Bettykins quietly sat down beside him. Bobby began letting his inward thoughts flow out to her, "I'm living such a big life, sis. I live in this big ol' world here with you, Mom, and Dad, and at the same time, I live in the amazing dream world that's within me. Sometimes the two lives blend. All in all, I have a *very* full life."

Bettykins has learned that Bobby is quite pleased with his double life, and she enjoys being part of it.

Suddenly, a voice from the house broke the pensive mood. "Bettykins, Bobby, breakfast is ready!" their mom shouted, loud enough to be heard above the crashing of the waves.

"Okay!" the siblings chorused.

The visit to Uncle Roy's was a great family gathering. Rufus and Roy shared stories about times together when they were young. They told tales rich with family and fun. Bobby and Bettykins enjoyed listening to them reminisce. Many of the stories they had never heard before.

About noon of the second day, Uncle Roy announced that he had heard that a temporary bridge had been built upriver from the old washed-out bridge. He said the road back to town was now open for traffic.

"Well, it's time to head home, guys!" Rufus said with purpose. "I've got a lot of work to catch up on."

So, the family packed up, said goodbye to Uncle Roy, and hit the road. The trip was smooth, except for rolling over the bumpy temporary pontoon bridge. When they cruised up their street, Bobby was glad to be home again. He was excited about making new memories with his dad in the days, weeks, and years ahead.

৵

The next morning, Bettykins needed to get back to school, so she left on the first bus. "I'll be back soon!" she shouted out the window as the bus pulled away.

After breakfast, Bobby showed his dad all the projects he had done over the last year or so. Rufus was impressed with the wide range of talents Bobby expressed in his hobbies and projects. His dad was amazed at the roller coaster made of thousands of little toothpicks and the newly built clubhouse. But he wasn't sure what to make of his talking plants – he himself had never heard a word from them.

As Rufus buried himself in office work, Bobby wandered outside with a plate of chocolate chip cookies his mom just baked. Just as the cookies were placed on the table, the real Cookie came running up.

"Hi, Bobby, nice to have you back!" she said warmly. "When the bridge washed out, I wondered if you would be able to come back at all!"

After small talk, they each picked up a cookie off the plate and strolled hand in hand to the clubhouse. They hung out inside for a while and shared stories about the events of the last few days. "Do you want more cookies, Cookie? I'll go get some," Bobby said.

He took off to grab a couple more, but there were only crumbs on the plate! "What happened to the cookies?!" Bobby asked out loud.

Cookie and Bobby looked around and walked here and there, hunting for the missing treats.

"Here's a piece on the ground," Cookie said. "And another one!"

They followed a trail of cookie crumbs which led to an oak tree.

Bobby gazed up and instantly knew what had happened to all the cookies. He saw a chipmunk sitting on a branch, fat as could be, chomping on a piece of cookie and dropping crumbs everywhere. The chipmunk stared down from its high perch and smiled a weird, chipmunky smile.

Unexpectedly, the chipmunk ran down the tree in a blur and sped between the two kids as if they weren't even there. It headed to the picnic table and jumped up. Without a care in the world, it sat down in front of the plate and picked up the remaining crumbs. The kids rushed over, but the chipmunk didn't move. It just stared at them.

"I hope Fluffers doesn't mind. It looks like you have a new pet!" Cookie said.

"I should have expected it because in my dream last night one of the kids just got a new chipmunk-like friend. Amazing."

"It looks like your dream keeps showing up in your real life. It's fascinating!" Cookie said.

"Hi, little chipmunk. I'm gonna name you Chip Chip, for all the chocolate chips you've eaten," Bobby said.

And so it goes.

Chapter 70

MONSTER IN THE BUSHES

❧❦

The four kiddos, with their backpacks heavy with goodies, were waiting on the trail for Violet and Topp to return. The evening shadows descended upon them as they looked for any sign of them. Even though they felt the urge to get going, they had to wait until Violet and Topp showed up.

The four impatient kiddos saw a lone figure coming toward them. It was Topp. As he skidded to a stop, he called out, "Hey Sugar, do you have a tire patch kit and bike pump in your emergency kit? Violet had a flat tire back there!"

"I sure do!" said Sugar as she handed them over to Topp.

"I'll be right back," he said. He turned his bike around and headed back at full speed.

"I'm going with him," Sugar said. "You three stay here so we have three here and three there!"

"Good idea," Taffy said, thinking about safety.

Topp and Sugar rode quickly to make the best time they could. When they arrived to fix Violet's bike tire, Violet wasn't alone. Next to her was Sugar's new friend, the biting chiperoo!

"Oh no," Sugar said as the chiperoo scrambled up to her and bit her ankle.

Topp ignored what was going on and made quick work of the tire repair. Topp, Violet, and Sugar took off abruptly, leaving the biting chiperoo behind in a cloud of rust-colored dust.

Back together again and ready to ride, the six kiddos picked up the pace. They rode at breakneck speed up the trail with Topp at the front of the pack. They rode on speedily for a while until Topp skidded to a stop in front of them.

"Oh no, there's a gate across The Gap!" Topp cried. "I think we're stuck!"

They dearly wanted to get home, but they were now trapped on the wrong side of the Charcoal Cliffs. The darkening was almost complete, and there would be no help from moonlight because the glowing orb was hiding behind clouds in the night sky. There were stars shining between clouds here and there, and their glow cast a mellow light around them. They were a long way from home and scared. The darkness consumed the land around them.

"What if we go down to Pperfume and Ddandy's house and see if they can unlock the gate for us?" Taffy suggested.

Without hesitation, the kiddos rode down to the island home of their friends. They stopped next to the water's edge where the steppingstones to the cottage began. From there, they had a clear view of the house.

"The cottage is dark," Taffy said. "I'll go check to see if anyone answers the door." She went hop, hop, and hop on the steppingstones to the front porch. She knocked several times, but nobody came. She could barely see the stones to step on in the darkness when she hopped back to the others. She didn't need to say anything, they knew that nobody was home.

"Well, there is another way to get to the other side of the Charcoal Cliffs," Topp said. "Through Rat Town, er, Roooganville."

Darkness fully filled the night air now, so if they wanted to get home they needed to walk their bikes through the town. They used the dim light from the stars and the yellow glow from the windows of houses to light their way.

They were frightened as they moved slowly in a bunch down the poorly lit road. They looked from side to side, as though they expected rats to come leaping out at them. The fact that the rats were called hamsters did not help them feel better – they know rats when they see them.

As they passed a house just outside of town, they heard lovely singing and laughing from within. That was comforting to the kiddos. If rats did attack, they could run to one of those well-lit houses.

Cautiously, they approached what seemed to be the center of town. The houses were closer together and brighter now which helped them to see. They heard children playing and singing songs inside homes as they moved along through the town.

In one house, they heard a man reading a children's book out loud. The kiddos paused and listened for a moment. It was a story about children getting lost while traveling in a faraway world. If they'd had more time, they would have lingered longer to find out if the kids in that story got home safely but they had to keep going.

The kiddos didn't say anything, but they all felt more at ease because they could hear comforting sounds all around Roooganville. They had no other choice, so they continued on their way, hoping to find the road that would lead back to Spooky Hollow.

"What was that?!" Sugar whispered, louder than she meant to.

"It sounded like a large creature scurrying around in the shrubs, like a tiger or a giant rat," Walnut said, looking at Sugar and speaking in a spooky teasing voice.

"They're hamsters here, not rats," Balooon said. That was a comforting thought, but Balooon was afraid, and he wished he were floating *over* this spooky place, instead of walking through it in the dark.

They continued quietly shuffling down the road but no matter what speed they were moving, they could still hear the rustling sounds of some type of creature in the bushes nearby. It seemed to be keeping up with them, just like a monster stalking children before it pounced.

"I think it's following us!" Violet said, her voice trembling. She shook her ankles and called out to her angels and fairies for protection.

Suddenly, a head with two glowing orange eyes peered out of a hedge only a few feet away from them. They were petrified with fear for a moment, seeing the eyes of an unknown critter staring at them from the shadows.

Then the creature crept out into the starlight.

"It's the chiperoo!" Taffy said. "It's Sugar's biting chiperoo!"

"Oh, my goodness!" Sugar moaned. She was glad that it wasn't a monster and somewhat happy to see her little friend again. "I guess I have a pet for life!"

She reached down to pick up the lovable little chipmunky-looking animal and received a kiss on her wrist in return. "Its name has to be Roo Roo but not *Biting* Roo Roo," she said. She placed Roo Roo in her backpack with its head sticking out, and then they moved on.

Violet spoke up, "If we can get to the Rat Town Trail, I know where there are fairy flowers near the road that can light our way home!"

The kiddos' eyes had gotten more used to the darkness, so they moved more quickly. They knew they were on the right track, and they weren't scared anymore. Maybe there *were* rats out there, but they never saw any and were glad for that.

Eventually, they reached the sign for the turnoff to Roooganville, so they hunted for the fairy flowers.

Walnut took in a deep breath and started whistling. Along the trail, a cluster of fairy flowers lit up. Oh, how Walnut can whistle!

Seeing the flowers glowing, the kiddos cleared their throats and started whistling too. They picked flowers (with their permission, of course), until they had all they needed. Using the string that Sugar carries with her, the kiddos tied bouquets of the magical flowers to the front of their bikes. The six kiddos whistled loudly as they rode down the trail toward the shady glade as if it were daytime.

It was late, but all seven of them (don't forget Roo Roo) made it back to the Big Abble in good shape. Ragamuffin and Smokey welcomed the kiddos but like most cats, they are wary of strange animals. Roo Roo calmly walked over to Ragamuffin and sniffed. Then she went over to Smokey and sniffed again. Roo Roo must have thought they wouldn't taste good, so she calmly lay down near them. It appeared that the three pets had become instant friends.

The kiddos emptied the contents of their packs onto the table and were amazed at all the treasure of zoooms and chocolate they had brought back.

They were exhausted, and their energy was long gone. "We have only one day to rest up to get ready to climb to the top of Ooga Mountain," Taffy reminded them.

The tired kiddos jumped into their beds and went to sleep straightaway.

Chapter 71

AMAZING BABY GRAVITY DAY

༄

"Wake up! Wake up!" yelled Taffy as she raced around the clubhouse waving her arms wildly. "Let's get going!"

"Wha-what's going on?" Walnut mumbled, trying to open either eye to see what the shouting was about.

"Is dark ow-side, Taff!" Sugar said, slurring her early morning words. "Whaz all the fuzz about?"

"It's Baby Gravity Day!" Taffy shouted. "It's time to get up and get going! It only happens once every seventeen years! Ooga Mountain, here we come!"

Topp wobbled to his feet and lit a candle in the complete darkness of the clubhouse. "Is this *really* what we planned to do?" Topp asked Taffy.

"It's *gotta* be the plan!" Taffy said. "A day is very short – so let's get going! When this special day is over, all the following days for seventeen years will be full-weight gravity."

THUMP!

"Baby Gravity Day is true!" Taffy screamed out. "I just leaped across the room in one hop!"

Taffy beckoned the others to wake up and try hopping around in less gravity than they'd ever experienced in their lives.

The kiddos who tried to go back to sleep soon realized it was pointless. Taffy was hopping around making loud thumps, and Walnut was doing the same thing. It took a while, but eventually all six kiddos got to their feet. They started leaping around and shouted with excitement as they experienced being almost weightless.

Even Balooon and Smokey came down from the treehouse after hearing all the commotion. You should have seen that cat-bird Smokey fly! In fact, Smokey took off, flapped her wings wildly, and didn't come back down again! Smokey was *flying* for the first time ever!

"The weak force of gravity (or whatever it's called) can't pull her back down. She's flying around the clubhouse just like a big plump fuzzy cat-bird," Balooon said proudly.

Have you ever seen a cat fly? I hadn't – until then.

"It's time to get started!" Taffy yelled. "Let's gather around for a final check and get ready to leave."

"I have a question," Walnut said, speaking to the entire group. "What *is* gravity, anyway?"

"It's what keeps us stuck on the ground," Sugar answered. "If gravity went away, we would just float up into the sky! That's about all I know about it."

"It's kind of like *time,*" Topp remarked. "You can't *see* time, but you know it's around somewhere. Gravity is like that."

"What I can say about *time* is that if time didn't exist, we would just stay frozen in one moment," Violet said. "There would never be a tomorrow or even a next minute!"

"It's kind of like *life,*" Taffy said, making things even more complicated. "We can't see life nor touch life but we know when it's there – and we know when it's not there."

"I sort of get what gravity is," Balooon chimed in. "When I go up in the balloon, I am defying gravity but when Vaporgas leaks out, gravity pulls me straight back down again – every time! Gravity never seems to get tired. It's always ready to pull me right back down – except not so much today!"

"All I know is that gravity today is less than what it *usually* is," Taffy said. "So, let's go climb to the tip-top of that there mountain!"

The day before, the kiddos had spent all their time preparing for today's journey. They had their big backpacks full of everything, anything, and whatever-thing.

They had packed plenty of chocolate and zoooms, as well as warm clothes for the cold on top of Ooga Mountain that they had heard about. They all had hiking boots too. Their bikes would have to be parked less than halfway up, at Lookout Rock. Of course, they had covered their bike tires with blob oil, to give them that extra riding ease. Eventually, they had everything ready. Knowing they had a big day ahead of them, they'd gone to bed early the night before.

Violet made pancakes to fill up everyone's tummies for the long day ahead. She added zoooms and chocolate chips to the pancakes. Why not, they had gobs of both!

They sat in silence around the table and concentrated on eating the pancakes quickly. They kept glancing at the window to see if there was any light of dawn out there yet. They were eager to hit the road when the first glow of daybreak broke through the dark sky.

"Let's go!" shouted Taffy.

The kiddos hopped out the door with big smiles and all. But Ragamuffin and Roo Roo looked quite glum, for they had been told that they could not go on this long trip. Smokey, on the other hand, had also been told she couldn't go but she didn't care. She knew she would be just as happy flying around the shady glade from tree to tree. All the hours she had spent strengthening her wings had finally paid off!

You might think the what-ers are weird to look at. Well, that's true, but a big, fuzzy, smiling flying cat ... now that's a sight to see!

The top of Ooga Mountain had turned golden from the suns rising over the Tot Tot Hills. This day, the suns were lined up right on top of each other, so it looked like just one sun. The mountain had never looked so beautiful in the early morning splendor.

"There it is!" Taffy shouted. "And today, we'll be at the very top!"

The other kiddos looked up at the mountain in awe – and with a little fear. They were thinking, *What's up there? Are there dangers we don't know about? Will we be strong enough to get to the top – and still be fit enough to get back down in one day? Will Baby Gravity Day really help us that much?*

Sugar stared up at the tall mountain and thought to herself, *Something always goes wrong – I wonder what it'll be this time!*

Many questions filled their minds as they sped off in an instant on their well-tuned three-wheeled bicycles. They left a small cloud of shady glade dust behind them in the cool morning air.

They made good time leaving the Village of Ooga Ooga. They crossed the bridge in record time and rode up the Wiggle Canyon Trail halfway to Lookout Rock in just a few minutes. They rode up the lower slopes of the mountain rapidly, almost as if the trail was downhill.

They carried their bikes across Whistle Creek so the blob oil wouldn't wash off. As they left the creek, they said "hello" to the fairy flowers (as if talking to flowers made sense).

Topp was prepared for the two-headed snakes should they appear on the trail this time – which they certainly did! Topp shook his pea rattle at the snakes, including the one with three heads, and they all ran off into the bushes on their ten little feet.

When the kiddos reached Lookout Rock, they were amazed at how fast and effortless the trip had been. They were also surprised to see the dozens of bikes parked there. "All the riders must have already left on foot to continue up the mountain," Taffy remarked. "Wow, there must be a bunch of people going to the top today. At least we won't be alone way up there."

The weather was warm but not hot, sunny but not too sunny. There were several patches of white puffy clouds around, giving them ample shade. It was a perfect day to climb to the top of the mountain. The kiddos parked their bikes and prepared for the formidable hike to the tippy top of the mighty Ooga Mountain – at last!

Chapter 72

MILLIONS OF SNOW BUNNIES

৵৵

Satisfied that their bikes were securely locked together (Rachett brothers safe), the kiddos wandered over to the edge of Lookout Rock. They crept just close enough to the overhanging edge to get that queasy, butterfly-in-the-tummy feeling, then they backed up a little.

"Look, it's the shady glade," Sugar shouted, "and there's the Big Abble in the shadows."

"I see the Ooga River Falls and the Bubble Bath too!" Violet said excitedly.

Looking farther to the north, Walnut said, "Look at Silver Peak, the Ooga River going through the Yeller Cliffs, the Fantasmo Sea, and Wow Mountain way out there."

Yes, there the kiddos were, far up on Ooga Mountain and it was still early in the morning. "Thanks, Baby Gravity Day!" Violet whispered.

The kiddos held hands and made a circle as they do from time to time. They lowered their hands then threw them above their heads and shouted, "Rainbow kiddos away!"

They moved up the trail quickly and with every step, they were higher on the mountain than they had ever been before.

Eventually, the slope of the mountain got steeper, and the trail became a switchback, which is a trail that runs back and forth across the slope's face. Zigzag switchback trails are dangerous because they're always on very steep grades such as this one. When a trail reverses course or switches back, there's always a dangerous drop-off at each turn.

The kiddos chugged up the mountain like the little train that could. As they moved up, Topp shouted out, "Whoa! Stop!" He put his hands out and signaled for the others to stop where they were. "There's a snake ahead – a saber-tooth rainbow snake at that! I saw a painting of one on display at the Museum of Everything!"

"Shake your pea rattle at it!" Violet suggested.

Shake it he did, but the rainbow snake just looked annoyed by Topp's antics. Its huge, colorful body was stretched across the trail, and its beady eyes stared at Topp with a menacing glare. It flicked its forked tongue in and out like snakes do when they are trying to pick up the scent of prey.

Topp recalled the lesson about being grateful for what the zoooms offered. He decided to be more diplomatic and try a little kindness, instead of rudely shaking his rattle at the snake.

Topp said softly to the snake, "Thank you for doing whatever it is you do, lovely snake. I do appreciate whatever that might be. We young children certainly mean you no harm whatsoever. So, now I ask and very politely do I ask, could you please kindly move a bit aside so that we may pass by and continue peacefully on our journey up this glorious pathway?"

The rainbow snake looked at Topp with what seemed like a frightening stare. Then it said in perfect Oogan, "Most certainly, young sir! I will gladly grant the wish for you and your companions to pass on by. Do have a wonderful journey." The snake lifted its head with dignity and slithered gracefully off the trail into the bushes below.

The kiddos didn't hesitate. They quickly moved forward and adroitly past where the snake had been on the dangerous switchback trail.

Taffy asked Topp, "How did you come up with that idea to get past the snake? That was genius."

"From the lessons we've learned about kindness, I suppose," he said.

When the zigzag trail ended, they found themselves walking through a pleasant, wooded area. Sugar moved ahead of the others, rounded a corner, and came to an abrupt stop, causing everyone to bang into each other in a chain reaction.

"It's a giant spider! Yikes!" Sugar shouted.

Right in front of her, suspended over the trail from an overhanging branch, was a massive spider that looked like a large ladybug with long legs. It was scary-looking but kind of cute too. It was just hanging there on a very thick strand of web.

"It's a fire spider!" Violet declared. "We have them around Purple Springs, on the west side of the mountain. I didn't know they lived up this high. They're harmless – *most of the time*, anyhow!"

Sugar began wondering what the fire spiders did when they *weren't harmless some of the time*. She didn't want to know bad things about them because she liked bugs and spiders, and she didn't want to hold a grudge against any of them for bad things they might have done in the past.

"They glow in the dark, don't they, Violet?" Balooon asked.

"That's right. They glow as brightly as fairy flowers."

"I sure do like the clothes, ropes, and thread we make from their webs!" Topp said. "Our lives would not be as good without them. I wish I had jujuberries to share with it."

As the kiddos moved onward into the wooded area, they were no longer afraid of the spider – it was now their friend.

As they continued climbing upward, Balooon remarked, "It sure seems dark in these woods."

"I agree – too dark!" Taffy said. "Something seems strange."

"It's the clouds!" Topp shouted. "The sky has turned gloomy dark!"

"Uh-oh!" someone said ...

CRRRAAACCCKKK went the thunder! A bright light flashed, and raindrops started coming down hard. It was a cold blue rain.

"Uh-oh!" someone said ...

The kiddos retreated down the trail and sheltered in the woods nearby. Knowing it would take a while for the rain drops to work their way down the leaves, they had time to tie a tarp from Sugar's emergency kit onto the branches to create a roof to hide under.

They built their little shelter a fair distance from the trail, and they were soon glad they did. As the rain got harder, droves of people showed up, hurriedly running down the trail to get away from the downpour. Perhaps as many as twenty-five people went by in a brief time. They were running in panic on their way down the mountain. The kiddos figured the people had given up on the goal to get to the top – just because of a little rain. Oh … and deafening thunder and bolts of white-hot lightning!

The six kiddos will not turn back, oh no! This is their best chance to reach the top because they know that full gravity will return tomorrow and last for another seventeen years.

It was wise to wait for the worst of the storm to pass. Not just because of the rain but for the dangerous lightning bolts that had been striking the mountain all around.

The time spent under their rain shelter gave the kiddos an opportunity to rest. Once they got going again, they rapidly ascended the steepest part of the mountain.

Oh, how close they were to the lovely ball rocks and the delicious mittenweed! They were also looking forward to having Ooga Mountain ice cream from the oozy ice cream glacier at the top. All was going well, the sky had cleared up, and the day was not even half used up.

As the steep trail passed through a lush green canyon, there was a distinctively tasty smell in the air. Violet reached down and picked a small sprig from a dark green clover-like plant that flanked them and popped it into her mouth. "It's mittenweed – very sweet, such a fresh taste!"

As the kiddos munched with delight on mittenweed, they knew that the top of the mountain was not far above them. They would be among the ball rocks and on top of the mountain within minutes.

Had *all* the other people gone down the trail? Were the kiddos alone? They listened but heard no sounds from above.

Now the trail was so steep, they had to crawl on all fours and inch their way up between the round rocks.

"Boy, I'm sure glad it isn't raining now!" Taffy said. "I don't think we could get back down if it was raining. It's always harder to go *down* a steep slope than *up* one, and it's impossible if it's wet or icy!"

They moved onward up the steep terrain until they reached a cluster of perfectly round rocks, big and small. Some were the size of houses, and others were as small as their heads. They also saw flat rocks stacked on top of each other. Grandpa Gabby had told them that when they come upon stacks of rocks, they are at the top of the mountain.

The kiddos had made it, and there was still more than half a day to go. Plenty of time, they figured, to get back down again. Oh, the wonders of Baby Gravity Day!

At the very tip-top of the peak of the mountain, there was one gigantic ball rock, the largest of them all. It was resting on a flat surface with several thick flat rocks placed around the base to keep it from rolling off the mountain.

The kiddos enjoyed the breathtaking views from the top. In one direction, they could see Candy Mountain. "See you soon!" Sugar shouted.

Taffy said, "Hey Topp, you brought the long-eye, didn't you?"

"Yes, I did! What a terrific opportunity to look for the *edge* from way up here."

Topp first looked toward the Valley of Ooga Ooga. He could clearly see the Tot Tot Hills at the far end of the valley and beyond the hills, he saw the Jolly Jungle. He saw miles and miles of jungle, all the way to the horizon. "Take a look, Taffy, and see if you can see an end to the jungle. It looks to me like it goes on forever."

Taffy looked for herself through the long-eye. "You're right. I don't see an *edge*, even though the air is clear." Then she turned her gaze to the north. She looked over the Yeller Cliffs and far out over the Fantasmo Sea. "I can see land on the far side of the Fantasmo Sea, but it just goes and goes, completely out of sight. I don't see an *edge* that way, either."

"Let me look to the south," Balooon said. He raised the long-eye and looked straight out over the Giant Step Mountains. "I can see the Ice Bug Sea clearly. It seems like it goes on and on. I don't see an *edge* this way, either, or the *edge* is so far away, we would never be able to get there anyway."

Balooon handed the telescope to Violet so she could look to the west. "It's cloudy out there, I can only see for a short distance because a white cloud is blocking my view," Violet exclaimed. "Oh, I know that kind of cloud, it's called a *cold-cloud* – and it's full of snow bunnies! That's perfect for cooling off Candy Mountain. It'll be cool and firm enough to go there any time we want."

Walnut was staring intently at the white cloud and its movement. He suddenly squeaked, "Look, the cloud's coming right at us!"

"Wow, it's almost on top of us!" Sugar cried out, startled by how fast it was approaching.

The visibility was getting worse by the moment as the front fringe of the cloud encased the top of the mountain. Things only got worse when the cloud lowered down on top of them!

"Oh no!" Violet shouted. "Snow bunnies!!!!!"

The kiddos huddled together to stay warm and shooed away any of the cold snow bunnies that tried to jump around on their heads.

There are always millions of snow bunnies when cold white clouds drop them on the mountains. Yes, they are adorable, however they are like fuzzy ice that hops around, making everyone feel cold. And being the rascals that they are, they tickle people with their icy ears.

With snow bunnies hopping around, freezing the ground around them, the kiddos were in a terrible predicament. Getting down the mountain was impossible. "The way down is slippery – way too slippery! We're doomed!" Taffy cried.

"If we don't get off this mountain, we're going to freeze into solid ice!" Balooon cried out in despair. "HELP!!!!!!!!"

Chapter 73

BOBBY, HIS DAD, AND MOUNT MYSTERIOUS

❧

Bobby woke up early in the morning shivering with cold, so he felt around to see what had happened to his blankets. He discovered that they were completely covering him, so he wondered why he was cold under his ample bed covers.

He thought for a few seconds and then remembered. *The dream, that's it. The dream-kids were freezing and stranded up on a massive mountain.*

He mumbled to himself, "I didn't know that dreaming about being chilled could make me cold in real life. But here I am, cold as can be, for no other reason *I* can think of."

He realized more and more how much his now long and ongoing dream was flowing over into his real life. The dream about the land with the funny name felt real to him every night.

He thought, *I'm warming up now. Maybe the dream-kids are getting warm too. I sure hope so.*

"Bobby, it's time to get up!" his mom called out. "You're going to Aunt Ferny's this morning with Dad, remember?"

"Okay, Mom, I'm up. I'll start gettin' ready."

His father hadn't seen his sister, Ferny, since his homecoming from the jungle. He wanted to see her again and catch up, and she wanted him to come for a visit. So, his dad planned a road trip and invited Bobby to come along with him.

Bobby and his dad were going to travel slowly on a gravel road to Theresville, the town where Ferny lives. Rufus knew the trip would take longer on the Coyote Canyon Road, but he wanted to take Bobby to an out-of-the-way mountain he had climbed when he was young.

Bobby, Rufus, and Mari cozied up to the kitchen table before they started out. They enjoyed a nourishing breakfast prepared by an incredibly happy wife and mom. The father and son could taste the love put into the breakfast, and it went down easily. Rufus and Bobby grabbed a few things for the day trip, thanked her, and headed out the door.

They rolled along outside of town on the main road for a while, and then his dad suddenly slowed down and made a sharp turn onto a gravel road. The tires grumbled as they headed up a switchback that zigzagged up a steep hill. After bumping along for more than an hour, his dad pulled over and parked.

"I brought you up here several years ago. You were just a baby then. You wouldn't remember."

They stepped out of the car and walked a short distance to a vantage point where there was an opening between a grove of tall trees. From there, Bobby could see a purple mountain looming high above them. It was very quiet where they were, so they let the serene peace that pervaded this small clearing settle in, all the way to their bones.

"That is a very interesting mountain, Bobby," his dad said. "It holds many mysteries. In fact, it's called Mystery Mountain."

"What do you mean by that?" Bobby asked. "What mysteries?"

"I suppose that's what some would call them. There are old tales about things that happened on this mountain, but nobody knows how true they are. Many of the stories are weird, and most of them are believable enough that people don't explore this mountain anymore. It might be just a normal old mountain, but … it might not be. Most people aren't sure, so they just leave it alone."

"It does feel a little spooky right here on the lower slopes," Bobby said, looking around side to side.

"When I was a young man, I climbed to the top of that mountain," Rufus said, pulling up memories from deep in his past. "The view from up there on top is so spectacular, I have never forgotten it."

"But it looks like sheer cliffs and rock faces near the top," Bobby said. "How could anyone get up there?"

"From the back side. I went with a small group, and we brought a clever rope ladder that enabled us to ascend a rock face on the back side. From there, an animal trail led to the top."

"Wow," is all Bobby could say.

"There's snow up there most of the year," Dad said. "But it's on the far side, so you can't see it from here. I remember how wickedly cold I got up there on the top – awfully cold."

"Wow, it must be really tall to have snow on it all year long," Bobby said. "Maybe I could go to the top someday, like you did!"

"Maybe we can do it together," Rufus said as only a father would say to his only son.

"That would be great and adventurous!" Bobby said.

Bobby stared intently at the top of the mountain for a long while. Like a block of granite, he stood there gazing. The mountain peak had triggered a memory inside of him. It was about the dream he'd had the night before. The dream-kids were stranded, cold and forlorn, on a towering mountain. He wished he could somehow help them and give them warmth. *Maybe tonight I'll help them somehow*, he thought.

"Are you okay, Bobby?" his dad asked.

"Yeah, I'm fine. It's the dream, Dad. The kids in the dream were stuck up on a mountain just like this one, and they were stranded in an awful snowstorm."

"It's *just* a dream, Bobby," his dad said.

However, Bobby knew he would feel better when the dream-kids were okay. His wonderful dream is *not* just a dream – it has truly become a real part of his life.

His dad broke the silence by telling Bobby more about the mountain. "It takes three days of slogging up rugged and steep terrain to complete the round trip. I'm sure you can do it. You're just about fully growed, Bobby!"

"Yes, I am," Bobby said with a modicum of pride.

"Well, we better head on to Ferny's. We still have a long way to travel to get to Theresville."

୭

Ferny was delighted to see her brother and nephew again. She gave Rufus a long hug and greeted Bobby with a very welcoming smile.

"How does this sound?" Ferny asked, "we'll go into town, and I'll show you my new candy store. It's almost ready for the grand opening. Then we can come back here and have a late lunch. Afterward you boys, er, *men,* can head on home." (In the middle of her sentence, Ferny realized that Bobby was no longer the young child she had babysat years ago.)

The tour of the new store was more of a construction viewing than a candy store viewing. There wasn't any candy there, except in Ferny's imagination. They returned to her house and enjoyed a tasty and filling lunch. Rufus and his sister took their time and talked and reflected on stories from their childhood.

"Ferny, I always wondered why your town is named Theresville," Rufus said. "Do you know why?"

"Well, if you can figure out why your hometown is named Heresville, you might find your answer," Ferny said cleverly with a chuckle.

They all got up and went out to the candy factory she had built in the backyard. From the outside, it looked like an old run-down barn. On the inside, it was a modern kitchen full of fancy machinery. She explained that she had obtained every kind of candy-making machine she could find, and she was learning how to operate them. Bobby noticed a tall man running noisy equipment.

The youngish man shut down the machine and introduced himself. "Hi, I'm Dirk. I'm a friend and partner of Ms. Ferny."

"I'd like you to meet my brother, Rufus, and his son, Bobby," Ferny said.

"I've heard a lot about you," Dirk said. "I'm so glad you're safe and could come visit our chocolate factory."

While in the barn, Ferny gave them an assortment of different candies to taste. She offered them so many goodies that Bobby and his dad regretted that they had taken up so much tummy space with lunch. After they said goodbye to Dirk, they waddled out of the chocolate factory like a couple of bubble-bellied quackers and headed for the house.

They were about to leave, when Ferny asked them to wait. She said she had something for Bobby. Ferny returned with three boxes, each about the size of a shoe box. Two of them were tied up firmly with twine. The third one was wrapped in colorful paper and tied with a curled ribbon.

"Happy birthday, Bobby!" Ferny said warmly.

"Wow, thank you, Aunt Ferny! What's inside?"

"You will find out when you open them *on* your birthday next week!" Ferny said with a sugar-sweet smile.

"I can't wait!"

"Yes, you can. I'll put your dad in charge to keep you honest!" she responded sternly with a wink.

The mystery boxes were loaded into the trunk, and they headed for home rather late in the day.

There were smooth little dips and wavy turns on the main road home that gave Bobby the sensation of being rocked in a rocking chair. His young body gently rested against the seat, and his head fell back onto a pillow he had made with his jacket.

With the memory of that mysterious mountain swirling in his head, Bobby closed his eyes and fell asleep. The gateway to dreamland was open to him once again. Can he possibly help the dream-kids from freezing in the snow on top of that mountain in the clouds?

Chapter 74

FROZEN, FORLORN, AND ALONE

ॐॐ

"STOP IT! Leave me alone, snow bunnies!!" Taffy shouted. "I'm not in the mood to get tickled! Stop it, you're so very cold! Brrr!"

The snow bunnies think they're funny, hopping around and tickling the kiddos with the points of their ears. The bunnies were quite comfortable and in a jolly mood, while the kiddos didn't find it funny at all!

When the kiddos first reached the top of Ooga Mountain, their spirits were high. They felt invincible. Then a white cloud came along, and now they were cold, forlorn, and alone.

"I'll call on my angels and fairies and see if they can help us out of this cold, white mess," Violet said. She knew that this might be too much to hope for from her imaginary friends. Violet stood shivering near the edge of a steep drop-off and stared up, up to the heavens where she supposes that her angels and fairies live. She whispered something quietly to the great beyond.

Trembling in the cold, the other kiddos watched in despair as Violet called out and invoked the power of the universe – or maybe nothing. Their thoughts and faces were blue, they were shivering, and they were dwelling on how far away they were from anyone who could help them get off the frozen mountain.

Walnut decided to share an idea that had crossed his mind. Rather sheepishly, he said, "We could try to get the giant ball rock at the very top to roll down the mountain toward Ooga Ooga. That would catch *somebody's* attention!"

"Yeah," Topp said. "They would probably say, 'Look, a ball rock came down off the mountain. We can put it next to the other one in Candy Mountain Park.'"

"Well, we could write *HELP* on it," Walnut said. He still thought it was a decent idea, considering how desperate they were.

"Write on the rock with what?" Topp asked. "With snow bunny flakes?"

Just then, a strange noise came from down below. It sounded like sticks being hit together in an odd rhythm.

Clickity, clackety, click, click, click! There was a silence, and then it started again, louder, and closer this time. *CLICKITY, CLACKITY, click, click, click!*

Topp figured they had nothing to lose, so he shouted out, "Hello there! Who goes there?"

The kiddos listened intently for an answer.

"ZIP HERE!" a voice burst out from below them. The kiddos' eyes were glued in the direction of the voice, when a nice-looking young man flowed through the misty white curtain of snow bunnies. "I believe someone sent for me. Who among you would that be?" he asked politely.

"Uh, well, uh, I guess I did," Violet finally answered. "I did call on my angels and fairies to see if they could help us. We're in a bad fix!"

"Well, I never think of myself as an angel, nor a fairy either, but somebody did ask for help!" the boy responded. "So, here I am!"

"Are you Zip, the boy who lives on the mountain?" Sugar asked.

"That be me!" Zip said proudly. "You are welcome to come with me to my cavedom and get away from these annoying snow bunnies and the painful cold they give out far too freely."

"But we think it'll be too slippery and steep to climb down, and that we will fall off the mountain and not have such a nice landing as we might like," Sugar explained, somewhat awkwardly.

"Nooo problem!" Zip said. "I have a special rope ladder to get off this steep mountain top. It's hidden away so it'll be there when I need it – like now. Come with me."

The kiddos followed Zip through the middle of a thick bush, growing between two ball rocks. When they reached the other side of the foliage, there was a ledge with a steep drop-off. Zip asked the kiddos to wait for him there for just a minute. He soon came back with a very sturdy-looking rope ladder that he attached to roots above his head. He hopped on it and told the kids to jump on and come down the ladder with him.

Down they went, oh so carefully, on the precarious rope ladder. The descent was surprisingly easy because they were almost weightless on Baby Gravity Day. They lowered themselves safely onto a large clump of mittenweed. Zip suggested they eat a handful of the leafy plant because it would help them get warm – and it did. The kiddos looked around and were relieved that there weren't any snow bunnies where they were now. With great timing, the suns shone through the cloud and warmed them even more.

Zip directed them to follow him down a skinny trail, one that was more like an animal trail than a people trail. The mini path wound between rocks, trees, and scrubs. The trail was small but quite manageable. The kiddos felt in good hands now because they figured Zip knew what he was doing. He and the kiddos made good time moving down off the mountain, and eventually they reached an open grassy meadow.

"Here we are!" said Zip with pride. "My cavedom!"

What the kiddos saw in front of them was a nice wooden cabin built right up against a giant boulder. There were gardens of pretty flowers here and there around the lovely cottage. The kiddos were startled when they realized that in one of the flower patches, there was a lovely young woman among the blossoms, camouflaged in a flowery dress.

"Hi, my name is Bonnet," the young lady said in a friendly singsong voice. "I'm Zip's friend."

"Nice to meet you," the kiddos all said, in each their own way.

"Most of the time, I live down low on the west side of the mountain, but sometimes I come up here to check on Zip and hang out with him. Zip told me that someone called for help. Was that you?"

"I guess so," Violet said. "We sure were in a cold mess up there at the top, and now we're safe and warm. We have Zip to thank for that."

"Come on into the cabin, and I'll show you the cave," Zip said.

The kiddos were fascinated by the cabin, the cave, and how nice and cozy it was inside. "Take a seat by the fire and have hot chocolate and Ooga Mountain ice cream," Bonnet said.

"So, Zip," Sugar said, "we knew that a mysterious young man lived on Ooga Mountain, but we didn't know if we would ever meet him – er, you."

"That's me," Zip said with a smile. "I'm the mysterious boy on the mountain!"

"I always wondered what your real name was," Topp said, "and where you're from, and why you came to live on Ooga Mountain."

"My real name is Alexander Puff, but it seems that people in Ooga Ooga call me Zip. I guess they call me that because I run, rather than walk, everywhere I go. I'm from Puff Island, which is far away in the Fantasmo Sea. Puff Island is beyond the far side of the Island of Wow, if you know where that is."

"Yes, we know where the Island of Wow is," Topp said. "But why did you leave your island and come to Ooga Mountain?"

"Pretty simple," Zip said. "Puff Island is small, so when I'd take off running, I'd be at the other end in no time. So, when I grew up a bit, I decided to live on this big mountain where I could zip around all day long and never run out of room to roam. I return to my island occasionally to see my family, but I like it here better."

"Thank you so much for your hospitality, and the ice cream is fantastic. Is this the ice cream that is supposed to ooze out from the top of the mountain?" Violet asked.

"Yes, it is, and lately it has been chocolate flavored. Sometimes it changes to other flavors," Zip said. "If you ever come up here again, I'll take you to the magic ice cream oozer. That's what I call it because it just oozes out."

"Fascinating!" Topp said. "Thanks for everything, but we gotta get going soon so we can get down to Ooga Ooga before dark. We'd like to invite you to a picky-nick we're going to have at the park in the village on the last day of summer. We hope you and Bonnet can make it."

"I don't see why not. I'll show you the way to get back down to Lookout Rock. Follow me."

From the cavedom, the trail to Lookout Rock led more sideways than downward because they had already descended well below the top of the mountain.

Before they reached Lookout Rock, Zip said his goodbyes to the kiddos. He pointed the way to go, and the kiddos thanked him profusely.

When they reached Lookout Rock, their bikes were still there, even though the Rachett brothers had been by earlier. The brothers were in the group of people who hurried down the mountain to escape the lightning and rain.

The kiddos jumped on their bikes and down the hill they went. It was still Baby Gravity Day, so they had to use a little of their own energy to keep going. There were no two-headed snakes this time. They must have been napping, so the kiddos made good progress on their descent.

As they neared Whistle Creek, darkness had settled in. They weren't worried because they knew they could get fairy flowers to light their way down that last part of the trail.

"Look, I see something ahead!" Topp shouted in alarm. 'There's something moving on the trail!"

The kiddos started whistling to light up the fairy flowers. A few flowers lit up but not enough to see what was ahead on the trail. They cautiously approached whomever or whatever was in the darkness.

"Look, it's someone waving their arms!" Taffy said, noticing a large figure in the middle of the trail.

"Who goes there?" Topp bellowed. "Friend or foe?"

"Friend – I hope!" a quavering voice called out. The kiddos walked up and saw that it was one of the Rachett brothers. "We got lost and now it's dark, and we can't see the trail anymore! We're scared!"

Without hesitation, the kiddos offered to share the fairy flowers they had begun picking. "Can you whistle? That's what makes them glow," Sugar explained.

Just then, from within a nearby hedge, whistles burst forth as the other five Rachett brothers came out into the light.

"We're going to go on and continue down the trail," Topp said. "You should be okay now. There should be enough light to get you to where you're going."

"Thanks so much!" a Rachett brother said with full-throated gratitude. "We'll be spending the rest of the night with our Uncle Bob in Ooga Ooga. Thanks again!"

"Hey! We're having a picky-nick on the last day of summer. You are welcome to come and join in," Sugar said.

"And all the folks from Bergville are welcome too," Violet added. "It'll be in the village park."

"Thank you," they said.

As the kiddos rode on toward the shady glade, they felt a great deal of gratitude. They were grateful for being warm, for meeting Zip and Bonnet, and for being able to help the Rachett brothers in their time of need. Maybe their act of kindness will be remembered by the rascally boys, from the little town of Bergville, on the shore of the Ice Bug Sea.

Chapter 75

CANDY MOUNTAIN AT LAST!

৵৵৽

The morning after the trip to the top of Ooga Mountain, the kiddos stayed in bed for a long time. For one thing, the full force of gravity was back, so when they tried to get out of bed, they felt too heavy to get up. Realizing that they didn't have to get to their feet, they just lay there under their warm blankets and thought back on the amazing journey they had just completed.

Violet got up first and began making a delicious breakfast. The other kiddos smelled the lovely aromas of her hotcakes, scrambled eggs, and biscuits. That gave them a reason to battle against the strong gravitational pull and get to the table.

After their tummies were full to the brim, they all went out in the garden to where they could look up at Ooga Mountain. There was a long silence as they stood there in awe of the mighty mountain they had just conquered. Yes, they climbed it when there wasn't as much gravity as usual, but at least they were smart enough to use that opportunity to reach the summit. They were the only children to have ever made it to the top, and due to the lightning storm, they were the only people to make it to the top on that special day.

As they peered up at the top of the mountain, they looked to see if there was still a white cap of snow bunnies up there. It was too far away to be certain.

On their way back into the clubhouse, Violet mentioned that the cold they experienced on the mountain was from the west, where Candy Mountain is. "The time has come to go to Candy Mountain!" she declared.

"Hooray!" shouted the kiddos. "Candy Mountain! Candy, Candy, Candy Mountain!"

Violet had gone there a few years ago, traveling by land across the Duney Desert. In those days, that's how everyone that traveled to Candy Mountain got there, but it wasn't easy. It is a long dusty trip through the desert and a long daunting trip back. Any candy that was to be brought across the desert got heavy on their legs, so nobody in those days carried much back with them.

Thanks to Balooon, Granny Bubbles, and her inventions, there's a better way to get to Candy Mountain now. Oogans can fly to Candy Mountain and back with loads of candy! It's still a long, difficult, and dangerous balloon float that must be left to expert balloonists. For this reason, Granny Bubbles will fly the kiddos on the trip to Candy Mountain.

Granny Bubbles really doesn't care about the candy from Candy Mountain, and she trusts that Balooon could get the kiddos there and back just fine. However, she was going on this trip for a special reason of her own.

For fifty years, Granny Bubbles had wondered what was out there, out beyond the Valley of Ooga Ooga. She has wanted to know how far the land goes.

When she was young, she heard about a group of adventurous Oogans who wanted to see if there was a final *edge* to the seemingly flat planet they lived on. Several of these explorers went off on long trips, one in each of the four directions: North, South, East, and West. They were prepared to be gone for a long time, to see what they could find far beyond the Valley of Ooga Ooga.

One of the explorers went east through the Jolly Jungle to find out how far the land went in that direction. He was gone for two years, and when he finally returned, he reported that the jungle just kept going and going, and that he never got to the end of it. He returned to Ooga Ooga safely, but his body was weary from the hot sticky jungle and the difficulties of jungle diseases and wild creatures.

Granny Bubbles knew another explorer who sailed south on the Ice Bug Sea. This seafaring lady captained a special ship made to sail long distances on the salty sea. She sailed with an able crew of sailors. Two years later, she returned to Bugg Town, tired, wet, and weary. She'd never found anything but sea and land, and more sea and more land. She had explained that there were a couple of times it appeared like the sea *was* coming to an end, but it turned out to be an optical illusion, a mirage. She saw that there was always more sea ahead and land ahead, so she turned around and headed back to Ooga Ooga.

Another explorer went on an expedition to the north, and she was gone for two years or so. She sailed across the Fantasmo Sea to the north and eventually found land. After crossing that land, she encountered another sea. She told Granny that she built another boat to sail that sea, only to find more land. A couple of years later, with no end to the lands and seas, she turned back to Ooga Ooga. She surmised from her travels that she didn't go far enough or the land never ends.

Granny knew another explorer, a poor soul who went westward toward Candy Mountain and beyond, to find out what was there. Two years passed, and he did not return. The bones of that brave soul were found scattered out in the Duney Desert, not far from the base of Candy Mountain. Among the explorer's bones, there was a sun-bleached note. Though the writing was illegible, some thought it suggested he had indeed reached the end of the land. He didn't live to tell the tale, so Granny never knew what he found out there.

Recently, Granny Bubbles had heard about an ancient map in the museum that showed an end or *edge* to the land in all directions. She had no idea that it was the kiddos who had found it, and the kiddos did not know anything about the earlier explorers and the one who perished.

Granny Bubbles was fascinated by the possibility that the far *edge* of their land had been discovered to the west of Candy Mountain. She wanted to go in the big balloon to see if she could find out if the land ended in the west. She decided to do it after landing on Candy Mountain with the kiddos. She did not mention any of this to Balooon or the other children.

The day before they were to fly to Candy Mountain, Balooon and Granny Bubbles flew *Miss Blimpy* to the shady glade. The kiddos began loading the big balloon for the trip. They planned on leaving early in the morning the very next day.

On the morning of the start of the adventure, Granny Bubbles and the kiddos awoke to blue skies. The weather could not have been more perfect for ballooning – there was a cool light breeze blowing directly westward toward Ooga Mountain.

With plenty of Vaporgas in *Blimpy*, the ten of them lifted off. The ten of them? Well, there were the six kiddos and Granny, that was seven. Ragamuffin made eight, Smokey made nine, and can you guess the tenth? It was Sugar's new pet chiperoo, Roo Roo, of course!

The balloon lifted easily in the morning air and rose above the treetops surrounding the shady glade. Walnut remarked, "Wow, gravity doesn't have a chance against this mighty balloon!" The other kids chuckled.

Balooon, the co-pilot for the trip to Candy Mountain, guided the balloon directly toward Ooga Mountain. He carefully steered it clear of the solid rock top of Ooga Mountain but close enough so the kiddos could see the ball rocks, the mittenweed, and a few snow bunnies still playing at the top.

"Maybe we should have just taken the balloon to the top of Ooga Mountain the other day," Walnut said. "That would have been much easier!"

"Yeah," Taffy said, "but we did it with just our feet. That was a great accomplishment that we can be proud of for years."

"I suppose," Walnut mumbled.

Leaving Ooga Mountain behind, the balloon began the journey across the desert. Walnut chose this opportunity to lay down and take a nap.

At last, the kiddos were on their way to Candy Mountain! They were now crossing a lonely, dry, dusty, foreboding, lifeless expanse of sand, called the Duney Desert. Several hours passed as they floated along. The wind picked up, and the once faraway Candy Mountain came ever closer!

"Wow! Look at all that candy!" Balooon screamed out. "It's times like this I wish my tummy was twice as big!"

"Me, too," Violet said, licking her lips.

"Look at all the bands of color on the mountain!" Sugar shouted. "I wonder if the yeller band is lemon drops or maybe yeller gummies."

"I bet the purple is some kind of grape candy," Violet said.

Candy Mountain had bands of colors indeed, dozens of colors. It was an ever-repeating rainbow, including white (coconut) and black too (licorice).

Violet stood next to Balooon and suggested that he land *Miss Blimpy* about halfway up on the north side of the mountain where there would be shade and the candy would be firmer.

As they approached the massive pile of candy, Balooon sighted a broad ledge made of what looked like giant candy bars. He brought the balloon down gently and landed on the wide stable surface.

Now the kiddos are about to find out if the candy is real. It *better* be real – or they'll what ...? Cry?!

Yeah, probably!

Chapter 76

CANDY GALORE AND TEN TIMES MORE

❧

"This is amazing!" shouted Taffy. "Even if the giants did eat a whole bunch of Candy Mountain, they sure left a lot behind for us!"

"Let's get our backpacks and head out!" Balooon said. "Don't wander off too far because we can't stay a long time. We need to get on our way home before the day is half over."

"Yes, yes!" Sugar yelled out, after she took a bite of the mountain. "The candy has sugar in it, or maybe the sugar has candy in it! It's *real* all right and soooo good!"

When Walnut looked around, his eyes opened wider than usual. With a ridiculous amount of excitement, he said, "There's soooo much candy here, tons of it! It shouldn't take long to load a whole bunch of it to take home."

After tasting the candy nearby, the kiddos ran off in all directions to look for their favorite kinds. Before long, they came back to unload what they had gathered. They then turned around and went back to get more.

Before Violet headed out for a third time, she stopped and asked Granny Bubbles, "We're loading mounds of candy into the basket, Granny, is it going to get too heavy to fly?"

"Don't you worry one little bit," Granny said. "She'll fly just fine. Just in case we need to lighten, there are heavy sandbag ballasts hanging over the edges of the basket that we can dump if we need to."

With that, Violet and the other kiddos continued running all over Candy Mountain like ants on a gingerbread house. Some of the loads of candy that the kiddos were carrying looked bigger than the kiddos themselves, the way ants look when they carry more than their own weight.

While all this activity was going on, Ragamuffin was lying around in the basket, feeling bored. As you know, cats don't like to eat candy, and Ragamuffin thinks he is more of a cat than a dog. Smokey, the real cat, didn't want any, either.

The kiddos brought along cat and bird food for Ragamuffin and Smokey. That's all they had to eat, the same as back home. So sad.

As for Roo Roo, the chiperoo, she does like candy but only candy with nuts in it. Roo Roo eats the nuts and leaves behind the candy part, for anyone who wants it *without* nuts.

Violet was right, the entire mountain *is* made of real candy. There are so many distinct kinds, it's hard to comprehend. Even *you* might not recognize some of the candy on the mountain. There are jelly beans by the billions (all flavors), bubble gum, hard candies, fruit drops, red and black licorice ropes, different flavored suckers, both sweet and sour gummy globs, and of course, every kind of chocolate – dark, milk, and even white!

That's just a few of the millions of candies scattered all over the mountain. When the weather is hot, the softer candies melt into other candies, making endless new combinations, like chocolate melted on gummy worms and fruit leather dripping onto suckers. They saw a mound of cotton candy full of chocolate chips, and peanut butter cups, brownies, and jelly beans all melted together.

Most of the candy was just lying around, ready to be picked up willy-nilly. Some candy was stuck in a pile of other candies and had to be broken loose. I know one thing for sure: The kiddos could make a million trips to Candy Mountain, and the mountain would still look the same size. That's how big Candy Mountain is.

Now if you're a kid, and a parent is reading this book to you, they might want to skip this list of other candies – but don't let them!

On Candy Mountain, there are candy canes, gum drops, chocolate mints, jawbreakers, malt balls, marshmallows, sweet tarts, candy corn, taffy (*Taffy!* She's a kiddo!), gum balls, tootsie rolls, sour worms, all-day suckers, caramels, orange slices, lemon drops, red hots, and more.

"Kiddos! Kiddos!" Granny Bubbles cried out. "Lunch time! Come eat lunch!"

Every one of the kiddos heard what Granny said and knew what she wanted them to do, but every one of them thought it was ridiculous that they would want or even have room for any lunch at all. What, with all this candy piled up miles high and for ten miles all around them! Duh, I don't think so!

"Children!!! Come eat your lunch – OR ELSE!" Granny yelled out sternly. The kiddos didn't know that Granny had made a promise to their parents. The agreement was that the children would have healthy lunches during the trip. So, Granny *will* insist on keeping that promise.

Something about Granny's tone or maybe because they wanted to come back to Candy Mountain in her balloon someday, motivated the kiddos to run back to the basket as soon as she called again. But they had no idea they'd have to eat *vegetables* for lunch!

Granny said, "I promised your parents that you would not eat just candy on this trip. That's why they gave their permission for you to come. Well done, children, thanks for coming for lunch."

"Granny, nobody makes veggies better than you," Walnut said. "You make them *edible*!"

Granny grinned as the kiddos headed back out to gather and eat more candy. "We need to leave in one half hour," Granny shouted, "got that, in one half hour!"

Long before the time was up, the kiddos came back to the balloon to rest. They sat around in the basket with tummies shaped like blimps and gazed upon the piles of candy they'd collected. It was in tall heaps all around the basket.

Yes, the kiddos do love candy, but most of this pile of sweets was intended for a specific purpose. The kiddos planned to give candy for prizes and gifts at the grand picky-nick on the last day of summer. Looking over their stash of goodies, the kiddos were sure that there was enough candy on board for ten picky-nicks.

They collected just a little more of their favorite flavors, and then it was time to go. So, the kiddos came aboard, and Granny counted heads to be sure they were all there. "Hang on, kiddies, we're going up! Balooon, let the anchor lines loose!" she shouted.

The kiddos knew Granny was in charge of piloting the balloon homeward. But they didn't know that she would be flying farther away from the Valley of Ooga Ooga – considerably farther. They didn't know that Granny Bubbles was going to go straight west for a while, to see what she could see …

Chapter 77

SOARING UP, FALLING DOWN

🙠🙡

When Granny Bubbles told them that they were going on a detour before heading home, the kiddos shrugged their shoulders like they didn't care. Her plan sounded like a bigger adventure which the kiddos are always enthusiastic about.

"Hang on tight!" Granny yelled to the kiddos. But they weren't paying much attention to anything other than the candy they had just put in their mouths. "Hold on tight, we're going to lift off!"

The kiddos ran to the edges of the basket where there were strong ropes to hang on to. They grabbed them tight and pulled themselves up close to the inner wall of the basket just in time. The balloon suddenly lurched, not up but sideways! The basket didn't go *up* at all, instead it scraped along the mountain surface like a plow and left a long groove of jumbled candies! The balloon finally went airborne, not because it was going up, but because the mountain surface dropped away as the balloon moved sideways.

"Whoops!" Granny said, hoping no one heard her. The takeoff was not ideal because the balloon was supposed to lift straight up, not slide sideways. It was clear of the mountain surface, but it still didn't go up, it kept going sideways.

Granny yelled out to Balooon, "Drop five sandbags!"

Balooon knew what that meant, so he ran around the basket and began dropping the sandbag weights that were hanging on the outside of the basket. Each bag or ballast dropped would lighten the load so the balloon could lift.

The other kiddos were amused as they looked over the edge of the basket and watched the heavy bags of sand drop down and smash candy when they hit the mountain slope below.

When Balooon finished dropping the five heavy bags, he ran to Granny to see if she had any more orders. The balloon seemed to lift a little due to the weight of the ballasts being dropped but not very much.

"Drop five more ballasts!" Granny shouted to Balooon. So, he took off again, ran around the basket, and dropped five more.

This time, the balloon lifted, and everyone was relieved because they were clearly free of danger and the mountain. The two suns above were beyond the midpoint of their daily arc as the big balloon headed westward. It picked up speed and headed away from Candy Mountain, and farther away from the Valley of Ooga Ooga.

The sky was cloudless, and the suns beat down with fierce desert heat on the balloon and basket. Heat helps the balloon rise, but the candy in the basket was starting to melt! The kiddos hurried to put the candy inside the cabin where it was cooler and protected.

"Where are we going, Granny?" Balooon asked. "It looks to me like we're going away from the Valley of Ooga Ooga."

"That's true," Granny replied. "We're going to see if we can find the *edge* of our land where it ends and goes off into space."

The kiddos standing nearby heard what Granny said. "Wow, Granny," Balooon said. "We've been on a quest to see if we can find the *edge*, too!"

"Oh, I see," Granny said. "Well, here we go!"

"But what is this thing called *space*?" Taffy asked.

"Well, it's kind of like other things that you can't hear or see or smell or touch," Granny explained.

The kiddos looked back and forth at each other because nobody understood what the heck she was talking about.

"Huh?" said Walnut. "That sounds weird."

"Well, it's kind of like time or gravity or life," Granny continued. "You can't see them, but you *know* when they're there. Space is like the air all around us, except without the air in it. Get it? It is like a place where there is absolutely nothing – empty – a void."

If you have ever wondered what a blank look on someone's face looks like, you could see nine of them – one on each of the faces of the kiddos and three on the faces of the critters.

"Okay, I know. I'll *show* you space," Granny said with a grin. "At least I *hope* to show you – if we can find it!"

The kiddos were clearly confused but excited about whatever it was Granny wanted them to experience. They carefully looked all around to see if there was something unusual out there that might be this thing called *space*, but right now everything looked normal to them.

"Have you ever seen space, Granny?" Walnut asked.

"Well, no ... not yet," she answered.

"Has anyone from Ooga Ooga ever seen this thing you call space?" Violet asked.

"I don't think so. We could be the very first to experience it – if we're lucky! Hang on tight, and we'll see if we can find it!"

About the only thing the kiddos understood were the words, "*Hang on tight,*" so that's what they did – until their knuckles turned white. The kiddos were growing concerned about what Granny was up to.

"Drop five more ballasts!" Granny called out to Balooon. "That should leave five more still hanging from the basket. Check on the count, too!"

So Balooon quickly ran around and released five more heavy bags of sand from the basket. IIe counted the remaining bags, which numbered five. "Five still hangin', Granny!"

"Excellent!" Granny declared. "Enjoy the ride, kiddos!"

The kiddos heard her words, but they were looking over the edge of the basket and were fixated on the sandbags that were smashing down on the desert floor below, one after the other.

"I'm glad I wasn't one of those sandbags – or under one!" said one of the kiddos.

When the five ballasts that Balooon set loose dropped away, the big balloon finally lifted upward and picked up speed. Granny knew what she was doing. She was raising the balloon to a new height, into a stronger air current, and it was working.

Miss Blimpy was now flying rapidly and in one direction – away from Ooga Ooga. The kiddos all stood by the leading edge of the basket and looked ahead to where they were going. There wasn't much below them but a desert, but a different kind of desert than the Duney Desert. This desert had lots of scruffy bushes, small hills with rock outcroppings, and no dunes. On the ground below, there were no signs of people or any forms of life, other than dry prickly bushes and cacti.

"Have you ever been here before, Granny?" Sugar asked and then wished she hadn't.

"Nooope," Granny said, in a spooky kind of way.

Their thoughts were spinning around. *Does Granny know what she's doing? Can we go home now? Is this a good idea? Might we end up like those falling sandbags?*

Without warning, the big balloon started losing altitude. It was as though the air or wind around the balloon had changed. *Something* caused the balloon to drop, and that didn't seem to be part of the plan. "Balooon! Drop three more ballasts, *please*," Granny said, saying *please* to try to hide her concern about the balloon's descent.

Balooon ran around the basket faster than ever and dropped three more bags.

The balloon leveled off a little, for at least a minute or two, and then it started to drop again. Yikes!

"Drop two more bags," Granny said with more urgency and obvious concern in her voice.

Balooon dropped the last bags quickly, but it had no effect. The kiddos kept staring at the desert in front of their path, when suddenly Topp shouted, "THE END OF THE LAND! OH MY GOSH! IT DROPS OFF ...... INTO ... NOTHING!"

Blimpy, still dropping, would have hit the desert had the land not come to an end. The balloon dropped even more and was now beyond and below the final *edge* of the land. In front of them, there was only black, indigo darkness, and a space filled with stars. In fact, the weird darkness was all around them, above *and* below.

"We have reached space!!!!!!" Granny shouted, sounding both fascinated and scared out of her wits. "There *IS* an end to our world! And, here it is kiddos, DEEP DARK SPACE!!!!!!"

The balloon dropped swiftly over the *edge* of the world and was floating down and away, into a dark purple void.

"OH MY!!! WHAT HAVE I DONE?!!!!"

Chapter 78

BOBBY AND HIS LOST DREAM-KIDS

৵৵

The first light of day woke Bobby up, and he found himself on his bed fully clothed except for his shoes. There was a blanket neatly tucked in on top of him. It quickly dawned on him what had happened. He had fallen asleep in the car on the way home from Ferny's, so his dad carried him in and put him in bed. Bobby slept through it all.

He was very comfortable and relaxed, so he rolled over onto his back and thought about what he remembered of last night's dream. Joy came over him as he recalled that the dream-kids had been saved from the cold and treacherous mountain top where they had been stranded in the freezing cold. However, he did not remember much more than that.

Usually, his recollections were full of detail and amazingly vivid. This morning, he had hardly any memories at all, beyond the dream-kids getting off the cold mountain safely. He had a few faint flashes of pieces of his dream beyond that, but they were so fragmented, he wasn't sure what was going on with the dream-kids last night.

Suddenly, an eerie feeling came over him. In the bits of his dream that he could recall, there was something that seemed scary. *Why can't I remember more of the dream? And why do I feel like something went terribly wrong with the dream-kids? I can feel it, but*

I can't see it. Maybe if I get up and get going, the dream will come back to me.

As boys often do, Bobby stayed in the clothes he'd slept in, put on his shoes, and wobbled to the bathroom to take care of ... well, you know, and brush his teeth.

He washed his hands and face, then moved on to the kitchen where his mom greeted him with a sweet hug and kiss. Bobby is a sensitive boy, so he doesn't take moments like that for granted. He gave her a kiss on the cheek and went outside to pick her a flower bouquet. He came back in with the flowers hidden behind his back.

"You sure left quickly, is something wrong?" his mom asked.

When he revealed the handful of flowers and gave them to her, he said, "Everything is just wonderful. I know I have the most loving and special mom ever."

As she took it all in, her eyes filled with tears of happiness. She was speechless, but her smile said it all.

After she composed herself, she said, "So your trip to Aunt Ferny's was nice, was it? I see you came back with a stack of presents from your aunt."

"Yeah, but I can't open them until my birthday in a few days."

"That reminds me," she said. "Dad and I are going to the cabin on the lake for a couple of days, so we'll be gone on your birthday. Bettykins will be staying here while we're gone. If it's all right with you, we could have your birthday celebration today and you can open all your gifts and such before we leave. Would that be okay with you, I hope?"

"Sure, Mom, you and Dad need time alone. The cabin sounds like a great idea."

"Thanks, Bobby. And of course, you know that your friends are planning a party for you *on* your birthday anyway. How does noon sound?"

"Can I invite Cookie?"

"You can invite whomever you like," she confirmed.

"So, I can invite Fluffers and Chip Chip?" he asked, with a rascally smile.

"If you have that little party *outside* – sure!" she said playfully.

He sat down for a millisecond, inhaled a small breakfast, and then rushed out the door to run to Cookie's house. He didn't get but two steps onto the street when Cookie came cruising up on a scooter.

"Hi, Cookie, I was on my way to invite you to a mini birthday party for me today."

"I thought your birthday party was in a couple of days. Let me guess – you're having two parties."

They walked down to the picnic table where his mom had put fresh cookies sealed in a container, so Chip Chip couldn't get to them. As the two friends walked by the table, they grabbed the cookies, and then strolled to the clubhouse with Chip Chip and Fluffers at their heels. They settled in to enjoy their cozy clubhouse, a place where neither the wind nor the hot sun could get to them.

After chatting, they talked about dreams, not just Bobby's dreams but Cookie's as well!

"Cookie, I'm afraid that something went wrong in my dream. This morning, I could only remember the *start* of last night's dream. The rest of it just faded away or something, or maybe I stopped dreaming."

"Well, it's the opposite with me. I haven't been dreaming much at all lately, but last night I had an amazing dream – as clear as real life."

"What was it about?"

"Well, this is going to sound a little odd, but it was like the dreams you've been having."

"Wow, tell me more! My ears are burning!" Bobby said.

Her dream was both long and clear in Cookie's memory. She started by describing the things in the dream and the surroundings she saw. Bobby sat there listening with his mouth stuck halfway open.

After she described each of the children in the dream, Bobby said, "Ooooooooh, my gosh, it sounds exactly like my dream, and you just described the dream-kids. Well, what happened?"

"It started with the kids riding in a balloon across a desert to a mountain made of candy!" she said. "After some older lady landed the balloon, the kids loaded a bunch of the sweets into the basket and floated away."

"I can't believe it!" Bobby shouted, astounded at what Cookie was saying. "That sounds exactly like the dream I've been having, except the part that you had last night, I never had. The trip to that mountain of candy was going to be their next adventure. It seems that *you* are having my dream now! Whooooa!"

"It was incredible, all right! It was so real, I wasn't sure if it was more real than my own life," Cookie said, reflecting back on her dream.

Bobby then said, "The fragments I remember from *my* dream last night hinted that something had gone wrong, and the dream-kids were in peril in some awful way. Did anything in your dream indicate to you that something might have gone wrong?"

"Well, there was one thing that did seem odd. When the kids left the mountain of candy in the balloon, they headed away from home not toward it. The odd thing was that that is what they *wanted* to do. Nothing really seemed wrong, and then the dream ended."

"Wow, amazing," Bobby said. "There was something scary in my dream. Maybe I'll remember what it was."

Suddenly, someone shouted, "Bobby! Are you out there in the clubhouse? It's party time. Do you know if Cookie's coming?"

When the two entered the kitchen, they saw colorful balloons, a birthday cake, and presents on the table. Dad even blew one of those party noisemakers that unrolls and makes a horn-like noise. "Whooot! Whooot!" he tooted in celebration.

"Happy birthday, Bobby!" his parents sang out.

Candles were lit, and candles were blown out. Presents had been wrapped, and presents were unwrapped. Amongst the gifts there were thoughtful, practical gifts from Mom (not socks).

Then there were the three boxes from Aunt Ferny. He chose to open the nicely wrapped one first. There was a card stuck in the ribbon that said:

For Bobby:

Inside these three boxes you will find a complete set of all the types and flavors of candy I make. I know you will be reasonable in how you eat your share, and I would like you to give the rest of it to your friends at your birthday party.

Love, Aunt Ferny

As he began opening the box, he said out loud, "Thank you, Auntie."

There was an exceptionally long skinny box on the table with a card attached to it. The note read:

FOR MY SON,

MAY YOU TRAVEL THE ENTIRE UNIVERSE & DREAM BIG!

LOVE, DAD

Bobby carefully opened the large box, and his eyes lit up when he saw what was inside.

"A telescope, wow! Thank you," Bobby said with a full heart.

"No! Thank *you*, Bobby! Thank you for taking such loving care of your mother while I was gone! Bless you."

Bobby blushed a little and then looked at the three people around him. He thought he must be the luckiest boy ever.

That evening the sky was clear and at least a billion stars were flickering above, so Bobby and Cookie set up the telescope out in the yard and looked up into the heavens.

As he focused on a sparkling blue star, he thought about his dream. "The dream-kids!" he blurted out. "I remember the end of last night's dream! They were lost in SPACE!!!!!!! They were helpless and floating away into outer space! Oh my! OH NOOOOO!!!"

"It's okay, Bobby," Cookie reassured him. "From all the stories you've told me about the dream-kids and how they get out of big pickles every time, I'm sure they'll figure this one out, too!"

With a worried look on his face, Bobby started to say something, but nothing came out. His facial features softened and then he whispered to Cookie, "I'm sure you're right. I do believe in them. The dream-kids *will* be okay ... "

Chapter 79

GONE FOREVER INTO THE GREAT BEYOND

The predicament that the kiddos were in was only getting worse by the minute. The giant balloon continued floating down and away as the *edge* of the land shrunk from view as they careened into space. The kiddos were frozen in fear because they knew there were no more sandbags to drop to help lift the balloon. They all felt like screaming, but their voices were completely petrified when they saw their world rapidly disappearing.

All the kiddos had their eyes glued on Granny. They hoped that she might somehow have one last idea to save them from the great beyond. But she looked as scared as they were. How can anything help them now?

$\backsim$

"THROW THE CANDY OVERBOARD!" Granny screamed. "HURRY!!!!"

Without hesitation, the kids ran out of the cabin faster than a swarm of killer bees. They grabbed armloads of candy and ran as fast as they could to throw the excess weight overboard.

As they approached the side of the basket to throw their treasure over the side, they lamented that they had to throw their precious candy away. They didn't mind giving away their valuables to charity, but they didn't like throwing their delicious candy away – to nobody – to outer space!

They quickly came to their senses and started throwing armloads over the edge. They threw lots of candy, tons of candy, out of the basket. They would have thrown away all of it to save themselves, but the balloon began to rise.

As the balloon moved ever so subtly upward, Granny saw Taffy lose her balance and almost fall out of the basket when she tried to throw out a large armload of sweets.

Granny cried out, "Stop, stop throwing candy!"

The last thing Granny wanted was to have to tell Taffy's parents that because of her, their daughter fell overboard and floated into the great beyond, into outer space … forever!

The kiddos stopped throwing the candy overboard and waited for more instructions from Granny. They stood there like lifeless mannequins, and the balloon continued rising slowly. Like a miracle in a children's book, *Miss Blimpy* rose and rose, until she was above the level of the desert they had just flown over. And then it rose up some more …

At this higher altitude, the balloon caught a strong easterly wind. This new stiff breeze floated them away from the edge and over the land, and they headed east over the desert toward Candy Mountain.

When the balloon went flying off into outer space, Violet had called on her angels and fairies for help. She thought they might be the reason they were kept out of harm's way. She may never know, as her angels and fairies never speak to her.

Although they were safe, the kiddos were completely freaked out from the ordeal they had just experienced. Their scary journey out into the dark black of space left them shaken. When they realized the drop-off of the land was far behind them, the kiddos let out a big sigh of relief and lots of cheers.

"What do ya think of space?" Granny asked six frightened children, a spaced-out dog, a sleeping cat, and a chiperoo munching on nuts.

" ... Odd, very odd ...," Violet squeaked, her voice barely audible. "I am very glad I live on land, I know that for sure!" The rest nodded in agreement.

The big balloon was moving rapidly now, and there was plenty of distance between the basket and the now cherished ground below.

At this point the kiddos were glad to still be alive, and they were thrilled they didn't have to throw any more candy overboard! After all, they need candy for the picky-nick, which will be in just a few days.

In full control now, Granny flew the balloon right over the top of Candy Mountain. The kiddos looked down as they passed by, and not one of them had the desire to go back down to get more candy. They all just wanted to get back to Ooga Ooga and the hometown where they live so happily.

Miss Blimpy maintained a rapid cruising speed, so it took no time at all to soar over Ooga Mountain. They peeked over the side of the basket and saw their cherished Valley of Ooga Ooga. It had never looked so beautiful to each one of them.

The brilliant sunset cast a deep scarlet red glow throughout the sky as Granny landed *Blimpy* next to the clubhouse in the shady glade. The kiddos, Granny, and the three furry little passengers had returned safe and sound from a thrilling balloon ride to Candy Mountain – and outer space!

Running around on Candy Mountain was exhilarating and delightful, but the trip out into space – off the *edge* of their world – was terrifying!!!

After the kiddos climbed out of the basket and jumped down onto the ground near their garden, they shuffled their feet and kicked up lovely Ooga Valley dust. The kiddos had never appreciated the shady glade as much as they did right then, and they don't care if they ever see space again – EVER!

The kiddos unloaded all the remaining candy from the balloon basket and carried it into the storeroom next to the kitchen. They were a little sad about the candy that they'd had to throw out, but after they looked at all that made it home, they knew they had more than enough for the picky-nick.

They realized that they'd had two choices out there: Keep *all* the candy and float off into space forever or toss most of it overboard and make it home to the shady glade. They couldn't be happier with the decision they had made.

I wonder if they will ever realize that the candy they threw into outer space will forever be part of the Milky Way galaxy.

After removing their belongings from the balloon basket, including Ragamuffin, Smokey, and Roo Roo, Granny Bubbles prepared to leave and float back to the Town of Trombone where she lives.

"Thank you, Granny!" the kiddos all yelled. "Thanks for the ride to Candy Mountain!"

However, none of them said a word about the scary voyage they had just survived in outer space. They were still confused about what had happened and what space was or what space *is*. They are extremely happy to be where they are, and they hope that outer space stays where it is.

"Granny," Sugar yelled out loudly and sincerely. "Thanks for getting us home safely!"

Granny Bubbles gave her a smile and a wink, then lifted off the ground and waved goodbye. She and her miraculous balloon disappeared into the darkening sky.

"All's well that ends well," one of the kiddos said quietly as they headed very humbly to their beloved clubhouse.

Chapter 80

THE BEAST THAT EATS OOGANS

෪෬

After they woke up the next morning with candy *on* their brains (and most certainly *in* their brains), the kiddos sat around the big table with smiles as big as a full-sized cotton candy. Each of them ate their favorite candy for breakfast, two helpings.

Hey, wait! Can it really be called a *breakfast* with only candy to eat? The kiddos think so.

"Heye-ever-bodey!" Taffy said with her mouth full of candy. With everyone's attention and all eyes staring at her, Taffy decided to stop talking for a minute. She had to finish eating the candy in her mouth because it tangled up her words when she tried to speak. She finally said, "We have the picky-nick coming up in a few days, so we better start preparing."

"Do we have enough brittles$ to put on the grand festival, the picky-nick?" Violet asked.

"I don't think so, not even close," Taffy said. "Especially if we're going to provide all the food, buy all the things we need for music, games, and sporting activities. We do have a few brittles$ left over from the coins$ we found on Fantasmo Beach, but it's less than half of what we need to make it a *grand* picky-nick."

"I have an idea," Topp said. "We can catch the giant fish in Wetwater Lake. There's a big prize for anyone who can catch that giant fish called Crunch. People don't like that mean ol' fish because it eats all the smaller fish that the Oogans like to catch for food."

"How much is the reward for catching it?" Violet asked.

"**Fifty** brittles$, I read it on a flyer posted by Mayor Boof of Old Town," Sugar recalled. "Not only that, whoever catches the huge fish gets the prize money *and* all the tons of wonderful fish meat."

"Wow!" Balooon said with excitement. "If we catch it, then we can barbecue fillets of Crunch at the picky-nick. That would certainly make it a *grand* picky-nick all right."

"I know *I* won't be able to catch that fish, but I know who can … " Topp said.

Walnut blushed a little and then assured them, "I'll do my best! I *can* catch fish. I *am* a good fisherman! I'll whistle, add a bit of pow pow, and gotcha big guy – you're mine!"

They all had a jolly laugh at Walnut's funny comment.

With Walnut-the-fisherman's help, the kiddos made a list of what they will need to catch the monster fish: 50 meters of the strongest fire spider rope available and a giant fishhook made of steel. They will also need to borrow a rowboat to use in Wetwater Lake, and someone will need to go to Old Town to see Mayor Boof and sign up for the contest, so they can try to win the official reward.

They sprang into action and headed off in all directions. Topp went home to ask his dad to help him make a giant fishhook, and Walnut went along, to explain to Mr. Topper what size and shape the hook needs to be.

Balooon took off for the Bun-Cha-Stuff store to buy the rope they need, while Taffy and Violet caught a Floatbus bound for Old Town to sign up for the contest.

Sugar went to see if she could borrow the rowboat floating in the Ducky Pond at Poppy Park. She had to get permission from the park ranger, Bob Bobber. When she asked to use it, he replied, "Yessiree, Bob!" which didn't make sense because her name isn't Bob. She *did* understand that he said "*yes*" so that was good enough.

When the kiddos returned to the shady glade, they'd all had success with their tasks. The hook was strong, made of steel, and taller than Walnut himself. The long fire spider rope was brand new and almost unbreakable. The girls learned that the prize money was still available, and Mayor Boof said he hoped that the kiddos would be successful in getting rid of that humongous pest. And Sugar got permission to use the rowboat on Wetwater Lake. Balooon said he could transport the small boat to Wetwater Lake right away, with his small blue balloon.

"Fishing is best during the cool of morning," Walnut said.

Believing Walnut (this time), the kiddos decided to take everything to the public fishing cabin at the pier on Wetwater Lake that afternoon. They would start fishing for Crunch at first light in the morning.

Walnut is missing one very important thing. Can you think of what it is? What else does Walnut need to catch Crunch, the giant monster-fish?

"Walnut, what are you going to use for *bait*?" Sugar asked, remembering it takes something delicious on a hook to attract fish.

"I have a secret plan for that," Walnut said mysteriously.

"Why can't you tell us?" Violet asked.

"Because, then *they* would know," Walnut said, which was even odder.

If there is one thing the kiddos have learned about Walnut, it is to let him do *his thing* any way he wants to. If you ask him questions about what he plans to do, he will often answer in an obtuse way. But Walnut has proven that he has clever methods and many of them work out somehow.

In the very early morning, while the other kiddos were sleeping, Topp woke up when he heard someone get up and walk across the floor. There was not a speck of light outside the window yet, though morning was going to break soon (poor morning). Topp wasn't sure who was walking around but when he heard the mysterious person go out the front door whistling, he knew exactly who it was.

The light from the eastern sunrise often wakes the kiddos up. This morning, it was especially true because they were going to Wetwater Lake early to catch that big fish. They jumped to their feet, splashed water on their faces to wake up, and met in the kitchen.

"Where's Walnut?" someone asked.

"I'm right here!" Walnut said as he walked in the front door with a strange box.

"What's that, Walnut?" Topp asked.

"It's a box."

"What's *in* the box … Walnut?" Topp asked, slightly perturbed.

"It's the bait to catch the fish, if you must know," Walnut said rather reluctantly.

"What kind of bait?" Violet asked.

"I can't tell you that – *they* don't want me to tell you," Walnut said, much to their surprise.

"You are an interesting dude, Walnut," Sugar remarked.

"Yes, I am. I *am* a fisher-dude!" Walnut said with a wide grin and an upbeat whistle.

When I heard Walnut whistle, I knew he had a good chance of catching that fish. What do you think? Can he really catch that monster fish? I think the huge beast Crunch will have something to say about that!

Chapter 81

ALL OF A SUDDEN, *WHAMOOOSH!*

ତ୍ଲ✍ଚ

The kiddos got dressed and ready to go to Wetwater Lake. Fishing sounds easy enough, but they are going to the lake to catch a gargantuan fish, one that is longer than a Floatbus and even fatter.

Violet made zooom omelets for them to eat at the lake near the boat launch. She put the omelets carefully into a picnic basket, and each of the kiddos grabbed a handful of their favorite candies and tossed them into the basket too.

Off they rode in the gloomy gray dampness of morning. They pedaled their bikes up to the little dock next to the fishing cabin on Wetwater Lake and skidded to a stop (but with no dust this time – I think the dust was still sleeping).

"Wow, look at that!" Taffy yelled out. "The rowboat is out of the water and upside down on the dock! Yesterday when we left, it was tied up and floating!"

"Who would've done something like that?" Sugar asked.

"The fish did it," Walnut said.

"How do you know that?" Violet asked.

"Because it *told* me – Crunch is sending me a warning!" Walnut said calmly and then resumed whistling.

"How big is this thing anyway?" Balooon wondered out loud.

"I heard it's as big as five Floatbuses end to end," Topp answered.

"Bigger, much bigger," Walnut said, licking his lips. "It will taste as good as it is big."

It was probably best that the kiddos didn't know any of the stories about the people who had previously tried to catch the terrible fish named Crunch. None of them died, but some wished they had!

Shush! Don't let the children reading this book know that – mustn't scare them so much!

"Time to eat breakfast," Violet said. She enticed the others to gather around the picnic table at the dock to fuel up for the exciting day ahead. Violet dished out generous helpings of her delicious omelet to the hungry kids. She scooped extra onto Walnut's plate, for he was about to embark on a dangerous mission.

"The lake sure looks calm," Topp said, staring out over the still water. "There's not a single ripple out there, it looks like a mirror."

"Not for long," Walnut said as he finished his omelet. He went to work tying the fishing rope onto the huge steel hook. He opened his mysterious box, and inside were four large blubberfish. The special hook was made so four fish could be put on it, and that's what Walnut did.

"Isn't that mean to the fish?" Sugar asked, always caring for every living thing.

"Not really," Walnut said. "They're *happy* to be the bait to catch that awful beast. Just look at their smiles."

"Oh, come on, Walnut!" Violet said. "They can't be happy about being eaten by a giant fish!"

"Yes, they can!" Walnut said sternly. "Crunch has eaten their relatives over the years: cousins, nephews, aunts, and uncles. As I said, these blubberfish are happy to catch Crunch – in fact, they *volunteered* to do it!"

That was the end of that conversation. It kind of made sense to the kiddos, but Walnut had such a big imagination, they were often flummoxed by his bewildering comments. Not knowing what else to say, Violet finished serving breakfast.

After they returned the boat to the water, Walnut climbed in with the rope and the hook, with the bait fish firmly attached. He asked Balooon to tow him across the lake to Skinny Island and let him go.

Walnut slowly coasted up to the narrow island after being set adrift. He whispered to himself, "Perfect!" Then he threw the hook with the bait on it into the water near the island. As soon as the four bait fish hit the water, they took off swimming toward the center of the lake, pulling the fishing line out behind them.

"Okay, here goes," Walnut said quietly to himself. Then he started whistling into a megaphone he'd brought with him.

The calm surface of the lake became agitated, but there wasn't any wind. Then waves started lapping up on the shore, and white caps covered the lake. A large mound of water rose from the center of the lake with something big and dark inside. Aroused by the smell of the bait, the massive creature surfaced and headed straight for the four delicious blubberfish on the hook.

WHAMOOOSH!!!

The enormous fish hit the bait at full speed. Then the menacing beast turned to face Walnut's little boat. With a giant splash from his enormous tail fin, the gigantic whale-of-a-fish took off at full speed toward the tiny rowboat and Walnut!

As loudly as they could, the frightened kids on the shore jumped up and down and yelled, "LOOK OUT, WALNUT!!!"

Chapter 82

THE WINNERS AND THE POOR LOSER

இ~ளு

When the giant fish saw Walnut, it knew who the enemy was and decided to take direct aim at the annoying little kid whistling in the rowboat. Crunch lurched forward with great force at his puny target. The beast picked up phenomenal speed as it headed for the little brat who dared to try to catch it!

"CRACKKK!!!" The huge fish Crunch hit the little rowboat with such power and brutality, the wooden craft broke into forty-four pieces! Half of the pieces landed in the lake, and the other half flew through the air and landed on the island!

Walnut was nowhere to be seen after Crunch violently smashed the little rowboat into bits with him in it. The kiddos wondered if Walnut had been eaten, broken into tiny pieces, or maybe just drowned. Oh dear ... what had happened to Walnut?!

Well, either Walnut knew what he was doing, or he was lucky. I think he knew what he was doing ... *and* I think he was lucky. At the last second, before the big fish struck, Walnut had jumped onto the island and hidden behind a tree.

The giant fish realized that the little runt in the rowboat had not been vanquished. Frustrated, it swam a short distance down the lake and turned around. It made such an abrupt turn, it created a huge white wave. The monster knew it had been tricked by the fisher-kid who whistled so annoyingly. So, Crunch swam back to look for the little pest.

Walnut did indeed get away to safety. Crunch had *always* made the fishermen and fisherladies pay heavily when they tried to catch it. Perhaps it had finally met its match with Walnut, the fisher-dude.

Crunch cruised back to the island again with the hook and bait fish still deep in its mouth, but that didn't seem to bother it. Walnut peeked out from behind the tree and looked sheepishly into the eyes of the vicious monster.

The beast got *really* mad when he saw Walnut hiding behind a tree.

Undeterred, the big brute had a plan that had worked before. In the past it had attacked *on* the island and blasted trees and everything else that got in its way. To pull off this most dramatic maneuver, the fish needed to start from the farthest end of the lake. That way it knew it could build up enough speed to skid across the island and take out everything, including that annoying fisher-twerp.

So, in a fit of anger, it turned around and roared down the long lake to the far end. As it sped down the length of the lake, the massive fish Crunch made quite a spectacle. *That little fool kid thought he was safe behind a tree on the island. Hahaha,* Crunch thought. When it reached the end of the lake, Crunch would turn around and start its charge to attack the island.

By this time, a few Oogans, Old Towners, and others had gathered on the shore to watch the drama as it unfolded. The crowd was totally aghast at how fast the fish was swimming.

SPEEEEEEE – ROING!!!! That was the eerie sound the rope line made when it reached its full length! The huge hook was embedded deeply in Crunch's mouth, and Walnut had already tied the end of the rope securely to a stout stump.

When the rope suddenly pulled tight, the head of the fish snapped around abruptly. With its massive weight moving lightning fast and the forceful whiplash of its neck, the great beast Crunch was killed instantly!

The crowd on the shore had been watching the battle between the giant behemoth and the little kid, and they weren't disappointed. The crowd broke into an explosion of cheering and applause, for they had just witnessed the end of the mighty Crunch!

Then Balooon flew over to the island, picked up Walnut, and headed down the lake to the motionless fish. Balooon towed the vanquished beast over to a dock where the crowd stood cheering.

"Hooray!" the throng shouted. "The wicked fish is dead!"

Mayor Kee Kee from Ooga Ooga and Mayor Boof from Old Town trotted down to the edge of the lake to congratulate Walnut for his incredible accomplishment. They also proudly presented him with a hefty bag filled with fifty brittles$!

Walnut was both excited and delighted to have won the prize. Now the kiddos certainly had plenty of brittles$ for a *grand* picky-nick, after all. They also had enough brittles$ to buy Bob Bobber a new rowboat for the Ducky Pond!

The triumphant, joyful kiddos felt giddy with happiness as they headed back to the shady glade to begin preparations for the picky-nick, which was only two days away.

Giggling and shouting, the kiddos entered the Big Abble full of excitement from all they had just seen. They each had a glass of water to soothe their throats from all the yelling and cheering. As they sat around the table, Topp stood up and lifted his glass into the air. "Please join me in raising a toast to Walnut, the greatest fisher-dude there ever was!"

Everyone stood up, raised their glasses, and yelled, "Hear! Hear! To Walnut, the greatest fisher-dude ever!"

Walnut stood up slowly and raised his glass slightly as he glanced around at everyone. With the hint of a smile – he blushed. Walnut's display of humility was quite charming.

Chapter 83

THE OVERWHELMING CHALLENGE

The celebration at the lake after the conquering of Crunch had been jubilant. The kiddos were hailed as heroes, especially when they gifted the two mayors ten brittles$ each to help their townspeople. The kiddos kept thirty brittles$ for themselves – that was plenty to put on a picky-nick, and a grand one at that.

At the Big Abble, after the toast to Walnut, they settled in around the table and started yawning. Each time one of the kiddos yawned, the rest had to yawn too. There wasn't much talking because of all the yawning.

"We got up soooo early this morning (yawn)," Taffy said. "It will be dark soon (yawn), so maybe we should just go to bed (yawn). We can get up early tomorrow and have a full day to get ready for the picky-nick (yawn)."

They were half asleep already, so it didn't take long before the kiddos slipped into their beds and fell asleep for good.

In the first light of morning, Violet made hot peppy-mint tea and chocolate waffles for the kiddos. While they ate breakfast, they worked out the details of hosting the grand event in Poppy Park.

All the many friends they'd made in each and every distant place they'd visited were invited to the picky-nick. From Zip on the mountain to Vine Boy in the jungle, from the Island of Wow to Bugg Town, they spread the word about the picky-nick to be held on the last day of summer. The kiddos made it clear that not only were their new friends invited but people from all the villages they'd visited as well. The kiddos couldn't be sure how many would show up, so they needed to plan for the possibility that *everyone* they'd invited might show up.

As they sipped and munched, Sugar said, "We hope that all those faraway friends will be able to come. For the locals, we can put up flyers around town to let them know what's happening at the park."

"I have an idea," Violet said. "Let's bring out our art paper and colors and get to work making posters that we can pin up around the village."

Violet went to the cupboard where they keep the arts and crafts stuff and brought supplies to the table. "They can simply say: *Everybody is invited to the Grand Picky-Nick on the last day of summer in Poppy Park. All are welcome! Food will be provided, and there will be music, games, balloon rides, and fireworks.*"

"I have a question," Walnut said, sounding concerned. "How are the people who live far away going to get home at night after the fireworks?"

"I have a solution for that," Balooon answered. "Granny Bubbles has four balloons, so when the fireworks are over, all the guests visiting from faraway lands can be flown back to their towns. With the full moon and the city lights below, it will be a delightful night to fly. Granny, Mom, Dad, and the PetTunias can pilot the four balloons to take them home."

"I talked to Mr. Stufff the other day about getting some tents," Topp said. "When the guests arrive, they'll have their own shelter to use for the event. And if some of them want to stay the night, they'll have a tent for shelter."

"That's brilliant, Topp. We can set up the tents on the outer edge of the park," Walnut said.

"I think it's time to discuss the activities we plan to offer at our grand event," Taffy said. "Let's make a list of all the ideas."

"Okay … pencil and paper are ready," Violet said. "I'll write them down."

"I think we should provide lots of food and drinks," Walnut said. "We'll have Crunch burgers and other barbecued delicacies. We'll have plenty of grilled steakettes and hotty totty dogs too. We'll need a giant kitchen area to feed everyone all day long, and we'll need lots of food of all kinds. And of course, we'll have a large table covered with candy from Candy Mountain for all to enjoy and take home if they wish."

"We should have games for young kids: swings, slides, jungle gyms, and such. And everyone should get a colorful balloon, oh, and let's have balloon animals too," Sugar said.

"Okay, and I think we should have music, dancing, and a dance contest. Also, we must have a bonfire and a sing-along," Violet offered. "And we should have a slip 'n slide that goes right into the Ducky Pond, a diving board, and a swimming area in the pond too. Oh, and water balloon fights."

"I agree, and we should have a soccer field set up with nets, and a basketball court. We should have a miniature golf course too," Topp said. "We'll have a free raffle with prizes galore, that's for sure."

"It would be nice to have a special visitor's tent with information and maps of the picky-nick to show where everything is in the park. A guest book would also be nice. The tent can also be used for first aid, if needed," Sugar said. "And it would be nice to give each guest a basket to carry their food, prizes, and other stuff. Name tags could be on the table, so guests can write down their names and hometowns. That way, everyone can get to know each other more easily."

"We can also have an area for people to sell things, like jewelry or pottery they've made. A play area for pets would be nice, plus large areas to have three-legged races and play tag or hide and seek," Topp said. "We can give nice prizes for the winners of the races. A horseshoe throwing pit would be fun too. Oh, and talking about horses, we should have six-legged pony rides through the woods on the edge of the park for everyone."

"Don't forget we'll be offering balloon rides around the valley, too," Balooon said. "And we can let kids tour our clubhouse and try out our three-wheeled bicycles."

"How about bubble machines that make bubbles all day long? Kids like bubbles, so we'll have soapy water for them to blow bubbles too," Walnut said. "And of course, we'll have fireworks when it gets dark and lots of sparky-sparks for everyone. There'll be a closing ceremony, and we'll give out gift boxes when our guests leave, including a thank you card and a souvenir picky-nick token."

A long, heavy, uncomfortable silence suddenly came over the room.

Then Violet said glumly, "And when are we going to have all of this ready? Tomorrow? Really??? What an imagination we kids have! How in this or any other world are we going to be able to prepare all of that, and be ready for the picky-nick tomorrow? I guess I'll call on my angels and fairies but sadly, it will take more than a miracle for even a little bit of our list to be ready in one day!"

Downhearted and sad, the tearful kiddos knew that Violet was right. This picky-nick would not be so grand after all. A gloomy silence filled the clubhouse.

Suddenly, there was a *TAP-TAP-TAP* on the door! The kiddos went silent and froze. They didn't have time for a what-er! They did not move nor did they make a peep. The knocking continued two more times. They figured that the what-er would get tired of knocking and then leave them alone with their sad thoughts and disappointments.

There was one more knock and then someone said, "Hey, Topp, you in there?"

They all knew whose voice that was. It was Topp's father, Mr. Topper.

Topp and the others rushed to the door and opened it wide to greet his dad. To their astonishment, outside in the shady glade, there were hundreds of people smiling, waving, and staring up at them.

"We're here to help!" Mr. Topper said. "We want to help you put this picnic event together. You kids deserve it, so how can we help?"

Mayor Kee Kee, who was standing next to Mr. Topper, spoke up, "Tell us what you want us to do, and we will be your tireless and able workers! We're here to get 'er done and support this wonderful event."

The kiddos were amazed at how many Oogans were there in front of them, and they were delighted by what Mayor Kee Kee had said. There must have been three hundred or more town folk standing in the shady glade, all with eager and glowing faces. A miracle indeed!

"Come on in, welcome to our humble clubhouse," Sugar said warmly. "We call this place the Big Abble, and *all* are welcome."

There were more people outside than could possibly fit inside. Everybody was interested in touring the kiddos' special abode, so it took a while for everyone to have their turn admiring the clubhouse. It was great fun showing the Oogans everything inside and out, and it lifted their spirits to the heavens.

All of the kiddos' parents were there, even Violet's parents, Blue and Rose Indigo, and her brother, Gray. They had come all the way from Purple Springs to help.

When all the tours were complete, Mayor Kee Kee instructed everyone to gather around her outside. "The children have handed me a list of all the activities and events they have in mind for the picky-nick. It's quite a lot, but I'm sure if we all work hard, we can do it. Let's head over to Poppy Park and make this grand event happen!"

The giant crowd turned around and headed toward Poppy Park, leaving behind a big ol' cloud of fragrant shady glade dust.

The kiddos stood there frozen in place, simply staring at the mass of people heading down the trail. They didn't know what to expect, but their glum disappointment and worries had vanished. They headed back into the clubhouse with joy and amazement sparkling in their eyes.

"I had no idea your angels and fairies look like the people of Ooga Ooga!" Taffy said with a wink.

"I didn't, either," Violet said with a sweet grin and a tear in her eye.

Chapter 84

READY OR NOT, HERE THEY COME

❧❦

"It looks like we don't need to put posters around town. After what we just saw, the word is out about the picky-nick!" Taffy said.

"I hope we get a good turnout from all our faraway friends. We can only hope," Sugar said.

"Maybe I should have flown around to drop off invitations ahead of time," Balooon said. "But it's too late now!"

"They'll all show up," Walnut said casually.

"How do you know, Walnut?" Topp asked pointedly.

"You know …," he said.

"*They told you* – right?" Topp said.

"Yep."

"Really? Oh … never mind!"

The others were laughing as they listened to Walnut and Topp. They were glad to hear that Walnut thinks that their friends from faraway places will be at the picky-nick tomorrow. As quirky as he may be, Walnut often knows what he's talking about.

The kiddos hoped that the young visitors will want to tour their clubhouse. They thought it might inspire their distant friends to create a special hideaway of their own. They worked most of the day to clean up the clubhouse, spruce up the garden, and freshen the entirety of the shady glade.

Topp painted a nice new sign to hang over the front door that read:

> # The Big Abble - Everyone is Welcome

He had wanted to add **except what-ers!** but he didn't, partly because it wouldn't be nice, and partly because he liked JoJo, the giant purple frog, and he wanted to invite her inside the next time he saw her.

Sugar polished the glass on the inside and outside of the glasshouse, and even washed the leaves of the healthy, happy planana tree and its two babies. She was happy her planana tree wasn't lonely anymore, and she gave them a good soaking of fresh Silly Creek water to perk them up.

Because the kiddos were busy with travels to so many lands (and outer space), the weeds in the garden had grown out of control. The overgrown wild plants were no longer getting along well with the veggies. The kiddos worked hard and pulled the tall, tangled weeds from all the rows in the garden. They got rid of the weeds around the fruit trees as well, made circular dams, and gave them a good soaking.

"My goodness goodshoes!" Sugar shouted. "Boy, does our farm look good!"

"It sure does. Now visitors will know for certain that we are *farmers*, not gardeners," Walnut said emphatically.

Later in the clubhouse, Violet was busy in the kitchen, tidying up, when she called out to the others, "We should take a nap and rest up for the big day tomorrow. What do you guys think?" But no one answered.

To her surprise, all five of the kiddos were curled up like little balls, fast asleep on the big soft rug in the middle of the room. *My, my, my, aren't we a tired bunch.* She found some space between Topp and Taffy, curled up into her own little ball and fell asleep.

Time passed, then a loud *CRASH, JANGLE, CLANK* rang out from the kitchen. Sugar woke up and went to see what had happened.

"Ragamuffin, you tipped the garbage can over!" she scolded, and then she noticed his empty food bowl. "I'm sorry, boy!" she said and fetched his dinner.

The commotion woke the others, who got up slowly and stretched to wake up their tired muscles.

"It's getting dark – nearly bedtime," Topp said.

They decided to clean up and organize the clubhouse for a while before going to bed. They busied themselves by straightening books, leveling the map and pictures, and sweeping the floor. They wanted to show their visitors the pride they have in their cozy shelter.

When the work was done, they started getting ready for bed.

Then Balooon said, "I'm not really that sleepy."

"Me, too," Sugar said.

The kiddos were restless and nervous about the next day. It was the eve of the grand picky-nick, after all!

So, instead of going to bed, where they would just toss and turn, they decided to walk up the trail to see what the park looked like after their neighbors, friends, and families had worked so hard to get everything ready. The brightly shining moon was straight overhead and the air was clear, so they could see whatever they wanted to see.

As they approached Poppy Park, their hearts were *tap-tapping* rapidly. The first thing they saw was a boldly colored sign which said:

Welcome to the Grand Picky-Nick

A few steps farther along, there was a sign in front of a large tent:

Welcome – Information

Inside the tent, there was a table with a list of activities available at the picky-nick. There was a stack of maps as well, showing where to find all the exciting stuff in Poppy Park. There was even a guest book and name tags for those who want to wear one. At the back of the tent was a first-aid station.

They also saw all kinds of interesting things set up throughout the park. All they could say was, "Wow."

It was getting late, so they headed home to the shady glade.

After entering the clubhouse, it couldn't have been more than ten seconds before they were fast asleep. Happy dreams, you delightful kiddos.

Chapter 85

LET THE GRAND PICKY-NICK BEGIN

❧

The two suns eased themselves silently over the Tot Tot Hills as they have for millions of years and turned the top of Ooga Mountain to gold. It was just before the break of dawn, and the kiddos were already up. The morning of the special event had come, and the kiddos were ready. They left the shady glade in the scant bit of early morning light and walked single file toward Poppy Park and the welcoming tent.

Were they excited? As excited as they were when they went into outer space, but everyone was *happily* excited this time.

As they approached the tent in the damp morning dew, they were surprised to see that Mayor Kee Kee was already there.

"Good morning, Mayor!" Taffy said cheerfully. "We're here and ready to get to work!"

"You kids are up early, and a good morning to you!" the mayor said warmly. "But, nay, nay, nay, you are *not* here to work!"

"But there must be a great deal to be done," Sugar said, eager to get going.

"It's all finished – all figured out!" the mayor said firmly, with a nice smile on top. "You children have done enough to get this delightful event off the ground. Now the people of Ooga Ooga want you to just enjoy yourselves and visit freely with your friends from far and near. You have been reaching out to the peoples of this whole greater land,

and that is all we ask of you today. Therefore, you are hereby proclaimed: *The Ambassadors of Ooga Ooga!"*

The kiddos looked back and forth at each other and then moved away a short distance for a private huddle.

"What do you guys think?" Topp asked. "I think they just want us to hang out and have fun. Do ya think we can do that?"

"Heck, that's our *favorite* thing to do!" Walnut said with a broad smile.

"It seems like they've taken care of everything – so why not?" Violet added.

"Works for me," Balooon said.

"We are taking part in the closing ceremony on stage after the fireworks. Otherwise, I'm for having fun," Sugar said.

"Sounds wonderful and easy," Taffy agreed.

They walked over and let the mayor know that they would be quite pleased to be *The Rainbow Kiddos, Ambassadors of Ooga Ooga*. They thanked Mayor Kee Kee and started wandering around the park.

Even though it was early, they noticed quite a few people milling around and heading toward the tent area. The kiddos walked to the gazebo where there was already a breakfast buffet set up and helped themselves. They forgot to ask for chocolate chunk waffles on their big list, but there they were anyway, along with a lot of other delicacies, too many to mention.

"Hi there, friend-ies!" someone shouted to the kiddos from within a boisterous group of strangers.

"Hello! Well, if it isn't Ddandy and Pperfume!" Sugar said with delight. "I'm so glad you could come today! Are your mom and dad here?"

"Everybody from Roooganville is here!" Pperfume said. "Everybody! We're so happy to be here. We hope that when the Oogans meet the Roooganvillers, that old Rat Town thing will be over and done with for good!"

"Let's hope," Violet said with sincerity. "We've never met anyone nicer than you and your family. We are big fans of our wonderful Rooogan neighbors."

"Is your dad wearing the hat with those rat ... er ... hamster ears?" Taffy asked.

"He wanted to wear it to be funny, but Mom gave him that stern look, so he didn't," Ddandy said with a sigh of relief.

"Hey, could we visit your clubhouse – if it's not too many troubles?" Ddandy asked.

"Sure, go right ahead. It's open for all to see," said Topp. "It's not far. Here's a mini map that shows how to get there from the park."

Pperfume gratefully took the map, looked at it and said, "Thanks, we've been talking about building a little clubhouse for ourselves on a tiny island in the pond and thought maybe your clubhouse could give us ideas." She and Ddandy then took off toward the trail to the shady glade.

After saying adieu to the Rooogan kids, the kiddos strolled around the park, here and there. They eventually ran into their parents and siblings, at one point or another. It looked like everyone was having a grand time.

They met Sugar's Grandma Mossy, who knew all about the fairy flowers at Whistle Creek. Taffy thanked her for saving them from the darkness on their way down from Lookout Rock. "Oh, my pleasure," she said.

"Look over there, it's Mr. Bark!" Violet said. "He's walking his green cat on a string. That looks *so* funny."

Mr. Bark came their way and introduced his cat, the one they knew he loved so much. "This is Leafy, my buddy. I want you to know that I think of you kids often and want to thank you again for saving me – and finding my cat."

"Thanks for coming, Mr. Bark," Sugar said. "We hope you are doing well. Thanks to you, we found an interesting artifact from ancient Dirt Town in the canal where you were stuck. We'll tell you more about that someday when we have more time."

"I look forward to it," he said and slipped away with Leafy prancing close behind.

"HO HO HA HA HA!" somebody shouted in their direction. All the kiddos turned around at once. It was the young chap, Vine Boy. He was laughing and giggling almost out of control.

"Hi, Vine Boy from the jungle, so nice you could come!" Violet said. "You seem in a happy mood."

"Always! You know – the jungle mist! This picky-picky event thing you're doing is super. Thanks for inviting us to come. Most of the people from Bog Town are here. They wanted to check out you *dry-landers*."

"But you're not *in* the jungle right now," Balooon said. "Why are you still laughing?"

"If you breathe enough of the jungle mist (hee hee hee), it stays with you for days. Hey, Violet, are you still doing miracles like you did when you walked on top of the bog? Hahaha ... that was incredible!"

"I suppose," she said softly and humbly and then handed him a mini map to the shady glade. "Here's a map to our clubhouse if you care to see it. The happy planana tree lives there now."

"Thanks, I just might do that. If you hear a group of people laughing out of control, it's most likely the other jungle Bog Towners who are here!" He then chortled a joyous goodbye, wandered off, and disappeared into the crowd.

Wandering among the gathering mass of visitors, it wasn't long before the kiddos ran into Buggy and Cricket from Bugg Town. During their chatting back and forth, one of the kiddos asked if they'd brought their ice bugs with them.

"No, our 'cats' (as you call them) were napping, so we left without them," Cricket said with a grin.

At their request, the kiddos accompanied Buggy and Cricket to the shady glade and gave them a full tour of the clubhouse, where they met Smokey, the kiddos' very own ice bug. "Your ice bug has little wings!" Buggy said in amazement. "Can Smokey fly?"

"Kind of," Balooon answered. "She mostly flops around *trying* to fly but on Baby Gravity Day, she actually flew around from tree to tree!"

"Look, Cricket, it's a biting chiperoo!" Buggy said. "How'd that get here?"

"She bit me, and now she goes with me everywhere," Sugar said. "Just like you said. But I don't mind, she's my sweet Roo Roo now."

"Maybe we oughta get a pet chiperoo, too," Cricket said to Buggy.

He laughed and said, "No thanks, two ice bugs are enough."

"Hey, we should warn you that we saw the six Rachett brothers a little while ago," Buggy said. "Watch out for them and their friends from Bergville."

"Thanks for the warning," Topp said. "But I think their rascally behavior is over – with us anyway!"

Just then, they saw the Rachett Brothers coming their way. Cricket and Buggy slunk down low, said a quick "bye" to the kiddos, and headed into the busy crowd.

The Rachett brothers came up to the kiddos rather brusquely but said "hello" in a friendly tone, I might add.

"Thanks again for helping us get down the trail that night on the mountain," one of them said. "And thank you for inviting us to your fun picky-nick."

"You are quite welcome," Walnut said. "Did anyone else from Bergville come?"

"Yes, they did, most everyone. It looks like they're having fun too. Hey, could we see inside your clubhouse, we've heard all about it, and we're thinking about building our own."

So, the kiddos gladly gave them the tour. When the Rachett brothers saw their three-wheeled bikes parked outside, they decided to explain why they took them that day at Rusty Canyon. They told the kiddos that they wanted to try riding their three-wheeled bikes because they wanted to rebuild the bikes that they had. They admitted that they were being a bit rascally, too, and apologized again.

The kiddos, the gracious ambassadors that they are, gladly accepted their apologies, and let them ride their bikes up and down the trail in the shady glade.

When the kiddos got back to the picky-nick, they were amazed at how many people were there. Hundreds? No, thousands! Poppy Park was full of people having fun everywhere. *So far, so good,* they thought.

Their tummies directed them to the food tent again, where they could get lunch. They each put together a delicious Crunch Burger made from the fillets of that mean ol' fish. They filled the rest of their plates with all kinds of other fine delicacies served from the picky-nick kitchen. The food was fabulous.

When nobody was watching them, the kiddos entered the secret opening that leads under the gazebo floor to a hiding place. And it was a very cozy place to eat their lunch and take a break from their busy ambassadorship duties.

They had been quite hungry and possibly eaten too much. So, they lay out on their backs to stretch out and make more room for all the tasty food they'd just consumed. As they lay there, one by one, they fell asleep, right in the middle of the picky-nick! Oh my!

Chapter 86

THE GRAND FAREWELL OF WISDOM

৵৵৶

BAM BAM, THUMP THUMP, CLANG, CLANG went the drums and cymbals of the band that was set up next to the gazebo to play dance music.

Taffy was the only one tall enough to hit her head on the floor framing above them, and that's what she did when she sat up! "Ow," she moaned. The other kiddos woke up to the band but not quite as quickly as Taffy did.

"I guess we took a nap," Walnut said, annoyed. "I like to take naps, but I don't like being woken up like that!"

"Back to work, kiddos," Taffy said. "It's time to do our duty and go out there and greet more guests." The kids picked up their lunch plates and such and crawled out from under the gazebo, while the racket of the band grew louder with each beat.

When they returned their plates to the kitchen, they looked up and saw Grandpa Gabby. He was sitting and enjoying all thc goings on from his favorite spot on the gazebo.

"Grandpa Gabby, what do you think of this?" Violet asked him, spreading her arms outward and pointing toward the crowd.

"Quite grand, me thinks!" he said. "You kids really whipped up a fine turnout of people from all over the land. Congratulations!"

The kiddos beamed as they looked out over the multitudes. They couldn't have asked for more.

"We owe a lot of this to you, Grandpa Gabby," Sugar said.

"Aw, shucks, no," he said. "You young'uns brought everyone together, me knows that."

They started to leave Gabby at the gazebo when a young girl came up the steps.

"Goldie!" Violet blurted out. "We were just visiting with your wonderful grandpa."

"That's nice, I was just bringing him a drink," Goldie said. "How are you guys doing? Hey, thanks for finding the silver coins$. Grandpa gave me my share, thanks!"

After sharing pleasantries with Goldie, the kiddos wandered on.

Moving into the crowd, the kiddos accidentally (and literally) bumped into two small children and almost tipped over their plates of food. Looking down, they saw that it was Tammy and Teddy Toast.

"Whoa, sorry about that – glad you didn't drop anything!" Walnut said. "I'm thrilled you two made it. So very good to see you again and under better circumstances this time. Do you think it will flood today?"

"That's silly," Tammy said with a wide grin. Then looking up at the sky, she said teasingly, "But who knows!"

Sugar enjoyed the little joke and then asked, "Did anyone else come from the Village of Ghosts, er, Toasts?"

"Yes, we are all here, all twelve of us," Teddy said. "And watch that *ghost* comment. They just might show up …!"

They all had a good laugh, and their tummies hurt a little that time.

I think their tummies were still too full to laugh comfortably.

The kiddos politely excused themselves after a bit and wandered over to the Ducky Pond where they saw familiar faces out on an island in the pond.

They walked over to the narrow bridge leading to the island and shouted out, "Hey, hello there, Wowettes!"

"Look, Tolly, it's those kids from Oogoo Oogoo," Golly cried out. "Hey, thanks for inviting us. This is grand!"

The six Wowette kids were standing on the island in the pond. "Glad you could come," Topp shouted back. "I see you prefer to be on an island – just like home but smaller."

"How'd youse know?" Biff Wowette said, standing next to his sister, Kiss.

"We'll cominty over the walken way to seez you," Polly said. (I *think* it was Polly, but maybe it was Golly.)

The younger Wowettes, Biff and Kiss, had met all six of the kiddos at some point, but Tolly, Golly, Polly, and Rolly had only met Violet and Taffy.

They chatted for a while about how the kiddos had made it home, and how the Wowettes had traveled to Ooga Ooga for this event. The kiddos had another opportunity to thank the Wowettes for their kindness, and they did. And the Wowettes thanked them again for the great raftie and the strong ropie.

"Have a great time!" said the kiddos. Then they started strolling around the park again, looking for more friends.

"Hey! Look, guys, it's Zip, and he's holding Bonnet's hand!" Violet said.

"Let's go over to them quickly before Zip zips away," Walnut said with a smarty-pants grin.

"The kiddos from the valley! Hello!" Zip said as they approached. "Hey, this is a great whooperoo – a special whoop-dee-do! I bet I could have heard all this noisy gaiety from up at the cavedom!"

Bonnet asked the kiddos, "Did you all get down off the mountain okay? Oh, silly me, here you are, and looking just fine. I guess I answered my own question!"

"If it weren't for Zip," Sugar said. "I don't think we would have ever gotten off that – beautiful to look at but dangerous to climb – mountain."

"We are thoroughly enjoying ourselves," Bonnet said. "Are you going to have one of these picky-things every year?"

"We'll have to ask *who* because *who* knows!" Walnut quipped. He might have been the only one who got his cutesy comment.

"You'll have to come and visit us up on the mountain – at the cavedom – not at the top," Zip said and winked. He mentioned that they were on their way to the kitchen. "We want to eat a little more of the great food – especially those Crunch burgers!"

Walnut's eyes smiled when Zip mentioned how good the Crunch burgers were.

As the kiddos continued moving about, there were two older gentlemen asking around, looking for the kiddos. Someone pointed them out, so the old guys walked up and said, "You kids sure know how to put on a shindig. This is wonderful, all these people coming together – and from all over the place. Thank you." It was Old Man Gruff and Captain Float.

"No ... thank you, Mr. Gruff," Taffy said. "I know for sure that if you didn't let us build our clubhouse in the shady glade, none of this would have happened. We give the credit to you and your generosity."

"And thank you as well, Captain, for all your help with our travels," Topp added.

The kiddos hoped their thanks sank into the hearts of those wonderful old men: Mr. Gruff, who is anything but gruff, and Captain Float, the nice old skipper of the waterways.

Violet bumped into Blubba from Gem Town and shared a few pleasantries. "Congratulations on finding more pink gold," he said. "I know one thing for sure, I'll never find any more because I won't go anywhere near that evil pink desert!"

From a distance, the kiddos saw Mr. Float giving a balloon ride to Mr. Funny, the mayor of Swampyville. They also saw Bob Bobb, and all his brothers and sisters named Bob. All the Bob and Bobb families were all over the place. There was no need to say "hello" to everyone since they all live in the Village of Ooga Ooga, and they bump into each other all the time.

And they ran into the Haywire kids who asked about their raft trip and if they still had all their toes.

The kiddos knew a lot of the people wandering around, like all the kids from school who often play with them at the Ooga River Falls and the Bubble Bath.

This fine summer had started at the Ooga River and was now ending in Poppy Park. The suns had just set below the horizon of Ooga Mountain, and the sunset colors were beginning to spread throughout the sky like wet paint. Darkness was certainly nigh, so it was time for the fireworks to begin.

Was this not the best summer ever? the kiddos thought to themselves.

To watch the fireworks, the kiddos walked over to the bandstand and climbed the ten steps to the raised platform where the band had been playing. The kiddos will say a final farewell to their guests, after the last rocket showers the lovely valley with sparkles of light.

POW! POP! PITOOOOO! went the first fireworks, and it only got more exciting and louder from there.

Earlier, Ragamuffin had been hanging out with his cat friends. But he was at Sugar's side when the fireworks started. He didn't like them very much – maybe he thought that the world was ending. A new era in the Valley of Ooga Ooga and beyond was just beginning.

The kiddos were glad that Smokey, the cat-bird, was back at the clubhouse with the chiperoo. Smokey was sleeping, and Roo Roo was eating the nuts that Violet had accidentally dropped on the floor (on purpose). The two pets think that their little party is better than the one in the park, I bet.

BIZZZ! BOP! ZEEEEEEE! went the fireworks for a few minutes longer.

Then Bob Bob, who was setting the fireworks off, gave a signal to Mayor Kee Kee to indicate that the last one would be next. Up it flew, and it was the most beautiful of all! Every color of the rainbow sprayed throughout the night sky.

A row of fairy flowers and light-wands was lit at the base of the stage. The light shone brightly up on Mayor Kee Kee, the six kiddos, and Ragamuffin.

The mayor picked up the sound projecting device and pointed it toward the huge crowd of people who had been alerted by the stage lights. The huge throng of guests became quiet, and everyone was now looking up at the stage.

"Hello to you all! Thank you for coming. To those of you who might not know me, I am Mayor Kee Kee, from the Village of Ooga Ooga," she said loudly so all could hear. "I hope everyone had a great time!"

The crowd exploded with applause, clapping, whooping, and yahooing. It was so loud I'm sure it could be heard all the way to the top of Ooga Mountain.

"It sounds like you did have a great time!"

And the crowd erupted again and filled the air with festive joy.

When the cheers subsided, the mayor spoke again. "For those of you who don't know this group of children, I will introduce them. And I will say that, if not for them, this incredibly grand picky-nick would not have happened."

The crowd went crazy again, shouting and whooping.

"I will say their names one by one, and then I'll read something they wrote for everyone to hear. The children, often called the kiddos, are Taffy, Sugar, Topp, Walnut, Violet, and Balooon." The crowd started cheering when the first name was read, so the rest of the names were just a sound-blur – but a lovely one at that!

"Here is a message from the kiddos to all of you," the mayor said and then began reading.

Dear fine and wonderful people of the Valley of Ooga Ooga and Beyond:

All of you have given us hope for our lives going forward. Yes, we are just kids, but what that means is that we will be living here on this land or whatever you want to call it, for a long time to come. Our future is here – here where there are gentle valleys, jungles, deserts, mountain ranges, and vast seas.

As many of you know, Granny Bubbles recently found the **edge** of our land to the west. This is where our land ends into outer space. This is where there is nothing – no dirt, no water, no air, no nothing, absolutely nothing! Having learned this fact, we assume that our land ends at an **edge** in all four directions, not in just that one direction. Our land does **not** go on forever in all directions as was believed for many years. Our land is **not** boundless. This means that this place, this piece of land we live on – is all we have!

So, it is more important than ever that we **all** take good care of this precious land and take good care of others who live here with us.

We all live on this small bit of land, and even though we look different and may speak differently, we are ALL very special living things, and we **must** see this truth in EVERYONE we meet. That has been our wish ... and today by coming to this picky-nick and gathering together, you made our grandest wish come true. Thank you ALL!

The crowd was silent and remained that way for a long time. They were deeply touched as they pondered the wisdom of these children and their vision of the world in which they wish to live.

Chapter 87

BOBBY'S BEST DREAM OF ALL

ↄ·ↄ

Bobby woke up early to the first light of day, not because of his rascally cat, Fluffers, but because he wanted to. It was his birthday, and he planned to spend the day with his friends. They would be meeting him at a picnic spot south of town, to celebrate his special day.

He slid out from under his bed covers and placed his feet on the cool floor. After his head cleared a little, he stood up and walked gingerly toward the morning light beaming through his window. He leaned down to see what kind of weather was in store for today. His nose touched the cold glass as he looked into the yard and then up at the enormous purple mountain in the distance. He noticed that the sky had few clouds, so he knew then that his birthday would be a bright and sunny one.

"What a morning – what a life!" Bobby whispered, so as not to wake up his sister.

He walked, almost danced, to the bathroom where he splashed his face with cold water, more to wake himself up than to get clean. He brushed his teeth, combed his hair, and got dressed. To be comfortable in the warm weather, he put on shorts and a sporty tropical shirt that Cookie gave to him last year.

Eventually, he wandered leisurely down the hall. Mom and Dad were at the cabin on the lake, and his sister was snoring in her bedroom, so the kitchen was all his. He looked in the freezer to see if there was any ice cream, his favorite but naughty breakfast. There in plain sight was a new carton of cherry-chunk chocolate ice cream. To his surprise, it had a note attached that read:

HAPPY BIRTHDAY, BOBBY – HELP YOURSELF!

He has the greatest parents, doesn't he?

He headed to the kitchen table with a massive pile of ice cream dumped into a deep bowl. When he scooted his chair up to the table, he saw a small, bright red present on top of an envelope with his name on it. He dug into the envelope and pulled out a birthday card. It was handwritten, and he read it out loud:

Happy Growin'-up Day, Bobby!
Much loviness, Cookie

He slowly peeled off the red wrapping paper and uncovered a shiny white box. When he shook it from side to side, he heard *thunk, thunk*. He tried to guess what was inside, but he couldn't figure it out. He lifted off the lid and screamed out in delight, "A new harmonica – a *real* harmonica!" He was ecstatic with the wonderful gift from Cookie.

Bobby has a little kiddie harmonica that he played when he was younger. It was of inferior quality and wasn't quite in pitch, but he played it often and his family closed their doors whenever he did.

He raised the new harmonica to his lips and gently blew into it. The pure sound it made was beyond delightful. "Wow – what a difference!" he said.

For the next hour, Bobby played many a tune, some he knew and some he made up. Between the musical ditties he played, he ate the ice cream, and then went back to his room.

Bobby figured it was nearly time for him to head out to see his friends on the far side of town, so he put a few things into a cloth bag to take with him. He put his swim trunks and a towel in the bag in case they go swimming. He also included the gift boxes of candy from Aunt Ferny to share with his friends.

He didn't put his harmonica in the bag. No way! That went in his back pocket for easy access. He often played his kiddie harmonica while taking walks, and that's what he planned to do today on his long jaunt to the party.

Before he went out the front door, he left a thank you note for his mom and dad, for the ice cream and the telescope. He also wrote one for Cookie to give to her when she arrived at his birthday party. He left his house, started skipping, and blew a happy tune as he started down the road.

Playing his harmonica all the while, he walked several blocks to River Road, turned left and headed toward town. Within minutes he passed by a large field of flowers alongside the river. The flowers were once pretty, but now their heads are turned down and their leaves are limp, having succumbed to the dry, late summer breezes. The street was strewn with fallen leaves in all colors of the rainbow. He playfully kicked them into the air as high as he was able as he strolled along.

He continued walking and tooting his harmonica until he came to the intersection of Moon and Brick Streets. He turned right on Moon and followed it until it ended at a park.

Stopping at the edge of the open space, Bobby looked up and saw that the view to the stately mountain was wide open. To his surprise and delight, he saw an enormous rainbow over the mountain, and it looked like both ends touched the ground. "Wow," he whispered softly.

All six colors of the rainbow were displayed brilliantly before him. *What color am I?* he wondered. *I've heard that if all the colors of light are combined, the resulting color is white. I like that. I am the color white then – that's my choice – I am all colors!* He couldn't be happier as he tooted out a sweet melody for the rainbow to hear.

Bobby stood there in the park, looking at the rainbow for what seemed like a lifetime. He thought deeply, *I should get going, but what could be a more special birthday gift than this moment right now? Could every moment of my life be as peaceful and fulfilling as this one? I'm going to strive for that!*

Suddenly, a scary streak of lighting flashed in the sky, followed by a loud, deep, booming crack of thunder. Bobby didn't flinch. He was so deep in his special moment, he continued to feel the calm beauty of nature in its many forms. *What a day – what a life!* he thought.

He slowly moved on and passed a gazebo on the bank of a pond. He stopped and stared at the perfect mirrorlike reflection of the majestic purple mountain and the rainbow. When a frog jumped into the water, it made ripples in the stunning reflection. It was time to move on.

Playing a waltz-like tune, he gleefully strolled on a path that disappeared into a grove of trees beyond the park. He followed the shady trail until it opened into a lovely sun-drenched field. At the far end, there was an old funny-looking shack hidden in the shadows.

As he slowly wandered on, Bobby was struck by the beauty of this place. The grandeur of the view of the mountain was magnificent as was the mix of blue sky and tall puffy white clouds. In and around the meadow was a multitude of green foliage and colorful flowers. He took a slow, deep breath, then slowly let it out with a quiet *aaaah*.

Arriving at the shack, Bobby approached the door with a smile and *tap, tap, tapped* on the door … and waited in anticipation.

The door opened slowly, and a girl stuck out her head to see who was there. "Bobby! Bobby! So happy to see you!" she exclaimed.

"Nice to see you, too! I hope you're having a nice morning, Taffy," Bobby said warmly.

"I'm having a *great* morning!" she said cheerfully.

Bobby was welcomed inside and paused to greet everyone.

"Hi, Topp!" Bobby said. "Hello, Sugar! Hello, Walnut!"

A girl came out of the kitchen and shouted, "Happy birthday, Bobby! Come on in, and have birthday pancakes, chocolate chip ones, just like you like 'em!"

"Thanks, Violet, I will!" Bobby said with delight.

"Welcome and happy birthday, Bobby," Balooon said. "I was up in the treehouse with Smokey when I heard you arrive."

Ragamuffin also said "hello" to Bobby with his weird but happy meow-ish sound. Smokey and Roo Roo sniffed his pockets, hunting for hidden treats.

The kiddos, now seven of them, sat around the big table in the clubhouse. Violet served a large stack of birthday pancakes with candles on top.

After the candles were blown out, and the birthday song was sung, Sugar said, "What have you been up to lately, Bobby? I haven't seen you around in a while."

"Just been home helping out – and having fun too. Cookie got me a fancy new harmonica for my birthday! I love it! Now I can play along with Walnut's whistling!"

Walnut smiled, and the kiddos chuckled.

"Where's Cookie? Is she coming?" Taffy asked.

"She'll be on her way soon. She had to help her mom until a little later."

"You *were* at the picky-nick, weren't you?" Taffy asked Bobby. "I never saw you there."

"Of course, Cookie and I were there, but there were sooo many people. We never saw you until you were up on the stage with Mayor Kee Kee after the fireworks. What a great celebration, and you guys gave such a wonderfully wise message for the people of Ooga Ooga!"

Sugar and the others nodded their heads in agreement and smiled.

Between bites of pancake, Topp asked Bobby, "Anything else going on in your life? You usually have interesting tales from your part of town."

"There is one intriguing thing that's been going on in my life – every day!" Bobby said. "Every night – it's been quite fascinating and hard to believe – I've been having an amazing dream!"

"We all have dreams, Bobby," Sugar said matter-of-factly and smiled sweetly.

"But have you had a dream that comes back right where it left off when you go back to sleep the next night? And not only that, it's a dream that continues over and over for weeks – one long dream – all linked together." Bobby explained his epic dream the best he could.

"That *is* very interesting," Taffy said with a puzzled look on her face.

"What's the dream about?" Violet asked.

"Well, in my dream, I had a great big bedroom, and I lived with my mom. I had a cat named Fluffers and a pet chipmunk. In my bedroom, there were stars and planets stuck on the ceiling, and I built a roller coaster made of toothpicks and glue. I grew plants near the window and talked to them. I did a puzzle of a monkey, and I had ice cream for breakfast every day!"

"Wow, what detail!" Walnut said. "Tell us more!"

"Outside the house in the dream world, I did all sorts of things. I built a new clubhouse and added a greenhouse, moved a big sandbox, and got stuck in the mud. In the dream, my dad was lost in the jungle and when he returned, we traveled to a big ocean, went up a mountain, and visited my auntie's chocolate factory. The dream was like – real life – really real!"

"Sounds amazing!" Balooon said in awe. "Anything else, birthday boy?"

"Well, it seems that the dream has ended now. I had two different lives for a while – the dream life and this life. That amazing dream was fun and exciting, and I did love it. But *this* dreamy life, the one I am living with all of you here in the Valley of Ooga Ooga, is by far the best dream of all.

Made in the USA
Columbia, SC
21 August 2023

21908664R00237